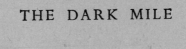

THE DARK MILE

THE
DARK MILE

By

D. K. BROSTER

❖

A Sequel to
THE *FLIGHT* **OF** *THE* **HERON**
and
THE **GLEAM** *IN* **THE** *NORTH*

❖

WILLIAM HEINEMANN LTD
MELBOURNE :: LONDON :: TORONTO

FIRST PUBLISHED 1929
REPRINTED 1930 (twice), 1932, 1933, 1934, 1935,
1937, 1938 (twice), 1940, 1947, 1949
1952

PRINTED IN GREAT BRITAIN
AT THE WINDMILL PRESS
KINGSWOOD, SURREY

To
G. W. TAYLOR

NOTE

David Maitland is not an historical
character, though the rôle assigned to him
before the story opens was actually played
by some man whose identity and motives
have never been established.

CONTENTS

Chapter		Page
	PROLOGUE. THE THIRTEENTH CHIEF	1
I	WHAT THE MOON SAW	14
II	ON HIS VERY HEARTHSTONE	22
III	BRANDED	32
IV	THE LADY FROM THE LOCH	43
V	WOULD SHE WERE GONE!	57
VI	THE FIELD OF DAISIES	75
VII	AN EXPLANATION AT THE GOATS' WHEY	86
VIII	THE ONLY SAFETY	100
IX	OTHER PEOPLE'S LOVE AFFAIRS	115
X	FATHER AND SON	124
XI	IAN STEWART LISTENS TO THE DEVIL	135
XII	"OUT, SWORD, AND TO A SORE PURPOSE!"	147
XIII	CASTLE DANGEROUS	158
XIV	"WILL YOU WALK INTO MY PARLOUR?"	173
XV	ON THE VERGE	190
XVI	ANOTHER IN THE TOILS	200
XVII	DELIVERANCE	210
XVIII	IAN DOES SOME HARD THINGS	223
XIX	FINLAY'S TOOL . . . ?	235

Chapter		Page
XX	IN A GREEN RIDING HABIT	247
XXI	TORMENT	255
XXII	THE COUNTER THRUST	270
XXIII	THE STREAM IN SPATE	287
XXIV	" ASK MR. MAITLAND. . . ."	304
XXV	" HE FORGAVE. . ."	318
XXVI	A LIFE FOR A LIFE	329
XXVII	LIGHT IN THE DARK MILE	340
XXVIII	THE KING OF LOCHLANN'S DAUGHTER	352

Several of the chief characters in this book appear also in its two predecessors, *The Flight of the Heron* and *The Gleam in the North*.

The Dark Mile

PROLOGUE

THE THIRTEENTH CHIEF

§ 1

ITS own peculiarly vehement and gusty wind was curvetting about Edinburgh this October afternoon of 1754, forerunner and abettor of the brief but whole-hearted squalls of rain which now and then were let loose upon the defenceless city, and sent every pedestrian running to the nearest doorway. Yet between these cloud-bursts it was fine enough, and during one of these sunny intervals a young man in black, holding on to his hat, walked quickly up the slope of the Canongate. His long stride accorded well with his fine height and build, and though his mourning was new and very deep, there was no trace of recent bereavement in his air. Indeed— despite the difficulty with his hat—he held his head with a sort of natural arrogance, and his glance at his surroundings in general was something that of a newly-crowned monarch surveying his territory and subjects. For only six weeks had elapsed since the earth had been shovelled down upon his old father's coffin in the roofless chapel of Holyrood, and the son who bore him no particular affection was come at twenty-nine into his in-heritance as thirteenth Chief of Glenshian . . . into possession of a ruined castle, an empty treasury, and

1

immense prestige in the Western Highlands. But he already possessed some very singular assets of his own.

Just where the High Street, having succeeded the Canongate, gave way in its turn to the Lawnmarket, this Highland gentleman came to an abrupt and apparently unpremeditated halt in front of a small shop-window. It was rather a dingy window with bulging panes, evidently, from its contents, the property of a vendor of almanacs and broad-sheets; but the new Chief's attention was pretty plainly engaged by a roughly-executed wood engraving which was propped, unframed, against a pile of books in the very centre of the window. There was nothing about this to distinguish it from any other equally bad print of the time; one could only say that it was a stock representation of a man of early middle age. But the inscription ran, " A True Effigies of Doctor Archibald Cameron, who lately suffered Death at Tyburn for High Treason."

At this "effigies" the young man in black stood looking with a frown, and a deepening frown. Regret, no doubt, was heavy upon him (since he too was a partisan of the White Rose) and a natural if vain desire for vengeance upon the English Government which, only a year and four months before, had sent his fellow-Jacobite and compatriot to the scaffold.

It would have required a more than human insight to discover what was really causing that scowl; more insight, certainly, than was possessed by the middle-aged, down-at-heels and partially drunken Edinburgh chairman who was lounging at the entrance of the close by the shop, and looking at the tall, stationary figure with a gaze half sodden and half cunning. Once, indeed, he detached himself from the dark and greasy wall of the entry as though to accost it; then, muttering something inaudible, relapsed once more against his support.

Yet, for all that, he was to speak to the gentleman in black; the Fates would have it so, desiring no doubt to show that they at least could read the mind of Finlay MacPhair of Glenshian. Nevertheless it would not have come about but for this day's inclement weather. For while the young Chief, his hand at his chin, yet stood looking at the dead Jacobite's portrait, the heavens without warning opened afresh, and there descended such an unmitigated flood of water that no one, save an amphibian, would willingly have endured it. Mr. MacPhair in his new blacks uttered an exclamation, took hold of the handle of the shop door, discovered that it was fastened, cursed strongly, and turning, hurled himself into the mouth of the adjacent close, almost colliding with the lounger already there.

" A bit o' a shooer! " observed the latter in a wheezy voice. He looked as if neither internally nor externally was he over-familiar with the fluid of which the cataract was composed.

Mr. MacPhair gave him a contemptuous glance and said nothing. The rain flashed in sheets past the entry and drummed and bounced upon the cobbles.

" Sae ye were keekin' at the puir Doctor's picter in the windy," commented the chairman, who, unlike most of his kind, was plainly a Lowlander. " Dod, yon was a fearfu' end, a fearfu' end! Mony's the time Ah hae re-gretted it—mony's the time Ah hae been near greetin' ower it."

" You must be uncommon tenderhearted," observed Finlay MacPhair indifferently, and, looking out, cursed the downpour with precision.

"Nae mair than anither!" returned his companion in an injured tone. "Nae mair than yersel', sir! Hendry Shand is no' gi'en tae greetin'. But Ah'd hae ye ken that there's whiles sic a thing as remorrse—aye, remorrse." He sighed windily. "The worrm the Guid Buik tells o' . . . Ye'll be ower young, Ah'm thinkin', tae ken it yersel'."

"I may run the risk of knowing it very soon," returned Glenshian meaningly. "If I have to throttle you to stop your havers, for instance. Damn this rain!"

"Ma havers!" exclaimed the chairman with deep indignation. "Havers!—me that's been stane-dumb a' this while, and never tellt a soul aboot the letter——"

"Continue your reticence, then," said the Highlander, very much bored. "I have no wish to hear your reminiscences."

This word, with which he immediately grappled, seemed to offend the toper still more deeply. "Remis— remishenshes. . . . They're nathing o' the sort! What for suld the Lord Justice-Clerk hae gi'en me a gowden guinea when Ah brocht him yon letter, gin it had been a matter o' remyshish——"

But the tall gentleman in black was no longer bored, no longer even on the other side of the alley. He was beside the speaker, gripping his shoulder. "What's that you said about the Lord Justice-Clerk? For what letter, pray, did he give you a guinea?"

The other tried to shuffle off the hand. "But that wad be tellin', " he murmured, with a sly glance. "Forbye, sir, ye said ye werena wishfu' for tae hear aboot ma remorrse. And indeed Ah hae nane the noo, for Ah've refleckit that Ah was but a puir body that was ready tae oblige the gentleman and earn a piece of siller." He wriggled anew. "Ye'll please tae let me gang, sir!"

For all answer his captor laid hold of his other shoulder, and thus held Hendry Shand's unsavoury person pinned against the wall. The rain, winged by a momentary gust, blew in upon them both unheeded. "Since you have chattered of your remorse and of Doctor Cameron's death, you'll tell me before you leave this place of what letter you were speaking, and why Lord Tinwald gave you a guinea for it. And you shall thereby earn two . . . if you tell the truth . . . and it's worth it," added the young Chief in a couple of afterthoughts.

In the semi-darkness Hendry Shand's eyes glistened. Finlay MacPhair saw the phenomenon, released him, pulled out a purse and, extracting two gold coins, held them up. Mr. Shand moistened his lips at that fair sight. But, half drunk as he was, he had not mislaid his native caution as completely as had at first appeared.

"And wha's tae judge if it's warth it?" he enquired. "And why sud ye be sae wishfu'——" He broke off. "Are ye for Geordie or Jamie? Ah'd like fine tae ken that first."

"You cannot know who I am that you ask that," replied the young man with hauteur. "I am MacPhair of Glenshian."

"Gude hae maircy on us!" ejaculated Hendry. "Ye'll be the new Chief, then! The auld yin was for Jamie, they say, although he never stirred for him himsel'. Aiblins then ye were a frien' o' puir Doctor Cameron's?"

Finlay MacPhair bent his head. "I knew him well. And I am aware that he was informed against, and so captured. If the letter you took to Lord Tinwald had to do with that matter,"—his voice sank until it was almost drowned by the rain, "—and it had, had it not?—and if you will tell me who gave it to you, you shall know what it means to be for the rest of your days in the good graces of the Chief of Glenshian."

There was a pause, filled by the drip of the now slackening rain from overfilled gutters. Hendry passed his hand once or twice over his mouth, his eyes fixed on him who made this promise. " Aye," he said slowly, " and what guid will that dae me when Ah hae ma craig yerked by the next Whig, or lie shiverin' i' the Tolbooth? What for did Ah no' haud ma tongue a wee while langer! "

The coins jingled in Glenshian's impatient hand, and when the chairman spoke again his voice betrayed weakening.

" Forbye Ah canna tell ye the name, for Ah never lairnt it."

" Nonsense! " said the young man roughly. " You are playing with me. I warn you 'tis no good holding out for more than I have offered."

" Gin ye were tae dress me in jewels," replied Mr. Shand earnestly and inappropriately, " Ah cudna tell ye what Ah dinna ken masel'. Bit Ah can tell ye what like the man was," he added.

There was another pause. " I doubt 'twill not be worth the two guineas, then," said Glenshian, in a tone which showed his disappointment. "But I'll give you one."

" For ae guinea Ah'll tell ye naething," responded Hendry with firmness. He seemed a good deal less drunk than he had been. " But—hear ye noo!—for the twa Ah'll tell ye what was intill the letter, for Ah ken that. And aiblins when Ah describe the gentleman tae ye, ye'll find that ye ken him yersel'."

" It was a gentleman, then? "

" For sure it was a gentleman like yersel'."

" Very good then," said the new Chief, " the two

guineas are yours. But "—he glanced round—" this is not a very suitable spot for you to earn them in. Is there not a more private place near?"

"Aye, there's ma ain wee bit hoose up the close—though 'tis hardly fit for the likes o' yersel', Chief of Glenshian. But you an' me wad be oor lane there."

"Take me to it," said Finlay MacPhair without hesitation.

§ 2

Although it necessitated a change of scene to an environment even less pleasing than the unclean and draughty alley-way, Hendry Shand's was not a long story. Late one evening in the March of the previous year he had, it seemed, been accosted by a gentleman—whom he described—and offered a crown if he would take a letter to the house of Lord Tinwald, the Lord Justice-Clerk. At first Hendry had thought that the gentleman was ill, for he was as pale as a corpse and his hand shook, but afterwards came to the conclusion that he was merely agitated. On Hendry's asking if he should say whom the letter was from, and suggesting that the name, however, was probably inside it, the gentleman shook his head, and replied that the name was of no moment, though the letter was, and urged him to make haste.

"Aweel," continued Hendry now, as he sat upon his frowsty bed in the one tiny dark room which constituted his " hoose " and gave himself to the pleasures of narration, " aweel, Ah set ma best fit foremost and gaed doun the street. Syne Ah thocht Ah heard ma gentleman cry efter me, 'Come back, come back!', but Ah'd nae mind tae

lose the croun he'd gi'en me, sae Ah took tae ma heels. A'
the way Ah was wonderin' what micht be i' the letter—
for ye maun mind Ah hadna the least notion—an' it may
be that as Ah rinned Ah held the letter a wee bit ower
tight in ma hand, for a' on a sudden Ah heard the seal gie
a crack. Syne Ah stoppit, and losh, the letter was open!"

" In short, you opened it," observed his listener.

" Na, na," denied Hendry; but an eyelid fluttered for
a second. " Never say that, Chief o' Glenshian! But,
seein' the bit letter was open, hadna Ah the richt tae lairn
what for Ah was earnin' a siller croun? . . . Aweel, ye
can jalouse what was intill the letter—it sent the Doctor
ootbye i' the windy tae the gallows."

Mr. MacPhair drew a long breath. " You remember
the wording? "

" Aye, certes. '*If ye wish tae tak Doctor Cameron,
send wi'oot delay tae the hoose o' Duncan Stewart o'
Glenbuckie in Balquhidder, where the writer saw him no'
ten days syne.*' "

" That was all? And there was no name of any kind
—not even initials? "

" No' a letter! Ye may be sure Ah keekit inside an'
oot. There wasna a scratch. . . . Aweel, Ah cam tae
Lord Tinwald's hoose, an' Ah thocht tae masel', Gin this
letter is sae important, the Lord Justice-Clerk may gie me
anither croun tae lie beside ma gentleman's. Sae Ah tellt
his man there wad aiblins be an answer, ' though Ah
dinna ken for sure,' Ah says, ' for though the bit seal is
broken, Ah canna read ae ward o' write.' (Yon was a
guid lee, but it was better tae say that.) Syne the auld
judge sent for me, and Ah cud see he was fair uplifted;
and he speired what like was the man who gied me the
letter. Ah tellt him, a douce sort o' man, yin that Ah'd

never seen afore in ma life. Then he gied me na croun, but a hale gowden guinea. . . . And when Ah heard that Doctor Cameron was ta'en by the redcoats i' Glenbuckie, and a' the Whigs in Enbra was sae cock-a-hoop, Ah had a mind tae gang tae Lord Tinwald and speir if the bit letter wasna worth mair, but Ah thocht better o' it, for Ah micht hae fand masel' i' the Tolbooth for meddlin' wi' affairs o' State. . . . And unless ye keep a shut mouth, Chief o' Glenshian, Ah micht find masel' there yet! "

And he looked anxiously at the listener in the dirty wooden chair.

" It's for you to keep that," said the young man, leaning forward. " This is to be kept a secret betwixt you and me, Mr. Shand; and you shall not find yourself the worse of that, I promise you. You have not condescended much to me upon the particulars of your gentleman's appearance, but I suppose that you would know him again if you saw him? "

" Ma certie Ah wad that."

" And you could write a letter? "

" Aye. . . . mebbe Ah cud."

" If it were made worth your while, I presume? What I propose, then, is that if you see this gentleman again you shall use every endeavour to find out who he is and where he lives. You will then communicate these facts to me, by word of mouth if I be still in Edinburgh, by writing if I have taken my departure for the Highlands, as I am about to do. Do you understand? "

" Aye."

" You undertake to do that then? I will pay you well for it." The guineas jingled.

" Ah'd like fine tae ken first what ye intend tae dae wi' the gentleman gin Ah find him for ye? "

" I shall do him no harm. I merely wish to have a conversation with him, by which he will not suffer; on the contrary. 'Tis not vengeance that I am after, man! What's done is done, and Doctor Cameron cannot be brought to life again. Is it a bargain? "

" There's aye twa sides tae a bargain," observed Mr. Shand, wriggling on the bed. " What wad Ah get, noo, for a' this wark an' the fash of sendin' a letter tae ye in the Hielands? "

" You shall have three guineas for it," responded his visitor. " That's paying you well—overpaying you, in fact."

Once more Hendry was seen slightly to lick his lips. " Yon will be as well as the twa ye're tae gie me the noo? "

Glenshian hesitated a moment. " Yes," he said at last reluctantly. " You shall have the three guineas in addition, making five in all. Three more guineas when I receive the gentleman's name and his direction."

Hendry licked his lips openly this time. " Five guineas! " he repeated below his breath. " Ye swear that, Mr. MacPhair? "

" My word is my bond," responded Mr. MacPhair haughtily. " Nevertheless, I swear it." He pulled out a pocket-book, scribbled something and tore out a leaf. " Here is where I lodge in Edinburgh; should I be gone for the Highlands, you'll address your letter to me at Invershian."

His agent did not immediately take the paper. " Ah'll need ye tae be swearin' too that ye'll never tell the gentleman, if ye get this bit crack wi' him that ye're ettlin' after, wha 'twas that fand him for ye? "

The young Chief rose. " I am willing to swear that too,

and by the sword of Red Finlay of the Battles, my ancestor. A MacPhair who breaks that oath is like to die within the year. Take this paper, hold your tongue, and be diligent. Here's your two guineas."

Hendry held out his dirty palm, bit the coins severally, stowed them away in some recess inside his shabby coat, then seized the unwilling hand of his visitor and dissolved into maudlin tears.

"Ah'll scarce tak bite nor sup nor sleep o' nichts till Ah find him for ye, Chief o' Glenshian," he hiccoughed. "Ah'll hunt like the tod efter him—wi' the Lord's assistance—and ye sall ken his name near as soon as Ah lairn it masel' . . . . Ye're awa? Ah'll unsnib the dure for ye, sir. Gude bless ye, Gude bless ye in a' yer undertakin's! "

§ 3

The rain had quite ceased, and a tremulous sunlight was now gilding the pools and the wet pebbles beyond the archway as MacPhair of Glenshian, with this benediction upon his head, closed the door of Mr. Shand's retreat behind him. People had even come into the streets again, for, as he then emerged into the mouth of the close, he was aware of a figure standing where he had stood a little while ago, in front of the shop window. But this figure was a woman's.

For one brief second Finlay MacPhair studied her from the mouth of the wynd. He was looking at a gentlewoman of about thirty, whose bare hands were loosely clasped in front of her, and who was undoubtedly gazing at the print of Doctor Cameron; from his position in a

line with the window Mr. MacPhair could even see the
deeply sorrowful expression on her face, and guessed that
her eyes were brimming with unshed tears. If sad, she
was uncommonly pretty. But was that a wedding ring
upon her left hand, or was it not?

He stepped out from the archway, and was aware that
the lady never so much as moved an eyelash, so absorbed
was she in her mournful gazing. The young Chief knew
a stab of pique; he drew up his fine figure and cast a
glance, as he passed, at the lady's back. So doing, he saw
an excellent opportunity of breaking in upon that unflattering reverie, for on the stones between her and the
gutter lay a forlorn little grey glove. He picked it up and
approached the fair owner.

"Madam," he said in the most courtly tones, "I think
this glove must be your property."

Startled out of her pre-occupation, the lady half turned.
"My glove, sir . . . have I dropped one?"

"I believe so. Allow me the privilege of restoring it,"
said Glenshian with a smile. He put it into her hand, took
the opportunity of directing an appraising stare under her
bonnet, then swept her a low bow, replaced his hat, and
walked slowly away.

A few seconds later, while the lady, holding her recovered glove, was still looking after the figure of its
rescuer, who by now had crossed the Lawnmarket and was
walking down the other side, the door of the shop opened
and a very tall and broad-shouldered man was stooping
his head to come out of it.

"So you finished with your mantua-maker sooner than
you expected, my dear," he observed with a smile. "And
whom, by the way, were you talking to just now? I did
not see."

" I have no notion," replied the lady. " 'Twas merely a gentleman who was kind enough to restore the glove I had dropped. There he goes! "

The newcomer turned and looked, and instantly the most remarkable change came over him. At first he stood as still as death, staring after the departing figure of Finlay MacPhair; the next moment he had taken a couple of steps forward and was at his wife's side.

" Let me have that glove, Alison," he said in a suffocated voice,—" the one he gave back to you! "

Overcome with amazement, Alison Cameron made but a half movement to comply. Her husband took the glove from her hand and went instantly and dropped it, as one drops something repellent, into the rain-swelled gutter in the middle of the street, where, in company with cabbage-stalks and other refuse, it began to voyage along the Lawnmarket.

" Ewen, what ails you? " exclaimed its owner, looking up in alarm. " My poor glove was not poisoned . . . and now you have left me with but the one! "

" Anything MacPhair of Glenshian touches is poisoned! " answered Ewen Cameron between his teeth. " And to think he dare come within a mile of that portrait! " He indicated the window; and then, making an effort to curb the fury which had so suddenly risen in him, said more quietly, as he drew his wife's arm through his, " Come with me, *m'eudail*, and I will buy you another pair of gloves for your little cold hands."

CHAPTER I

June 15th, 1755.

" IF the moon looks through the roof she will see us all in bed! " a little boy had gleefully announced this evening, sitting up suddenly in that retreat. "—*Can* the moon look through the roof? "

Nobody knows for certain, though it is commonly held that she cannot. Yet, even if she has that power, and high as she was riding on this clear June night above the old house of Invernacree in Appin, she would not have seen all its inmates in bed. The child who had spoken of her, yes, and his elder brother, both very soundly and rosily slumbering; these she would indeed have seen; and in their respective apartments their great-uncle, old Alexander Stewart of Invernacree, to whom these, his dead sister's grandchildren, were paying a visit; and his two daughters, Grizel and Jacqueline, between whom there lay twenty-five years' difference in age, seeing that Invernacree had married twice; and Morag Cameron, the children's nurse, who had come with them from their own home of Ardroy, in Lochaber, while their mother lay in of the daughter whose presence would be such a surprise to Donald and little Keithie when they returned. All the servants likewise would the moon have seen laid out on their truckle beds or pallets—all save a young maid who was awake with the toothache, and wishing she had access to the skill of the wise woman at home.

But in one of the larger bedrooms there were two

persons—two men—who had not even begun to undress, though it was fully an hour since they had come upstairs. The younger was sitting on the edge of the old four-poster bed, with an arm round one of the columns at the foot; it might be presumed that he usually occupied this bed himself, and so he did; for he was Ian Stewart, the son of the house. He was of the dark type of Highlander, lithe and dark-haired, with deep blue eyes under black lashes, lean and sensitive in feature and looking about five and twenty. The other, of larger build altogether, un-usually finely made in fact, fair complexioned and some ten years his senior, was his first cousin and very good friend, Ewen Cameron of Ardroy, the father of the two little boys in the green bedchamber, come to fetch them both home again. He was now leaning over the back of a high chair, gazing at his kinsman with eyes more markedly blue than his, because they were not so dark.

"Yes, my father is set upon my marrying soon," said the young man on the bed with a sigh. "One can well understand it, Ewen; he is old, and desires to see a grand-son before he dies. But if Alan had lived——"

"No, there would not then have been the same necessity," agreed Ardroy. Alan Stewart, the elder brother, had been killed, unmarried, at Culloden, nine years before. "Yet, Ian, you have taken no vow against wedlock, have you? Or is there someone . . . ? "

Ian Stewart ran his finger round and round a detail of the acanthus carving on the bedpost. "There is no one," he confessed. "Indeed I wish there were. My father would not then have to look about for a suitable match—for which the choice is none so wide neither, since I naturally cannot marry a lady from a Whig family."

" And has Uncle Alexander found anyone?"

" Two," said Ian with a little grimace. " Miss MacLaren, and Maclean of Garroch's second daughter— the eldest is promised. I have no objection to either of them . . . save that I do not desire to marry either. I want someone of my own choice. Now do not, Ewen, tell me that arranged matches generally turn out very well, as I can see that you are upon the point of doing, for you have no right to possess an opinion on that subject, you who had the luck to marry the woman you chose for yourself and waited for! "

Ewen Cameron smiled and, coming round, threw himself into the chair on which he had been leaning. " I was not going to say anything of the sort. I wish I could help you, Ian; and I am sure that Alison would if she could. She'd not be a true woman if she did not hanker after the chance."

" If only I had the means to travel a little!" said his cousin regretfully. "Still and on, to go from place to place looking for a wife as one might search for a brood mare would not content me neither. A spaewife once told me that I should love a woman who would be other than she seemed—not a very pleasant prophecy, was it?—But enough of my affairs. Tell me, Ewen, how are matters between you and the new Chief of Glenshian since he succeeded his father last autumn, and is now become almost your neighbour?"

Very likely Ewen Cameron of Ardroy could prevent his sentiments from appearing on his face if he so wished —he looked as though he could—but with his present companion there was evidently no need to hide the signs of a most uncompromising antipathy to the individual just named. His bright blue eyes seemed to change colour till they were the match of his cousin's dark blue ones; his already decided chin appeared still more decided. "I am glad to say that I have not seen even his shadow near Ardroy, and I think it will be many a long day before Finlay MacPhair of Glenshian comes near my house. I know too much about him."

Ian looked at him curiously. "But is he aware of that?"

"Very well aware of it. I sometimes wonder that in the couple of years which have passed since I was enlightened as to his true character he has neither made overtures to me nor——" Ewen paused.

"Nor what?"

"——Nor found means to send a gillie behind me some dark night with a *sgian dubh*. We were both in Edinburgh last autumn—in fact I saw him, though he did not see me." Ardroy seemed to be going to add something else, but apparently changed his mind. "However, I know now that he will not touch me, and I have sworn not to touch him. It is checkmate."

Ian had got off the bed. "Ewen," he said, and his tone was grave, "are you jesting? Do you indeed go in danger of that man, because if so——"

"No, no," said Ardroy lightly. "I was not meaning that about the gillie; my tongue ran away with me."

"Then 'tis the first time I have ever known it do so," retorted his cousin, surveying him doubtfully. "And what is the discreditable secret that you know about Glenshian?"

Ewen put his elbow on the arm of the chair and shaded his brow with his hand. "There is nothing to be gained by sharing it." His voice had grown all at once very sombre. Ian stood still and looked at him.

"Oh, very well," he said at length, a trifle piqued. "I have no wish to pry into your relations with Glenshian, though they seem devilish uncomfortable ones. And why you should have sworn not to defend yourself against him passes my comprehension. I always thought you had more common sense than most."

"I did not swear that," answered Ewen after a pause. "I made a vow, two years ago, that it was not for me to take vengeance." He dropped his hand now, and young Stewart could see that he was very pale. "I cannot explain why I took such an oath . . . perhaps I was fey with grief . . . but I have never regretted it, and even if I should regret it in the future, still I must hold by it."

"Two years ago," "fey with grief"—Ian realised to what his cousin must be referring, to the execution of his kinsman, Archibald Cameron, which had been so great a sorrow to him and which he had risked his life to avert. His own slight resentment vanished; he laid a hand for a moment on Ewen's shoulder, and then went past him and, drawing the window-curtains aside, looked out. Yet he wondered what could possibly be Finlay MacPhair's connection with the tragedy—no, he must have misunderstood Ewen; there could be none. And he would not reopen so painful a subject.

"I hope we do not disturb Uncle Alexander by our talk," observed Ewen, rousing himself. "Is not this room of yours next to his?"

"My father grows a little hard of hearing," said Ian in reply. He dropped the curtain. "And the wind blows to-night. Speaking of my father's deafness, by the way, I think that was the reason why I overheard you telling him something about your brother-in-law, Hector

Grant—that he had come into an inheritance; or was I mistaken?"

"No, you were not mistaken," answered his cousin, and rose suddenly to his towering height. "Hector has been left a small property in Glenmoriston by some remote kinsman of his father's, and he will soon be coming over from his regiment in France to visit it. Indeed, Alison wonders whether he will not resign his commission and settle in Glenmoriston."

"Oh, indeed," said Ian drily. "But Mr. Grant will find the existence of a Highland laird but a poor thing after his life as an officer in France. Would he not be better advised to think twice before taking such a plunge?"

Ewen swung round on him. "I never knew that you disliked Hector!" he exclaimed in a tone of surprise.

"My dear Ewen, I don't. But I cannot think him, somehow, suited to the Highlands."

"He's as Highland as yourself, *laochain;* his mother was a Macrae."

"Maybe. But a lifetime spent in France has given him . . . too much French polish for my taste."

"Is that your objection?" said Ewen, laughing. "I had not noticed the defect myself; and as to a 'lifetime,' why, he is only about two years older than you. He is younger than my wife."

Ian made a gesture to dismiss Mr. Hector Grant. "Talking of Lady Ardroy, is the daughter like you or like her, Ewen? Your boys, I think, favour you both, one apiece."

"You had better come with me when I return and see for yourself," answered his cousin. "I shall insist upon Uncle Alexander sparing you for a night or two.

You have not visited us, I think, since you gave Donald that claymore hilt which Keithie threw into the loch, two years ago last autumn. Now, if you'll forgive me, I am going to bed!"

On that announcement his host remorsefully snatched up a candle to light him to his room, excusing himself for having selfishly, as he declared, called him into his, by the fact that he saw him so rarely.

But, coming back, Ian Stewart did not follow his kinsman's example and go to bed. He sat down on the window-seat, where the curtain was already drawn aside, and gazed for a long time at the silver road which led across Loch Linnhe to the mountains beyond. The Celt in him had gone dreaming; dreaming as a girl is supposed to dream of the ideal lover. But *his* romance had never come to him, and soon it would be too late for it. He must mate, since it was his duty to beget children to come after him, without ever knowing that high rapture of which the poets sang, and the moonlight, and the flight of wild swans over the pool. There would be no Deirdre or white-breasted Bronwen for him, only a decorous young housewife, a MacLaren or a Maclean, whom he would respect and cherish, and to whom he would be faithful. In time, perhaps, would come affection too. Well, perhaps that was better in the end than passion, but youth was slipping away, and he had never known youth's prerogative, to give, and hazard everything in the giving. His marriage would be as tepid an affair as that impassive moon now looking at him over the mountains of Ardgour.

Yet under that same roof, up in her little turret room, Ian's young sister Jacqueline was smiling in her sleep, having heard something that evening

which had pleased her. For her sentiments about Lieuten-
ant—now Captain—Hector Grant differed entirely
from her brother's. In her dreams she did not seek the
ideal lover, for it seemed to her that she had already
met him, here in her father's house, more than two years
ago. She had been but seventeen then. If, on his way
to his recent inheritance in Glenmoriston, he should come
this way again? . . . She was dreaming that he had.

And away in northern France, where the same moon
was silvering the steep-pitched roofs of Lille, a handsome
young man in uniform was going home to his quarters,
after a game of cards, with pockets somewhat lightened.
But what did that matter? He was almost a man of
substance now—no longer, at any rate, a mere landless
Jacobite. In the deserted streets, whence all good
burghers had long ago departed, and where his footfalls
woke such echoes on the cobbles, he began to whistle a
Scots air. And who knows whether, when at last he
reached his couch, he was not visited by the image of
a girl in far away Appin? But the moon could not be
sure of this, for she sank to rest before he did.

She missed, therefore, by the hour of her setting, the
conclusion of a novel and most interesting experiment in
cattle-lifting not far from Ewen Cameron's home at
Ardroy in Lochaber.

CHAPTER II

ON HIS VERY HEARTHSTONE

June 17th.

"Eh, Alison, my lass, she's going to be a beauty!"
declared Miss Margaret Cameron, indicating a red and
puckered object in which only the eye of faith or of close
kinship could discern any such promise. Both these re-
quirements, however, were fulfilled by the keen gaze of
Miss Cameron, the infant's great-aunt, who had brought
up Ewen Cameron himself from a child.

"You really think so?" asked Alison Cameron as,
propped up in bed, she stooped her pretty becapped head
with a smile over the sleeping baby in the crook of her
arm. "I am afraid that Donald and Keithie may not
be of that opinion when they return to-morrow. It was
to-morrow that Ewen said, was it not, Aunt Marget?"

"To-morrow it was, my dear. Now, shall I open
your window a wee, since 'tis such a fine afternoon?"
Erect, silver-haired and comely, she went to the window
for that purpose, and gave an exclamation. "Preserve
us, there's about half a score of gillies or what not down
below there! Now, might they but wear the tartan
again, one could tell whose they were."

She continued to look out, uttering various surmises
as to the identity of the invaders, until bent old Marsali,
who had the entrée, came into the bedchamber.

"There's a gentleman below asking for Mac 'ic

Ailein, and he from home," she announced in the Gaelic and unemotionally.

"A gentleman? Who is it?" inquired Miss Cameron with interest.

"By what he says, it will be MacPhair of Glenshian."

Alison uttered a little exclamation, and her arm tightened round Miss Cameron the younger.

"Glenshian!" exclaimed the elder lady. "And what's Glenshian wanting here?"

"He's wanting the laird on an affair of business," replied the old woman. "Then he asked could he see Lady Ardroy."

"The idea!" exclaimed Miss Cameron. "I will come down, Marsali, and find out what he desires. Am I sufficiently *à la mode*, think you, Alison? This is the first time the present Glenshian has set foot in this house, and I must not disgrace its master."

Alison beckoned her to the bed. "Aunt Margaret," she said in a rather troubled voice, "I do not know how much you know, but Ewen and Glenshian are . . . not good friends. I wonder what has brought him?"

"Not good friends? Since when?—Aye, I have fancied something of the sort. Then 'tis as well that Ewen is away," deduced Miss Cameron briskly. "Glenshian can't but be polite to an old woman, and he a young man too."

"But you say he has brought a number of gillies with him!"

"Isn't he but nine months or so Chief, and likes to swagger about with his tail on? Never fash yourself for that, Alison, my doo," replied Aunt Margaret, and, after setting her cap carefully to rights at the mirror, she left the bedchamber.

2

As she entered the big living room below, a tall, red-haired young man turned round from his contemplation either of the antlers over the hearth or, possibly, of the worn escutcheon on the stone, where the motto *Fideliter* could more clearly be read than the half defaced bearings of the shield. For a second or two he stared at the elderly lady as if surprised ; then he bowed politely in response to her rustling curtsey.

"Good day to you, sir," said Aunt Margaret pleasantly. "My nephew Ardroy is from home, as I expect you'll have been told already, and his wife lies upstairs with a newborn bairn, so the task of welcoming you here falls upon me. I am Miss Cameron. Will you not be seated?"

"When you are, madam," replied the Chief of Glenshian politely, and waited until Miss Cameron had disposed herself. Then he sat down at no great distance and looked at her, drawing his light eyebrows together in a contraction that was half puzzled, half annoyed.

"Ardroy will be sorry to miss you," observed Miss Cameron after a moment. "We do not expect him back before the morrow."

"Aye, that makes my errand the more awkward," responded the visitor, fingering his chin.

"Perhaps your errand can wait, sir?" suggested Aunt Margaret. "Though I would not wish to give you the trouble of bringing yourself and your tail"—she gave a glance through the window—"these many miles again. Can I not give my nephew a message?"

Finlay MacPhair shook his head. "My business is not an agreeable one for a gentleman to come upon to another gentleman," he remarked.

"Then perhaps," suggested Miss Cameron, quite unperturbed, "you'll find it easier to transact with a lady?"

"Not at all," said the new Chief, frowning. "Not at all. 'Tis no matter for a woman."

"Improper, do you mean?" queried his hostess. "I am old, Glenshian—nearly sixty-five. You may risk scandalising me."

Mr. MacPhair gave an impatient movement. "Has Ardroy no factor with whom I could deal?" he demanded.

"I'm all the factor he's ever had in the past," replied Aunt Margaret with perfect truth. "He's his own grieve now. See now, if it's some matter of affairs, I'm sure he'll be pleased to wait upon you at Invershian when he returns from Appin."

The young man's lip curled in a sarcastic smile. "I doubt it, madam. And that would not serve, neither; the business cannot be transacted anywhere but here."

"Then you'll e'en have to put yourself to the trouble of coming again, sir, or stay until Ardroy returns. This house is at your disposal."

"That's out of the question," said the visitor rather rudely. "I must then do what I have come for in Ardroy's absence."

The very tiniest stiffening was apparent in Miss Cameron's upright figure as she sat there. "If you will kindly enlighten me as to what you propose, sir, we will see about that," quoth she.

"Madam," returned Mr. MacPhair with emphasis, "I will enlighten you. You have lived in the Highlands, I daresay, for——"

"For well over half a century," filled in Miss Cameron.

"And you will not be a stranger to the fact that Lochaber has always been noted for cattle-lifting."

"Aye, nearly as noted as Glenshian," agreed the lady, smiling.

The Chief of that region could not have relished the quite justified retort, but he could affect not to show that he felt it. "All that," he pursued, "is supposed—*supposed*—to be old history now, but . . . I'm wanting two of my best steers this week past, and I have but just come upon proof of where they went to. I regret to have to say it, madam . . . but you'll find them amongst Ardroy's cattle!"

Miss Cameron jumped up, a sparkle in her eye. "You accuse——"

The young man also rose. "No, no, madam," he protested with apparent sincerity. "I should be loth to bring such an accusation against a gentleman. But what laird in these parts knows precisely what his tenants will be about when his back is turned . . . and you say Ardroy is from home now. Yet, since the steers are branded——"

"Aye," broke in Miss Cameron with vivacity, "that alone proves, my good sir, that you are talking nonsense—and very offensive nonsense too! Had the cattle come here, by straying or even by reiving, you would have had them back by now, branded as you say they are."

"Yet I have not had them back."

"Then they never came here."

Glenshian looked at her loftily. "I have the best of reasons for knowing that they did . . . I should like to see Ardroy's herdsman."

"I have no authority to allow that in his absence," replied Miss Cameron. "I perceive," she went on with

warmth, " that you're almost upon saying that I went and
lifted your steers myself one dark night, and have them
hidden—in my bedchamber belike! You may go and
look, sir. But warrant you to interfere with Ardroy's
dependents I cannot."

" Then," said the visitor still more loftily, " I regret,
but I shall have to do it without your warrant, madam.
I am not going back without my steers."

" You'll go back without much reputation for civility,
Mr. MacPhair!" retorted the lady. " But as you have
brought some sort of an army with you, and we are only
women in this house . . ." She made a gesture. " Forbye, are you sure you did not know all the while that
Ardroy was from home?"

To this suggestion Glenshian deigned no answer. He
said, looking black, " There are men on Ardroy's land,
at any rate—the men who drove off my cattle."

" And do you think, sir, that they are going to help
you find those phantom beasts?"

" Someone is going to help me find them. I have
come for that!"

And like two duellists, the young man and the old
woman faced each other. Miss Cameron made the first
lunge.

" Very good then," she said after a moment. " Take
your tail that's out there, and go up the braeside, Glenshian, and look for your steers. But if you think that
one of Ardroy's gillies will lift a finger to help you without orders from him you are sore mistaken! In the
latter end you and your gathering will likely all spend
the night in a bog!" And she followed up this attack
by a second. "Here's another point for your consideration: God knows what sort of faces my nephew's tenants,

and particularly the MacMartins, will show you when you go marching over his land and driving his cattle!"

"You will please to send word in advance, madam, upon what errand I am come."

"And have the look of countenancing it! I shall do nothing of the sort!"

To the ears of the disputants, both now thoroughly roused—and the younger and stronger aware, too, that this damned old lady had him at something of a disadvantage by her refusal of support—there came in the momentary silence the rumble of carriage-wheels. Miss Cameron, if her older hearing did not perceive it quite as quickly, was, however, at once aware, from the way he turned his head, that the intruder had heard something or other.

"That's maybe Ardroy returning before he's expected," she remarked casually, though she did not think it was. "You will be able to make your request to him in person, which will no doubt be more agreeable to a gentleman like yourself than trying to bully an old woman."

"Request," said Finlay MacPhair, throwing back his head. "I'd have you know, madam——"

But, then, out of the corner of his eye, he perceived a chaise pass the window, and did not finish the sentence.

"Losh, it *is* Ardroy and the bairns!" exclaimed Miss Cameron in genuine surprise. "What brings him back before his time?" She went to the parlour door (the vehicle having meanwhile passed out of sight, and being presumably by now in the act of discharging its occupants) and called out, "Ewen, come away ben at once; here's a visitor to see you!"

And so, a moment or two later, Ewen Cameron

entered to find the enemy who, as he had declared only two nights ago, was not likely ever to trouble his house, standing in a very haughty manner almost upon its hearthstone. He had not seen Finlay MacPhair face to face—though he had seen his back—since the revelation of his treachery, two years ago, in the Chief's London lodging, when he himself had interposed between his sword and Hector Grant's.* He stopped, speechless, in the doorway.

"You are surprised to see me, Ardroy?" said the visitor, showing no embarrassed consciousness at all of their last meeting. "But when you hear why I am come, I can't but think that you will put fewer obstacles in my path than your good aunt here has seen fit to do."

"I wonder!" thought Aunt Margaret. Her nephew's dour expression suggested that there was one path at least in which he would place no obstacles, and that was Mr. MacPhair's homeward one. His lips were so firmly closed that, to her, it seemed as if he were only keeping back with difficulty the utterance of this sentiment; but the traditions of Highland hospitality were too strong for him to give way to his visible desire.

"In what then can I serve you, Glenshian?" he asked in the most frigid tones, laying his hat and a riding whip upon the table as he spoke.

And Finlay the Red answered him with much directness: "By restoring to me the cattle which your tenants have lifted from me."

A quick flush dyed Ewen's fair skin. "I think I cannot have heard you aright, sir. My tenants do not lift cattle . . . from anyone!"

The young Chief smiled a half pitying smile. "Not

*See *The Gleam in the North.*

with your knowledge, perhaps; I do not suggest that. But, as I was just remarking to Miss Cameron, who knows what goes on behind the laird's back?"

"In the case of a man with so many dependents as yourself, that question may perhaps be asked," retorted Ewen. "But I, with my mere handful "—there was no humility, rather the reverse, in his tone—" I flatter myself that I know their employments pretty well."

Glenshian sniggered. "I would not be too ready to claim that knowledge if I were in your place, Ardroy. In the end it might prove awkward for you."

But, before her nephew could reply to this innuendo, Aunt Margaret, already standing at the door, had slipped out of the room. Although by nature she relished a fight, it seemed to her that Ewen would prefer to have out this preposterous business unhampered by the presence of a woman. Moreover she must prepare Alison for the onslaught of her small sons. The sound of their excited voices and of racing feet was even now audible upstairs, and the hall door had just opened to admit a man in riding costume whom she recognised, without much surprise, as young Invernacree.

"Is that Ian Stewart?" she asked, and, Ian coming forward to salute her, she went on, in a voice which, despite herself, showed signs of trouble, "MacPhair of Glenshian is here, making a great pother about a couple of steers which he swears Ewen's people have lifted from him. Whether you'd best go in on them or not I don't know. Ewen looks very angry, but I suppose they'll not come to blows—at least I hope not."

Ian hesitated a moment; then he remembered something which Ewen had let fall about a dark night and a *sgian dubh*. "I can always leave the room if necessary," he answered, and opening the parlour door, went in, on the sound of a voice which was not his cousin's, to catch the words, ". . . if you refuse to put it to the proof!"

By the inflection it was the end of a sentence, and then he saw the speaker, standing at the far end of the room, young, arrogant-looking, red-haired and tall. Ewen (still taller) who faced this visitor, swung round for a second as the door opened, saw his kinsman, then turned back and said, rather as if he were hurling a missile at the man on his hearthstone:

"Very good, then! It *shall* be put to the proof—and here is a witness. Ian, let me present you to Mr. MacPhair of Glenshian, who has come here to accuse me of stealing two of his cattle. Glenshian, this is my cousin, Mr. Stewart the younger of Invernacree."

CHAPTER III

BRANDED

§1

June 17th (continued).

IAN STEWART knew his kinsman well enough to divine that he was in a towering rage, though a stranger might not have guessed it. Across the room the red-haired young man returned his own bow by a slight inclination of the head.

"Your servant, Mr. Stewart.—Perhaps hardly an unbiassed witness, Ardroy, in view of that kinship; but let that pass. Truth will always out."

Ian heard his cousin give an exclamation under his breath. "Is it possible that you are learning that at last?" he asked.

The new Chief moved forward a little from his stand by the hearth. "You'll not advance your cause by being offensive, Ewen Cameron!" he retorted, his eyes lighting up. "There's one thing *you* have certainly no need to learn, and that's the advantage of having some relative or other at your heels in your dealings with me! This time, however, I trust that your intervention will not be required to save me from assassination by your henchman, as it was in the case of Mr. Grant. I owe you thanks for that intervention, if for nothing else."

A brief but tingling silence succeeded this speech, to Ian so startling that he almost thought his ears could not have conveyed its purport aright. But one glance at Ewen's face and pose convinced him that battle was now joined between him and the speaker over a matter more serious than a few supposedly stolen cattle.

"Since you have brought up what occurred at our last meeting, Mr. MacPhair," said Ardroy with extreme grimness "—though I should have thought you would have preferred it to remain in oblivion—we had best go into it thoroughly. If you wish, I will ask Mr. Stewart to withdraw."

"By no means," responded Finlay the Red, folding his arms. "For I do not know what account you may have given him of that occasion." He turned to Ian. "Your kinsman here, Mr. Stewart, most unwarrantably invaded my premises in London, and his satellite, Mr. Hector Grant, took from me, at the point of the sword, a treacherous paper of his own writing which, since it came by good chance into my hands, I had been able to hinder from fulfilling its black purpose. I——"

He got no further. Ewen had stridden forward, overriding him. "Don't listen to him, Ian! God's name, this impudence surpasses everything.—Who stole that letter, Finlay MacPhair, who deciphered it and sent it to the English Government, who——"

"'Tis much more to the point," broke in Glenshian with an unpleasant smile, "to ask who wrote it, full of secret information as it was, and handed it over, under pretext of having been robbed, to a Government agent in the Highlands? Mr. Stewart had better know the answer to that. It was the same Mr. Hector Grant who was so anxious to get his damning property into his own hands again that he was ready to cut my throat for it!"

"That's a foul lie!" cried Ewen passionately.

" Hector Grant's letter was written and intended for the eyes of Cluny Macpherson and no man else."

" And had no direction upon it!" sneered Glenshian. " A curious kind of ' letter.' 'Twas nothing else but a paper of information, and if I had not rescued it——"

" ' Rescued it!' " burst out Ardroy, unable to contain himself. " You ' rescued ' it from your ally, Mr. Pelham, I suppose! Did you also 'rescue ' the letter from that dirty traitor, Samuel Cameron, which was in your pocket that day? You did not save him from being drummed out of the regiment for his complicity. And the noblest blood that has been shed in England this many a year . . . do you ever look at your hands, Glenshian? "

At that unmistakeable insinuation the much perturbed Ian expected the Chief either to spring at his accuser's throat or to crumple up entirely. He himself felt both bewildered and revolted, for he knew Ewen Cameron too well to suppose that he would ever make random accusations of such terrible gravity, especially against a fellow Jacobite. But Finlay MacPhair, though his face seemed suddenly drained of colour, neither sprang nor flinched. He again moved forward a little until he was quite near the table, and, drawing himself up to his full six feet of height said, with surprising coolness:

" If by that hyperbole you mean the late Dr. Cameron's blood, then I can only assume that your affection for that unfortunate gentleman has unsettled your intellects, and that I need not therefore take with you the course I should pursue with any other man who had made such a suggestion to me." Here his hand fell upon Ewen's riding-whip, which was now lying within his reach, and he fingered it significantly, looking the while at its owner, who stood with clenched hands well within range of a slash across the face. Ian, afraid to move for fear of precipitating such a catastrophe, nevertheless braced his muscles to fling himself upon the assailant the moment he should grasp the handle.

But Finlay MacPhair went on contemptuously, "You were once good enough to assure me that some day in the Highlands we should settle accounts over the question of the late Dr. Cameron's connection with the Loch Arkaig treasure. But I don't think I am disposed ever to go out with a man who has not yet disproved that he is . . . a cattle-thief!"

The word came out with all the sting of the lash which had not been lifted from the table. Ewen took a step backward and gripped one hand hard round the wrist of the other. With an immense effort he succeeded in answering quietly, though he was exceedingly pale, and his eyes sparkled like blue diamonds.

"I have already undertaken to disprove that. If you will wait a moment, I will go and give the necessary orders." And, turning abruptly on his heel, he went out of the room. Ian followed him.

"Ewen," he burst out, "that man—he's insufferable! What are you going to do now?"

There was sweat on Ardroy's brow. He put up his hand and wiped it off. "Give orders instantly to have all my cattle driven in and go through the tally," he answered, gritting his teeth together. "God give me patience! . . . And I have not seen Alison yet . . . I'd best not, I think, till this business is over, and he's out of my house." And he flung through the porch, almost into the midst of Glenshian's waiting gillies, and Ian heard him calling, "Angus—where is Angus MacMartin?"

§ 2

An immense, blood-red and ominous sunset was towering in the west, high over the heads of antlike men and their dwarf cattle, ere the business of disproving the Chief of Glenshian's accusation was finished. Yet a warm brown dusk was already beginning to rest upon the great spaces of bloomless heather, seeming, indeed, rather to be breathed out by the ground itself, just as from Ardroy's own little loch, Loch na h-Iolaire, the Loch of the Eagle, there was already rising a ghostly film of mist. Ewen's shaggy cattle, thus unusually driven down and herded together in this comparatively level stretch not far from the loch, lowed uneasily, pushed at each other with their spreading horns, or looked about from under their tawny fringes in mild perplexity. Hours of the hardest and hottest work had gone to their collecting, not because they were so numerous, but because they were so scattered in their grazing.

"There still want three," said Ewen, glancing at the list in his hand. He and Ian stood on the edge of the herd, with never a glance behind them, where on a little knoll Glenshian sat with a gillie at his back. The only person who occasionally turned his eyes that way was eight year old Donald, who, heated from his assistance in the chase, now stood by his father's side and perpetually counted the cattle, reaching a different total every time.

"Those will be the three," said Ewen, "which gave Duncan the slip up there. But he sent a couple of men after them."

"And there they come, I fancy," observed Ian, pointing to a small group of cattle and two men who were making their way slowly round the end of the loch.

" But your list is incorrect, Ewen, or else the beasts have been miscounted, for there are five steers there instead of three." He said this in all innocence, suddenly realised the possible significance of what he had seen, and ejaculated under his breath, " It's not possible!"

As for the laird of Ardroy beside him, he might have become one of the pines by the loch, he was so still. Nearer and nearer came the five steers, in a leisurely, lurching fashion, and the sunset glowed upon their lion-coloured pelts and touched their enormous horns with light. They were all of the same breed, indistinguishable save to the eyes of a herdsman. " They *must* all be Ewen's!" thought Ian. " Someone has miscounted."

Ardroy roused himself and beckoned.

" What is the meaning of this, Duncan?" he asked hoarsely. " Why have I two more beasts than the tally shows?"

Duncan looked at his master with eyes at once shrewd and visionary. "Witchcraft, Mac 'ic Ailein," he replied. " Four days ago you had them not. Yet they may have strayed into the herd."

" They have been stolen!" said Ardroy in a fierce, ashamed voice. "They could never have strayed so far from Mac 'ic Fhionnlaigh's land. Stolen by one of my men—in effect, then, stolen by me! And I so certain———"

" Father," broke in Donald's little voice by his side, " here is the gentleman coming down to speak to you."

And Ewen Cameron turned to meet the bitter chagrin and humiliation he saw falling upon him. Glenshian, descending leisurely from his mound, walked towards him through the rustling heather-stems, his hair glowing like fire beneath the red canopy spread above them all.

"It was well I had patience until the end," he observed with a very disagreeable smile. "Yet, as I said, truth will out. Here come two of my best steers, Ardroy —well hidden away they were, no doubt."

"Prove your ownership!" said Ewen, short and sharp.

"Seumas!" called the Chief over his shoulder. The gillie went forward, seized one of the beasts by a horn, tugged it nearer, pushed it sideways, and, lifting the shaggy hair on one flank, disclosed a large "G" roughly branded there. In the same dead silence he repeated the performance with another. A long breath went up from the assemblage of hot and weary men, and Glenshian's gillies began to talk excitedly together. Ardroy's were silent. And the colour on their master's face was not from the sunset.

"You'll allow my men, I suppose, to take my stolen property home?" queried Fionnlagh Ruadh. "And, since you were so insistent that you knew all about your people's doings, Ardroy, I must conclude that this petty theft—one can hardly dignify it with the name of a *creach*—had your connivance."

This he said so that all could hear; stepping closer, he added in a lower tone, "Your own glove will be the better of a wash in the gutter now!"

He swung on his heel, went to his horse, which a gillie brought forward from the mound, gave an order, and mounted. With sulky, puzzled faces the Camerons watched the two alien steers being separated from the rest and driven off after him. Ian and little Donald saw Ewen himself, as if stung by a gadfly, go striding away from all of them, under that yet tremendous sunset which might have been painted for the setting of some great tragedy rather than of this ignominious little exposure.

Ian took his small relative's hand. "Come home, Donald; we'll not wait for your father."

And Donald, knitting his brows, came obediently. He asked questions, of course, which young Invernacree did his best to answer, in spite of his own bewilderment. What an odious and inexplicable scene! . . . Poor Ewen!

"Cousin Ian, Cousin Ian, our house is on fire!"

For they were now come in sight of the House of Ardroy, and its western windows did flame and glitter as if a conflagration raged within.

"'Tis only the reflection of the sunset, *laochain*," answered the young man. ("Or else the house is angry, like its owner, at the affront put upon him.") But he did not pass on this fancy to the astonished and excited little boy at his side.

§ 3

The burnt out sunset was only a memory, for even the tall candles were dwindled down nearly to their sockets that night ere Ian put to his cousin the question which had been secretly tearing at him all evening. For up till now they had spoken of nothing but the problem of the stolen cattle.

"Ewen, is it true about Finlay MacPhair—that he has Doctor Cameron's blood at his door?"

Ewen's eyes met his. The angry mortification still alight in their blue depths gave way to another emotion.

"It is quite true. I will tell you how I know it. First of all, it was common talk among the Jacobites in London that Archie would never be brought to trial because the English Government would have had to produce evidence whose source they did not wish to reveal—in other words they had some valuable spy whose usefulness they did not intend to curtail by disclosing his identity. Next, with my own eyes I saw Finlay MacPhair coming secretly one night out of the house of Mr. Henry Pelham, my Lord Newcastle's brother—he who died last year. When I charged Glenshian with this, in Hector's presence, he denied it absolutely, and told us some fairy tale about a ' double.' Upon that we discovered in his lodging the very letter whose loss had caused some most damaging reflections on Hector's honour—the cipher letter which he had written to Cluny Macpherson and which was stolen from him in the Highlands the previous autumn, when Archie came over, by some man who was either an agent of the Government's or of Glenshian's himself."

" That, I suppose," commented Ian, " was the letter which Glenshian pretended this afternoon contained intelligence really meant for the Government, because it was not openly directed to Cluny? "

" Yes. You see how he twisted that unlucky business, cunning as he is, in order to carry the war into the enemy's country. I need not tell you that you might as well suspect me of purposely giving information as Hector Grant.— To resume, on finding this letter of his in Finlay's possession Hector drew his sword upon him; I contrived to separate them before either had injured the other. Glenshian, who was recovering from an illness, swooned from the exertion, and Hector, going through his pockets in search of further evidence, found undeniable testimony that it was actually through his agency that he had been slandered. Finlay had taken steps to try to put the blame, or part of it, for Archie's capture upon poor Hector's shoulders. Why should he have done that, if it were not to ease his own? "

One candle expired guttering in an overflow of wax. Neither of the men at the table even noticed it.

"You mean to say, then, it was Finlay MacPhair of Glenshian who betrayed Archibald Cameron to death?" said the younger in accents of horror. "Ewen, I can scarce believe it! And if it be so, why in God's name have you not warned everyone against him—why have you so kept your knowledge to yourself? I know you too well to suppose that it was from fear of any consequence to yourself; moreover if Glenshian knows that you know—and indeed you have now charged him with it to his face—you go always in danger of some measure of retaliation on his part, as you hinted a few nights ago at Invernacree."

"It looks somewhat as though that retaliation had already begun," agreed Ewen with a wry smile. "Your question is very natural, Ian. But it is a different matter to be convinced of Finlay's responsibility, as I am in my very bones, and to possess sufficient proof to warrant my accusing him directly to the King, or even to Secretary Edgar. I have warned a few friends, privately. But my only proofs are that I saw him coming out of Mr. Pelham's door, and that Hector's deciphered letter—and Samuel Cameron's—were in his possession. Moreover, as I told you after Archie's execution, the man who sent to the authorities intelligence of his actual whereabouts in Glenbuckie is still to find. He was probably in collusion with Glenshian, or even in his pay—but I have no proof of that whatever. Yet Finlay's was the hand—I shall believe that to my dying day—though this unknown man was the dagger in it."

Ian sighed. A lost cause, indeed, whose adherents could so shamelessly betray a comrade. . . .

"What was it," he asked dully, after a moment, "that

Glenshian said to you, as he was going away, about a glove and the gutter? "

Ewen pushed back his chair and rose. " Oh, that! In Edinburgh last autumn he picked up a glove which Alison had dropped and returned it to her. I took it from her and threw it into the gutter. He must have seen me do it . . . I thought he had not . . . though I should have done it just the same. . . . Well, 'tis all one . . . and perhaps he is even with me now."

CHAPTER IV

THE LADY FROM THE LOCH

§ 1

June 19th—21st.

THE tide was running out very strongly from Loch Leven at Ballachulish two evenings later, and the passage across the ferry was consequently prolonged, so hard did the rowers have to strain to keep the ferry-boat even moderately in her course. Between the necessity of coaxing his mare to stand quiet for longer than usual in this craft, and the memory of the day before yesterday's scene at Ardroy, which continued to play itself over in his brain, Ian Stewart had little thought to spare for the sunset across Loch Linnhe, which was transmuting to red gold the sentinel heights at the entrance to Glencoe. If he noticed it at all, it was but to be reminded of that, even more splendid, by the Loch of the Eagle, and what it had witnessed.

One could not disembark on the Appin side of the passage without seeing what dangled from the gibbet on the hillock there; a thing which had once been a man, and a Stewart too—chained bones which testified to Campbell vengeance for a murdered Campbell. To-day Ian hardly looked up, but took the road by the gate of Ballachulish House and under the flanks of Lettermore, past the very spot where Campbell of Glenure had fallen, without thought of that three-year old tragedy. Another tragedy was engaging his mind—Archibald Cameron's—and the incredible part which Finlay MacPhair seemed to have

43

played therein. Really it was less abhorrent to think that Ewen had been mistaken, that his strong affection for his dead kinsman had led him into fixing the guilt of his judicial murder on a man who had indeed behaved in an equivocal fashion, but who, in his position and with his traditions, surely could not have deliberately betrayed a comrade. Besides, as even Ewen had admitted, there was always the actual informer to account for. If Finlay's hands were smeared, his were dripping.

The cousins had not spoken again of that black business. The whole of yesterday had been spent in trying to find the man who had so smirched his young laird's honour by cattle-stealing, but all attempts had proved fruitless, and had only tended to injure the good feeling which existed between Ardroy and his dependents. Ian's belief that the culprit must have been tracked by one of Glenshian's people was shaken by the universal denials, not only of the theft, but of any smallest knowledge of it. The mystery of the stolen steers raged like a plague through the house as well; it seemed as if no one could talk of anything else —save, naturally, Ewen's infant daughter, whom Ian had been allowed to see, and even, to his secret terror, to hold. It was a thoroughly uncomfortable, even unhappy day, and had, Ian feared, sown seeds of mistrust and ill-feeling between Ewen and his tenantry whose harvest might not easily be rooted up. Finlay MacPhair could hardly have planned a better revenge, upon a petty scale, than this which Fate had planned for him.

But had the planning been entirely Fate's? Ian went so far as to wonder whether the Chief of Glenshian could possibly have bribed some very poor gillie of Ewen's to steal the animals, so that he, as owner, could come to Ardroy with the triumphant foreknowledge that he should find them there? Surely no Cameron or MacMartin would have lent himself to such a transaction! And yet . . . it had all fallen out so pat. . . .

Immersed in these speculations, Ian rode on at a good pace. Duror of Appin was behind him; he would be home before long. The sunset had withered slowly, but now the mountains across Loch Linnhe were once more cloaking themselves in the grape-hued mystery of twilight. Young Invernacree, who loved them, and had something of the poet in him, came for a moment out of his absorption, some Gaelic verses about the high hilltops recurring to his memory; and then poetry and cattle-lifting were alike driven out of his mind by a distant sound ahead of him resembling that of horses galloping at a rate very unusual on this rough road, accompanied by a rumbling noise such as a heavy vehicle might make. He rounded a corner and saw that his ears had heard aright. Swaying and banging, a coach was fleeing away in front of him along the loch-bordered road—and fleeing was really the word for its progress behind its obviously runaway horses. Ian decided that he must already have heard the hoofs of these before they had broken into their mad gallop, but had been too preoccupied to realise the fact. Now . . . he struck spurs into his mare and sent her forward after the receding vehicle.

It was instinctive, his pursuit, though even in its course he knew that he could do little good. The ill-fated coach had had too much start of him. He could not see the postillion for its bulk, and wondered whether the latter had lost his seat, and that this accounted for the coach's wild career; but in that case he must have come upon him by the roadside. Now he saw a man's head emerge for a moment from the left-hand window, the furthest from the loch and go back again; then a hand sought for the handle of the door and opened it.

"Is he going to jump out? Uncommon dangerous!" thought the pursuer. "And is he alone in there, or is there another occupant?" For the man was with one hand keeping the door open, no easy task at that rate of progress; yet, as his head and shoulders remained within, it almost seemed as if he were occupied with some other person in the interior of the conveyance. And then, before he could jump—if such were his intention—the end came, and in a more catastrophic manner than the rider behind had anticipated. For the road again made a slight bend, and, to Ian's horror, the rocking coach, instead of following it round the curve, plunged straight ahead. The horseman uttered a shout of dismay as he saw the vehicle go clear over the brink; it lurched, half stopped, then toppled over on to its side on the stones of the shore. There was a splash as it struck the shallow water—luckily the tide was out. Nor was the actual drop from the road, mercifully, more than a very few feet.

But, before it actually went over, the man who had been trying to get out had succeeded in doing so—half scrambling, half thrown—and was now picking himself up out of the road. The postillion—he was there after all—had stuck to the horses, and by the time Ian arrived he was cutting the traces of one, which was lying struggling. The other had wrenched itself free and was making off. Seeing that the gentleman on the road was, if not altogether unhurt, at least able to get to his feet, Ian, as he swung himself off his own mount, was for making to the assistance of the postillion. But he found his arm gripped, and a hoarse, desperate voice said in his ear:

"Help me, for God's sake! There's a lady—my

daughter, inside the coach . . . drowning perhaps . . ."

Horrified, Ian ran down to the shore. A lady in there —how was one going to get her out? The upper wheels of the coach as it lay on its side reared themselves at about the level of his head; one could only see the underneath of the vehicle, and its great springs.

"I'll climb up, sir," he said to the traveller, now at his elbow. He perceived him to be spare, middle-aged, rather harsh-featured, with a grey wig somewhat awry from his tumble.

Young and agile, Ian swung himself up and clambered on to the side of the coach, now become a roof, and stood there like a mariner boarding a derelict. In the accident the door had slammed itself to. Ian stooped, wrenched it open and looked in.

Down at the bottom of the species of large, ill-lighted box thus presented to his gaze, amid fallen cushions and wraps—and a glimmer of water also—there was a lady in a blue cloak. She lay on her side without stirring— yet surely there had not been time or water enough to drown her! She must have been thrown against something hard and have struck her head as the coach went over. But which was the quickest and best method of getting her out?

A distracted voice below was saying, "Is she hurt? Help me up . . . get her out, man! Why, the coach is half in the water!" And there was the elderly traveller trying vainly to emulate his own gymnastic feat.

"Stay where you are, sir," said the young man hastily. "I will pass her down to you. Postillion, leave that horse to shift for itself now, and come up here to me."

"Do as the gentleman bids you, James," said his employer, and the postillion left the now freed horse, which, subdued by its recent experience, got to its hind legs and remained there trembling. Ian had thought at first that by bending in through the window, with the man to hold him, he could haul the lady out, but he soon saw that she was too far away from his reach in this position. One of them must get down into the box and lift her up to the other; he had only been deterred from doing this at once by the fear that he should trample on her. However, he must risk that. He tugged off his riding boots, and taking a careful view of what lay beneath him, lowered himself through the door and felt about with his stockinged feet until he encountered something flat and solid upon which to rest his weight. He did not know what it was; it was enough that he stood neither upon the lady nor the broken glass of the undermost window. Water lapped cold about his ankles as he removed his arms from the doorway.

And there at his feet was the girl, as pale as the swansdown collar of her cloak. Ian stooped and very gently lifted her by the shoulders; her head fell limply back. He touched her face; it was not even wet. Thank God, her mouth and nose had not, then, been under water, though he could feel that parts of her clothing were saturated. Laying an inexpert hand upon her pulse he found it beating, as it seemed to him, regularly enough. But it was not too easy, in that confined space, and with uncertain footing, to raise the injured lady and hold her up to the postillion leaning ready to receive her at the aperture above, and Ian was afraid that the man might let her slip; however he himself supported most of her weight from below. At last the postillion had her safe and drew her through; the rescuer scrambled after her to the upper side of the coach, and together they lowered her into the arms of the agitated gentleman waiting to receive her.

A moment or two later young Invernacree, somewhat breathless, was once again looking down on the girl. Now, however, she lay on the pebbles of the foreshore, half supported in the arms of her father, who had taken off her bonnet and was gazing with deep distress at the cut, scarcely more than a scratch, which its removal had disclosed above one shapely eyebrow. Ian went and dipped his handkerchief in the loch, and the traveller, accepting it, wiped away the blood.

"I think the wound is but slight, sir," said Ian earnestly. "A splinter of broken glass, perhaps. But we will get the lady at once to shelter. My father's house is a bare mile from here. There is no vehicle obtainable, but surely the postillion and I could carry her upon a cloak; and on the way there is a small farmhouse whence I could despatch a messenger to warn my sister to have a bed ready, and where I could also arrange to have your missing horse sought for."

The traveller thanked him warmly, premising only that he himself would assist the man to carry his daughter, in order that the rescuer should ride on ahead as messenger. But, on attempting this arrangement, it appeared that the gentleman's own fall from the coach had not been entirely innocuous, and that a slight wrench to one knee, of which in his devouring anxiety he had hardly been aware, would prevent that modification being carried out. He, and not Ian, must therefore ride the latter's mare; yet, having mounted, he did not push on ahead, preferring to ride behind, leading the remaining carriage-horse, as Ian and the postillion slowly carried his daughter along. It was a strange little procession, greeted with sympathetic outcries at the farmhouse when they stopped to exchange the cloak for a more convenient hurdle, and to send on a messenger to Miss Stewart.

When at last they came up the avenue at Invernacree, there was Grizel in the open doorway, with Jacqueline behind her, capable Grizel, skilled in leechcraft and nursing. She already had a bed prepared. Ian and the postillion carried the hurdle with its light burden up the stairs, the gentleman following them. The young lady was laid upon the bed, and Ian, descending again, gave orders that a man should ride at once for the doctor. Then he returned to the landing to wait for the young lady's father to emerge, and to conduct him downstairs. His own father, he had ascertained, was out.

He had not waited long before the bedroom door opened and the traveller came forth.

"I think you were right about that cut, sir," he said. "I thank God it is so little. But she is still senseless. Can one have a doctor here?"

"I have already sent a man on horseback for one, sir," said Ian, looking sympathetically at this poor father's haggard face. "Meanwhile, will you not come downstairs, and let me offer you a glass of wine or eau-de-vie after your accident?"

The gentleman thanked him and they went down. Old Invernacree, evidently just come into the house, was standing in the hall.

"I was out, and have but this moment heard of your mishap, sir," he said courteously. "I hope your daughter is not severely hurt. Will you please to come in here?" And he opened the door of his study.

The stranger sank into a chair and rested his brow on his hands, and there was silence for a moment or two. A servant brought in brandy; Ian took it from him and advanced to the guest's elbow.

" May I pour you out a glass of eau-de-vie, Mr.——
sir?" he corrected himself.

" Thank you, I should be glad of it." The traveller
raised his head. " My name is Campbell—Campbell of
Cairns."

Ian's hand shook suddenly, and he poured a little
stream of brandy on to the salver which held the glass.
He heard his father draw his breath sharply, and saw
that, standing there, he had put a hand to the table as
if to steady himself. Mr. Campbell of Cairns, between
past shock and present anxiety, noticed nothing; with a
murmured word of thanks he drained the glass and a
little colour came into his thin, hard face.

" I thank you, sir," he said, looking up at Ian. " When
my brain is a trifle clearer . . . I have a great deal, I
know, to thank you for. I think I heard the name of
Stewart used. Am I right?"

" Yes, our name is Stewart, Mr. Campbell," said the
old laird, standing very still and regarding him fixedly.
" Stewart of Invernacree. This is my remaining son,
Ian. My firstborn fell on Drummossie Moor."

" Like many another brave man," murmured Mr.
Campbell. At that moment the door opened, and he
turned his head and got up. It was Grizel.

" Madam, what news of my daughter?"

" I think, sir," said Miss Stewart, " that you may be
easy. She has come to herself. We may expect the
doctor—if he is at home—before nightfall."

" She has come to herself? Then I will go to her,"
exclaimed Mr. Campbell. " That is, unless you think it
inadvisable?"

" No," said Grizel, " I think you might well see her
for a few moments, sir, for she has asked for you and is

anxious for your safety." And on that, with a murmured apology to his host, the anxious father followed her out.

"Ian," said old Invernacree when the door was shut, "do you realise who that man is?"

"Yes," answered his son very gravely. "But even Alan in his grave would not have us refuse him and his daughter shelter."

"No," acquiesced the old man. He seemed to have aged by ten years in the last few minutes. "No, that is the worst of it! . . . O God, give me charity!"

Once more the door opened; this time it was Jacqueline who came in, looking even prettier than usual in her excitement. "Father, Ian, the young lady has recovered her senses! Did you pull her out of the coach, Ian—and was it running away all the while—and who are they?"

It was her father who answered the last query.

"That is the man, Jacqueline," he said, with a deep and steady sternness, "who commanded the Campbell militia at the battle of Culloden; and they, as you know, were the troops who shot down your brother Alan."

§ 2

Supper that night at Invernacree was an uncomfortable meal, at least for all the Stewarts at the board, though it was not in old Invernacree to show a grudging hospitality. As for Mr. Campbell of Cairns, his anxiety for his daughter and his own recent escape from serious accident, joined to the probability that he was not himself aware that Alexander Stewart regarded him as having the blood of his eldest son upon his hands, pro⌐

tected him in some measure from the full realisation of the prevalent malaise, though naturally he could not suppose that one of his name would ever be very welcome under the roof of a Stewart, more especially of one who had lost a son at Culloden. Whatever he perceived, however, or did not perceive, he excused himself soon after the meal and retired to bed, while the old laird withdrew with a clouded face into his own study, whither no one liked to follow him. Grizel returned to the bed-side of her patient, and Ian and Jacqueline were left alone together, she to enquire of every particular of the accident, and he to deplore the strange and unfortunate chance which had thrown Campbell of Cairns and his daughter, of all people, upon their kindness.

" Not that one could hold *her* responsible for anything, Ian," observed Jacqueline almost pleadingly. " She can have been little more than a child when Alan was killed."

" No, naturally not," agreed her brother. " Yet I wish, chiefly for our father's sake, that it had been any-one—any Campbell even—but Campbell of Cairns!"

Jacqueline sighed. She herself had been but ten years old when the Cause went down in the sleet and the wind. She remembered her brother Alan well, of course, but nine years seems a long space of time to a girl not yet twenty. Ian had never replaced Alan in her father's heart—she knew that—but he had in hers.

" She is very beautiful, this Miss Campbell," she re-marked after a moment.

" Is she?" asked Ian indifferently. " I had not time to observe it."

He was not speaking the truth. If there had not in-deed been time in the overturned coach to see whether the huddled girl he had lifted out were plain or comely, he had not helped to carry Miss Campbell all the way to Invernacree without observing the face upon which he had looked during that slow transit. And even viewed upside down, even with a handkerchief bound about the forehead and half obscuring the beautiful pencilling of the eyebrows, that face was one which a man would not willingly take his eyes from. Young Invernacree, therefore, was quite aware that the lady of the coach was lovely; and quite unmoved by the fact. She was a Campbell.

The invalid, reported Grizel next morning at breakfast, had passed a very fair night; the headache from which she had suffered yesterday was gone, nor was the slight cut on her forehead troubling her. But the doctor had decreed last night that she was not to leave her bed for a couple of days, nor to take her departure from Invernacree for a week or more.

"We shall be very pleased, shall we not, Grizel, to keep the young lady for as long as it suits her to remain?" said the laird at breakfast, with no trace of hostility in his tone. Nor was the speech due to the presence of the young lady's parent, since Mr. Campbell was breakfasting in his own room.

"But what about her father, sir?" queried Ian.

Invernacree's fine old face grew dark. "God forbid that I should turn even the slayer of my son from my door when he is in need of succour. Since Campbell of Cairns has broken bread beneath my roof, I cannot hasten his departure, but I can hope that he will soon take it of his own motion, for last night I seemed to see Alan's wraith behind him at every turn."

"If Mr. Campbell had shot poor Alan with his own hand our father could not feel it more acutely," observed

Grizel with a troubled face a little later, when she found herself alone with her half-brother and sister. "I cannot quite so regard the matter; it was the fortune of war that he and not another should have commanded the Campbell militia and thus——"

"Was it the fortune of war which made the Campbells prostitute themselves to the service of the Hanoverian?" demanded Ian, suddenly fierce. "No, it was another kind of fortune, that which they have always known where to find—the profitable, the winning side in every quarrel!"

"My sorrow!" sighed Grizel. "I know that as well as you, Ian. Yet Cairns seems a decent man enough, and it's likely has regrets now."

"Grizel is over douce," pronounced Jacqueline, twining her arm in her brother's. "For my part, I shall be very glad when Mr. Campbell is gone, but I have no desire to see his daughter drive away. She has a face like . . . like moonlight on the loch yonder."

"Your enthusiasm has betrayed you into a very unsuitable metaphor," said Ian coldly, and somehow his arm disengaged itself from the girl's. "I cannot but feel with my father in this matter, and wish them both gone as soon as may be."

And half of Ian's inhospitable wish found itself fulfilled with more promptitude than he had dared to hope. Whether Mr. Campbell made the urgent business of which he spoke an excuse, or whether it really was as pressing as he asserted, at any rate he alleged himself bound to depart next morning. He was well satisfied with his daughter's condition, and ready to leave her behind under Miss Stewart's care with full confidence and, as he added with much feeling, with deep gratitude.

He departed in a postchaise, his coach, though now fished up from its ignominious position on the shore of Loch Linnhe, being still lamentably wet and muddy and having a broken window.

His host omitted no courtesy at his departure, but the courtesy was stern and strained, and Campbell of Cairns' own leave-taking was not free from embarrassment. He, or one of his sons, was, however, to return to fetch his daughter in about a week's time.

CHAPTER V

WOULD SHE WERE GONE!

§ 1

June 22nd—24th.

THE sun was coming into the bedroom, and Olivia Campbell, lying on her couch near the window, watched it with delight—the sun and the sweet air from the hills. Their presence seemed to dispel the last traces of that haunting memory of darkness and confinement which had hovered over her during the last few days. It had quite lifted now, and she could laugh at it, and say, as she had said to kind Miss Stewart, that nothing less romantic or more ridiculous could happen to any girl than the accident which had brought her to Invernacree. To be imprisoned in an overturned coach with the possibility of being drowned, before she could be extricated, in six inches or so of loch water! And how *had* she been extricated—how had Mr. Ian Stewart, the actual rescuer, as she had heard from her father—how had this agile young man contrived to extract her from the bottom of her prison without trampling upon her?

Grizel indeed scarcely knew, for her brother had not been expansive on the subject; she could only be thankful that her patient had been extracted. "You were in real danger, dear Miss Campbell, seeing that you were unconscious." "But in such a ludicrous kind of danger," Olivia had responded, laughing. "Not, indeed, that I wish to underrate your brother's skill in getting me out of it!"

Olivia had laughed a good deal in her two and twenty years of life, for she had a happy disposition and a keen sense of the ridiculous. People said that her widowed father loved her, his only daughter, better than any of his four tall sons, whom, like most men, young or old, she could generally charm into doing what she wanted. Wilful she was, more than a little, but at the core of too fine a temper to misuse her power very seriously, and exercising it much too spontaneously to be vain of it. So loth was her father to part with her that, though she had arrived some time ago at full marriageable age, he neither made plans for a match nor smiled on those gentlemen who were so willing to make the plans for themselves. Olivia did not smile upon them either with any permanency, being wont to say that the only man who always pleased her was that friend of her father's, Mr. Maitland of Strathmory, whom she had known from a child. But she was safe in saying that, for there were three very solid obstacles in the way of her ever uniting herself to that kind and personable gentleman—he was forty-five at least, was a Jacobite, and had a living if bedridden wife, not to speak of a son just grown to manhood. Olivia called him Godfather, though he had no right to that title, nor indeed any kind of relationship with her. Just occasionally it had occurred to her to wonder how Mr. Maitland, holding such very different political views from her father—having, in fact, been "out" in the Forty-five, could be on such friendly terms with him. But it was quite a couple of years now since he had paid them a visit at Cairns.

It was perhaps not surprising that she should suddenly

think of her Jacobite friend, here, in a Jacobite, even an ultra-Jacobite household. Before the Rising, so she had been told, relations between the Whigs and the adherents of the White Rose had been much easier, a case of live and let live; but the events of 1745 and 1746 had wiped out that tolerance and hardened the line of cleavage. And Olivia knew, of course, that, as a field officer commanding at Culloden, her father could not be welcome in a house whose men had certainly fought on the opposite side. That its eldest son had fallen there she fortunately did not know. But no trace of political animosity had coloured the kindness and care of the two Miss Stewarts, and it was only when she looked at the very unflattering oil painting of the ill-fated "Pretender's son" over her mantelpiece that Olivia remembered where she was.

She glanced round the bedroom now in search of something to occupy her. It was not often that she was left thus alone. Grizel had lent her a book, but she was tired of reading—tired, too, of lying on this couch, when she felt perfectly well. She slipped off it and went and sat down by the open window.

How delicious the air was! And, absurd though she might find her adventure, it had not been free from genuine peril. That rocking, swaying coach . . . Yes, indeed there had been a possibility that she might not now be breathing this air, feeling the warm sunlight on her throat, looking at those distant blue and purple mountains . . . nor watching with pleased eyes the dove which suddenly alighted on the sill outside and began to walk about there.

It was this bird which induced Olivia to lean out. "You pretty creature!" she said impulsively, and put

forth a cautious hand, hoping to stroke its sleek neck.
But, though the pet dove was indifferent to her presence
just inside the window, the stretching out of that strange
hand alarmed it, and it flew off. Olivia leant out still
further to see where it had gone to, and thus became
aware of a young man almost immediately below her,
who was engaged in fastening up against the wall of
the house a detached spray of something or other. And
this young man, though his face was a little turned up-
wards, did not see her. His brow wore a slight frown as
he worked, and between his lips was a piece of twine.

And so Olivia looked down upon her rescuer's
countenance as he had looked upon hers—though not in
this case exactly upside down nor for nearly so long a
period. In fact it was only for a moment or so. Some
instinct caused Ian to look up, and he instantly beheld
Miss Campbell gazing down upon him. A blush sprang
into the lady's cheek, and she made a movement to withdraw. Ian stepped backwards; he could not doff his
hat, since he was already bareheaded. But he removed
the string from his mouth, bowed, and said rather
formally:

"Good morning, madam. I am glad to see you recovered."

"I . . . I was trying to stroke that dove," said
Olivia, with a natural idea of accounting for her situation at the window. "But it flew away." (It was to
be hoped that Mr. Stewart did not know the number of
seconds which had elapsed since its flight, but he probably
did.) "I think I see it in the cedar tree yonder."

"My sister Jacqueline could catch it for you," Ian
assured her gravely. "It will not come to me. I will
find her."

"No, no, Mr. Stewart," said Olivia in haste. "I do not want the bird. I want . . . when shall I have the opportunity of thanking you for what you did for me?"

"Thanking me!" exclaimed the young man, looking up at her more fully. "Miss Campbell, you have nothing to thank me for. I fear my sisters have been exaggerating a very simple and natural action, and one that in no way warrants gratitude."

"But I think differently," replied Miss Campbell in a soft voice—she had at all times a very pleasing one. And from the window she gave young Invernacree a glimpse of the charm of her smile, which, though he knew it not, was reported in the neighbourhood of Cairns —and further than that—to have the power to coax a man's heart out of his breast. Then she withdrew from the window rather suddenly, for Grizel had just come into the room behind her.

"I have been talking to your brother, in the most romantical fashion, out of the window," confessed Olivia, laughing. "When, dear Miss Stewart, will you allow me to go downstairs and thank him in proper form for his rescue of me?"

Grizel looked at her standing there. For a Campbell, she was dark; tall and of a beautiful shape, and held herself like a princess. She wore on her simple grey gown a plain muslin kerchief; but the gown had little green paniers too. Good, homely Grizel thought it very pretty. She smiled back.

"The doctor said that you might leave your room on the third day. To-morrow, then, if you sleep well to-night."

Olivia Campbell slept well enough when the time came. Strange to say, Mr. Stewart the younger did not. The recollection of a glance, a smile, sent down from a window, had been with him all the rest of the day, and he resented the impression which he could not shake off. There she had stood in that grey gown, grey like the dove's plumage—but she did not at all remind him of a dove— and had given him that smile which seemed to smite down from the window into his very vitals. "The girl's a finished coquette!" he said indignantly to himself. "Thank God she will soon be gone!"

But, saints above, she was lovely—lovely beyond a dream! Yet he did not thank God for that.

Miss Campbell's leaving her room next day was something of an event. Alexander Stewart, forewarned of her approach, met her at the foot of the stairs, made the most paternal enquiries after her health, and gave her his arm to the drawing-room, where Jacqueline awaited her with a cordial, and an English spaniel which she had never seen before—it was Ian's—greeted her, after the manner of its kind, as a dear and seldom-seen friend.

After a little while dinner was announced. The spaniel's owner came into the dining-room and duly kissed her hand. She sat upon her host's right, Grizel upon his left, young Invernacree at the bottom of the table. The light from the window was behind him, and Olivia observed how well his head was set upon his shoulders. They ate roast muirfowl, but the old laird had broth. The spaniel sat by her side throughout the meal, and gazed up at her with eloquent but sycophantic eyes. Young Mr. Stewart did not say much. Was he shy, or sulky?

Olivia herself was neither, and Jacqueline, who already thought her the most beautiful being she should ever behold, was equally enraptured with her conversation. Even Invernacree, who was not accustomed to hearing brilliant talk from ladies, though at first a trifle mistrustful, ended by being subjugated by it too. After dinner the convalescent was allowed to take a turn in the garden, the old laird with his stick on one side, Jacqueline on the other, Grizel and Ian more or less in attendance. Miss Campbell was delighted with the view over Loch Linnhe, and asked the names of all the mountains she could see. Ian had to supply the names of some which his father's old eyes could not quite distinguish; he did so with a polite readiness, but nothing more. But the old man was pleased with her enthusiasm for Appin, and forgot what blood it was which coursed through the veins of the little hand lying so lightly upon his arm. He was sorry to deliver her over to his eldest daughter, who then bore her off to her bedchamber again.

Without Miss Campbell's presence, something seemed lacking at supper that night; old Invernacree went so far as to put the lack into words. Ian neither agreed nor dissented; and his spaniel lay heavily on his feet under the table. But his light burnt late that night, and he read himself almost into a state of stupor before he ventured to get into bed.

§ 2

It is true that, in consequence of this precaution, Ian slept; but he woke early. Only three days more, however, and he would no longer be forced to look at that pale, sparkling face, that mouth with the curve which took his breath away, the arch of those slender eyebrows, black as a raven's feather, nor the wonderful grey eyes beneath them. She would be gone from Invernacree for ever, and this haunting fear—it was hardly less—would ebb back from his heart, and all would be as before. . . . Yes, and he could go and begin his wooing of Maclean of Garroch's second daughter.

The young man groaned, and flung himself out of bed. He must be bewitched. He plunged his face into cold water, threw on his clothes, and, early as it was, went out of the sleeping house and down to the edge of the loch with some idea of having a swim. But when he was there the intention abandoned him, and he walked for a long time to and fro on the pebbles, his hands clutched behind him. The tide was coming up Loch Linnhe, sucking gently sideways over the stones, little patches of mist were wreathing away before the sun, a gull or two was crying, and all at once, quite near the shore, Ian was aware of a dark, sleek, rounded head in the water—a young seal's. And into his mind sprang a medley of seal legends which as a child he had drunk in from his nurse, a woman of the Outer Isles, where seals were human creatures under spells, princes and princesses, the children of the King of Lochlann, who yet married sometimes with ordinary mortals; for if a man saw a seal-woman in her shape as she truly was (and three times a year she must assume it) he went mad for love of her. Ian stopped his pacing and threw a stone at the sleek head, which vanished instantly.

Ian was late for breakfast, an offence in the laird's eyes. Apologising, he said that he had gone down to the loch betimes to have a swim, and had walked farther than he had realised. He forgot to add that he had not fulfilled his intention, so that Jacqueline was caused to wonder why his neatly tied-back hair was so evidently bone dry. She thought he looked rather strange, almost ill, but she knew better than to remark upon this.

After breakfast Ian went off to one of the farms. As he returned through the garden he saw Miss Campbell sitting in a chair, which had apparently been brought out for that purpose, by some old stone balustrading, whence there was a good view down over the loch. He had to pass near her to reach the house, to pass near or to turn back altogether; and this latter he could have done without being seen, for she was not looking his way. But he did not. It was uncouth, uncivil, to avoid her; was a Stewart to show himself lacking in breeding, and before a Campbell? He approached.

Olivia heard his step, and turned her beautiful head—like a lily on its stalk, the young man was thinking even then.

"Good morning, Mr. Stewart. I am a shocking late riser, whereas you, no doubt, have been about much earlier."

He had, indeed, and she was the cause of it. Ian said, "You are under the doctor's orders, Miss Campbell. I hope he would not disapprove of your sitting in the open air on such a morning."

"I regard myself," returned Miss Campbell cheerfully, "as now emancipated from the doctor's care. And your kindest and best of sisters, Mr. Stewart, in whose judgment I have the greatest faith, permits it. I even have a book to read while she and Miss Jacqueline are about their household duties, so you see that I intend remaining here for some time."

"Nevertheless, I fear that we shall have rain before long," said Ian doubtfully, looking westwards at the mountains beyond the loch.

"Let us not anticipate calamity," answered Olivia gaily. "Yet, since you are looking in that direction, Mr. Stewart, will you not be my dominie, and rehearse me the names of the peaks over yonder which I tried to learn yesterday. I desire to know if I remember them aright." She looked up and sent him a little smile, like a flower only half unfolded; but the same shaft sped through the young man again, and, tingling as though from some actual physical impact, he sat down upon the balustrade beside her and obeyed.

From that he found himself talking of the region in general. Miss Campbell spoke of the peaks of Jura, an island which Ian did not know. Her brothers, she said, had climbed some of those heights; no doubt Mr. Stewart was familiar in the same way with some of the crests at which they were looking. "If I were not a woman," she said, pointing over the loch, "I should like to stand on that summit yonder. Have you ever stood there, Mr. Stewart?"

"No, never," confessed Ian. "I have not often been on the farther side of Loch Linnhe. But I think my brother Alan once——" He pulled himself up, his colour changing, then went on rather lamely, "My brother Alan once climbed Ben Mheon."

"Oh, I did not know you had a brother."

"Nor have I . . . now," said Ian, looking away. "He is dead."

"Indeed, I am sorry," came Olivia Campbell's voice after a moment, with real sympathy in its soft tones. "Recently?"

Ian had a savage longing to go on, "And it is your father who is responsible for his death," not exactly from a desire to shock and wound the girl beside him, but to remind himself that he had no business to sit here talking idly with Campbell of Cairns' daughter because she had smiled at him. Yet, instead of flinging that reproach at her he found himself, to his surprise, bestowing something of a confidence.

"No, not recently. Nine years ago. He was my elder—the heir, and my father's darling. If he had lived——" Again he broke off. Often and often as he had thought how different things would have been for him if Alan were not lying with all the dead of the clan in the great grave on Culloden Moor, there came at the moment a new realisation of what the difference might have been, so startling that he got up from the balustrade. The thought was mad, traitorous! Even had he been still the younger son. . . .

"The rain will really be here in a moment or two," he said in a strained voice. "It is sweeping fast over Loch Linnhe. Indeed you should go indoors—allow me to carry your shawl."

"Mr. Stewart," said Olivia, looking up at him with compassionate eyes, "I regret very much if I have trespassed upon memories——"

"No, no!" he broke in. "You have done nothing. . . . And here comes Grizel to hasten you. Pray take my arm."

He offered it, catching up her wraps with the other hand, as Grizel came running over the grass at the first drops of the shower.

That evening Miss Campbell was with them until eight o'clock, but no longer, so that, as yesterday, supper seemed a dullish meal. And yet Ian had a shamed sense of safety. When he could not see the King of Lochlann's daughter he could not, surely, be bewitched by her.

But when he went to bed he found this a most fallacious doctrine. He was in the toils of something which he shrank from putting a name to. Was it only a little more than a week ago, when Ewen Cameron was here, that he had sat at this window and reflected how rapture had passed him by, and he must make a mere humdrum marriage? *This* was not rapture, God knew—it was enslavement, sorcery . . . and all to no purpose. He must forget the spell-weaver as fast as possible, for she could never be his wife.

He descended next morning, after a wretched night, to find Miss Campbell at breakfast with the rest of his family. During the meal it transpired that she had already heard that one of her brothers was coming to fetch her away the day after to-morrow. Lamentations from Grizel and Jacqueline, and polite regrets from the old laird. Ian alone said nothing. ,What was he to say, he who was so much relieved at the idea?

But was he relieved?

At any rate, since Miss Campbell was leaving so soon, he might safely show her some civility. He thought of offering to accompany her and Jacqueline to some spot whence they would have a good prospect, but the morning, which early had been fine, deteriorated with that blighting rapidity characteristic of the Western Highlands, and by the afternoon the steady drizzle had become torrents of rain, loch and mountains were blotted out, and Grizel had a fire burning in the drawing-room.

And there, about four o'clock, Ian somehow found himself playing chess with their guest, while Jacqueline looked on and Grizel sewed at a little distance. Miss Campbell proved to be a moderately good player; Ian was usually something more than that. Yet since, against his will, he paid more attention to the fair hand which moved the pieces than to the pieces themselves, it was not wonderful that in the end he was badly beaten.

"I verily believe," said Olivia laughingly to Jacqueline, "that your brother has allowed himself to be defeated out of chivalry. Else he could never have overlooked the disgraceful blunder which I made some twenty minutes ago."

"I thought you were laying a trap for me," retorted Ian with a smile. "But indeed I have no pretensions to being a great chess player. I but learnt in order to please my father."

"And I to tease mine," averred Olivia. "He used to say that all women played chess (when they played at all) without judgment, and I thought to disprove it."

"I am sure," said Jacqueline admiringly, "that he cannot say so now!"

Miss Campbell laughed her low, captivating laugh. "Now he says that they play without *true* judgment, so I have not done much to convert him from his opinion!"

And for a moment there was merriment round the fire. The rain lashing against the windows only made this warm, cheerful seclusion the more desirable, in the pleasant and homely room with the faded carpet whose red and yellow roses Ian could remember as long as he remembered anything, except perhaps the twin ivory elephants which his grandfather had brought, so he had always understood, from the mysterious land of China itself. He could see them now in the cabinet behind Miss Campbell's head, as he sat opposite her in her gown of green silk with a silver shine in its folds. All these years, and the familiar old room had never known its proud destiny—to enclose *her;* nor the battered old knights and castles theirs—to be touched by those beautiful fingers. . . . The spell snapped, as like a bitter, searing wind there blew into Ian's soul the remembrance of the identity of the father at whose prejudices the girl here by the hearth was gently laughing, and he and his sisters with her—the man of that greatly hated race whose action had cut off their brother Alan from that very fireside, to lie for ever out in the cold and the rain. With darkening eyes he rose from his seat opposite her, and to give some colour to the movement, threw another log on to the fire. Perhaps the chill which had swept over his spirit, as well as the fact that he was thinking of something else, was the reason why he threw on so many. The flame shot up hot and crackling.

"Why, Ian," said Grizel in surprise, "you'll roast us all! I am sure Miss Campbell, near the fire as she is, will be incommoded by such a blaze."

"I beg your pardon," said her brother mechanically, glancing round for a second at the guest. "I was not thinking what I was about." No more did he seem to be thinking of it now, when he remedied his absentmindedness by taking hold of the last log which he had thrown on and pulling it off again, not without cost to himself.

"Mr. Stewart, did you not burn your hand then?" exclaimed Olivia Campbell, leaning forward. "Oh, why did you not leave that log where it was!"

"It had not caught fire," replied Ian carelessly, pointing with his left hand to the piece of birch. The right was already thrust deep into his pocket, for, though the log in question was not alight, the flame through which he had plunged that member had licked his wrist and scorched his sleeve.

"Yes, but something has caught fire," said Grizel,

putting down her work. "I can smell singeing. Ian, how could you be so foolish! Let me see what you have done to yourself!"

"Nonsense," said her brother. "'Tis only my sleeve. I felt nothing." He came and resumed his place at the little table opposite Olivia. "Miss Campbell, will you allow me the opportunity of my revenge, or am I too unworthy a foe?"

But Miss Campbell seemed in distress . . . and how lovely in it! "Mr. Stewart, I implore you to allow your sister to look at your hand!" And as Ian, shaking his head with a smile, and saying again that it was nothing, began to replace his pieces on the board with his left hand, she leant over and said in a pleading tone, "Do not refuse me this favour!"

Ian set his king firmly where his queen should have stood. What a fool he had been to cause all this pother —and, incidentally, this pain to himself! His wrist was smarting like hell. But he answered with polite nonchalance, "When we have had our game, Miss Campbell, with pleasure."

"Jacqueline," said Grizel, rising from her chair, "pray go up to the cupboard in my room and bring what I have there in readiness for burns.—If you will not seek a leech, Ian, the leech must e'en come to you."

"No doubt," observed Ian with a resigned air, as Jacqueline fled from the room. "You have had experience, Miss Campbell, of what it is to fall into the clutches of a female Æsculapius. If you want to make Grizel happy, contrive to scratch yourself, however slightly. I have sometimes done it with that object, when I was a boy."

He continued to arrange his side of the chess board,

still with his king and queen reversed; but Olivia made
no effort to set hers. He *had* burnt himself, she could
tell. How obstinate and crazy and generally incalculable
men could be!

Miss Stewart seemed to share this unspoken opinion.
" I have no patience with you!" she declared, suddenly
coming and standing over her brother, and looking as
if a very little more would cause her to withdraw his
other hand from its seclusion in his coat pocket. " And
what is that child about? I suppose I must needs go
myself." She went, and the chess players were left alone.

" You have not set your pieces, I see, Miss Campbell,"
observed Ian in a business-like tone. " Or is it that you
will not play with me again?"

" I certainly cannot play with you until you have had
your hand dressed," said Olivia gravely.

" But I can make the moves equally well with my left.
Or, for the matter of that, and to prove to you that it is
unhurt, with my right." And he plucked his other hand
out of his pocket and laid it on the table by the chess-
board. " You see, all this to-do is about nothing, but,
as I say, Grizel dearly loves——"

He got no further. Two swift, cool hands had his
imprisoned as it lay there, and fingers, with incredible
gentleness in their touch, were pushing the scorched cuff
away from his red and blistered wrist. " Mr. Stewart,
look at that!" said an accusing voice. " Now, was it
worth it!"

("If you will keep your fingers there, yes, it was
worth it, a thousand times worth!") thought Ian. They
were snowflakes . . . snowdrops . . . and what were
the grey eyes—soft now, not sparkling—which looked at
him so reproachfully? It was not the pain of the burn

which made his head swim as he ventured to meet them, and the chessmen dance wildly for a second or two in the firelight. *Ah, beautiful and kind, and for ever impossible to love, you shall not know that it is my heart which you have between those healing hands of yours!*

" . . . But you see how little damage has been done," he said, and knew not how dazedly he spoke. He tried to summon up resolution to draw his hand away. And there was a moment's silence; only the fire crackled, and, without, the wind flung itself against the glass. Then Grizel came in, and Jacqueline after her.

Ian rose to his feet at once. He did not intend any ministrations to be carried out in here. "I'll come with you as meek as a sheep," he said quickly, "if Miss Campbell will but excuse me. Jacqueline, will you not stay with our guest?" And he followed his elder sister out.

"Do you think my brother's hand is much burnt, Miss Campbell?" asked Jacqueline a little anxiously.

Olivia was thoughtfully fingering a chessman. "It was not his hand; it was his wrist. I wish he had not been so rash. If I may say so, one would not have expected it of him."

"But one is never quite sure what Ian may not do," explained Jacqueline, sitting down in Ian's place. "He appears so composed, and then suddenly he is not composed.—But when I say that one is not sure what he may not do, pray do not think I mean that he would ever do anything dishonourable—that he would, for instance, ever forsake a friend."

"I hope we should none of us do that," said Miss Campbell.

"No, indeed! Yet I meant something more than that. . . . I do not know how to put it."

"You mean perhaps, Miss Stewart, that he would never forsake a cause," suggested Olivia, leaning forward with her elbows on the table. "I do not forget that you are all Jacobites.—Perhaps you mean also that he would never forgive an enemy?"

"I don't know," said little Jacqueline, looking troubled. "We ought all to forgive our enemies, ought we not?—But perhaps I do mean that."

"Yet I hope Mr. Stewart will forgive me for that burn," said Olivia with a whimsical little smile. "You must intercede for me, Miss Jacqueline!"

"Oh, dear Miss Campbell, the burn was Grizel's fault, I think, not yours!"

"Then I hope he will forgive me for having called attention to the injury, for it was undoubtedly I who did that in the first place, and he was not best pleased, I think."

"Men," pronounced nineteen-year old Jacqueline with a great air of experience, "are very strange creatures in that respect. For if you neglect to notice their injuries they do not like that neither."

"In short," said Olivia laughing, "we women are the only sensible sex. (Yet men say that *we* are not over faithful to our friends.) Come, let us put away the chessmen, for something tells me that your brother will not come back, although he challenged me to another game."

And in this prediction Miss Campbell found herself perfectly correct.

CHAPTER VI

THE FIELD OF DAISIES

§ 1

June 25th—26th.

IF Ian slept ill that night he could, and did, attribute it to the smart of his burnt wrist. But he knew in his heart that that was not the cause.

The last day of Miss Campbell's sojourn at Invernacree was going, he saw, to be gloriously fine. The last day; yes, to-morrow would see her leave his father's roof for ever. If, therefore, he could only get safely through to-day, all would be well. The best thing would be to invent some excuse which would keep him out of doors most of the time, and at a distance; and after some casting about he succeeded.

But he had forgotten that his father had appointed this morning for going into the half-yearly accounts of the estate with him, and this there was no escaping. All morning Ian added, subtracted, verified and discussed; but in this unromantic pursuit he had less time to think of Miss Campbell, and at all events could not be in her company. His arithmetic, however, was not beyond reproach. At the end of their joint computations the laird began to talk of the sum which he intended in the future to apportion to his son when he married, for though he would not at first have a separate establishment he would need more money, and with economy Invernacree thought that he could allow him this.

Ian thanked him in a voice which even to himself sounded choked, and his father asked if by ill chance he had taken a fever of cold, as well as burning his hand so foolishly yesterday (for enquiries at supper, not to speak of the presence of a bandage, had disclosed that fact to Mr. Stewart; and in truth Ian had not found writing too pleasant this morning). The young man repudiated this suggestion.

"Indeed, I hope you are not indisposed," said Invernacree, "for it is so fine a day that I think a row upon the loch this afternoon might benefit as well as interest Miss Campbell, and Grizel thinks so too."

"Dougal Livingstone and his brother are both available," replied his son.

"I think," pronounced the laird, "that it would show more courtesy if you were to row Miss Campbell and your sisters yourself. Or at least (if the consequence of your folly last night incapacitates you) that you should accompany them."

"Since when," asked Ian, "have you laid store, sir, by showing courtesy to a Campbell?"

Displeasure sat upon the old man's brow. "One does not war with women, Ian. I cannot think that I have ever trained you in such a notion. And Miss Campbell is our guest."

She has bewitched you too, thought Ian. Aloud he said submissively, "No, sir, you are in the right of it. I shall be pleased to row Miss Campbell and my sisters on the loch this afternoon."

And even as he said it he knew that what he desired was to row Miss Campbell without his sisters. He caught his breath. But that could never be . . . mercifully.

" By the way," said his father, reverting to business, " you will have to go to Glasgow for me in a few weeks' time to see Buchanan about that affair I spoke of, and one or two others. I am too old for the journey now.— Where is that paper of memoranda I had under my hand a moment since?"

§ 2

Dougal Livingstone and his brother were the rowers after all, and Ian, steering, was unable therefore to feast his miserable eyes upon the King of Lochlann's daughter, where she sat beside him in the stern, as well as he could have done had he faced her on a thwart. On the other hand she was so close to him that his miserable body was only too conscious of the fact.

The boat slipped over the hardly rippled loch, stained in the distance by the reflected mountains with hues that had vanished when the spot was reached, leaving the water as clear and colourless as before. Jacqueline chattered, the rowers at Olivia's request sang a *iorram*, Grizel told legends of this place and that. All illusion, like this tormenting nearness on the other side of the helm—like the mirage on the water, pretence of what was not and could never be. . . . When he moved the tiller from him his hand all but brushed her; when a stray whisper of breeze caught a ribbon of hers it sent it across his face or knee . . .

" Ian," said Jacqueline, suddenly leaning forward and pointing, " why should we not land on Eilean Soa and show Miss Campbell the cairn where the ancient king was buried with his treasure? "

Land, and be released from this torturing and intoxicating proximity? No . . . yes . . . which?

His decision was not awaited. "Oh, let us land!" cried Olivia. "Of all things I love a buried treasure!"

"'Tis not there now," observed the practical Grizel.

"We need not go round the point to the flat shore," pursued Jacqueline. "You know the place this side, with the solitary pine tree. I have often got ashore there."

"It might be difficult for Miss Campbell," said her brother doubtfully.

"Why, Mr. Stewart, are you suggesting that I am less nimble than your sister!" cried the guest. "I am no town lady, and I insist on being put ashore where Miss Jacqueline is accustomed to land."

Ian yielded, and steered for the nearer side of the island, since to anyone young the place presented no difficulty. A slight spring up to an embedded piece of granite and a tiny scramble thereafter, aided by the tough stems of the tall island heather, and one was there. He got out, and, knee-deep in the heather a little above her, assisted Miss Campbell, half hoping that she would slip, so that he could catch her; but she showed no sign of such a thing.

It was Ian who slipped, or nearly, though it was not his fault. For, having put one foot on the lump of granite to extend a hand to Grizel in the boat below, he felt the stone, to his astonishment, beginning to give beneath him, and sprang back, clutching the heather, just in time to watch it slowly leave its place, slide down, and disappear sedately into the water.

"I had no notion that I was so heavy!" called Olivia's laughing voice from above him. "I am glad you did not follow it, Mr. Stewart!"

"So am I," observed Grizel from the boat. "But, Ian, can we land here now?"

"You cannot," replied her brother. "Go round the point to the beach. Miss Campbell and I will walk across and meet you there."

There was nothing else to be done, so the boat pushed off again and Ian was left alone with Olivia Campbell— alone, though but for a few minutes, in a world apart. His desire was equally to hasten to the other side of the little island . . . and to loiter here; not to speak or listen to her . . . and to detain her for hours. In this state of mind he preceded her from the landing-place, mechanically holding back a bramble or a branch when necessary, but really not conscious of what he was walking on, grass, rock or heather—till all at once he heard her cry:

"Oh, Mr. Stewart, how beautiful . . . and how very unexpected!"

And because she had stopped, he stopped too, and found that they were both in a little abandoned meadow full of moon-daisies, all swaying and nodding towards them in welcome. But in a few minutes the boat would have rounded the little green headland on their left, and he would never be alone with her anywhere again . . . thank God, thank God!

And was that why he took her hand in a cold, unsteady clasp, and without a word raised it to his lips and kissed the palm of it with a long, forsaken kiss? The touch of her fingers was like cool well-water to the burning lips of fever. She did not pull them away. But Ian dropped her hand, and stood looking at her among the knee-high daisies of Eilean Soa so wildly, so desperately, that for a second Olivia Campbell all but recoiled. She did not, however; she said gently, "The sun is very hot, Mr. Stewart; will you not put on your hat?"

"Do you think I have sunstroke?" Ian spoke so low that she could scarcely catch the words. "You know it is not that! . . . You are going away to-morrow?"

"Yes," answered Olivia gravely. "To-morrow, when my brother comes for me." There was pity in her beautiful eyes; that made it harder still. "I did not mean to do this to you—indeed I did not! . . . There is the boat coming to shore. I will wait here."

He still looked at her, for as long as it took a tiny breeze to run from side to side over the daisy heads and set them quivering. Then he turned, and strode through the flowers towards the shore.

But Olivia stood without moving, pressing her hands tightly together. No, indeed she had not meant to do this! And how had she done it—she had seen him so little, talked with him so seldom! In vain to ask that question of the thousand flower-faces in their white and golden dance; if they knew they would not tell her.

"Oh dear," said Olivia, "I *wish* it had not happened!"

And this was strange, for conquests were not distasteful to her.

But Ian continued to stride on, through a tangle of grasses, to the flat strand where the boat had already grounded.

"You have left Miss Campbell behind, I see," observed Jacqueline as she sprang to land. "Whatever can those flowers be among which she is standing?"

"I do not know," said Ian. "Are there any flowers?"

"Dear brother, you must be blind! One can see them from here—hundreds of them!" And she ran off.

Ian helped his elder sister out. "If you will forgive

me," he said in a low voice, " I will stay here by the boat while you go to the cairn with Miss Campbell. I . . . my burnt wrist is paining me somewhat; I should be poor company."

" Dear Ian . . ." said Grizel, looking at him in perturbation. He was so oddly pale beneath his sunburn. " Shall I stay with you? Why should your wrist . . ."

" Because I wrenched it," he lied, " when that stone gave way. The pain will go off in a little, but I think I will stay here. Go after Jacqueline and explain."

She looked at him again dubiously and obeyed; and Ian, after a careless word or two to the rowers, walked to a rock a little way off, sat down there and was very still. If only he could have left the island, and gone home by himself. But he could not take the boat and abandon the ladies, even for a time; and though the swim to land was not beyond his powers it would have seemed the most extraordinary proceeding, calling for investigation, and above all things he wished no one of his family to know what had befallen him.

For there could be no doubt of it—he loved Olivia Campbell to distraction, and fight against the avowal of that passion as he had done, he was glad in his heart that she knew it. He ought not to have betrayed his love, because of the long and bitter racial feud almost as much as because of the blood which cried from the ground between them, but she was too generous, too noble, to make of that avowal a subject for triumph or for mockery. She might soon forget his mad and wordless confession—he hoped she would—but she would never misuse it.

And now, a supreme effort, it only remained during the homeward voyage to behave as naturally as he could, and to lay any blame for his recent defection upon yesterday's now fortunate injury. Olivia, in her divine kindness and comprehension, would support him in that pretence.

Even if the young man were already attributing to the enchantress all sorts of noble qualities of whose existence he could not possibly have been aware, he was right as far as the homeward voyage was concerned. Miss Campbell made it as easy for him as she could, contriving somehow to change places with Grizel so that the latter, and not she, sat next the tiller; and encouraging Jacqueline to talk, to tell her again, for instance, about the empty cairn and what it had once contained.

"But the burial chamber was so small," she objected at one point. "I should have thought a king would have been taller! Were they dwarfs in those days?"

"It was only the burnt bones of the king—or his ashes, I forget which—that they found," explained Jacqueline, looking a little surprised, for she had distinctly heard Grizel already informing the visitor of this fact. "Isn't that so, Ian?—Ian, what are you dreaming about there?"

"You were talking of ancient kings," answered her brother slowly, his eyes fixed on the point for which he was steering, "and I was thinking of one, that is all. Yes, I believe that nothing but ashes was found in the cairn. None of us, after all, kings or king's daughters, can leave behind more of ourselves than that."

"What a horrid speech!" cried Jacqueline; and Grizel, also disliking the macabre trend which he had given to the conversation, observed drily, "You certainly made an effort to reduce yourself to that condition yesterday evening;" and began to talk about the prospects of a fine sunset. And at last, as all ordeals must, the voyage came to an end.

A surprise awaited them all at Invernacree, where they were informed that Miss Campbell's brother had already arrived, in order to be able to make an early start with his sister next morning. He had come to the house to pay his respects, finding no one, not even the laird himself, at home, and had, the domestic understood, taken up his quarters at the tiny inn down by the loch.

"But Mr. Campbell must not remain there!" exclaimed Grizel on hearing this news. "Ian shall go and bid him come up to the house for the night—will you not, Ian?"

Without waiting to find his father Ian went off. He had no desire at all for the company of a male Campbell, and his father, he was sure, would have still less; yet he knew that Invernacree would not be satisfied to leave the traveller to the mercies of the inn, more especially when his sister was already staying beneath his roof. And after all, thought the young man, nothing mattered very much to-night. His outburst had by now numbed him; he felt nothing. To-morrow the world would come to an end for him . . . if it had not already done so over there on Eilean Soa among the daisies.

He found at the inn Mr. Colin Campbell, a tall, fair young man of about his own age, who at first refused to put the laird of Invernacree to the trouble of receiving him for one night, and was stiff even when, unable to do anything else, he finally yielded. The two of them walked together up to the house, neither finding much to say to the other.

And through the evening, while Ian watched Olivia in a kind of dream, still numbed, but every now and again waking to a stab of pain, as though the blood was beginning to run once more in a frozen limb, it seemed to him not unfortunate, perhaps, that Colin Campbell was here, for the atmosphere was changed by it. The presence of that typical son of Clan Diarmaid seemed to draw Olivia so much further away from them, back into the circle to which she belonged; it showed things as they really were. It was better so.

She left early next morning with her brother in their father's coach, which by now had been repaired. Ian had no word alone with her. But as old Invernacree was about to hand her in she said, " I shall never ride in this carriage again, sir, without the most grateful thoughts of what I owe to you and . . . your family."

For a moment her gaze went past him to that member of it for whom no doubt her thanks were specially intended, where he stood by Jacqueline's side, saying nothing and not, apparently, looking at any one.

" My dear young lady," replied the old man, with an air at once courteous and paternal, " anything which my family has been able to do for you is their good fortune. God bless you, and may you have a better journey than the last! "

Their good fortune! Ian could have laughed out loud. If his father only knew!

Mr. Colin Campbell, a little less stiff than last night, but still not at ease, got into the coach and slammed the door, the postillion chirruped to the horses, and that fatal vehicle drew away from the old white house among the oak trees. Grizel and Jacqueline stood on the steps for some time, Jacqueline waving a handkerchief, to which, as the coach turned just outside the gate, there was an answering flicker of white. But Ian had not stayed to see that.

So she was gone, the enchanted, the enchanting. Up

in his own room he had only to shut his eyes, and he was back in the flowery meadow where he had kissed her hand. His heart still lay there among the daisy stems, in the place where the King of Lochlann's daughter had stood. But now that she was gone from Appin he had a half hope that it might creep back to his breast, even if it should never be the same heart again, but remain what it seemed now, as much ashes as any in the ancient tomb on Eilean Soa.

CHAPTER VII

AN EXPLANATION AT THE GOATS' WHEY

§ 1

Aug. 11th—13th.

IN his house in the Trongate, in the pleasant and prosperous little city of Glasgow, Mr. John Buchanan, Invernacree's "doer" for nearly forty years, sat, a little more than six weeks later, on one side of a table and looked at Invernacree's son, on the other, with a smile compounded of shrewdness and benevolence, as befitted a family lawyer of long standing. He had the round legal face, not the long; it was smooth and fresh, with no trace of eyebrows remaining, and he did not wear spectacles.

" You'll find those all in order, Mr. Ian," he said, indicating the packet of documents which he had just handed over. " Or rather the laird will. He still keeps the reins pretty closely in his own hands, I see."

"There is, thank God, no reason why he should not," observed Ian.

" Quite so, quite so," agreed Mr. Buchanan. " And indeed it seems but a few years ago that you were a wee bit wean in petticoats. Yet you are twenty-five years of age now, I'm thinking."

" Twenty-six," said his visitor.

" D'ye hear that now, Gib? " remarked the lawyer to the large sphinx of a tabby which sat like an immense paperweight upon his table. " Twenty-six! To think of it! And when shall I have the pleasure of drawing up your marriage contract, young man? "

86

"Oh, before very long, I expect," responded Ian in as colourless a voice as he could muster. "Then I am to tell my father that he will hear from you later on the subject of that wadset?"

"If you please. But, speaking of your prospective marriage, my dear young gentleman, who is the fortunate lady to be?"

Ian ran his hand down Gib's massive back, feeling the muscles under the fur ripple in the opposite direction at his touch. "I have to ask her, sir, before I can tell you that . . . It seems to me that I remember this cat of yours as long as I remember you."

"I wonder does he remember you—eh, Gib, ye rascal, do ye? And to think you are twenty-six! Aye, 'tis time that ye thought of matrimony now that ye have taken poor Alan's place."

Ian made no comment. "I see you have a map upon the wall there," he said. "I shall make bold to study it for a moment, if I may."

"Ye surely know your way home, Mr. Ian?"

"Yes, I know my way home," said the young man, getting up and going over to the map. Nevertheless he looked minutely at it, and there was something in his face as he did so which suggested that he was making calculations. "Thank you, sir; 'twas only curiosity. Maps have ever interested me."

He came back to the table. The cat Gib stood up, arched his back, stretched himself prodigiously, uttered a small sound and sat down again, fixing upon Ian a gaze of such apparent omniscience as almost to be perturbing. Then the topaz orbs blinked; with a twitch of the end of his tail the sage appeared to dismiss the matter from his mind, and lay solidly down again, folding his

4

paws inward. But Ian had a momentary conviction, quite difficult to shake off, that Gib knew, if his owner did not, why he had just been studying the map.

As he walked away from Mr. Buchanan's house, past the colonnades of the Trongate, with their cave-like little shops beneath, the papers entrusted to him safely inside his coat, his thoughts were busy with another paper—and that, not to mince matters, a stolen one—which lay nearer to his heart than they did, and was the sole cause of his consulting the lawyer's map just now.

About a week after Miss Olivia Campbell's departure from Invernacree, at the end of June, had come a letter from her to Grizel, which, among expressions of undying gratitude to the writer's dear Miss Stewart for her kindness and her skill, had contained the information that when the summer was a little more advanced she herself was, in deference to her father's wishes, going up into the hills of Central Perthshire to take that sovereign specific, goats' milk. "Papa is of opinion that my health—which is in truth perfectly sound, and never was better—would be re-established by a course of the whey. At any rate he so urges it, in order to counteract the possible effects of the coach accident, that I have not the heart to stand out against him; and so, my dear Miss Grizel, you may picture me next month up at Kilrain with my faithful Elspeth in attendance, drinking the whey as though I were some gouty old gentleman doing his annual cure. I trust there will be none of them there at the time, for they would surely think the presence of such a blooming young woman absurd, as I do. I promise you I shall be vastly bored."

It was for days a matter of puzzled conjecture to Grizel how she could so completely have mislaid that letter, though she knew that she had left it about for a short time. So did Ian, who, though he was never going to see Miss Campbell again, nor would ever write to her or receive a word from her, pounced upon that sheet of paper over which her hand had travelled and which seemed to carry the very sound of her voice, secreted it, and unblushingly declared his complete ignorance of its whereabouts. To such hopeless folly had he come who was shortly to woo Miss Margaret Maclean.

Miss Campbell's letter, since he always carried it upon him, went with Ian to Glasgow when, in August, Invernacree sent him thither to see his lawyer, as he had projected some time before. And it was in Glasgow that temptation came down upon Ian like a river in spate. Olivia Campbell was at Kilrain, not thirty miles away, out of his homeward path, it was true, but not so greatly out of it. He had hoped never to see her again, never to go within distance of the spell which she had cast upon him. Now—he felt he could not live unless he did. The reason he gave himself for yielding to temptation was this: he had allowed her (since he could not help himself) to see his passion, but he had not told her why he could never contemplate asking for her hand. It was almost an affront to have acted so . . . but he had lost his wits that day on Eilean Soa.

He did not pretend that he had found them again now. He knew that it was mad to go to Kilrain, and could lead to nothing but fresh suffering for himself. Yet he would welcome that . . . And he must make his explanation, justify his silence—or so he told himself. To another voice which said that he could equally well, and far more prudently, write this explanation, he shut his ears. He had little desire to combat the flood setting towards Kilrain; he was only too glad to be carried along by it. By the time he paid his second and last visit to Mr. Buchanan this afternoon his mind was made up, and he had consulted the map upon the lawyer's wall with entire composure. The detour might have been part of his original plan.

For all that, he had not left the green orchards of Glasgow behind him next morning, his face set north-eastwards, when his blood began to run faster. He knew his self-offered excuse for what it was; he was going to see Olivia Campbell because he could not keep away. And even how she would receive him weighed upon him but little, for she could not prevent him from resting his eyes once more upon her loveliness, though the moment of vision might be short. He could never have gone to Cairns to see her, whether she were like to refuse him admittance or to welcome him; but up in those hills which were neither Campbell nor Stewart territory, she could not entirely forbid his presence. And he fell to imagining the meeting, as, leaving the Clyde behind, he rode by glen or loch side, sometimes mounting, sometimes descending. Every stream which sang along his course or barred it seemed to utter her name, so liquidly sweet to the ear that he could forget the patronymic which followed it.

He halted at three o'clock to bait and rest his horse, for there was no haste, even though he should not reach Kilrain before dusk. It was even better so; he could more easily make enquiries as to Miss Campbell's whereabouts in the clachan without the risk of coming upon her unawares. He hardly knew what he should find at Kilrain, save goats.

And it *was* dusk when he came there, up the stony,

winding road. It was not too ill a track, for little Kilrain lay upon a minor highroad; otherwise, perhaps, it would scarcely have gained its reputation for "the whey." A curled young moon, and a star too, shone in the green sky over the rounded summit of Meall na Creige, and there was no wind to stir the pines which fringed that crest. All in the little village seemed within, if not abed, but a light or two still showed at the end by which Ian had entered. Had they not, he would willingly have slept on the hillside, but the sound of his horse's hoofs on the stones brought an old man to the door of one of the nearest cottages, and of him young Invernacree, representing himself as a benighted traveller, asked if there were an inn to which he could betake himself.

The old man replied in the negative, but offered to take him in himself, adding that he and his daughter were accustomed to do this for the gentry who came there for their health. Asked if there were any of these now visit-ing Kilrain for that purpose, he at first said that there were none—which was to Ian as though the moon had been struck suddenly out of the sky—but his daughter, correcting him, declared that there was a young lady, a bonny young lady, staying with her woman a little way higher up the hill.

From the tiny room assigned to him Ian could see up the slope, and gazed at the one faintly illumined window at some quarter mile of distance which he imagined—probably wrongly—to be Miss Campbell's until the light went out there, and the moon, as if waiting for this extinction, sank into the black arms of the pine-trees on the ridge; and all was as quiet in Kilrain as if a very imprudent and unhappy young man had not come to it.

§ 2

Though Olivia Campbell had written to her late hostess of her probable exceeding boredom when " at the goats' milk," it was only because she felt the absurdity of going there. It was fashionable to pretend to ennui, but in reality she hardly knew the meaning of the word, either in its French form or in its English.

Least of all did she know it this morning as she knelt by the little mountain pool which an eager burn, slackened in its course by a sudden outward thrust of the slope, had amused itself by forming on this kind of escarpment. She was watching the antics of a couple of kids who, in the intervals of staring at her across that mirror, sprang about it the most ridiculous gymnastics or butted each other with infantile fury. Olivia knelt there in a blue gown and a large shady hat and laughed; securely seated on a big stone, with a cloak folded beneath her, Mrs. Elspeth MacUre, who had been her nurse, knitted busily, and from time to time relaxed into a smile. And it was fine weather; fine with that loveliness-waking magic of the Western Highlands, which can wipe clean from the memory the days of mist and rain and storm, long and many though they be. Highlanders both, the two by the pool were not unmindful of this, though Mrs. MacUre, who was of a stout habit, had already remarked rather ungratefully upon the heat.

" You'll fall in, you wee thing!" warned Olivia, addressing one of the kids. " And I doubt you can swim. Are you prepared to wade in after this featherbrain if necessary, Elspeth?"

Mrs. MacUre shook her head with decision, but replied not in words. She was counting stitches.

" I see a man coming up the path who can act rescuer if one is needed," said Olivia in a lower voice. " But do not be so rash, creature," she went on, addressing the kid in Gaelic, as if she thought it could better understand that tongue. . . . " Although," she added with a little quick intake of the breath, " he who comes is something skilful in rescue . . . especially from water!" And, the colour leaping into her face, she rose to her feet. " Mr. Stewart, how . . . how come you here?"

Hat in hand, Ian stood on the other side of the pool. Everything in the scene was painted on his brain with pigments that would never fade, he thought—the azure pool, the crystal burn that fed it, the glowing heather, miles upon miles of surging mountains, clouds like ships in full sail, and soaring, limitless sky—and yet he only saw one figure, Olivia's.

" Kilrain lay upon my road yesterday," he replied, repeating what he had carefully rehearsed, " but I was belated in my arrival last night. And I bethought me this morning that you had written to Grizel of your intention of being here in August; and so I resolved that, if you permitted it, I would pay my respects to you."

If she had been alone, would she have sent him about his business, he wondered. And how much was she conscious of what had been virtually their last meeting, among the moon-daisies? He could not tell. She turned to her attendant, who was still knitting, and said with a smile, " Elspeth, this is Mr. Stewart of Invernacree, to whom I owe my rescue from that horrible coach, as you know. Pray, Mr. Stewart, come round to this side of the lochan and let Mrs. MacUre have a good look at you!"

Ian came round the pool—a very ordinary little High-land tarn, but more wonderful to him than all the stretch of the long sea-loch by which he dwelt, because she was upon its brink. Mrs. MacUre rose and curtsied to him. Even she shared in the enchantment, though to be sure he could have wished her away. And yet—she had perhaps her uses.

"And so you are travelling, Mr. Stewart," remarked Miss Campbell. "You have very fine weather for your journey. May one ask whither you are bound—for Perth perhaps?"

"No, I am upon my way home," confessed Ian. "I have been to Glasgow upon affairs."

"To Glasgow?" said the girl, and he saw those deli-cate eyebrows of hers lift a trifle. She recognised then that his homeward road had been by no means of the most direct. Indeed she showed her realisation of it next moment by adding, with a spice of mischief, "You too have perhaps been ordered to the goats' milk, Mr. Stewart, for your health?"

Before Mrs. MacUre Ian would not take up the challenge. He replied soberly, "No, Madam, that is not the case. I had a fancy to see Kilrain, that is all, and came this way, but it was almost dark last night when I reached it."

"Well, now you see it!" said Olivia, waving her hand towards the great sweep of view. "This is the prospect for which you have, I imagine—though indeed I am no geographer—come a good many miles out of your way!"

"And is there no other?" asked Ian, venturing to look at her rather directly. "Cannot one see more of the place from the pinewood yonder, for instance?"

On her answer to that simple question hung balanced, it seemed to him in some crazy fashion, the very continuance of the mountains in their solid majesty, the very preservation of the sun in the sky. He held his breath lest all should go crashing. . . . And though Olivia could scarcely have guessed at that exaggerated conviction of his, at any rate she weighed his suggestion before rejecting it—and did not reject it.

"One might perhaps see a little further down the valley from the other side of the wood," she conceded. "Shall we walk up that way?   I will come back to you here, Elspeth; but if you find the sun too hot, do you return to the cottage."

Ian did not know what Mrs. MacUre said to this proposal, nor did he care. The sun still shone, and the hills were secure. Miss Campbell, when she could easily have avoided it, had granted him an interview alone; that was all that mattered.

§ 3

They walked up the winding path towards the wood, a path so narrow that two could not go abreast. But Ian went by Olivia's side through the heather. She asked news of all at Invernacree, and he answered in a dream. She was graver than she had been by the pool; yet surely she could not be greatly displeased, or she would not have vouchsafed what she was vouchsafing.

To go into the pinewood out of the sunshine was like leaving the fair land of what might have been for the region of what really was. It was so much darker and colder here, and the pine stems stood stark and straight, like signposts pointing a man to his duty. Yet the sun did enter, in places, and the wood was beautiful, if with an austere beauty. And when they had walked a little way into its aisles Olivia Campbell stopped and said seriously: "Mr. Stewart, why have you come to Kilrain?"

He said, equally gravely, and quite calmly—at first: "You know why; it is because I could not keep away, knowing that you were here. If I died for it I had to see you again—once again. But there is another reason too. You must know, since that day on Eilean Soa, that I worship you; yet I allowed you to depart next morning without explaining why I could never give you the proof of that worship . . . even though it should mean nothing to you . . . why I could not ask for what I had, doubtless, no chance of obtaining—your hand in marriage."

Olivia stood with her eyes cast down; she neither flushed nor paled; she appeared to be thinking. Then suddenly she walked on a little way, and Ian did not follow her. He was not here to plead with her, but to tell her, alas, why he never could plead. He stayed where he was under the stern, dark trees and watched her move slowly away. She crossed a glint of sunlight; her blue gown flashed with colour; then she was beyond the bright barrier. And there she came to a standstill, turned her head, and made a little sign for him to come to her. Ian came.

"I thank you for the honour you wished to do me, Mr. Stewart," she said gently, looking at him much as she had looked that day on the island. "And I thank you for coming all this way to tell me that it was impossible."

"I hoped you would forgive me for that," said Ian anxiously.

"Perhaps," said Olivia, looking away from him, "my forgiveness may depend a little upon the reason for your . . . abstention. You have not yet given me that reason, you know!" There was the faintest glimmer of a smile round her enchanting mouth. "I presume it is the very ordinary one that you are already affianced."

"Ah no," said Ian, "it is something more——"

"More irrevocable than that? You are married then —secretly, perhaps?"

He shook his head. "Miss Campbell, don't play with me! Does not your own heart tell you that one of my name and allegiance could never wed with one of yours, especially——"

"Is that it?" cried Olivia, and her eyes sparkled, with what emotion the young man could not quite divine. "Surely we have buried the old clan hatreds now; and shall bury those between Whig and Jacobite in time! Can it really be that you regard me as someone outcast because my forbears and yours, a hundred years ago——"

"How could I regard you as anything of the sort!" broke in Ian passionately. "You are everything that is lovely and desirable, and I would give the sun out of the sky, if I had it, and walk in twilight all my days if only you were beside me! But there's a river between us deeper than you know; there's no bridge can cross it, and no power can turn its course. I can only say farewell to you, and hope that God will bless some man with you who is worthy of you. . . if there be such a man . . . worthier at least than I should have been." He snatched up her hand and bent to kiss it; bent still further, and flinging himself on his knees, pressed the hand for a moment to his hot forehead.

" Mr. Stewart, what have I done? " asked Olivia, looking down upon him in a very perturbed fashion. " What is there between us, more than our names and our politics? For what am I to blame? "

" You? For nothing, for nothing! " answered the young man in a stifled voice. " But there is my brother Alan's blood between us. He fell on Culloden Moor, and it was the Campbells——"

Olivia gave an exclamation. " Culloden! He died *there!* I did not know. And you mean that because my father . . ." She did not finish.

" Yes, that is what I mean," said Ian. He had loosed her hand, and now got to his feet again; he was very pale.

She too was pale, and put the hand he had released over her eyes. " But," she said rather pitifully after a moment, " my father only did his duty, and it was not . . . not by his very hand that your brother fell."

" Not by his hand, perhaps. But by his orders, by his act. There is no difference. I would to God I could see it otherwise! You are Highland too—you must see that it is not possible."

Yes, Olivia Campbell was Highland too. Yet she did not assent to this doctrine. She said, shivering slightly, " This wood is very cold. I think we will go out into the sun again."

All the way out of the wood the young man beside her struggled with the desire to snatch her suddenly into his arms. All the fire, the melancholy of the Celtic nature, its passion for the hopeless and the intangible, its willingness to lose everything for a dream, and that not always a worthy dream, all surged up in him as he walked beside his Deirdre, his Bronwen, found at last, when he had thought the chance of it was over—and found in vain. Yet it was just that inheritance which kept him from a ravished kiss.

So they came in silence to the edge of the wood, and saw the sunshine spread over all the scene beyond it like a veil of gold.

"Where are you lodging, Mr. Stewart?"

He told her.

"You are remaining at Kilrain to-night?"

"No," he said with an effort. "Now that I have seen you I shall continue my journey to Appin this afternoon."

"I should like to have spoken with you again about this matter," said Olivia faintly. "There are considerations . . . I cannot bear your thinking of my father in this way . . . If I had not such a headache I think I could make you see it differently." She put her hand once more to her head, and it was quite plain that she was not acting a part.

But if he stayed, if he stayed! . . . Oh, could he be held to blame when she directly asked him to remain? And did he care if he were blamed? He offered his arm, his heart leaping so wildly that he almost felt its pulsations must quiver down to his finger-tips.

"Allow me to take you back to your lodging," he said quietly. "And, to avoid the sun, let us descend the hill inside the wood, if it is possible."

Murmuring some excuse for her "foolishness," Olivia accepted his arm, and, going back a few paces, they turned and went down the slope through the solemn pine boles. So there she was, walking beside him in the twilight, as he had said. But the sun of heaven was not his, to cast from the sky; he could do nothing, nothing. . . .

CHAPTER VIII

THE ONLY SAFETY

§ 1

Aug. 13th—14th.

STRANGE that it should often take an obstacle in the stream's path to show the stream which way it is flowing! This, at least, was what had happened to Olivia Campbell, and it was the matter which she sat deeply pondering at her bedroom window that evening, while the stars strove faintly overhead against the long-drawn Northern daylight.

She could not tell herself that she loved Ian Stewart, but she did recognise that she had been devoting a good deal of thought to him these last few weeks. And now she had been informed that she must not do so any more. Human nature being what it is, there could hardly have been given her a more powerful specific for ensuring that she should.

But he—he was in earnest, and she had lost what she had never known that she possessed. She would never see him again after to-morrow . . . unless to-morrow she could persuade him to view differently that tragic gulf which in his eyes separated them. In her heart she doubted her power to do that, although he had agreed to stay until she could see him again. Besides, why was she about to try to make him see it differently? The attempt, thus formally arranged for, had the appearance of an endeavour to persuade him to make her an offer of marriage after all; and, since she had no intention of accepting such an offer, why should she try to provoke it? It would be no satisfaction to refuse him.

Olivia got up and began to move about her tiny low-ceiled room, her hands clasped together and her chin resting upon them. She somewhat prided herself upon being clearsighted. *Why* was it that she was loth to let him go? Surely it could not be some unworthy form of coquetry or pique? What was it, then, since she did not love him?

With that question still unanswered she sought the stuffy little box-bed in the wall which was all that the cottage—and many a dwelling better than a cottage—had to offer. But she could not sleep; and in this confined space the sudden headache of the morning, which had been perfectly genuine and had continued most of the afternoon, came on again. Her own hot forehead, when she put her hand on it, recalled young Invernacree's when he had pressed that same hand to his brow; and the remembrance brought back the hopeless passion in his voice as he had knelt there in the wood, renouncing her. . . . But why should she think of that again now, and so insistently that she could see once more the top of his dark head bowed over her hand, even the very way in which his hair-ribbon was knotted, and feel a longing to lay her other hand in consolation on that bent head? Good God, had she really been conscious of such a feeling at the time, or was it a mere trick of memory? For what was hopeless passion to her, when she did not share it? She had met it before; and after a while felt glad to be rid of the tribute.

But this particular tribute she did not want to be rid of: that was the conclusion of the whole matter. It was not a conclusion which made for peaceful or refreshing sleep.

Its effects, indeed, were apparent next morning, for Mrs. MacUre observed that she doubted Miss Olivia was getting as much benefit from the whey as her Papa would wish, and added, " Did ye not sleep well, my dear?"

" Not very well," confessed Olivia. " It was so hot in my little room. But I shall be myself again when I am in the fresh air."

" Would ye not do better to stay in the house the morn?" suggested her attendant. " 'Tis going to be a hot day again. But at any rate ye'll need to stay until ye have drunk your whey."

Olivia assented, knowing that Mr. Stewart would not arrive to wait upon her until after that hour.

The rite over, she brought out a piece of embroidery and sat down to watch for him. Elspeth and she had the cottage to themselves, Mr. Campbell having hired it in its entirety, which had enabled Mrs. MacUre to bring it to a state of cleanliness not known for many years. The sun climbed a little higher; the goats could be heard bleating as they were driven to pasture; a few people went by; still Ian did not come. A panic seized Olivia; suppose he had not kept to the compact, if compact it could be called, which they had made yesterday? She flung down her embroidery, looked out of the window several times, took up a book and dropped it again after a page or two.

" Ye're unco restless, Miss Olivia," observed Elspeth MacUre, who was in and out of the room enough to observe this fact. " If ye're ettlin' to go out, why not go out now? 'Twill be hotter by and by."

" I think I will not go just yet," murmured her

charge. To herself she said, "But, upon my soul, if he does not arrive within the next five minutes, I will . . . and he can come and search for me!"

But in that case he might fail to find her; or, worse, he might not even try, but ride away discouraged.

"This is too tiresome!" she exclaimed aloud.

"What's tiresome, my dear? And who's keeping you in the house if ye're set on going out? I'm sure 'tis not your old Elspeth. She's ready to put on her bonnet the moment ye give the word."

Olivia looked at her in mute despair. The five minutes had already fled away and another three been added to them. Save that convention forbade, even here, she would have gone to the cottage where Mr. Stewart was lodging, not exactly to hasten him, but to ease her mind of this ghastly suspicion of a misunderstanding somewhere. But of course even she, who was somewhat of a law unto herself, could not outrage decorum so far as that. Should she send Elspeth? But that would be to reveal . . . too much.

The middle portion of a man's figure—more was never visible of any passer-by—came past the minute window. Olivia's heart leapt up; higher still when there came a knock at the door, which opened directly into the living room. Elspeth hastened to open it, and there he stood, slim and strong against the sunlight, and doffed his hat. His hair was not as dark as she had thought—not so dark as her own—for the sun struck a gleam of brown from it. . . .

"I called to enquire for Miss Campbell, whether she is recovered of her indisposition of yesterday?" came his voice.

"Miss Campbell is quite recovered," called Olivia

gaily from the corner of the room. "Will you not come in, Mr. Stewart?"

§ 2

In the clear air above Meall na Creige a speck was hovering—a large hawk, perhaps even an eagle. Olivia looked up at it fixedly, because if there are tears in your eyes there is in this attitude a more reasonable hope of their not descending your cheeks.

It was all in vain: in vain that she stood here alone with Ian Stewart by the great lichened shoulder of rock on the other slope of the glen, surveying this fair sunlit world; in vain that she knew he loved her, and that she . . . that she was conscious without looking at him of that reserved and sensitive profile of his. The phantom of a young man whom she had never known stood there with them, a cold, shadowy presence, the green Stewart tartan on his breast all reddened with Campbell musket balls, and, since she was Highland too, she knew in her heart that the dead Alan's only brother, now the heir, could never go back to his father and his clan and announce that he had asked in marriage the daughter of the man whose command had winged those bullets. Nor was it merely the ban of his family and his race which was ranged against her; Ian's own fidelity to conviction, despite the way in which it racked him, was unshaken—she saw that; and though he had come to Kilrain with no other aim but that of seeing her, such a concession to his own weakness would never happen again. All was over before it had begun.

Olivia would not weep; she called to her all her pride of clan and of womanhood. Allow a man . . . any man—a Stewart least of all—to see. . . . The bird above the mountain soared unexpectedly out of sight. Yet she must still look hard at something; and, her hearing assisting her in the quest, her eyes fell upon a horseman going at a walk upon the road below. He seemed, as far as one could tell from a distance, to be gazing up at her and her companion; then—yes, surely, he was trying to attract their attention! Could it be news of some kind from Cairns?

"Mr. Stewart," she said rather breathlessly, "do you see a man down there on a grey horse who . . . why, I believe he is dismounting and coming up to us!"

Until she spoke Ian had not been conscious of the rider, nor, indeed, of anything much in his surroundings. Now he looked down the heathery incline and saw the dismounted horseman starting quickly up it. And very soon, to his surprise, and by no means to his gratification, he heard Olivia say animatedly, "Why, it is my dear Mr. Maitland! Whatever can he be doing here?"

In spite of his renewed act of renunciation Ian felt a sharp pang as he heard these words. Who was this Mr. Maitland of whom Miss Campbell could speak in these terms, and whose advent could cause her, even at this moment, so much evident pleasure? The newcomer had the figure of a young man, and he mounted the hillside with all the speed and agility of one, but before he had arrived at their level Ian saw that his face was that of a man of five and forty or so—and a very attractive face it was too, even if its beauty was almost too ethereal for masculine taste. (But it occurred to Ian that a woman might not think so.) A very sweet smile dawned upon it now as, just a trifle out of breath with haste, he arrived at the rocky shoulder.

"My dearest Olivia!" he said, and kissed her hand.
"I feared I should not find you. I went first to your
lodging at the cottage, and was fortunate in happening
upon your good Elspeth there, otherwise——"

"But how did you know that I was here at all—and
still more, why are *you* here?" asked Olivia, laughing,
and slipping her hand in a most intimate manner into
the newcomer's arm.

"I knew that you were here from a letter of your
father's, and I am here because Kilrain lies on my way
to Lochaber, whither I am bound on affairs," the gentleman replied, putting his other hand over the one reposing
on his arm.

"What good luck!" cried Olivia gaily. "But, dear
me, what a centre of travel this little spot is becoming!
For here is Mr. Ian Stewart of Invernacree, of whose
prowess and kindness I wrote to you. He also was
passing through the clachan. Mr. Stewart, let me present
you to my oldest friend, Mr. Maitland of Strathmory,
whom I sometimes call my godfather."

Ian came forward and bowed. Mr. Maitland held
out his hand.

"Indeed I have heard of you, sir, from Miss Campbell; and if I may, as so old a friend of hers, I should
like to add my thanks to those of her family!"

His manner and his look a good deal disarmed Ian.
And, after all, Olivia could hardly contemplate marriage
with a man of twice her age whom she called, even
occasionally, her godfather!

There was some further talk up by the rock. Mr.
Maitland wished to know if the young lady were really
in need of a sojourn "at the whey"; he had hoped that
it was only a whim of her father's, to which Olivia

emphatically responded that his hope was justified. She seemed to Ian quite to have shaken off the sadness consequent upon their recent interview, in the pleasure of seeing this elderly friend of hers. It was no doubt just as well. . . .

Presently they were all going down the side of the hill together, for Mr. Maitland announced that he must push on at once. Miss Campbell asked him where he was going and on what business, but the traveller returned no definite answer.

"Well, my dear Olivia," said he when they reached his busily grazing horse, "I hope that the rest of your stay will be agreeable and beneficial to you. It has been a great pleasure to have had this glimpse of you; I am only sorry that it must be so short."

"You might have had a glimpse before this, and a longer one," replied Miss Campbell with a little pout. "Do you know that you have not visited us at Cairns since some time early in '53—more than two years ago!"

"Is it really so long!" exclaimed the gentleman. "I certainly deserve censure for that." He began to alter a stirrup leather, and then to examine his horse's girths, and Ian, who, since he happened to be at the animal's head, had put an instinctive hand upon its bridle, was struck by the swift change which came over his face. As he turned away from the girl it was as though a mask had slipped off it, and, when he raised himself from his examination, Ian's impression of sudden metamorphosis was even strengthened. Why, the man looked tragically harassed, as well as ill! Ian was startled by it. Then Mr. Maitland turned round again to Olivia, and she too must have observed some change, for Ian heard her say,

"I don't think you look very well, Mr. Maitland. 'Tis you should be staying here, not I!"

"A touch of tertian fever, my dear, which I had a few days ago," replied he carelessly. "'Tis nothing—save perhaps a sign of advancing years. So, by your leave, I'll not let myself be overtaken by the night." He kissed her hand again (Ian wondering whether he were not accustomed, at any rate in the absence of strangers, to kiss her cheek or brow) gave her a message to her father, mounted, saluted Ian and was off.

Ian looked after him and his vanishing grey horse. He too ought to be riding along that road. Why prolong this pain? He said: "I think my own mare must be reshod by now, a thing I found she needed; but the smith was indisposed this morning and could not shoe her." It was in fact the discovery of this necessity and of the difficulty in remedying it—for, in more brutal language, the blacksmith was drunk—which had caused his delay in coming to Olivia's cottage. "May I escort you back to your lodging before I set out?" he added.

Olivia assented, and they began to walk back along the road.

"There is a path," said Ian after a moment or two, indicating one on their left which began to mount from the road. "I fear this is rough walking for you, and the path would be somewhat shorter too, probably."

"Do you wish it to be, I wonder?" murmured Miss Campbell to herself. But she did not say it aloud.

It was a wider path than some, and they went along it side by side. For a while it pushed by great bushes of broom, whose golden glory was now departed; ahead was a little wood, a mere copse of oak and hazel.

"Do you know, Mr. Stewart," said Olivia suddenly,

as Ian held aside a branch for her to pass, "that the gentleman who has just left us is a living argument against the conviction which . . . which you hold, for Mr. David Maitland has been a friend of my father's for as long as I can remember; yet he is a Jacobite."

"There are Jacobites and Jacobites, Miss Campbell."

"But Mr. Maitland is not one of your theoretical Jacobites," returned Olivia with vivacity. "He was 'out' in the Forty-five; he fought at Falkirk. I believe he only escaped proscription through the good offices of my father. And yet you see," she ended with a little sigh, "he is our intimate friend."

"It was not a friend that I wished to be," said Ian in a voice unlike his own. The sentiment, or something else, produced a silence between them, during which they reached the coppice; and the path, dipping slightly, brought them to the banks of a little woodland stream which it immediately crossed by means of stepping stones. They came to a halt.

"And so," said Olivia slowly, looking at the sparkle of the water, "you will not in future be able to think of me as a friend?"

Ian caught his breath. "I hope that I shall be able to avoid thinking of you at all," he said harshly, a man in pain not always measuring his words. Olivia bit her lip and turned her head away; then, not answering, she placed her foot on the first of the stepping-stones. It rocked a little, even beneath her light weight. The next moment she was caught by both elbows and steadied.

"Step on to the flat stone in the middle," came Ian's voice. She obeyed, and he instantly released her.

"The stone was loose," she said, excusing herself.

" Indeed I can usually cross a burn without falling in."

Her companion was standing in the shallow water beside her. " I do not doubt it. But, lest there be other loose stones. . . ." He offered his hand.

Olivia took it, and next moment was safely on the opposite bank. Before she could make a remark of any kind Ian, still holding her hand, began to speak again, the words tumbling out, and checking, too, like the watercourse at their feet.

" Forgive me . . . forgive me for saying that! It is not true. I shall always think of you, I am afraid. It would be too much to expect you to think of me, sometimes . . . just from kindness . . . as one thinks of the very unhappy. . . . Perhaps I should know it—but perhaps it would be better if I did not. . . . And if you will forgive me, I will leave you, now that you are over the burn; there is your way back plain. . . . I cannot walk any further with you . . . there is a term to what one can endure—and so I will go back the other way."

He looked indeed absolutely exhausted, as a man might do after prolonged torture. Olivia's hand was still in his; after the first, she had not attempted to withdraw it. She tried to say " Good-bye then," but no words came. And whether Ian drew her unconsciously towards him by that captive hand, or whether she as unconsciously came, or both, next moment her head was on his breast, and remained there.

Then with his other hand the young man gently turned her face up to his, and she did not resist; she only shut her eyes. So, in the oak copse by the stream, Stewart and Campbell kissed each other without a word; and equally without a word did Ian's clasp relax. Olivia

heard footsteps splashing quickly through water. . . .
She put her hands over her face, in a gesture of possession,
not of concealment. The air should not so soon obliter-
ate that gift—that gift which she had returned. When
she removed them she was alone.

But the world was changed—how changed! She walked
home in a different one, whether a gladder or a sorrier,
she hardly knew. Mrs. MacUre, after looking at her
once or twice, forbore to ask what had become of her
escort.

§ 3

Twenty minutes after he had kissed Olivia Campbell
Ian was standing in dismay before the little forge in the
village, to find that the blacksmith had not yet recovered
from the effects of his drunken bout of the previous day,
that the mare had not in consequence been reshod, but
that her shoes, most unfortunately, had been removed in
readiness by the smith's boy, and could not be put on
again. So he could not ride her away with the old shoes,
as he had intended. There was no other saddle horse in
Kilrain, nor could he get home on foot. The smith's
wife, saddened and apologetic, was, however, sure that
by sundown her man would have sufficiently recovered.
If the gentleman would have a little more patience. . . .

The gentleman flung away distracted. If he stayed
he was lost. With that honey of Olivia's kiss still on his
lips, the touch of her tingling in his veins, nothing but
flight would save him. If he went near her again now
all his defences would go down with a crash, and he saw
himself imploring her to marry him out of hand, by a

mere Scots marriage before witnesses, anything. . . . There was no hope for him but to leave this sweet and fatal place at once. Yet because of this ridiculous and vulgar contretemps of a drunken blacksmith he was pinned here.

Patience! as if he would not have given his right hand to stay! Was Fate plotting against him to drive him into dishonour? For Olivia Campbell could not be indifferent to him, or she would never have allowed him, as she had, that moment by the stream which made his head turn when he thought of it. *Now*, if he asked her to be his wife, would it, in her eyes, be out of the question? He knew that it would not.

There was nothing to do but to go striding away up into the hills, too far away to run the risk of coming upon Olivia, till such time as that sun which had seen her lay her head against his heart should put an end, behind the shoulder of Meall na Creige, to this wretched and ecstatic day.

He did walk, for hours, in the peace of the high hills, but still the sun rode the heavens, though by Ian's watch it was time to turn. And at last he came once more in sight of Kilrain. The smoke of evening was beginning to rise from the thatched roofs as he descended, steering his course at random. By now he was very tired, for he had scarcely slept the night before, and emotion, joined to fasting (since he had not dined that day) can exhaust even a vigorous young man of six and twenty. And with fatigue a sort of trance came upon him, and he recognised without surprise that his returning steps had somehow led him into the little copse of the morning. It seemed appropriate. That surely was the very spot where he had stood with her when the wonder of the world had happened to him—yes, there were the stepping-stones.

"*Olivia*," said the burn, hurrying gently along. "*Olivia . . . O . . . liv . . . i . . . a . . .*"

Ian threw himself down for a moment, to listen to that cool and gliding music.

Strange! He must actually have fallen asleep! Yes, he did remember, now, changing his posture and stretching himself out under an oak tree for a few minutes' rest. But by the change in the light it must have been much more than a few minutes' sleep. It had been long enough to hold a dream, also, one of those particularly vivid and sudden dreams which come with daylight slumber and partake of day's reality. Ian lay still a moment recalling it, for it was sweet.

He had dreamt that Olivia was standing there, looking at him, and he had tried to speak to her, to ask her for some memento, since he had none. But the chains of sleep held him fast, and he could not utter the words; he could not even open his eyes; yet he knew that she was there. Nevertheless, being in his dream the King of Lochlann's daughter out of the old tales as well as Olivia Campbell, she gave him as a token that grey, mottled skin of the seal, her other self, the possession of which enabled her at will to go back to the sea from whence she came. And the gift meant that she renounced her right—for him.

Ian lay still a moment longer, smiling rather bitterly. Of what odd elements were dreams compounded! It was time to relinquish them, to face reality, and to ride away. With a heavy sigh he raised himself on to his right elbow . . . and remained there motionless, the blood rushing into his face. Between the fingers and

the palm of that open right hand lay a freshly plucked
sprig of bog-myrtle—bog-myrtle, the only too familiar
badge of Clan Campbell.

.   .   .   .   .   .

A little later, between sunset and moonrise, Ian
checked his mare for a last look at Kilrain before the
drop of the road should hide it from his view. Like
to like—the sprig of gall was in the folds of Olivia's
letter over his heart. He stayed a moment, wrenched
with longing; then tugged the mare round again and
rode on down the slope.

CHAPTER IX

OTHER PEOPLE'S LOVE AFFAIRS

§ 1

Aug. 14th—19th.

To every lover his own love affair is naturally the only one in the world. Yet while Ian Stewart, surrounded by goats, was dallying with the foeman's daughter up in the hills, a young man rather older than himself, whose existence he had temporarily forgotten, was approaching Invernacree with intent to pay his addresses to Ian's sister. And because of Ian's absence, he was going to find his path at first a good deal smoother than it might otherwise have been.

Of Captain Hector Grant, of the régiment d'Albanie in the service of His Most Christian Majesty of France, Ian himself had not long ago said that he was too French for his taste. Hector had indeed a slightly French air and French manners—what wonder, since most of his life had been spent upon Gallic soil? In the uniform which he had left behind the former was probably even more apparent. Yet, as his brother-in-law Ewen Cameron had pointed out, he was Highland to the backbone for all that. Did not, indeed, the three motives which had now brought him to Scotland prove that fact? He was on his way to take possession of his recently-inherited Highland property, to satisfy his desire for vengeance upon another Highlander who had injured him, and to discover whether a certain Highland girl in Appin remembered him as well as he remembered her. And if he found Miss Jacqueline Stewart, that pretty, shy thing, ready to welcome him, and if her eyes still held the smile he had seen there more than two years ago—well, he was no longer, as then, a penniless French officer unable to think of marriage. She was a very charming girl, Miss Jacqueline; and Hector had had plenty of opportunity of comparing her with the French demoiselles. Mercifully, perhaps, his poverty had prevented him from marrying one of these, so that he was still free to woo a Highland lass.

And thus he came within sight of the tree-surrounded house of Invernacree, which had sheltered him after he had escaped with Ewen Cameron of Ardroy from captivity in Fort William on the Christmas Day of 1752.* It was only fitting, therefore, that he should pay his respects to old Alexander Stewart, and renew acquaintance with the son of the house, who—mainly, of course, on his cousin Ardroy's account—had so materially assisted in that escape. At the very outset fortune gave him a favourable omen, for as he rode up to the gate he perceived, under the oaks of the avenue, two ladies walking towards the house—the two Miss Stewarts, there was no question. Better of course had it been the younger alone—but that would come later! Hector stooped from the saddle, opened the gate and rode through.

The sound of the gate falling to again caught the ladies' ears; they both turned their heads and stopped. Mr. Grant rode on a few paces, swung out of the saddle and advanced, hat in hand. And on Jacqueline Stewart's face, for one brief moment at least, was sufficient warranty for his welcome.

*See *The Gleam in the North.*

§ 2

Two days later Hector Grant was still at Invernacree, and in those two days, thanks to an intensive system of wooing pursued under favourable circumstances—though Hector was not sure that old Invernacree would prove altogether tractable to handle when it came to the point—had achieved, as far as Jacqueline herself was concerned, the position of accepted suitor. In this he had been greatly assisted by the fine weather, since one cannot sit or walk with a lady in a garden—a locality very favourable to courtship—during persistent rain; in such the lady, at least, is condemned to the house, where love-making is more liable to interruption.

Now the sun which shone upon the pair was, naturally, the same which had shone for Ian in his more clandestine commerce with Miss Olivia Campbell among the rocks and the heather of Kilrain. Yet that ill-starred lover, when, returning home on the third day, he left his horse in the stable and crossed the garden on his way to the house, was by no means pleased to perceive the result of this equality of solar benefits; indeed, he stopped dead, astounded, scandalised, and then angry at what, himself unseen, he saw taking place.

Upon the seat encircling the trunk of the cedar-tree in the middle of the lawn was sitting his sister Jacqueline; she held an arm outstretched, and upon the wrist thereof perched, like a hawk, one of her doves. A handsome young man, whom Ian instantly recognised, with one knee upon the brown carpet of cedar needles, was laughingly tendering his arm also towards the bird; he appeared to be trying to tempt it away. The hands of these two arms were very near each other, their owners' heads not far apart.

And somehow Ian felt that he would have been less stirred to anger if he had come upon the intruder wholly upon his knees to Jacqueline, making an impassioned declaration in due form, or if Jacqueline's dove had not been so inextricably, so sacredly bound up in his mind with his own bright vision of Olivia leaning out of her window here, the day her smile had enslaved him. After that, this scene was sacrilege!

"Curse his impudence!" he said under his breath, and advanced.

The dove saw him first and flew off its mistress's wrist; the culprits, looking for the reason of its flight, became aware of a third person. Hector sprang to his feet.

"Good afternoon, Mr. Stewart! If it were my place to do so, I would say, 'Welcome home!'" And, not in the least abashed, he came forward, holding out his hand.

Ian bowed rather stiffly as a preliminary to taking it, which he could not in common civility refuse to do. ("No," he thought, "it is not your place to welcome me, Mr. Grant, and never will be!") Aloud he said, "Your servant, sir! Good-day, Jacqueline; are you teaching Mr. Grant to be a bird fancier?"

She, at least, was rosy in the face which she put up for his kiss.

But it was in no placid frame of mind that Ian went off to see his father, and to give an account of his mission to Glasgow. It was hard to return from renouncing the love of one's life to find a love affair—minor, of course —going on in one's own home; it was doubly hard when the suitor was a man whose name had been a source of irritation for the last two years. For that name was connected with the fiasco which had left his cousin Ewen, that December morning, stranded on Ardgour beach in great danger of recapture, a fiasco which his father had never ceased to make a source of reproach to him, though indeed the consequences to Ewen had not been lastingly serious, nor did Ewen himself bear his cousin the slightest grudge for a mishap which the latter could hardly have foreseen. But old Alexander Stewart, who had a great affection for his nephew Ardroy, had more than once muttered, " Ah, your poor brother Alan would have seen in time what was going to happen!" It was all part and parcel of the feeling which Ian knew to exist in his father's mind, that he was no worthy substitute for his slain elder brother. Yes, it was bitter to come back to that knowledge, when it was partly to his position as Alan's successor that he had sacrificed his heart's happiness.

His father, however, greeted him affectionately enough, listened to his account of his interviews with the lawyer, received the papers and looked through them, remarking only that Ian had stayed longer than he expected in Glasgow, and surmising that Mr. Buchanan had been busy.

"Yes," replied Ian unblushingly, " he was somewhat throng with clients, and I had to wait his leisure, which delayed me." Here he tempered falsehood with truth by adding, " The mare, too, unexpectedly needed reshoeing, and a drunken blacksmith delayed me still further."

" Reshoeing! You should have looked to that before setting out. I must speak to them in the stables about it," said Invernacree, vexed. " And I imagine a drunken smith can hardly have shod her well! Where did you come upon him?"

5

"Oh, in some clachan on the way," replied Ian hastily, wishing he had not introduced the subject; and thereupon remarked upon the arrival of Mr. Hector Grant, partly, also, in order to see what his father thought of the attentions paid by the guest to his younger daughter. But the old man did not appear to be aware of them, and on the whole Ian was glad, not wishing, in reality, to discuss the subject of lovemaking.

He went out of the study to the privacy of his own room, and there took out of his pocketbook an object which the utmost care had not preserved from withering. Nothing droops more quickly than the bog-myrtle; yet it retains in death its sweet, half-bitter fragrance. So it was, so it always would be with the memory of those enchanted hours at Kilrain, ending, indeed, in frustration and parting, but yet with a talisman, a sign, magically given.

For how the sprig of gall came to be in his hand, unless Olivia had laid it there when he was asleep, Ian could not conceive. He rejected the idea that someone had done it as a jest—for who would have played such a prank? He could not in his sleep have reached out and clutched it, for there was none growing near; he had searched the spot. But there was a patch some way further down the stream; and it *was* the Campbell emblem. Never before, he imagined, had a Stewart cherished the gall; never before had one of his name been so besotted as to put a withered fragment of it to his lips as he did now, though he knew not even whether his love had laid it in his hand, nor what had been her meaning if she had. But it was the Campbell emblem, and she was a Campbell . . . O God, if only she were not!

§ 3

And now Captain Hector Grant's courtship began to prosper less conspicuously, for the home-coming of young Invernacree cast a perceptible blight upon its hitherto very rapid growth. It was not only that his physical presence was inconvenient, seeing that he was much more likely to come unexpectedly upon the lovers than was the old laird or Grizel, but it also reacted mentally upon Jacqueline herself, who began to close up as the anemone touched by a rash finger furls the pretty fringe which the tide has set waving in the pool. She was very fond of Ian, and sensitive to a disapproval which she felt the more, perhaps, that it was unexpressed. Hector cursed to himself, but he was unable to do much save see all he could of his lady, and as little as possible of her brother. He wondered how much longer he could with decency prolong his visit. Ian Stewart's covert hostility, which he could not quite understand, was additionally trying because he himself was in Ian's debt over the old Fort William business. And he had not yet approached the laird on the subject of his younger daughter—did not even know whether he suspected anything of his feelings. Suppose it was Invernacree's son who first enlightened the old man; that would be awkward in the extreme! Endowed with all the sensitive pride of a Highlander, Hector was uneasy lest he should have placed himself in a false position, and that in the house of another Highlander. And on the third afternoon after Ian's return he spoke of his perplexities to Jacqueline herself, driven to it by the knowledge that her brother was actually closeted with Invernacree at the very moment—at least, he had seen Ian go into the old man's study a little while ago, and, as far as he knew, he had not come out again. He and Jacqueline were seated in the window-seat of the drawing-room, and he was holding a skein of green silk for her to wind. But when he made the suggestion of asking her father for her hand without further delay the girl ceased winding, and looked intensely troubled.

" But I did not wish my father . . . anyone . . . to know just yet!" she objected.

" My darling! Yet your brother guesses, I think. I should have spoken to your father already," said Hector, slipping the skein off his hands.

" But," said Jacqueline, looking down at it, " I hoped . . . it is so short a time that you have been here . . . O, pray, Mr. Grant . . ."

" *Mr. Grant!*"

" Hector, then," she said in a small voice, her fingers all the while doing a good deal of damage to the skein.

He captured the little ravagers. " ' O pray, Hector ' —what then?" he asked smiling. " ' O pray, Hector '— silence! But, my heart's treasure, what if your brother has forestalled me!"

" He cannot—he would not do such a thing! Ian is too fond of me!"

" *Cela n'empêche pas le moins du monde,*" her lover assured her, in the tongue which was almost as natural to him as his own. " All the more reason, on the contrary, that he should. He does not love *me* with any great affection, I am sure, and he will be the less anxious to lose you. I should have been beforehand with your father. Directly I can be sure that your brother has left his room I shall ask for an interview and make a formal demand for—this." He lifted the little hand to his lips as he spoke.

"Yes, I suppose you must," murmured Jacqueline, still looking down. "But if my father should refuse——" She came to a stop, and when she raised her eyes they had become homes of tragedy.

"He'll not refuse," returned Captain Grant with much assurance. "But if he should, I'll get round him somehow. I will procure Ewen Cameron, for instance, to plead my cause."

"That would be a good notion," said the girl, brightening. "My father thinks a great deal of Cousin Ewen. . . . But you say that Ian is with him now. Suppose they were already speaking of . . . us!"

"That, *mon amour*," observed the young man, "as I was saying, is just what I am afraid of."

But before he could enlarge upon this possibility they were somewhat apologetically interrupted by Grizel, who needed Jacqueline's presence on household affairs.

CHAPTER X

FATHER AND SON

Aug. 19th (continued).

THE couple on the window-seat, however, need not have
been apprehensive. A delicate matter was indeed under
discussion at the moment in Alexander Stewart's study,
but it did not affect them. Indeed their affairs were
miles away from the mind of the young man who stood
there, somewhat like a criminal before a judge, and tried
to fend off for a while longer the necessity to which,
willing or unwilling, he would in the end have to yield.

" But if I understand you rightly," his father was saying, " you practically refuse to continue the prosecution
of your suit to Miss Margaret Maclean. Or do I not,
by good fortune, understand you rightly?"

Ian moistened his dry lips. " One cannot prosecute
what is not yet begun."

" Don't quibble with me, sir! In essence it is begun.
Before you went to Glasgow you assured me that the
match was not disagreeable to you, and that upon your
return you would pay your addresses to the lady. Acting
on your promise, when I met Garroch at Ballachulish one
day in your absence——"

" Good God!" cried his unfortunate son, " you have
not already opened the matter to him?"

" And why not, pray?" demanded Invernacree.
" Was I to suppose the word of a son of mine to be a

mere tuft of bog-cotton, blowing hither and thither in the wind? I was more than justified in sounding Garroch on the subject; 'twas the proper path to pursue, and he expressed much satisfaction at the prospect of the alliance. But if you are not man enough to win the lady for yourself——" He paused, perhaps expecting his taunt, by drawing blood, to rouse some angry reaction in this strangely reluctant and impassive suitor. But instead of displaying any healthy resentment (though indeed a slight quiver appeared to go through him) Ian Stewart turned his back and went and gazed out of the window in silence; and after a second or two put a hand over his eyes.

Whatever emotions of dismay or ruth were in the old laird's soul as he looked at the figure of all the son that was left to him, and whatever momentary compassion showed for an instant on his face, there was no faltering in his voice as he pursued mercilessly:

"If, as I say, you are not man enough, you must employ an ambassador. Shall I offer myself? "

Ian turned round. Against the faded grey paint of the folded shutters his face looked grey too, but Alexander Stewart's eyes were old. "Father . . . I will go . . . but not yet—not yet! Give me a little time, for pity's sake! " The desperation in his voice was unmistakable.

"Time! " exclaimed the old man harshly, though his heart fluttered at the note. "You have had time enough, my son. You assured me that you knew your duty—which ought, if you have the common instincts of humanity, to be something more than a duty. I am not proposing to you an ill-favoured or misshapen bride; I should be the last to wish such an one to become the mother of your sons. Miss Maclean is a modest and comely girl of good family. And you have been at liberty to choose elsewhere if you had so desired, and your choice had my approval. What more do you wish?"

"Or what less?" muttered Ian.

"Come nearer to me, if you please," said Invernacree irritably. "I cannot hear what you say, and you give the impression of trying to escape into the garden. Come and sit down here, and let us discuss this matter in a reasonable spirit."

Ian obeyed in silence. He sat down at the library table not far from his father, who was ensconced restlessly in a big chair near the empty hearth; but by leaning his elbow on the table's edge the young man was able easily to raise a hand at need to shade his face. "There is nothing to discuss, sir," he said dully. "I am ready to fulfil your wishes and my duty."

"Ready! You are not ready!" burst out the old man impatiently. "Why say you are? Your unreadiness is what I am complaining of."

"I am ready if you will give me a little longer," declared his son.

Alexander Stewart smote his hand upon the arm of his chair. "Delay, delay! A very gallant suitor to keep a lady waiting! Ian, procrastination always has a motive, however secret. You will kindly tell me, before we go further, what it is you hope to gain by yours."

"To gain? Nothing—nothing in the world," answered Ian a trifle wildly. "I only ask you not to press me to attempt what I cannot . . . yet. In a couple of months, perhaps. . . ."

"A couple of months! And why, pray, will you find it easier to ask for the hand of Miss Maclean in a couple of months?"

Ian shaded his eyes with his hand and said nothing. He

did not know that he *would* find it easier; and how could he explain? Through the open window came the murmur of Jacqueline's doves, which would always now bring back Olivia's face to him. The wind of Kilrain played again about his temples; under his feet was the hillside heather, and in his arms. . . .

Suddenly and most unexpectedly he felt his father's hand upon his shoulder. " Ian, my son,"—Invernacree's old voice was charged with the feelings which he had been combating all the time—" my only son, I would to God I had your confidence! I have nothing to complain of in your conduct hitherto. Can you not tell me what is at the bottom of this strange reluctance of yours? Are you—I can scarcely think it of you, yet I suppose it is possible—are you entangled with some girl, and asking me for time in the hope that you will shortly be free? I beg you to tell me frankly if it is so; you will not find me unduly harsh."

" No, I am not entangled with any girl," said Ian quietly. " I shall never be freer than I am now."

A pause. Ian heard Invernacree sigh. " I should like to know what you mean by that? "

Ian did not supply the interpretation.

" Do you mean, my boy, that you are in love, though not engaged in an intrigue, with some woman? "

His father's voice was so unusually gentle; besides, how could he say, No? Ian said, " Yes, I do mean that."

The words fell like stones; and Invernacree asked, as slowly, " Does she know it? "

" Yes."

" Is it impossible for you to marry her? I would not stand in the way of your happiness, Ian, if I could avoid it."

"And what about Miss Maclean, to whom you have practically affianced me?" asked his son, dropping his hand. "But it *is* impossible—quite impossible . . . and you would be the first to say so."

"Why should I?" asked his father, still gently. He could see now how ravaged the boy's face looked. "I could speak to Garroch of a prior attachment, unknown to me when I made my proposal.—But I suppose the lady is already married, or promised. Is that so?"

Ian shook his head. "Let us put her out of mind, as I have, or am trying to. That I have not yet fully succeeded is my reason for begging a little delay before . . . before trying my fortune elsewhere."

The unintentional turn of the the phrase inevitably brought upon him the question, "She refused your suit, then?"

A wintry sort of smile dawned round the young man's mouth. "No, sir. I never pressed it."

"Yet you say that you love her? This is a strange business. You do not, I expect, wish to tell me her name, and I suppose I must not ask it. 'Tis, perhaps, some lady whom you met while you were in Glasgow recently?"

"I did meet her while I was away, yes," admitted Ian after a moment's hesitation. He glanced up. His father was looking at him so wistfully that, against his better judgment, against his own desires and instincts, he was moved to add, "You will not be the happier for knowing her name, sir, but that you may not feel I am withholding my confidence from you, I will tell you. It is Miss Campbell of Cairns."

And with that, not wishing to see the change which his avowal would work on that old face, he got up and looked steadily at the clock on the mantelshelf, already feeling a traitor, to what he did not quite know, for having delivered up his secret.

And to one to whom it had dealt a shattering blow. The old laird had fallen back in his chair, his hand at his throat, " God, God, what have I done to deserve this!"

In Ian's heart two streams of pity were coursing at the same time—for his father and for himself. He had surrendered his heart's desire that no real stroke might fall upon that silvery head; it was he himself who was bleeding from it. " Father," he said, kneeling beside him, "you need have no fear! We shall never meet again, Miss Campbell and I. It was impossible, and I knew it; no one of our house could wed the daughter of Campbell of Cairns. I shall never of my own will set eyes upon her again. You can trust me, sir! It is over."

He gripped the old man's shrunken wrists in his eagerness, and looked into his eyes. Alexander Stewart still drew his breath as one who has been plunged into some icy current. " It was an evil day when Fate brought her here. . . . I might have known it. She was fair enough to bewitch any man. . . . Ian, Ian, you say this now, yet you ask for delay. If I should die before your two months' grace is up, what then? "

Ian winced, but he had to allay his father's fear without showing that the doubt hurt him. " It would make no difference," he said unsteadily. " If in my own heart I did not feel the impossibility of making her my wife, should I have thrust her out of it. . . . to break it, I think, as I am doing, solely for my duty to you . . . and Alan, and our house, and the clan? You have called me not man enough to win a bride—if it were not for that *here* which forbids me," he struck his breast, " I had ridden off with her to the Lowlands and lived with her in a shepherd's hut sooner than let her go! No, you need not fear to come back after death, father, and find a Campbell bride in this house! "

The passion with which he had spoken shook him, shook his father also. Alexander Stewart lifted a trembling hand and laid it on the dark head beside him. " Bless you, my poor boy. . . . I'll not press you . . . You shall have time. I will write to Maclean; I'll find something to say, too, that will not betray your——"

The door opened very suddenly. Ian jumped up. It was Grizel looking in, with a question in her face.

" One moment, my dear," said her father hastily. " Come again in a few minutes, if you will. Ian and I are just discussing something of importance."

If Invernacree had allowed his daughter to enter, and his interview with Ian had broken off upon that note of concord, subsequent events might have fallen otherwise. As it was it slackened the thread of it. The laird rose from his chair and took a turn up and down the room, while Ian stood with bent head by the hearth; then the old man stopped on the far side of the writing table and mechanically began to shift some piles of papers, looking at his son the while.

" I am deeply sorry for you, Ian. I only hope that time will bring healing, especially as you had known Miss Campbell for so short a space. By the way, what did you mean when you said that you had met her when you were in Glasgow? "

Ian raised his head. What a foolish admission that had been! Still, he had already bared his secret. " I did meet her when I was away. It was then that I made the resolve I have told you of. . . . Need we speak of the matter any more, sir? "

But his father was going on. " I could not quite understand why you found it necessary to spend so long in
Glasgow. What was Miss Campbell doing there?
And, by the way, how could she be there? I distinctly remember Grizel receiving a letter from her saying that
she was going to the goats' whey at Kilrain about this
time. It must have been her ' fetch ' that you saw in
Glasgow, my poor boy," concluded Invernacree, essaying
a mild pleasantry.

" It was not her fetch," answered Ian steadily. " Nor
was it in Glasgow that I met her—I never said so. It was
at Kilrain."

" At Kilrain! But you would not pass that way. Do
you mean to tell me that you went to Kilrain of set
purpose? "

" I did," answered Ian. " I went there in order to see
her. It was there that I took farewell of her."

" And you told me the other day," said his father, a
little colour coming into his cheeks, " that Mr. Buchanan
had kept you waiting in Glasgow! You went half a day's
journey out of your way after Miss Campbell, and spent
—how long?—in her company? "

" Does that matter? " asked Ian wearily. " 'Tis all
over and done with now."

" Do you think," enquired his father, roused and stern,
" that you can put deceit behind you as easily as that? And
what else, may I ask, have you put behind as ' over and
done with '? "

" What do you mean? " asked the young man, roused
also.

" Who else was at Kilrain—who saw you there? If
you have given cause for scandal—if you have compromised Miss Campbell——"

"——You fear that I might have to marry her!" finished Ian bitterly. "Then I wish to God that I had compromised her! Unfortunately I cannot think that I did!"

The wrath which could still burn in the old Highlander lit up like fire among summer heather. "You wish you *had* compromised her! I see what all your protestations are worth, all your fair speeches about my ghost and the barrier in your own heart! You have shown me the truth——"

Ian started forward. "Father—no, as God is my witness! I do mean every word that I have spoken. Cannot you understand—you were young once—I said good-bye to her for ever . . . but it was cruelly hard, and is still. . . ."

Alexander Stewart had become dry and cold now. "We had better look at this dispassionately. Apart from your lying to me, your action may have a consequence which you would evidently welcome only too eagerly. For Campbell of Cairns, thickskinned like all his race, would probably raise no particular objection to his daughter marrying a Stewart—indeed, if matters turn out as you evidently hope, he would have to swallow any such objection. What if he holds that you have fatally injured her reputation—what then?"

Ian gave no intelligible reply. He had turned his back and laid his head against the hands which gripped the mantelshelf.

"Answer me what I have already asked you! Who else was at Kilrain?"

"Miss Campbell's woman—no one else."

"How long were you there?"

"Two days."

"And two nights?"

"Yes."

"And you mean to tell me that there was no one else at Kilrain then, taking the whey? It is a fashionable enough occupation for gouty, scandalmongering old men!"

"There was no one else."

"And no traveller passed through the clachan? It lies on a highroad, I believe."

"One traveller passed."

"He did not see you together, I hope?"

"Your hope is not justified."

"He *did* see you! But—please God—he did not know either of you?"

Ian was silent.

"Answer me that, if you please—and try not to lie again!"

Ian suppressed all retort. "He knew Miss Campbell— well, it seemed, and she him. He had known her since she was a child."

"My God! A friend of the family—of her father's?"

"Apparently."

"Then if he did his duty he would go straight and tell Cairns what he had seen!"

"As it happened," said Ian, with infinitely more coolness than he was feeling, "he was on his way into Lochaber. In any case he did not appear at all perturbed about Miss Campbell."

"'He did not appear '," repeated his father scornfully. "How can you tell what was in a stranger's mind, and what he would report? Your madness has—but there, what use to speak of it? I will give you credit for meaning what you said just now about having put away the idea of marrying Miss Campbell—you could not be a Stewart and my son, with a brother lying under the sod of Culloden, without meaning it—but your disastrous folly has rendered all that unavailing. But the day that you are forced to marry Olivia Campbell, if it disgracefully comes to that, will see me carried to my grave . . . and I think you will not greatly care! ".

Ian turned round; he was the colour of chalk. " I will never marry Olivia Campbell—not if Cairns begged me to!—Father, I have done more than cut off my right hand that I might not fail in my duty to you and to the blood in my veins . . . and you can say such a thing as that about your death! "

" You have shaken my confidence too severely," was the old man's unmoved reply. " You may have done what you say, and I do not doubt your sincerity at the time, but——"

" In short, you don't trust me!" said Ian, flaring up. " I have trampled my life's happiness under my feet—for you—and this is all the thanks I get for it! 'Tis true I never looked for thanks . . . but reproaches and distrust are a little too much to swallow quietly.—I think we had best bring this interview to an end! " And, seething with indignation, but impelled, too, by a fear of saying to his father what he would afterwards regret, he crossed quickly to the door and went out of the room, out of the house altogether.

CHAPTER XI

IAN STEWART LISTENS TO THE DEVIL

§ 1

Aug. 19th (continued).

BEREFT of Jacqueline, Mr. Hector Grant had meanwhile sat down again upon the window-seat in the drawing-room, wishing, for once, that he had someone to advise him—Ewen Cameron, for instance. But unfortunately Ewen was not immediately available.

Jacqueline, sweet, half-timid creature, had left her silks behind. The young officer took up and began to play with one of the balls which she had been winding. His thoughts ran to the little estate in Glenmoriston which his kinsman had left to him. He had never seen it; none the less he began to imagine the house—with Jacqueline in it . . . The silken ball slid presently from his fingers and bounced lightly upon the floor; Hector stooped to recover it, and, just as he came upright again, was aware of a man's figure going rapidly past the window—young Invernacree's for sure. So the interview in the study was over; he could go in and have his.

Hector got up, and then sat down again. Was it wise to rush in upon the old laird just now? How if he were to go instead after young Stewart, and find out from him whether the moment was propitious or no; even, perhaps, whether he and his father had already discussed the situation? It occurred to Captain Grant, for the first time, that quite possibly the covert hostility in the young man's demeanour was due to that very fact—that he, a suitor, had not spoken of his intentions in the proper quarter. Ian Stewart might conceivably be thinking that the visitor was only amusing himself with his sister. In that case he could not bear a grudge against the suitor for revealing to him that he was in earnest, and for tacitly asking his assistance in proving it.

Yet even then there came to the impulsive and light-hearted young man a whimsical idea of letting chance direct his course. The ball of green silk was still in his hand; if he could roll it exactly on to a particular rose of the carpet he would go after young Invernacree; if not, he would seek the laird. To lay the matter still more upon the knees of the immortals Hector shut his eyes, and, slightly stooping, bowled his silken projectile gently along the floor, reflecting that, thus self-handicapped, it was very unlikely that he should judge either his goal or the necessary pace correctly.

He opened his eyes and received a shock. On the very heart of the faded rose stood a little sphere of vivid green. Hector did not know whether to be pleased or sorry. But having settled to abide by this test, he left the ball where it was and went out of the house in quest of Ian Stewart.

§ 2

When he left his father's presence Ian had gone striding up the hillside behind the house so fast that, mountaineer though he was, his breath began to give out —but not his anger and his sense of injury. Finally he came to a standstill under a clump of pines on a little plateau, and flung himself down upon a long-fallen trunk. The hills of Appin, softly contoured and warmly coloured, looked at him kindly, the line of strath below was green and pleasant, and between the trees he could see the pointed turrets of his home. But the young man's heart was too hot to feel a sense of peace or graciousness in anything. His father had been unjust and cruel; and his own great and difficult sacrifice, made so largely for his sake, was to go for nothing—because of Kilrain. And the magic of those few short hours with Olivia Campbell, already more bitter than sweet, was now, and always would be, bitter only. Ian hid his face in his hands.

Someone was coming up the slope. Ian rose hastily to his feet, and turning his back, pretended to be absorbed in examination of the trees above him. Meanwhile the steps came nearer; their author was whistling a little tune between his teeth. And at the sound of it Ian faced round as if he had been stung, because he knew the air for French, and only one man hereabouts was likely to be whistling it. What the devil did Hector Grant mean by intruding himself on him at this moment of all others?

" Ah, 'tis you, Mr. Stewart," exclaimed the whistler as he arrived on the level of the little plateau. " I was taking a stroll in this direction, and saw someone up here." For Hector had decided that it might be wiser to conceal the fact that he had not come upon his quarry by accident, but as the result of enquiries.

" Yes, I was looking at these old trees," said Ian shortly.

Hector perceived that his brow was overclouded. Nor did his manner diffuse geniality. Evidently the interview in the study had not been a pleasant one, whether the subject were timber or . . . Jacqueline. He began to doubt whether the green silk ball had sent him in pursuit of young Invernacree at a propitious moment; and indeed, had he but known it, that ball had done him no good turn by causing him to stoop after it just as Ian passed the window, for had he seen the latter's face he would have thought more than twice before coming after him. However, here he was, and must go on with the business.

He seized upon the topic just introduced. " Are they in danger, then, these trees—are you proposing to fell them? "

" Not immediately," was the reply.

" I am glad of that," responded the young officer. " One does not see pines like these everywhere in the Highlands. But you of Appin are fortunate in your trees. How well, for instance, those oaks set off your house down there." He turned and threw a glance at it.

" You think so? " enquired Ian, indifferently. Why did Captain Grant not continue his walk, if he had really been taking one, instead of standing here making conversation?

Now Hector did not at all relish this curt manner, and decided to learn the reason for it. " Mr. Stewart," he asked, looking his contemporary straight in the face, " have I offended you in any way? " In view of the object of his mission he went so far as to add immediately, " I regret it very much if I have."

" Offended me? " returned Ian, lifting his straight black brows. " No, not that I am aware of. Why should you think so? "

" Because you are pretty short with me this afternoon," returned Hector with truth. " And, to be candid," he hesitated a moment, " my own conscience is not quite clear."

" I am sorry to hear that," replied Ian, folding his arms and leaning against the pine stem. But he did not sound sorry, he sounded bored, and Hector was piqued.

" I should be obliged if you could give me a few moments of your time, sir," he said stiffly.

" Willingly," answered Ian at once, but without changing his attitude. " Only I am not, you know, qualified as a confessor—if you are a Catholic, that is."

" You must know that I am not a Catholic," retorted Hector with some warmth, scenting the erection of an imaginary barrier between himself and Jacqueline. " From your acquaintance with my sister, who is your cousin Ardroy's wife, you must be aware that we are Episcopalians! "

" I beg your pardon," said Ian, his manner suddenly as mild as milk. " But I did not know what you might not have become after so long a residence in France."

" I have never become anything but what I always was—a Highlander. Yes, and one thing besides. That is what I wish to speak to you about. Perhaps you can guess what I mean? "

" Not in the least," said Ian with annoying lack of curiosity. " Unless you mean that you have turned Whig or something of the sort." He put up a hand to hide a yawn. " In that case it would be better to confess to my father."

" It would indeed be better to tell Mr. Stewart what I have to tell, though it is certainly not a change in my politics," agreed Hector, gathering momentum. " Aye, I ought already to have told him—that is where I fear I have acted other than I should. . . . You have perhaps been speaking of the matter in your recent interview? "

Lightning came from the cloud at that. " Interview? What do you know of any interview of mine? " flashed Ian, starting forward from the pine-tree. The merest reference to that scene flicked him on the raw. " You were not present at it, so far as I know! "

Hector was brought up short. " 'So far as you know!' " he repeated frowning. " Pray, Mr. Stewart, what do you mean by that expression? "

" Whatever you please," replied Ian, resuming his pose against the tree. " But, since you have somehow discovered that I have had a conversation with my father this afternoon, let me assure you that, from first to last, your name was not mentioned in it."

It is certain that Hector Grant, that least pacifically-minded of young men, merited at this moment a good deal of commendation for keeping his temper in the face of provocation. But it was not his cue to quarrel with Ian Stewart if he could avoid it, so with an effort he passed over this suggestive speech, and said, " May I be permitted to ask without offence, was there no mention neither of your sister, Miss Jacqueline Stewart! "

" Why should there be? " retorted Ian impatiently. " And if there were, why should I be supposed to remember it—and be interrogated upon the point? "

"I had no intention of interrogating you," said Hector, biting his lip for a second. " I only wished to ascertain . . . but, in short, Mr. Stewart, I think you must be aware that I intend to ask in form for the hand of your younger sister."

It was out now, and there was a silence under the pine-tree—charged, for all that the sun shone there and a bee was droning near, with a hostility almost sinister. Ian had not thought the affair between Jacqueline and the young soldier serious, but, on thus learning that it apparently was, an immense and unreasoning resentment surged up in him. His own love had suffered shipwreck at his own hand; why should another's immediately prosper; why should he help to give his little sister to a man whom he did not particularly like? The devil, moreover, suddenly showed his sore and tormented soul how he could prevent it.

He began with one hand to finger the crest of a tall stem of bracken beside him, though his eyes never moved from the figure of Hector Grant, standing before him against the background of space and hills. And at last he said slowly, " Yes, I was afraid that that was the case."

" Afraid? " interjected Hector. " Why ' afraid ' ? "

" However," went on Ian with the same unwinking gaze, and a curious evenness of tone, " since you have not yet approached my father on the matter there is no great harm done."

" But I am going to approach him! " exclaimed the other.

The head of the fern bent and broke. " I cannot prevent you, naturally. But I advise you not to do so."

" And why, pray? " cried Hector, with one of his occasional half-French gestures. " Are you so sure that Invernacree will refuse? I love your sister sincerely, I have every reason to believe that the feeling is returned, I have the means to support a wife, a home to take her to—"

Ian struck. " And what sort of a name to give her? " he asked in a voice of steel. " No sister of mine marries a man of whom it can be said that he once gave or sold information to a spy of the English Government!"

Hector Grant reeled back as though a thunderbolt had fallen between them; and he blanched slowly to the colour of ashes, as the guilty might blanch. "Where . . . how did you hear that lie?" he gasped.

"Why, from a fellow-Jacobite—from Finlay Mac-Phair of Glenshian," answered Ian, the devil still looking out of his eyes. "So it is a lie, is it? Ardroy said it was. But then you are his brother-in-law; you were that before your transaction with the spy. Let me tell you, however, that you shall never be mine after it!"

Hector's pallor was now less that of ashes than of white-hot fury. He came right up to Ian where he stood under the pine-tree, with the scrap of bracken crushed in his hand. "Glenshian, my worst enemy, told you that, and you believed it! Ewen told you that it was a lie, and yet you believe it! . . . No, no, you *pretend* to believe it, thinking to keep your sister from me! You are a damned dirty scoundrel, not worthy of the name you carry!" And he struck Ian with the back of his hand across the face.

§ 3

For long after his son had flung indignantly out of the room old Invernacree had sat at his writing table, turning over papers with shaking hands, and then, when he was a little recovered from his agitation, really trying to give his mind to them in order to fend off other thoughts. But the effort, though he kept it up doggedly, was vain, and by the time the last ray of sun had slid from his southern window he was sitting there motionless, thinking—and thinking of his own first wooing, so many years ago. Yes, he had been too harsh with Ian ; the boy had done his best. And, if he had gone after the enchantress, he had cut loose in the end. Ian himself had seen that the marriage was out of the question. Surely he could trust him not to go back upon his word, surely he could ! Surely if, at Kilrain, Ian had not acted as he averred, he would have kept silence about the whole matter instead of admitting the meeting, as he had done. He had been too hard with his son over the small measure of deceit which he had employed ; and he must tell him so.

Half abstractedly, as he reached this decision, Alexander Stewart observed the figure of a man coming hastily across the lawn from the stile which gave on to the hill path. For a moment he thought that it might be Ian's ; then he saw that it was young Grant, and that he seemed to be in considerable haste.

A moment or two later there was a knock at the study door, and Invernacree's, " Come in," brought the young man in question with the same air of haste about him.

" Is anything amiss, Mr. Grant ? " asked Invernacree in some surprise, for there was discomposure as well in his visitor's mien.

" I am sorry to say, sir," replied Hector, " that I have just received news from the factor of my little estate in Glenmoriston which necessitates my immediate presence there."

" But you will not set off this evening, surely? " asked Alexander Stewart, glancing at the clock.

" I fear that I must, sir. There is full time at least to cross the ferry at Ballachulish, even if I get no further, and that will be so much gained in the morning. I deeply regret the necessity of so sudden a departure, but I must pack my valise without a moment's delay, and, if I may, order my horse to be brought round while I make my adieux to the ladies."

There was no doubt that the haste was genuine. "I am very sorry indeed, Captain Grant, to lose you thus suddenly," said the old laird courteously. "The news from your factor is not, I fear, of a very welcome order?"

"It is . . . disturbing," admitted Captain Grant, but did not particularise further. He was fidgeting as he stood there.

"You met the messenger somewhere on the road, I suppose? But where is my son? Does he know of this?"

"Mr. Stewart," said the young officer quickly, "was with me when I . . . received the news a while ago. He will meet me later; I think he intends to set me on my road a little."

"That is well," said the old man, nodding his head. "Go and pack your effects, then, Mr. Grant, since you must. I will give orders about your horse, and Grizel shall have some refreshment set ready for you."

"I fear I'll not have time to partake of any, sir," said Hector even more hurriedly. "But I beg you to receive my deep apologies for this unceremonious departure."

"Needs must, Captain Grant, I suppose, when affairs drive one. I trust it is not the devil in this case," said Invernacree smiling, and going much nearer to the truth than he knew. "I will see you again when you are ready, and speed your departure. I wonder where my daughters are." He went to the door of his room, calling, "Grizel, Grizel!" and next moment, when Grizel appeared at the door of the drawing room, announced, "Here's Mr.

Grant must leave us at once, unfortunately. Tell your sister——"

Hector stayed to hear no more but ran up the stairs. At the top he met Jacqueline, who had overheard, preparing to descend. She turned a scared face on her lover. He caught her hands and drew her quickly into a dark corner of the landing.

"There is nothing wrong, *mon cœur*," said he, but despite all his efforts his voice and manner belied his words. "I am urgently summoned to Glenmoriston on affairs. No," he sank his voice, "nothing has been said to your father about us—'tis not that which causes my departure. I'll be back here, please God, before very long, and we'll get his blessing and fix the marriage day. But if I do not leave at once there may be no home to take you to when that day comes."

"'Tis you I want, not the home," cried Jacqueline rather pitifully.

In the shadow of a curtain which hung there Hector pressed her to him. "I hope, my darling—" he began, then seemed to stop himself from saying more, and, catching his breath, kissed her passionately. Disengaging himself, he rushed into his room at the other end of the passage, and could be heard dragging open drawers, and presumably flinging their contents into his valise.

A quarter of an hour later that object was being strapped behind the saddle of his horse, already at the front door, and Hector, cloaked and booted, holding his hat and a cane, was bending over Grizel's hand uttering mingled thanks and apologies.

"Be sure, Mr. Grant, to let us know how your business prospers," said old Invernacree genially, as the young man mounted. "And if you come south again this way, do not pass this door without knocking upon it. You say that you are to meet Ian upon the road—good! " Standing at Hector's stirrup he touched the long and solid cane of polished wood in the rider's hand. " Do you usually encourage your horse with so stout a switch, young man? " he asked. " I wonder he does not throw you."

" 'Tis not for my horse, sir," Hector assured him with a rather curious note in his voice. " I have found it useful ere now against animals more noble . . . or less, according as you look at the matter. Again a thousand thanks to you, sir, and to Miss Stewart, for your hospitality; and present my compliments, if you please, to Miss Jacqueline."

He lifted his hat, bowed from the saddle with a somewhat foreign grace, touched his horse with the spur and went down the avenue at a trot.

" Well, whatever has gone' wrong with that young man's affairs let us hope that he will succeed in putting it right," observed Invernacree, looking after him. "A good seat on a horse—but he rides as though he were glad to escape from us! "

" Preserve us! if he has not jumped the gate! " exclaimed Grizel aghast.

" Young fool! " commented her father, turning round again with a frown. Then all at once he looked at his middle-aged daughter, with something a little wistful in his gaze. " Yet I was young once, Grizel, and did many a thing as mad. But one forgets . . . one forgets as the years go by." And shaking his head with a sigh, he went back to his own room to wait for Ian's return.

CHAPTER XII

" OUT, SWORD, AND TO A SORE PURPOSE! "

§ 1

Aug. 19th (continued).

AFTER his exhibition of horsemanship, of which, directly it was over, he felt somewhat ashamed, Hector Grant rode at a hard, pelting pace for about a mile and a half along the lochside road to the north. Then he pulled up to a slower gait, and went glancing about as though looking for someone or something. The light had waned a little, but for hours now it would not greatly diminish; over the loch on his left hand a clear saffron sky extended behind the peaks of Morven. On his right the road was pressed towards the water by slopes and thickets.

At last he came to a place where the shore widened considerably, because a stream had formed a small delta there. A rough bridge spanned this stream where it crossed the road, and by it a man was standing waiting. Hector pulled up.

" Is this the place? " he asked.

Ian nodded. " If you will dismount I will lead your horse down to the shore; it will be best not to leave him here."

Hector swung off, and young Invernacree, taking his horse's bridle, led the animal down a rough path to the shingle below. Here he hitched the reins on to a tree stump projecting from the bank.

"No one passing can easily see him from above, I think. I can find no spot convenient for our business in the wood beyond the road. But the shore is level enough, and will serve." Ian's voice was perfectly expressionless; he might have been reading out of a rather dull book.

Hector looked round. The worst that could be said of the chosen ground was that it was stony. At its mouth the little river was continually rearing up a bank of pebbles, which any especially high tide in Loch Linnhe as continually dispersed over the foreshore.

"'Twill serve very well, provided we are not interrupted," he pronounced. "Here is my sword; you had best handle it a little to become accustomed to it. I have brought the swordstick of which I spoke for myself." Laying his sheathed sword on the ground, he took hold with both hands of the stout cane on which Invernacree had commented, touched a spring and drew out a long, sharp steel blade.

"I cannot accept your sword," said Ian, with at last a sign of life in his dead voice. "The weapons are not evenly matched. Give me the other."

For since no resident Highland gentleman might possess any arms, this coming bloodshed had only been rendered possible by the chance of Captain Grant's having brought with him on his travels a sword-stick, as well as the more usual weapon at his side. Up under the pine clump, after Ian's accusation had provoked him to the blow which rendered a meeting inevitable (provided neither of the two had tried to strangle the other out of hand, which for a moment or two seemed probable, though actually they did not touch each other again) this expedient had been decided upon, and the pretext for Hector's sudden departure invented also.

But Hector would not subscribe to this theory of in-equality.

" No, on the contrary I assure you they are well enough matched," said he. " See, the length is the same, or very near." He unsheathed the sword, and held the blades up together.

" No, no, I will not use your sword," declared Ian. " The sword-stick has no guard, for one thing; you could not parry with safety to your hand."

" Then, since you think it inferior, I cannot consent to your using it either," retorted his opponent. " In that case, what are we to do? "

His tethered horse—the nobler animal or the less noble —turned its gentle, intelligent head and looked at them with the air of mildly wondering what he had been brought down here for. Then, swishing his tail, he resumed his search for nourishment among the stones. Nearer the loch a pair of oyster catchers, disturbed in their fishing, were running to and fro like mechanical toys and keeping up their insistent cry. And for a moment, under the influence of this disparity of chances, when either duellist was unwilling to take a supposed advantage for himself, and the whole tension of the situation was lowered by their having to make and discuss their own arrangements—formalists were wise who did not allow parties to a quarrel to speak to each other again after the challenge—even, perhaps, under the influence of the peace and loneliness which brooded over this lake shore, it seemed as if some kind of truce might have been patched up. In fact the hot-tempered Hector actually made a step towards that consummation.

" I suppose," he said in a voice shackled with embarrassment, looking at the oyster-catchers by the water's edge, " I suppose, Mr. Stewart, that you would not be willing to apologise for what you said to me—which I cannot believe that you really meant?"

" Apologise—after a blow!" exclaimed Ian, flushing up; and in spite of himself his hand went to the little abrasion on his lip which Hector's signet ring had set there. " No, by Heaven—not even if you apologised for striking me!"

Hector stiffened at once. " There is no question of that," he returned coldly. " Apologise because you insulted me, *parbleu!*—Take my sword, and let us delay no longer! " And, laying down the two blades, he tore off his coat and waistcoat.

But Ian had put his hand into a pocket and now held out a coin. " Let this decide the question of weapons. Otherwise I insist on having the swordstick."

" Very well," agreed Hector. " Do you spin. Head, you take the sword—shield, I do."

Ian threw up the florin so that it fell tinkling upon a flat stone at his side. The young men both bent over it. His Majesty King George II, whose effigy was to decide this matter for subjects who denied his suzerainty, presented to them his unbeautiful profile.

" The sword is yours," said Hector with relief. " Now you need hesitate no longer, sir. And don't fancy," he added, " that you have the advantage on account of it, for I wager I have had more practice at this game than you."

He only meant to appease his over-scrupulous adversary, but his words savoured too much of patronage to be palatable to the latter. Ian said nothing openly in reply, but, inwardly cursing the speaker's insolence, he flung off his outer garments until he, like Hector, was in shirt and breeches, caught up the naked sword, tested the poise and made a pass or two with it in the direction of the bank. Then, perceiving that there was more breeze blowing than he had thought, he laid it down again and, removing the ribbon from his queue, tied his hair back more securely, lest a loose wisp might blow suddenly across his eyes.

Captain Grant meanwhile was carefully examining the surface of the ground which they had chosen, picking up or kicking away a loose stone here and there. He had no mind that either of them should slip and bring about a catastrophe, for he intended merely to give his calumniator something to remember him by, no more. To inflict a serious wound upon the brother of his lady-love, however badly that brother had behaved towards him, would scarcely be a passport to the good graces of any-one in the family. Before he had come down from the hillside where they had quarrelled Hector was aware of that awkward fact.

But Ian had no such consideration to restrain him. The recognition of his own culpable folly, which he had had plenty of time to make, did not, for all that, tend to repentance. The child nature which survives in all of us cried in a small, ashamed but angry voice that just because he had been "naughty" he would go on being "naughty" still; and all the more so because he was faced with the possibility of a very unpleasant payment for his naughtiness. That he was in the last resort hazarding his life in this course must atone for the wilfulness. Never in all his days had he suffered the indignity of a blow, or imagined one being offered to him; and he shut his eyes to the knowledge that never in all his

6

days had he afforded another man such justification for dealing him one.

Hector, having now ceased his scrutiny of the ground, had picked up the swordstick and was rolling up his right sleeve in a business-like manner. Since he wore a wig he had no need to emulate Ian's precaution; yet even so the sea breeze suddenly lifted the ends of his lace cravat. He untied it, threw it off, and looked at his antagonist.

"Are you ready?" he asked. Ian, without a word, saluted and came on guard; and in the silence the blades clicked together and engaged.

They had not clicked many times before Ian became aware that his adversary's recent boast (as he termed it) was justified. If not a better theoretical swordsman—for young Invernacree had learnt of a good *maître d'armes*—Captain Grant was a much more experienced duellist . . . and small wonder. Ian had never fought in earnest before. The knowledge angered him extraordinarily, and even the realisation of the peril in which he consequently stood, instead of sobering him, merely infuriated him still further. Yet, lunge or parry as he might, he could not get rid of the menace of that evershifting steel at the level of his breast, directed by the same hand which had given him the recent blow across the mouth. He felt, in fancy, the tingle of it still. God! if he could only mark that handsome, intent face opposite as his had been marked! He began to consider by what feint he could best get past Captain Grant's very competent guard to accomplish this amiable design; neglected his own defence for a second—and immediately paid the penalty. Quicker, almost, than the eye could follow, Hector's watchful point had slipped over his blade, and was sliding and tearing its way along his forearm to bury itself above the bent elbow. . . . It was plucked out again at once, and Hector, springing back, lowered his sword.

"It's nothing!" cried Ian furiously, though the sensation was like redhot wire, and the blood was streaming down his bared arm. Yet he managed to retain hold of his weapon. "Come on—we have not finished!"

"No, that must be tied up first," declared his opponent, his point nearly on the stones. "Have you a handkerchief?"

But something told Ian that if he stopped for bandaging he would never be able to continue. Already it was difficult to grip his sword. All the more, therefore, did he say threateningly, "On guard again, if you please, Captain Grant! This is not the end!"

But Hector, instead of complying, held up his left hand for silence. "*Chut!*" he said in a quick whisper, "I heard voices! Someone is coming along the road up there."

"Damnation!" muttered Ian. But in that at least he and his foe were at one; neither had any wish for witnesses. He too listened, he too heard voices . . . Clutching hold of his right arm—the hilt of the sword was now sticky with blood—he went reluctantly towards the bank, which, when one was close under it, would probably shelter one from view. Then only did he let fall his weapon, and thereafter himself sat down rather suddenly upon a large stone projecting from the bank. The loch had all at once begun to glitter strangely; indeed it seemed to be invading the shore with its brightness. But the voices on the road above, instead of coming nearer, died away altogether. He fumbled vainly with his left hand at his right shirt-sleeve, essaying the impossible task of tearing off a piece of the linen to staunch the blood. Then someone else seemed to be tying up the wound, and, though the process hurt, the fingers were not, he felt, ungentle. Ian leant his head back against the bank and shut his eyes. After a space there was the taste of brandy in his mouth.

"Have they passed?" he heard a voice asking—perhaps his own.

"Some time ago," was the reply made to him. "But, Mr. Stewart, we cannot continue this affair. It is out of the question." He knew this voice now for Hector Grant's. It sounded grave, and quite near him. Ian opened his eyes, triumphed over the strange difficulty he found in focussing them, and saw his late opponent kneeling on one knee beside him, with a little flask of eau-de-vie in his hand. He himself was still sitting against the bank. From Captain Grant's face his gaze went to his own right arm, round which were neatly and tightly fastened two pocket-handkerchiefs, both considerably reddened.

"Why is it out of the question?" he asked stupidly.

"Corbleu, look at your arm!" expostulated Hector. "You are worse hurt than you know, though I think it is only a flesh wound. Moreover, we *have* fought. For myself I regard my honour as satisfied . . . and I am willing to express regret for having struck you."

Ian thought, in what seemed left to him of mind at the moment, "I suppose he expects me to say that I am sorry I practically charged him with espionage," but he knew that he was not going to. Out of his pallid lips there came only a muttered, "If only I had learnt to fence with my left hand too!"

The successful swordsman took no notice of this aspiration. He seemed to regard the business as at an end, for he rose to his feet and said, with a certain visible anxiety, "I do not quite know, Mr. Stewart, how you are to get home again."

"What does that matter?" asked Ian, looking at his bandaged arm, which now seemed to belong to someone else—and yet, every now and then, to be only too unpleasantly his own property. "Naturally, I shall return as I came." And he rose to his feet, only a little care being necessary for this proceeding. "There is your sword," he said, pointing to it, for it seemed wiser not to attempt to pick it up. "You were right after all; there was not much advantage in its possession."

Hector stood in front of him. "I beg of you," he said earnestly, "to accept the loan of my horse as far as your own gate. I will accompany you on foot, and afterwards——"

"Indeed you will not!" said Ian sharply. "I am perfectly capable of walking back to Invernacree on my own feet." And, passing Hector, he returned to the spot where he had thrown down his coat and waistcoat, but made no comment when Hector, hastening after him, picked them up and assisted him into them in silence. But when the operation was finished the victor made a last appeal.

"Mr. Stewart, I was greatly in your debt once. You helped me to freedom. I beg of you——"

"Debt?" said Ian harshly. "I think you have remembered that somewhat late. No," he added, his better self rising for a moment to the surface, "I will not say that; I brought this on myself. But I ask you to excuse me the further humiliation of returning to my home as the captive of your bow and spear. I wish you good speed on your journey; I'll be about mine." And, slightly raising his hat with his left hand, he walked with a firm step away from his antagonist across the little strip of shore, and went slowly up the path by which they had descended, Hector making no move to follow him save with his eyes.

But standing there alone in his shirt and breeches, he swore softly to himself in French, adding, "*Eh bien*, if Monsieur Lucifer falls by the wayside, as I think he probably will, *Dieu sait que ce n'est pas ma faute!*"

"It is clear," he soliloquised, as he untethered his horse a moment or two later, "that they are right who regard green as an unlucky colour. Though I suppose, *mon ami*, that it is your favourite one!" He wrenched down a handful of grass from the bank, gave it to his steed and then tugged him up to the road above. There was no sign upon it of his wounded antagonist; so Hector flung himself into the saddle, and was off in the other direction on the second of his quests, the settling of his score with Finlay MacPhair of Glenshian. But now it was a double score.

§ 2

Monsieur Lucifer, however, did not fall by the wayside. It was not indeed easy, that mile and a half back to Invernacree, but Ian compassed it somehow, and, about three-quarters of an hour later, stood upon the doorstep of his own home, sick and giddy, full of the miserable knowledge that he had behaved abominably, that he deserved sympathy from none, that his father, when he

learnt how he had treated their guest, would feel inclined to disown him, and that Jacqueline, whose life's
happiness he had probably jeopardised. . . . But Jacqueline, at least, he did not intend to encounter.

With a swimming head and patches of mist floating
most inconveniently across his vision, he opened the outer
door. And there, mist or no mist, there was Jacqueline
in the hall, caressing his spaniel. Ian paused irresolute on
the threshold; then, leaving the door open, he advanced,
fending off the bounding dog with his left hand.

" Ah, there you are, Ian," said his young sister. She
looked as if she had been crying. "We did not
wait supper for you, but—Mercy on us, how pale you
are! What has happened?"

"I have met with a slight accident," said Ian con-
fusedly. "Nothing to be alarmed about." Encounter-
ing a settle, he sank gratefully upon it, and, as Jacqueline
stared at him in dismay (for in truth his appearance was
enough to alarm any female, sister or no) Roger, the
spaniel, completed his overthrow. For, putting his fore-
paws on the settle, he poked his nose violently under his
master's right elbow in order to draw attention to himself. A cry which he could not wholly suppress broke
from Ian; he half rose, fell back again, and then, to
Jacqueline's horror, slid completely off the settle and lay
in a huddle at her feet. Roger, with tucked-in tail, first
fled to a safe distance, then turned and barked long and
furiously, on which there came out Invernacree, anxious
to know if Ian had returned; and what he saw was the
son from whom he had recently parted in anger lying
motionless on the floor, with a young girl clasping one of
his hands and crying his name distractedly to ears which
did not hear.

CHAPTER XIII

CASTLE DANGEROUS

§ 1

Aug. 21st—27th.

IT was two o'clock of the afternoon when Hector
Grant, in the rain, rode his weary horse up to the doors
of the House of Invershian and, without giving his name,
demanded to see the Chief. On being told that Mac 'ic
Fhionnlaigh was out at the moment he said firmly that
he would await his return, and was shown in to do so.

Finlay MacPhair, for all his importance, possessed no
dwelling commensurate with his dignity—but that was
not his fault. The ancestral castle of the MacPhairs
had been half destroyed and gutted before his day; after
the Rising still further vengeance had been wreaked upon
its ancient stones, and the Chief of Glenshian consequently lived in a house scarcely to be distinguished from
the farm of a well-to-do tacksman. He talked very
largely about rebuilding at least the keep of Castle Shian,
but it was not evident whence the money was to come for
this reconstruction.

The old man who now ushered in Captain Grant
dwelt with apologetic intent upon the transitory nature
of the present habitation, but Hector happened to know
that the old Chief, Finlay's father, had also lived in
these modest surroundings—and no shame to him. If
the English had rendered the pile reared by Red Finlay

of the Battles a mere resort for owls and toads, its owner still abode almost within sight of what had been for centuries the home of his race.

For some time Hector walked restlessly about the room, his wrongs reviving within him. At last he heard a voice outside the door saying in Gaelic, " A gentleman to see me? Aye, I know who it is; I have been awaiting him. Bring him to me in the other room, and fetch a stoup of wine also."

Awaiting him, forsooth, and a stoup of wine! Not much of Mr. MacPhair's wine was going to pass *his* lips! But Glenshian could not have been expecting him; it was a mistake.

The old servant entered and said that Mac 'ic Fhionnlaigh would receive Mr. Maitland.

" But my name's not Maitland!" cried Hector. The old man, however, either heard not or decided to pay no heed, but flung open a door; and as Mr. MacPhair would soon discover who this alleged " Mr. Maitland " was, Hector stepped into his presence with a certain pleasurable anticipation.

The room, surprisingly large and long for the size of the house, had a deep hearth at one end on which, in deference to the bad weather, a newly-lighted fire was burning. The Chief had evidently just flung on some fresh fuel, for a blaze shot up behind him as, turning round quickly, he came forward a few steps and said, " I bid you welcome, Mr. Mait——" Then his jaw dropped, his outstretched hand also.

" My name is not Maitland," said Hector, beginning to enjoy himself. " You were not expecting me, Mr. Finlay MacPhair, were you? We are now going to have the explanation which you have owed me since May, '53, and in addition a fresh one of the slander you put upon me not many weeks since! "

" Explanation! " repeated Glenshian haughtily. He had recovered from his surprise. " Do you really imagine, Mr. Grant, that you can come and demand ' explanations ' from me in my own house?"

" I do, indeed," retorted Hector. " But I can well believe you will find them so difficult to give that this," he tapped his sword-hilt, " will prove the only key to the situation."

" If you are planning another murderous assault upon me," observed his enemy, " let me warn you that—besides not being able to run away after it this time—if you so much as touch me——"

" A cock that won't fight, eh?" queried Hector contemptuously. " Don't be afraid, Mr. MacPhair. If you must shelter yourself behind a hedge of gillies, then you are not worth the crossing swords with again. Nevertheless, I intend to have satisfaction, in some form or other, both for your black treachery in London two years ago, and for your libelling me here in the Highlands before Ian Stewart of Invernacree!"

" Will you be so good as to leave this room?" inquired Finlay in a tone of suppressed passion.

" When I have had what I came for, not before! " retorted Hector.

" You may very well get more than you came for! " said his involuntary host threateningly. " Set down the wine, Roderick," for the old man had just come in with the stoup, " and show this gentleman out at once! "

" If I consent to go now," declared Hector, " I warn you, I shall remain in the neighbourhood, and tell you before witnesses—not servants—what I think of your conduct!"

But at this the young Chief merely turned his back and went and held out his hands to the fire.

The action infuriated Hector beyond bearing. He strode up to him, swung him round by the shoulder, and said through his teeth, " I *will* have it out with you, you go-between and traitor!"

The old man near the door uttered a shrill exclamation, flung it open and called out in Gaelic. Almost instantly the sound of running feet could be heard in the passage, though Hector, occupied in glaring into eyes which glared back at him, was scarcely conscious of the sound. But Finlay heard it, and, without removing his wolf's gaze, called out a brief order to those whom the feet were bringing:

" Remove this gentleman to some place where he will not molest me!"

Then did Hector become aware of his danger. Six or seven shaggy and unkempt individuals were precipitating themselves into the room from the door at the further end. But he had small intention of being "removed" tamely. Springing back from the Chief's vicinity, he tugged out his sword and faced the gillies, gratified to see that the two foremost, who appeared to have no weapons, showed marked signs of hesitation at the appearance of the naked steel. The next moment a shock ran along his arm and his sword snapped off short near the hilt. Glenshian, half behind him, had snatched up the long, heavy bar used for stirring the peats in the big fire, and had brought it down upon his blade. And the famous sword-stick was fastened to his saddle outside. . . .

Hector flung the useless hilt at Mr. MacPhair's face and launched himself unarmed into the thick of the Chief's retainers, in a gallant effort to fight his way through them to the door. He never reached it; at least, not of his own volition. . . .

Five minutes later the Chief of Glenshian sat down by the hearth in the now empty and quiet room, with the stoup of wine beside him. The hilt of a broken sword still lay on the hearthstone; he smiled scornfully, and pushed it away with his foot. Then, pouring himself out a glass of wine, he pulled forth and re-read a very dirty and ill-written letter with the Edinburgh postmark; and afterwards, drumming his fingers impatiently upon the table, sat looking into the fire with a frown.

" He *must* be on his way by this time," he muttered. " He dare not neglect to come;" and so sat, the glass of claret untasted at his elbow.

§ 2

Four empty wine-barrels (on one of which stood an unlighted candle) and one empty keg; a pallet with a couple of blankets, a rough ewer and basin and an armchair which, being upholstered in red leather, was, even if shabby, scarcely of a piece with this retreat—these, its only furniture, the occupant of that retreat was this morning surveying, for perhaps the two hundredth time, with the emotions proper to a captive of singularly unresigned temperament. But he had ceased to relieve that temperament by swearing, for even the resources of three languages had by now proved unequal to so prolonged a strain upon them, since this was the morning of the sixth day which Hector Grant had spent in the Chief of Glenshian's disused wine-cellar. Partly below the level of the ground, it had all the disadvantages pertaining to that situation, save that it was not especially damp; but it was cold, and filled at the brightest hour in the day with an extremely depressing twilight, and at all hours with a chill draught which filtered into it through a small grating about a couple of feet from the floor.

Hector was leaning, silent, against one of the walls, his hands in his breeches pockets, looking at the wine-casks. He was thinking what delight it would have given him, had they been full, to remove a spigot and let Finlay MacPhair's good wine run about the floor, not to speak of drinking a proportion of it. But alas, neither French wine nor French brandy were his for the broaching; that keg of Nantes had long been dry. Having the first day, however, heard the sound of liquid falling into a vessel, he had stooped and peered through the grating, and had made out, in what seemed to be another cellar, the rotundities of barrels which were not, evidently, empty like these in his prison. And once every day, after that, there had come thither for a supply of wine—as he could see by screwing himself into an uncomfortable position—the old man called Roderick, who had both admitted him to the House of Invershian and summoned the retainers to eject him from the Chief's presence.

If Captain Grant was at all tamed by the experience to which his rough handling by these gentry had been the prelude, no sign of it had been vouchsafed to any eye which so far had rested upon him. Whatever fits of rage, indignation or quasi-despair passed over him in secret lay between him and the regard of heaven; most certainly the mocking gaze which he must shortly encounter would be permitted to discern nothing of these emotions. For about this time Glenshian daily arrived in person to enquire of his contumacious prisoner whether he had yet come to his senses and to a proper recognition of the outrageousness of his behaviour. The moment that he was ready to apologise for this and to withdraw his allegations against the Chief, Hector was given to understand that his stay among the barren wine-casks was over.

If this were the only gate through which he could regain his freedom, Hector saw little prospect of ever beholding the blue sky again, for even had Glenshian's finger been on the trigger of a pistol held against his breast, the young officer would not have consented to apologise nor to withdraw his charges. And since his attempts both at breaking out unaided and at bribery had proved futile, and the chances of rescue (seeing that no one knew for certain where he was) were exceedingly small, the only real hope he cherished was that his obstinacy would in the end wear down Glenshian's patience, and that he would at last set him free of his own motion. But that consummation was unlikely to occur just yet, since this—curse it!—was only the sixth day of captivity.

Think of the devil . . . was that Glenshian's step already? Hector started away from the wall, passed a condemnatory hand over his chin—he had no razor— congratulated himself (in the absence of a comb) that he was wearing a wig and not his own hair, pulled down his waistcoat, and, going over to the ancient chair, seated himself therein with an air of being much at his ease and quite content with his surroundings.

The door was unlocked; Somerled, the stalwart,

bearded gillie who was in charge of him, entered and stood aside, and when Glenshian had stepped in, closed the door and stood with his back against it. Finlay surveyed his prisoner for a moment under half-lowered lids, his head thrown back—a favourite attitude of his. A faint smile just touched his lips.

" Good day, Mr. Grant."

" Good day, MacPhair," responded Hector, in the cheery tone which one might use to a superior servant come for orders. He knew quite well that any display of rage was merely gratifying to his captor, and had very soon abandoned even the sulky dignity in which he had at first clothed himself. His present attitude was that his sojourn in this cellar was perfectly indifferent to him; and if this pretence did not lack transparence, it undoubtedly gave his enemy less ground for open triumph.

Very stately and upright, Finlay continued to look at him. He, on his side, was now sustaining the rôle of the just, patient and not unmerciful judge, who is still amenable to some sign of penitence in the reprobate.

" Well, Mr. Grant," he said at length, " are you ready to apologise and withdraw? "

" I beg your pardon? " enquired Hector, leaning a little forward, as though he did not quite catch the words. Then, their meaning having apparently penetrated, he smiled indulgently. " My dear Mr. MacPhair, I should really have credited you with more intelligence than to waste your time like this! Surely you have something more profitable to do with it—some other man of your own party whom you could vilify to his associates behind his back! Fix up a notice here in your best handwriting inviting me to do as you say—'twould be every whit as effective—or send a gillie each morning with the invitation. 'Pon my soul, I am not sure that I should notice the difference!" he concluded drawlingly.

The Chief of Glenshian took no notice of this piece of rudeness. He said, in a manner which combined the most lofty-seeming detachment with a subterranean grimness which was not at all detached: "You anticipate my intentions in the most remarkable way, Mr. Grant. This *is* the last time that I am coming in person to offer you so simple a means of regaining your liberty. I have been much too easy with you; had you lived in the time of Red Finlay of the Battles you would certainly not be alive five days after laying hands on the Chief of Clan MacPhair—no, not one day! So you are going to learn something of the methods which—if he had spared your life at all—Fionnlagh Ruadh nan Cath would have employed. After a short experience of them you are likely to desire to exchange them again for mine; but you will then have to send and beg me to receive your apology."

"Indeed?" said Hector, crossing his legs. "It still has not dawned upon you that when I am traced here there will be a pretty heavy reckoning to be paid by the present Fionnlagh Ruadh?"

"As I observe no signs of your being traced anywhere," retorted Glenshian with perfect truth, "I am not disturbed at the notion. And if they do come, your friends will undoubtedly find that you have already procured your release on the terms which I have stated. I will, therefore, wish you good day . . . until you send for me."

He was gone, and the captive was left again to the uninspiring society of the winecasks. The only bright spot in the twenty-four hours was Hector's brief daily passage of arms with his enemy. And now he was apparently to be deprived of that. He was faintly uneasy also; what change for the worse in his circumstances was Glenshian proposing? The times of that early and bloody-minded MacPhair, Red Finlay of the Battles, had not been remarkable for humanity, as Hector well knew, and his descendant now seemed disposed in some way or other to revert to them.

" 'Tis preposterous!" exclaimed the captive, leaping up from his chair. "Glenshian is downright mad—he ought to be in Bedlam . . ."

Perhaps, but he was not in Bedlam; he was at liberty, and a petty king in his own way. Hector had not as yet suffered any actual bodily ill-treatment, beyond that incurred in the initial struggle with the Chief's gillies; surely it was not possible that Glenshian, in this civilised eighteenth century, was really contemplating a return to the barbarities of the fourteenth!

Yet a distinct chill, creeping over his intrepid spirit, reminded Hector that he could do nothing to prevent such a reversion. For the first time he began seriously to wonder whether it was possible that he should never set eyes on the inheritance which had been left to him— never see again the charming Appin girl whom he designed to bring there as its mistress . . .

"Nonsense!" he thought, squaring his shoulders. "Things which could be done with impunity in Red Finlay's day cannot be done now. For one thing, there is the English garrison at Fort Augustus to reckon with. If only I could communicate with them in some way. . . ." And then, with genuine dismay, he realised what he was doing—he who had never lost an opportunity of denouncing the presence of the Sassenach in-

vader, with his hated redcoats, in the Highlands. . . .
It was something of a shock, and he sat soberly down in
his shabby armchair again. All the same, if Governor
Traupaud only knew. . . .

His rather shamefaced pursuance of this thought was
broken into by a clinking sound which came through the
grating. That was old Roderick fetching wine—and not
drawing it from the cask this time either. There must
be bottles of it also in the adjacent cellar; Hector felt
he could well have done with one in his. Voices too. . . .
Somerled, his gaoler, had evidently gone in after
Roderick—a conjuncture which had never taken place
before. Hector had not, therefore, had the opportunity
till now of discovering how clearly he could hear what
was said in the next cellar, even in Gaelic, a tongue of
which he had a good working knowledge, but which,
owing to his residence abroad, he rarely had the chance
of speaking, and did not indeed follow with quite the
same ease as English or French. But he quickly made out
that Somerled was giving expression to precisely his own
sentiments about the wine.

" Though indeed," Hector heard him add in his big,
gruff voice, " I have drunk it, and that not longer ago
than last June."

" You surely did not steal a bottle, Somerled!" said
the aged retainer in shocked tones.

" Indeed no! But Mac 'ic Fhionnlaigh sent out a
bottle from his own table that Seumas and I might drink
his health. You cannot have forgotten that, Roderick.
'Twas the night he came back so late from Ardroy with
those two missing steers of his."

The old man gave an exclamation. " Aye, I remember
that now, to be sure. Indeed, I do not know how I came

to be forgetting it, for I was asking myself at the time why Mac 'ic Fhionnlaigh should be doing such a thing when there was plenty of usquebaugh to hand."

Hector, attracted by the mention of the word "Ardroy," had pricked up his ears. What on earth had Finlay been doing with steers at Ardroy—buying some from Ewen?

"*Usquebaugh!*" Somerled was saying with a contemptuous laugh. "That evening's work was worth something better than usquebaugh, and so the Chief thought. By St. Bride, you should have seen the laird of Ardroy's face when Seumas showed the brand on the beasts!"

"Aye, I heard of that," assented Roderick. "Ardroy's men had stolen the steers—though he swore they had not. No doubt Mac 'ic Fhionnlaigh was glad to be getting them back; I remember his look at supper that night. And yet," he pursued, with the persistence of an old man, and one who was jealous of his master's best wine, "yet I do not know why you and your half-brother should have been given a bottle of this claret, which Glenshian brought specially from London with him last year."

"Do you not, then!" retorted Somerled half-mockingly. "What if I were to be telling you——" But here he stopped, and, no doubt pointing to the grating, said, in a lower tone, "The gentleman within there can hear us, I'm thinking."

"No matter if he do," retorted old Roderick. "He is but a French officer from over the sea, and will not have the Gaelic, though he has the English well enough. There's no word of Erse in his mouth, now, is there?"

"No, that's true." Evidently reassured, Somerled

went on: "Well, then, we drank the Chief's health that night with a will, for it's he that has the cunning; and we pledged each other too, Seumas and I, for doing his work to his liking."

"For bringing back the steers, you mean. *Dhé!* that was no great feat."

"Nay," said Somerled with a laugh," for something better than that. For putting them there for the Chief to find!"

"Putting them there! *putting them there!*" repeated Roderick incredulously.

"Aye, Seumas and I had driven them over two nights before, by Mac 'ic Fhionnlaigh's orders. 'Twas not difficult, for there was a moon. And we left them in the grazing grounds of Ardroy's own cattle—two good steers such as a thief would have chosen. And when Ardroy in his wrath had all his beasts collected together to prove that the Chief's were not among them——" He broke off, perhaps with a gesture to complete his meaning.

Moving like a shadow, Hector went on to his hands and knees and took a quick glance through the grating. He could see old Roderick's back, with the end of a bottle showing under either arm. Somerled he could not see.

Roderick was cackling appreciatively. "I wish I had been there . . . he, he he! And Ardroy never guessed?"

"How should be? He thought that his men had been helping themselves to Mac 'ic Fhionnlaigh's cattle without his knowledge—which was just what the Chief wished him to think—and he was exceedingly angry and ashamed. It was a good jest."

"And it was only for a jest that the Chief was after doing it?"

"Why else?"

"Because he is so clever," quoth Roderick admiringly. "Cleverer than the old Chief, God rest him. I am wondering, therefore, why he should have taken so much trouble."

And Hector, listening open-mouthed, was wondering too.

"Was it not worth trouble to humble the Cameron, who had sworn that his men were not cattle-thieves?" enquired Somerled. "It was a good hour for a MacPhair like myself, that, and to Mac 'ic Fhionnlaigh it was even better, as I could see."

"Well, I never heard the like," commented the old man, beginning slowly to move towards the door with his bottles. "Yes, 'tis no wonder he was pleased, and sent you the wine."

"Here, don't be leaving your keys, man!" said Somerled, "otherwise I might be helping myself to another bottle of the Chief's claret; or my fine gentleman in there, if he should take a fancy to try again to break through the grating, would find the door unlocked.—Not, indeed, that he will be able much longer to play any such pranks."

"Why not?" asked the old man, stopping; and it is certain that Hector prepared every nerve of hearing to catch the answer. He also took another comprehensive look through the grating in question; and so, both men now being within his range of vision, he saw with disappointment the hitherto incautious Somerled stoop his bearded lips to old Roderick's ear and whisper something inaudible. The old man gave an exclamation of surprise. Somerled laughed, drew back, and laid a finger on his own lips; upon which Roderick, shaking his head with what appeared to be disapproval, hobbled out without another word, followed by his informant.

On the other side of the grating Hector raised himself slowly from his hands and knees, and sat back frowning. That was an extraordinary affair—that of the steers . . . but he wished very much he did not feel that he was soon going to hear of one perhaps even stranger, in which he himself was destined to play the central part.

CHAPTER XIV

" WILL YOU WALK INTO MY PARLOUR? "

§ I

Aug. 28th.

AND meanwhile he *was* on his way, the man whom Finlay
MacPhair had been expecting. He was not even very far
off, but his progress had been delayed by a recurrence of
the fever of which he had spoken so lightly to Olivia
Campbell that day at Kilrain. It was in fact a recurrence
so severe that David Maitland had collapsed at the door of
a little cottage near Letterfinlay, on Loch Lochy, four
days before Hector Grant made his ill-fated attempt to
settle his score with the Chief of Glenshian.

It was to require ten days' stay with the very poor but
hospitable couple who lived in that miserable dwelling,
and such rudimentary care as they could give, before
Maitland was well enough to think of resuming his interrupted journey to Invershian. Just a week after Finlay
the Red had sat reflecting over Hendry Shand's epistle
announcing that he had seen and contrived to discover the
identity of the gentleman who had given him the fateful
letter for the Lord Justice-Clerk, Maitland himself, in-
tending to resume the road next morning, was re-reading
with a sombre and harassed face a missive which he, too,
knew by heart already. It was short and stabbing.

Dear Sir,
Circumstances having put me into posession
of yr. Secret, which I should supose you would pay

173

*any price to kepe from the knowledge of your Frinds
and of yr. Enemys also, if you wish it to remain a
secret you will please come to confer with me at my
house of Invershian as soon as you conveniently may.
If you dow this I shall show you a way of disposeing
of it that it shall troble you no longer.*

   I have the Honour to be, Sir,

      Yr. frind and wellwisher,

        MacPhair of Glenshian.

*If you dow not come I shall be forced to other Steps
which will not prove so agreeable to you.*

This letter, whose phraseology seemed engraved upon
his brain, David Maitland put back at last in his breast,
his face gone greyer than before, its delicate and attractive
features all pinched as though by cold. And indeed he
was cold, cold to the marrow of his bones—but not from
his late indisposition. " God have mercy upon me! " he
whispered to himself, and leant back in his rough chair,
his eyes closed, his hands open on the table, in the attitude
of a man beaten, defenceless and despairing.

His surroundings were indeed not out of keeping with
despair—the dark little room, with its floor of trodden
earth and its walls blackened by years of peat smoke, the
rickety old table at which he sat, the few poor necessities
for cooking and eating, all evidence of the most grinding
struggle to live. Through the half open door there
streamed in the damp, sweet, soft air, and the cries of
children playing outside, which he was in a mental region
too far away to hear. He was not, therefore, aware of the
sudden hush which had fallen upon these shrill voices,
nor of the sound of wheels upon the rough road below,
and started violently when there came a quick step outside,

a peremptory knock upon the open door, and a voice asking in Gaelic, "Is there a sick gentleman staying here?"

Not understanding Gaelic, Maitland could not reply to an unintelligible query; all he could do was to say in English, "Will you not come in? The good people of the place are out in the croft."

"Ah! you are perchance yourself the man I am seeking—Mr. Maitland of Strathmory?" asked the voice at once, and the speaker stepped in—as well as could be seen against the light, a tall, red-haired young man carrying himself very upright, and by his attire a gentleman.

Maitland got up, a hand to the table less because of his weakness than because he was come, he suspected, very near the brink of the precipice.

"You will be perhaps from the Chief of Glenshian, who has heard that I am here, sir?" he enquired. For, owing to a misunderstanding of the scanty English of his hosts, he had received a totally wrong impression of Glenshian's personal appearance, and never divined this fine and well-built young man to be the Chief himself.

The newcomer stared, and after a second gave a brief laugh. "Yes, I am certainly from the Chief. He desires me to bring you to him, if you are well enough to travel the remainder of the way. I . . . he is very sorry to learn of your indisposition." He came further in, and Maitland saw him better, and liked him less.

"I am at Mr. MacPhair's disposal," he said quietly. "Indeed, I had fully purposed resuming my journey to-morrow."

His visitor, who had been studying him very hard with eyes whose like the elder man had never seen before, now transferred his gaze to the convalescent's wretched surroundings. "You'll not be sorry to be out of this hovel,

I should think," he said contemptuously. " What a sty!
I have no shieling, I think, on my estates as miserable as
this! "

" The good man and his wife here, despite their
poverty, have done their best for me, and I am very grateful to them," responded Maitland, resenting the tone,
though he knew that the place was a hovel. And then the
newcomer's last words came home to him with fresh
meaning. " Are you then perhaps Mr. MacPhair of
Glenshian himself? " he asked.

" Well, Mr. Maitland, since I have no wish to keep the
fact from you, I am," admitted the young man with a
careless laugh. " At your service, and vastly sorry if this
long journey, which you have been good enough to take at
my suggestion, be the cause of your indisposition. I have
only just heard by chance of your presence here, or I
should have made shift to remove you ere now to better
quarters. I have an equipage waiting now upon the road,
so, if you will allow me. . . . ? "

He was urbanity itself. Maitland looked at a knot in
the table and spoke with difficulty. " Could we not have
our conversation here, Mr. MacPhair? "

" And be interrupted by *that* every moment? " queried
Glenshian, swinging an arm towards the door, round
which a bevy of dirty and awestruck children was
collected. He came nearer to Maitland. " Moreover
these walls do not even keep out the wind," he added
meaningly. " Don't you think that, for your own sake,
something more solid is desirable? "

David Maitland bowed his head. " I will come with
you. Let me but get my effects together and find and
thank the kind folks who have tended me."

The young Chief strode instantly to the door, the

children scattering wildly at his approach, and called out an order; then, turning, asked, "Have you a horse, sir? One of my gillies shall ride it—or, if you prefer not to entrust it to a servant, I will do so myself."

Maitland's pale face flushed. "I *should* prefer you to ride him, Mr. MacPhair, if you would be so good." For so he would be alone in the chaise, and defer yet a little longer the moment that was coming.

Solitary, as he had designed, in the chaise bumping its way a quarter of an hour later along Lochy side, David Maitland stared in front of him with blind eyes. He could not understand Glenshian's manner to him, for the young Chief had not treated him as an outcast whom no decent Jacobite would admit within his doors—he seemed to be welcoming him with every civility. And yet he knew . . . or said that he did. A wild hope showed its head every now and then above the choking waves of shame and misery, a hope that Glenshian did *not* know that secret which was eating his soul away, and that his letter had referred to something else. But to what else could those guarded phrases have reference, save perhaps . . . Yet that was scarcely possible; for *that* secret was none of his, did not even concern himself directly, and was no burden to his conscience. Indeed, until this moment, the idea had never occurred to him since he had received, at Strathmory, the summons which had brought him here. Well he remembered that sunny day; he had hardly been aware of the sun since. . . .

But how the Chief of Glenshian had got upon his track Maitland could not imagine. He had not put any name to his own letter of intelligence on that March day more than two years past, nor had he taken the letter in person to Lord Tinwald's door; and though it was true that he had acquaintances in Edinburgh, whither he was accustomed to go about twice a year, that was no solution of the mystery. He was not there frequently enough for his face to be familiar to the town caddies and chairmen who were reputed to know everyone and everyone's business; he was sure that it was not familiar to the rather dingy messenger to whose charge he had committed the letter. Yet it was undeniable that Finlay MacPhair's summons had reached him a couple of weeks or so after his recent visit to the capital, whither he had gone to consult a physician about his wife's malady. Nevertheless, as the chaise conveyed him on towards whatever it was that Glenshian wanted with him, Maitland put that particular question from him. It was more important to be resolved to walk warily, in case there should be a door after all. . . .Yes, he must walk warily when he came to grips with this smoothspoken young man who had written that he would show him a way to dispose of his burden. . . . O God, if only he could!

§ 2

There was no sign of coming to grips during the good meal which followed Maitland's arrival at the House of Invershian. Much solicitude did the young Chief show, on the contrary, in pressing meat and drink upon his guest, advising him, now that he was free from fever, to eat in order to strengthen himself, and recommending the claret which, as he said, he had brought from London last year. But at last, when Maitland, who had drunk little enough, and eaten less, would drink no more, Glenshian rose.

" Well, now, sir, if you are not too much fatigued,

will you come to my own room, and we can have our discussion, which I'm in hopes you will find not without profit to yourself."

He was so damnably pleasant about it! Could it—could it be something else . . . not *that*? Yet Maitland passed out of the door which his host held open for him with the feelings of a man going to the gallows, an impulse to get the business over quickly. None the less he knew that he ought to resist that temptation to leap from the cart, as some did, in the hope of breaking their necks at once; for there might be a reprieve. There *was* another secret which he knew. . . .

In his own room Finlay MacPhair drew a couple of chairs up to the fire which burnt there, arranged tobacco and two long pipes on a small table between them, and then went and locked the door.

"Now we'll not be disturbed," said he cheerfully. "Pray sit down, Mr. Maitland. Do you use tobacco?"

Maitland, complying, said that he did not.

"'Tis a solace at times," observed the Chief, filling one of the pipes. "When a man has something on his mind, for instance. But perhaps you are not troubled in that way, Mr. Maitland?"

"No," answered Maitland defiantly. "Not unduly. But you, sir, I observe that *you* use tobacco!"

"To be sure I do, for I *have* something on my mind," avowed Finlay with frankness. "Poverty, Mr. Maitland, for all that I'm Chief of Glenshian, with lands that run from the Great Glen to the sea. You have but to look at this house to see that I am absurdly poor for my position."

Taken aback, Maitland murmured he knew not what.

"Aye," went on his host, "I'm in the case of a man wanting something he has not. And you"—here he turned full upon his guest those curious light eyes of his, " you, on the contrary, are in the case of a man who has something he would give a deal to be rid of. Am I not right? "

After all, reflected Maitland bitterly, he must know that I would not have taken this journey at his bidding unless he were right. It was not much use fencing, when it came to it. " Will you not be more explicit, Mr. MacPhair? " he asked, digging his further hand deep into the pocket of his coat and clenching it there. But he did not look at him.

" Indeed I will, since you thus invite me," replied the Chief pleasantly. " Time, they say, is money—though I have not found it so. . . . Well now," his voice dropped, but was no less suave, " well now, would you not gladly be rid of the responsibility for a certain letter which on a night in March of the year before last you caused to be delivered to the Lord Justice-Clerk in Edinburgh, a letter which———"

He paused, for it did not seem necessary to continue. Maitland had pulled out that clenched hand and put it over his eyes; the other he stretched out in a wavering gesture. " You need not go on." His voice was quite quiet. Then that hand too joined its fellow, and both covered his face as he bent forward, his elbows on his knees. This *was* the gallows after all.

Finlay MacPhair sat on the other side of the little table, pushing the tobacco down into the bowl of his pipe. At moments his lips were compressed; at moments there was a smile about his mouth, especially when he cast a glance at the bowed figure on the other side of the hearth. Time passed; the fire glowed; Finlay lit his pipe with a pine chip and began to pull at it.

" Come, Mr. Maitland," he said at last, removing it from his mouth, " I hope you do not think that I have caused you this long journey either to reproach you for the sending of that letter, or to spread the knowledge of it. There's but one man besides myself, I suppose, who knows that you sent it, and he is a nobody who would not be believed."

The hands fell. " Then why *did* you cause me this journey? " asked Maitland in the voice of the dead.

" Because," replied his host equably, taking another pull at his pipe, " I thought you might be glad to be quit of the memory of that letter—if it irks you."

Maitland looked at him across the fire. " Do you by chance fancy yourself to be Almighty God? " he asked bitterly. " —Yet even God Himself could not compass that! "

" On that I can express no opinion," replied young Glenshian. " But I see that you're not quite easy lest it be known that it is you and none other, a declared Jacobite, who have upon your hands the blood of that excellent if misguided man, Doctor Archibald Cameron of Lochiel."

" ' Not quite easy ' ! " repeated Maitland. " My God, you have a gift of phrase! "

" I have no wish to exaggerate," said Finlay modestly. " Nor to wound your feelings. If I did not put the matter strongly enough, I apologise."

" You have not put it even correctly," said the other, with sudden passion. " Although, when I took the step I did, I never thought—nay, as God is my witness, I never even dreamed—that it would mean the scaffold for Archibald Cameron, yet I have suffered so much these two years that I could scarce suffer more if what I did became public, and if all men, Jacobite or Whig, turned and hounded me out of Scotland! And how you, a Jacobite and a Highlander, who know what I did, can have broken bread with me passes my comprehension! "

For the first time Finlay MacPhair appeared a little perturbed.

He laid down his pipe and leant across the table. " Mr. Maitland, you would do well to compose yourself, and not to give way to such feelings. I have broken bread with you because I desire to help you, not to denounce you.—I trust that you do not contemplate denouncing yourself? That would be madness! "

" I sometimes think it would be the only sanity."

" *Dhé!* what good could it do to you or anyone else? " expostulated Finlay. " What's done cannot be undone now. You had your motives, doubtless, for writing that letter; 'tis not for me to enquire what they were. At any rate they were not mercenary ones, for since you never signed your name to it you cannot have expected payment for your information. Or did you put in a claim for reward afterwards? " There was a real and anxious enquiry in his eyes, and he leant a little further over the table.

" A claim for reward! " exclaimed David Maitland, his delicate features contorted with disgust. " You think I *sold* him! "

Relief, a profound relief, was perceptible on the young Chief's face. " No, as I say, I am sure you did not. Yet, had you allowed your name to be known, you would not have found the English Government ungrateful. They were desperately anxious to capture Archibald Cameron. But I might have known that you were above taking money for your action. . . . I suppose you are . . . still of that mind? "

Maitland rose suddenly from his chair. "Mr. Mac-Phair, I don't know what this conversation is aiming at, but you cannot be ignorant that it is exquisitely painful to me, and I should be obliged if you would cut it as short as possible. I am in your power; is it a written confession that you want from me?"

Finlay was up too. "No, no! Pray sit down again! You quite misapprehend my attitude, sir. I want no vengeance on you; it may be that after all you did not do a bad day's work!"

"*You* can say that!" exclaimed Maitland, almost in horror. "*You* can look at it in that light—the light in which the Devil showed it to me!"

"Oh, I would not be so sure it was the Devil! I am a trifle more behind the scenes than you, I fancy, Mr. Maitland. However, to recur to my purpose. You have read, I suppose, of the scapegoat of the Jews, on which were laid the sins of the people? . . . What would you say to my finding you a scapegoat for yours?"

In sheer astonishment Maitland sat down again. "I don't understand you!"

"'Tis plain enough. A scapegoat—one who would be ready to shoulder the blame of the deed, if necessary; to swear that it was he who sent that letter to the Lord Justice-Clerk—you of course furnishing him with the requisite details, lest his story should be challenged. Surely that is simple?" His face was eager.

"I'm not a rich man, Mr. MacPhair," replied Maitland drily. "Nor would such a piece of pretence ease my mind in the least. How could it? Nothing can alter the fact that it was I who wrote that letter."

"But only I and one other—a nobody—know that!"

7

"I have said that I almost wish, sometimes, that all the world knew it!"

"That's a mere sick man's fancy," pronounced Finlay rather scornfully, yet again with visible uneasiness. "You, a gentleman well thought of, a Jacobite that's been 'out'—did you not tell me so?—to brand yourself publicly as an informer without reflecting what it would mean to your family and relatives—for I suppose you're not without kin of some sort—pshaw, my dear sir, you've the fever still in your veins! And all the while you could rid yourself of the burden with such ease, and do a good turn to a poor devil who——"

"*Do a good turn!* Are you crazy, Glenshian?"

"——who wants to earn a little money," finished the young man quickly.

"I've told you I have none to spare. And, if I had, do you think I would pay a fellow-creature, even the lowest, to take my guilt upon his head?"

"'Tis not a question of *your* paying him, man!" exclaimed the Chief, sounding rather exasperated.

"Then who *is* going to pay him? You?"

Finlay's eyes began to gleam, and his manner became all at once charged with excitement. "I?—I, to whom . . . No, by God! The English Government, who contrive to get inestimable services for nothing, who make promise after promise, and because a man cannot prove up to the hilt that he carried out his work to the very end, sit on their money-bags, damn them, and draw up the strings the tighter! 'Tis they that would have to pay!"

"And how, pray," asked Maitland coldly, "have you this knowledge of the methods of the English Government with its spies, Mr. MacPhair?"

Like a rider who has been giving his horse too much

rein, and suddenly perceives it, Finlay MacPhair pulled up. He said somewhat shortly, " Because this poor wretch of whom I spoke was in their pay—or rather, was not paid."

And at that there came over Maitland's ravaged face the look of one who begins to guess that he has stumbled upon a nest of something poisonous and unclean. " In their pay . . . and in your confidence!"

" In my confidence, no. But I cannot avoid knowing his circumstances. He is . . . a kinsman of mine, on the wrong side of the blanket."

" And you wish to do him what you call a good turn— enable him to claim from the English Government blood-money which he did not earn?"

Glenshian bristled at the tone. " He all but earned it," he retorted sulkily. " All the preliminary work was done by him, and if you had not had the luck to forestall him by being in Glenbuckie at the right moment——"

Maitland sprang up, pushing his chair so violently that it screeched on the uncarpeted floor. " I cannot go on with this conversation, Glenshian. It brings me near vomiting!"

Finlay jumped up too. " Sit down again," he snarled suddenly across the table, " sit down again and remember what you are yourself! How dare *you* ape virtuous indignation! How dare you, just because you were too timid to claim the money—how dare you come and play the saint over a better man than yourself, who had not your luck!"

David Maitland stood quite still, gripping the back of the chair, his eyes fixed on the figure of the angry young man, who was leaning over the table and emphasizing his points by banging it with his fist, so that he broke the pipe lying there.   Horror and incredulity were in the elder man's gaze; then his face stiffened into a mask of despair and self-loathing.

"Is it possible? " he said hoarsely. "You—*you* want the blood-money yourself—*you* were in the pay of the Government!   Now I *know* that I am in hell!"   He subsided again into his chair and once more buried his face in his hands.

Finlay MacPhair, with a touch that was not quite steady, took up the two halves of the snapped pipe, threw them into the fire, and flung himself down with outstretched legs and hands deep in his breeches pockets. For some time he studied the flames playing round the tobacco in the bowl; at last he removed his hands, sat up and said briskly:

"Well, now that we know the worst of one another we can get to business, Mr. Maitland. Perhaps you are by this time come to a proper appreciation of the service I propose to do you?"

Maitland dropped his shielding hands. "I believe I do appreciate it at its proper worth," he said very slowly. "And I will take my leave of you, Glenshian." For the third time he stood up, horribly pale, but quite composed.

"Nay, 'tis too early to go to bed," said his host without moving. "Moreover, we have not arrived at an understanding."

"I think we have," answered Maitland, still more quietly. "And I was not proposing to go to bed under this roof. I prefer . . . anywhere else."

And at that Finlay rose too, looking dangerous.

"Indeed?   If I choose to risk the contamination of my house by harbouring an informer, that is surely my affair, not yours! "

Maitland faced him unflinchingly, though his features were fallen in like a corpse's. "Your house harbours something worse than an informer, MacPhair. Even I have not sunk to enduring the society of a paid spy who is trying to get the credit of a crime which he never committed—for money!"

"You'll have to endure it," retorted Finlay coolly. "The door is locked, Mr. Informer, and the key is in my pocket."

"Yes, I know that. But I am going nevertheless."

"The last man who offered violence to me," observed Finlay menacingly, "is regretting it now. He too thought he would leave at will—and could not."

"I should not dream of offering you violence," replied his present visitor. "I would liefer not touch you. If you are afraid to let me go you must, then, keep me prisoner. But at least I shall not in that case be your guest."

"Afraid?" Finlay took him up. "Afraid of what? That you will go and drop hints about the countryside? You can't do that without publishing your own indubitable shame; and nothing that you can say against MacPhair of Glenshian is going to be believed out of *your* mouth! Why, even Ard—even a man with a clean record who has a private grievance against me dare not air it in public. (And, by the way," he added to himself, "his record will not be so clean presently.) You are a Lowlander, Mr. Maitland," he finished loftily, "and must be excused your ignorance of the position of Mac 'ic Fhionnlaigh in the Highlands!"

Maitland said nothing, but stood waiting. Finlay changed his tone a little.

"Mr. Maitland, I have been at a good deal of expense

and trouble to secure this interview with you. Come, sit down again and reconsider your foolish and hasty decision! You can leave this house, if you wish, to all intents and purposes cleared of your guilt. You have only to——"

"I prefer to leave it with my guilt upon my own head!" broke in Maitland with all the impetuosity of a young man. "At least it is my own shame. And I will not be implicated in another man's infamy. Informer as I am, *I* never took pay from the English Government! "

" And who's to prove that I did?" retorted Glenshian with an insolent tilt of his head. "You are a double-dyed fool, Mr. Maitland, for I have you in my hand, body and soul. And yet all I desire is to come to an accommodation with you."

"Either give me the key of this door," said Maitland sternly, " or summon your servants and have me made captive, if such is your intention. I will not resist them. But to stay longer in the same room with you is a punishment too great for my sin, and I'll not endure it!"

" And what will you do to prevent it?" enquired the young Chief with a sneering smile. " If I have a fancy to contemplate Doctor Cameron's murderer for a while longer, you cannot hinder my indulging it. 'Tis a privilege given to few . . . Are you not anxious to know how I came upon your track? No? Is there then nothing I can do to pass the time for you? Details of the execution—you have had all those, I expect, being naturally anxious to know how your plan succeeded, but if I can furnish——"

" Will you give me that key?" demanded Maitland. " If you keep me here till Judgment Day I shall not consent to what you propose!"

A sudden gust of rage—the rage of the defeated—swept over Finlay MacPhair. He pulled out the key and flung it on the table between them. "Go, then—and take your shame elsewhere! I am glad to be rid of a fool as well as a scoundrel!" He turned his back; Maitland picked up the key and without a word went straight to the door, opened it, and was gone.

And the man who from the moment of Archibald Cameron's landing in the Highlands had sent the English Government all the information in his power about him, and yet had failed to secure the reward for his apprehension—and had failed again now—began to hammer the remaining pipe which lay upon the table with his clenched fist until it was in a score of pieces; and continued, his face distorted almost to frenzy, to hammer until his hand was grazed and bleeding, and the little table rang and tottered with his blows. The fortunate chance meeting with Hendry Shand in Edinburgh on which he had so congratulated himself had brought him no luck at all—on the contrary; and the thought of those unremunerative guineas was like vitriol on a wound.

CHAPTER XV

Aug. 28th (continued).

RAIN—fine, driving, soaking rain. David Maitland was glad of it; it was clean . . . a kind of lustration.

But no. No rain, no water in the world could wash him clean again—less now than ever, after that hour with Glenshian. For two years there had been blood on his hands, those delicate, scholarly-looking hands which had tied a noose about a man's neck as surely as the English hangman; this fact he had known, had faced, had kept at bay every hour of those two years. The only weapon which he had against it was the knowledge of his complete innocence of such an intention, for he had very truly told Finlay MacPhair that he never dreamed he was sending Archibald Cameron to death. He had thought that in informing the Government of his whereabouts he was merely condemning him to imprisonment, removing thereby the menace of a recurrence of that terrible and useless waste of life of the Forty-five, in which he himself, as a Jacobite, had played his part. Should another such hopeless attempt be made, fostered by the endeavours of Doctor Cameron, he knew that his own young son would be sacrificed in it, and many another like him. But, through a chance meeting on a March day of 1753, an angel had put it in his power to prevent such a calamity by checkmating the conspirator who was working to bring it about. Racked with scruples, yet arguing that he must not let them stand in the way of the good of hundreds of his countrymen, Maitland had posted off to Edinburgh, written a brief, unsigned message to the Lord Justice-Clerk, found a casual messenger to deliver it . . . and had soon learnt that there are two kinds of angel. . .

And now to the blood upon him was added mud. He seemed to have stepped into some festering bog of infamy. He himself had played the informer, it was true, yet—ironical though it appeared in view of the consequences to his victim—he had played it with the best intentions. But behind him in the house which he had left was a young Jacobite of high standing, the head of a great Highland clan of like traditions, who had apparently been in the pay of the English Government for God knew how long, who regretted that he could not show to them his fellow-Jacobite's blood upon his hands in order to get paid for the stain, and who, to that end, had planned how best to simulate the appearance of it there! It was so nearly incredible that once or twice, as David Maitland stumbled away in the wet dark from the House of Invershian, he began to wonder whether the whole thing could be a delusion. But there came over him again the shuddering remembrance of the words, the looks, the innuendoes—of the final half-involuntary disclosure and the assumption of a common bond of turpitude. *"Now that we know the worst of one another."* Yes, that was hell—to be condemned by one's own act to the company of those even more vile than oneself, who had the right to call one comrade.

Maitland had now come, he perceived, to the borders of the loch by which he had driven that afternoon, and heard, though he could not see, the little waves, whipped by the small wind which blew the rain against him, flinging themselves gently along the shore. Water, water on every side; for he heard the voice of a burn also, lamenting in the night. And he came to a stop. Why not the loch? The deed would have some semblance of purification. If his body were found it would only be supposed that he had stumbled in by accident in the darkness. He had but to wade out into that whispering water which he could not see, save as a kind of greyness. Wife, son, friends and kindred—no one need know otherwise. Only the man whom he had just quitted might guess differently.

But merely to walk into the loch would not be sufficient, for he divined it too easy to turn back and to drag himself to land again, though he was not a very good swimmer. He needed a bank from which he could throw himself, not a flat shore like this, and the weight of stones in his pockets in order that his resolution, if it shrank from the cold embrace of the water, should shrink in vain. And he remembered having seen, as he drove along this afternoon, the ruined keep of a castle, standing above the loch on higher ground than this. It could not be very far from here, that loftier shore, and the ruin would supply him with his other requisite.

Maitland walked on again, and pictures went with him through the half-darkness—his ailing wife, his son, so full of promise, whom . . . it seemed such bitter irony . . . he had named after the Prince, Olivia Campbell, whom he loved as a daughter, the man whom he had betrayed. On the scaffold Archibald Cameron had said (so Maitland had heard) that he forgave any who had helped to bring him there. Perhaps he himself would soon learn if that had been a mere figure of speech.

The world seemed a trifle lighter now, though the rain

kept on as steadily as ever. Maitland, a man just recovered
from a long bout of fever, was by this time wet nearly to
the skin. Well, he would be wetter soon. . . . He
plodded on, and found that his memory had served him
correctly. He was going slightly uphill, and before long
there loomed upon his left hand the dim shape of some
high building, doubtless the tower he had seen that afternoon.

He went up to this and stood there until he could make
out a little more of it. Its base seemed to be thickly
fringed with nettles and brambles, and was probably rich
in fallen stones and fragments of stone. Groping, and
getting stung and scratched, and wondering that he should
care enough to be faintly annoyed at these small tribula-
tions, his last on earth, Maitland found several bits of
masonry of a size to stuff into his pockets. These were
half filled when he suddenly gave a violent start and
dropped a stone which he had just disembedded from the
nettles. Surely that was a cry!

It must have been, for in another moment a voice, a
man's voice, a little muffled but not, apparently, very far
away, called out:

"Is anyone there? If so, come here to me, for God's
sake!"

"Where are you?" asked Maitland after a moment's
astonishment. "What is amiss?"

"I am inside this old tower, on the ground," replied
the voice eagerly. "The entrance is on the side away
from the loch. Come quickly—but do not let anyone see
you!"

"There is no one who can," answered Maitland, looking round as he made this statement, which it was too dark
to substantiate or contradict. He began to take the stones

out of his pockets, but slowly. Did this mean that he must renounce his purpose—for the time?

" Are you not coming—are you in his pay also? " asked the voice on a note of desperation. " If you go away and leave me you may have my death at your door! "

" One is enough," thought Maitland with a grim humour somewhat foreign to him. The stones clattered down from his pockets. " I am coming to you immediately."

For all that his progress was largely a matter of groping. It was naturally even darker inside the tower, roofless though it was. A portion of one floor still remained in place about twenty feet up, and this projection was discernible, from below, against the sky.

" Where are you? " asked Maitland, once well inside.

" Here," replied the voice, which came from his left hand. " Down by the wall, under the shelter. I can just distinguish your figure. Do not fall over me."

Maitland at that remembered that he had his tinder box with him, and that it was probably dry, since he usually carried it, when travelling, in a wrapping of shagreen. He got it out, and after some difficulty succeeded in obtaining a momentary illumination. It showed him a sufficiently startling sight—a man whose clothes, though draggled and dirty, were well cut and of good materials, a young man too, despite what looked like a week-old beard, sitting against the naked masonry of the tower among nettles and stones and débris. Then all was dark again.

" What is wrong? " inquired the surprised Maitland. " Cannot you rise—have you injured yourself? "

In the darkness the young man gave a somewhat unsteady laugh.

" Could you rise if you were chained by your middle to the wall? I can lie down—on these damnably hard stones —and I can kneel (and will kneel to you with pleasure if you'll get me away) but more than that I cannot do."

" How long have you been here? "

" Two days and a night—no, a night and a half now, I should suppose."

" Good God! And who—no, I think I can guess that," said Maitland, for suddenly he remembered a hateful voice saying something about a man who ' found he could not leave at will.' " But are you not starving? "

" No, only hungry. I have a pitcher within reach, and they bring me bread once a day; but I must fight to keep the rats off it. If you have any humanity in you, sir, waste no time, I implore you, but go to—"

" Wait a moment," interrupted the elder man. " Now that I am here I can surely do something towards freeing you? "

" Not unless you have the strength of a giant, or suitable implements," said the prisoner discouragingly. " I have spent hours in wrenching, and taken most of the skin off my hands."

" Nevertheless you must allow me to try," responded Maitland, and again he procured a spark from his flint and steel. It was not of much use. " I must feel, then," he said; and kneeling down in the nettles traced the stout chain which encircled the prisoner's waist, too tightly to be slipped off, to the point, about three feet away, where it was fastened immovably to a staple in the wall.

" Like a monkey, eh? " asked the young man, speaking with a somewhat forced lightness. Maitland took up a stone and hammered, but he could not make the slightest impression on any link; nothing but a file or very powerful pincers could do that. He desisted and got up again.

"But have you not shouted?" he asked, in a sort of disbelief at this extraordinary thing. "Have you not cried out for help? You are not gagged in any way?"

"I shouted nearly the whole of yesterday, till I was as hoarse as the crows which came and looked at me from the top there. But this tower is believed to be haunted, and not a Gael will come near it—superstitious wretches that we are!—and the less if they hear any cries coming out of it. My only hope has been that a party of soldiers from Fort Augustus might pass within earshot, but they naturally take the other side of the loch where Wade's road goes; and perhaps none have passed, at that. . . . Whatever good fortune sent you this way, sir, at so late an hour, too?"

To this question David Maitland might have returned a sufficiently startling answer, but in point of fact he made none. In any case he had for the time been shocked almost out of thought of his own affairs. He said with determination, "I must get you released at once. Where is the nearest house or village?"

"You'll get no one to help you here," opined the voice from the ground. "'Tis all Glenshian's territory, where he is absolute king still, although the English have taken away the hereditary jurisdiction of the chiefs. You must go on further, into Cameron country—best of all, go, if it is not asking too much of you, to my brother-in-law Ewen Cameron of Ardroy on Loch na h-Iolaire. The shortest way to get there—"

Cameron, Cameron—the name beat in David Maitland's ears like a gong, and he hardly heard the directions which were emanating from the captive among the nettles.

"But do you think," he objected, when at last their purport became clear to him, "that I shall find my way in the dark over this pass you speak of, which is quite unknown to me?"

There was silence for a moment. "No, that is quite true," said the captive. "'Tis to be feared you might not, and I would not have you endanger yourself for me. Yet the other way to Ardroy is so long—for after this loch comes near seven miles, I should suppose, of Loch Lochy, before you bear away to Loch Arkaig through the Dark Mile. After that—" He proceeded to give further instructions, and ended: "At any rate, sir, if you push on until you find yourself in Cameron country on Lochy side, you may come on some dwelling whence you could send on a messenger to Ardroy. I do not myself know the district well enough to indicate any particular house, but I am sure you will find one somewhere along the loch before you come to the Water of Arkaig and the Dark Mile."

"I scarce like leaving you," said Maitland, hesitating a moment. "Are you sure that the man who put you here will not have your throat cut. . . . I know something of him."

"Do you? I am sorry for you! No, he'll not do that, if only for the reason that a man with a slit gullet cannot apologise, which is what he is hoping I will do . . . and which," added the captive with concentrated fire and fury, "is what I shall not do even if I have to sit here until I am a skeleton!"

"We'll have you away before that," Maitland assured him. "I had best be off, then. You can reach that pitcher and platter?—May I learn your name, by the way?"

"Hector Grant—Captain Hector Grant of the régiment d'Albanie in French service . . . God bless you, God bless you, sir! "

The words rang after David Maitland somewhat hollowly as he felt his way out of the keep and once more set his face south-westward against the wind and the fine rain. He had already repressed a shiver or two of cold as he stood talking to the unfortunate prisoner. Like a fool (as he said to himself now) he had walked straight out of the House of Invershian without his cloak, which was with his other baggage in his bedchamber there. Well, it did not much matter, provided the exposure and exertion did not bring on a recurrence of ague before he had fetched help to the young man—help from a Cameron source! What would any of these Camerons into whose territory he was going say if they knew his own story? He would be dirked, if there were any dirks left in Lochaber. . . . But that, again, would not greatly matter.

Dirks of another sort were beginning to stab through his veins and limbs as he hurried on in the rain. He almost wished that he were going to attempt the shorter way by the pass of which young Grant had spoken, but his legs would certainly not compass an ascent, though they would carry him awhile yet on the level. But would they ever carry him far enough on this much longer route of which he rehearsed the various stages to himself? He had not yet come to the end of the loch which he had thought to make his grave; then there should be a couple of miles without the companionship of water until the length of Loch Lochy began. And, nearly at the end of Loch Lochy, if ever he got so far, he was to turn aside and go through this strangely named Dark Mile. He might be in it now, for all the light he had, mental or physical. Only, at the end of the tunnel in which he felt himself, there did shimmer a light of some kind, though whether it were death or the accomplishment of his present mission he could not tell.

Whatever it was, it had sufficient power still to drag him forward, an hour and a half later, drenched and stumbling, under the flanks of the relentless, stream-scored mountains whose feet were in the grey glimmer of Loch Lochy, mountains over whose base he crawled on-wards like a fly. The Dark Mile, the Dark Mile. . . . It was not one, but many . . . and it had been two years long.

CHAPTER XVI

ANOTHER IN THE TOILS

§ 1

Aug. 26th.

ROGER, the Invernacree spaniel, had taken very little exercise of late, his master having so inexplicably retired to his bed. Hence, in default of longer rambles, he was glad this morning to accept an invitation to accompany Miss Grizel Stewart down the avenue. It did not seem much of a walk, but she might, for all Roger knew, be meaning to go further than the gate, for he noted that she had a basket in her hand. Deciding to assume that she was, he inaugurated their departure from the house with the displays usually reserved for greater occasions.

" Foolish dog! " said Miss Stewart indulgently.

Roger moreover went through the pretence of discovering all sorts of novelties in the well-known undergrowth; and at the end of the avenue he did come upon something not of quite daily occurrence—a couple of horsemen advancing up it. As in duty bound, he barked at them.

Grizel, who had been absorbed in thoughts of Roger's master and the events and anxieties of the last week, looked up at the sound. The foremost cavalier was her cousin Ewen Cameron, the second his young piper and right hand man, Angus MacMartin.

" Cousin Ewen! " she exclaimed. " What a pleasant surprise! "

Her kinsman rode up, uncovered and, stooping from the saddle, gave her a cousinly kiss. " I was wondering when you were going to become aware of me, my dear Grizel," he said with a smile. " You appeared buried in thought."

" So I was," admitted Miss Stewart. " Or perhaps I am growing deaf. I'm not so young as I was, cousin."

" We none of us are that," agreed Ewen. But he himself, being ten years her junior, swung lightly out of the saddle with no sign of the encroachments of age. " Were you going out? "

" 'Tis of no consequence," said Grizel (speaking for herself, and not for Roger). " I'll turn back to the house with you." And she began to walk beside him and his horse. " And why have we the pleasure of seeing you to-day, Ewen? "

" Because I want some advice from Uncle Alexander," replied her cousin.

" Papa went to Duror this morning; I wonder you did not happen upon him as you rode through. But he may be back at any time."

"Is Ian in the house, then? If so, I'll have a talk to him first."

" Ian? . . . You have not heard about him, I suppose? "

" What about him? Do you mean that he is from home also? "

" No—very much at home," answered Grizel drily. " Ian has met with a misfortune . . . a sort of accident."

" *Dhia gleidh sinn!* I had not heard. A serious one? "

" There was a day," said Grizel gravely, " when the surgeon talked of the possibility of his losing his arm—his right arm."

" Good God! " exclaimed Ardroy, stopping dead.
" What had happened to him? "

" Perhaps he would rather tell you himself. Oh, he's
much better now, thank God; he left his bed yesterday,
and was out of doors a while this morning, but we have
been very anxious. . . . Well, since Captain Grant is your
brother-in-law, which perhaps makes it a little awkward
for Ian to approach the matter with you, I will tell you
this much: a week ago the two of them had a . . . a
disagreement—a quarrel, in fact, and a meeting down by
the loch in which Ian was wounded in the arm, rather
severely—or so it proved in the end."

Ewen smote one hand into the other with a vexed
exclamation. " Will nothing cure Hector of being
such a firebrand?—And, by the way, I did not know
he had been here; I have been wondering where he
was.—But to quarrel with Ian! Over what did they
disagree? "

" If anybody was a firebrand I am afraid it was Ian,"
said Grizel. " He confesses to having behaved extremely
badly. They quarrelled over Jacqueline. . . . Yes, it
appears that Captain Grant is in love with her, and she
with him; but since Ian admits that he insulted our guest
beyond bearing, one does not know whether, after that,
he will ever return to ask for her hand. (I can't think
what came to Ian; he must have been fey.) And
Jacqueline, poor child, has been terribly distressed over
Ian's condition—she's with him now—and my father
too, because in some way which I cannot fathom, he
seems to think he was partly to blame for the episode.
However, it may distract and cheer him to learn that you
need his advice, Cousin Ewen."

Her tall kinsman had listened to this recital with an

ever tightening mouth, which at this deduction tightened still more. "I very much doubt that, Grizel," he said with a good deal of grimness. "And I doubt whether Uncle Alexander can really do anything to help me, and whether in a few weeks' time you may not be ashamed to be seen walking with me."

"I—ashamed to be seen walking with you!" exclaimed Grizel, openmouthed. "You must be crazy, Ewen!—What have you done?"

"Precisely nothing. But the difficulty is to prove it!"

§ 2

Grizel Stewart had not used the language of exaggeration about her brother's condition. The wound which his folly had gained him, though painful enough, might not have proved dangerous had the weapon which inflicted it been clean. But there must have been rust on the seldom-drawn blade of the swordstick. Ian's arm on the second morning was swollen from wrist to shoulder; by nightfall he was delirious, and the whole household in despair. The surgeon said that nothing but a miracle could save the arm—could indeed save the young man's life if drastic measures were too long delayed. There were periods when the unlucky duellist was able to comprehend what was hanging over him, and declared that he would sooner die than lose his right arm—was even understood to say that he did not much care if he did die. . . . Yet by morning the swelling had begun to subside, the patient, if corpselike in appearance, was in his right senses, and the surgeon, who had spent the night at Invernacree (sharpening his knives in readiness, as Ian afterwards surmised) averred that he had had the greatest surprise of his professional experience.

It *was* a miracle; Ian recognised that. He put it all down to Jacqueline's agency—to her prayers, to her tears, to her sweet and entire forgiveness of the wrong he had done her, all of which had enveloped him in so healing an atmosphere that it had seemed to push away from him the heavy clouds of fever, remorse and pain. And he had come out of them once in that long, terrible night, during Jacqueline's watch, to find his young sister's tears upon his face and to hear her saying distractedly, " Ian, Ian darling, only get better and I'll give him up . . . I'll try never to think of him again! "

Drenched with sweat, Ian had opened his eyes and managed to utter the words, " I will bring him back for you, Jacqueline . . . Only say you forgive me. . . ."

He felt her cool face pressed instantly against his burning cheek. She kissed him with a long, clinging kiss, and gradually he fell asleep, really asleep, with his head on her arm.

After that he became unwilling to let her out of his sight, and so, on this afternoon of Ewen's arrival, though Ian was sitting in a chair in his room, having indeed already walked a little about the garden, Jacqueline had to sit beside him. She had even at his request attempted to shave him, but her nervous handling of the razor had been so unsuccessful and even dangerous, that a gillie had had to be summoned to finish the operation. So now she was mending one of his shirts, and Ian, looking at her bent head, sat thinking of Olivia and Hector, interwoven and flitting thoughts which dazzled in his brain like the patterns in a kaleidoscope.

" Ian, here's a visitor," announced Grizel, opening the door.

The young man looked round, saw who it was, flushed up with the quick flush of the convalescent, and attempted to rise.

" Don't get up!" said Ewen, and, " Don't think you have to explain to Ewen," said Grizel simultaneously. " I've told him. Jacqueline, has he had his broth? "

" Yes, and finished every drop. Good day, Cousin Ewen." Jacqueline tendered her cheek. " Oh yes, you may talk to him as much as you like. 'Twill do him good; he's had overmuch of women's society of late." She threw her brother a glance which showed that she neither meant nor believed this, and slipped out of the room. Grizel had already gone.

" My poor Ian! " said Ewen after a moment, looking down at the invalid and his bandaged arm.

" My poor fool, if you like," responded Ian, but without bitterness. " 'Tis good to see you; sit down, and rate me as much as you wish. I have been worse than a fool. But I hope to make amends."

" Did Hector try you past bearing? " asked his cousin. " I have known him to be pretty irritating."

Ian leant back in his chair. " It was not he. It was something which had naught to do with him, and that is why my conduct was so indefensible. Directly I can use my hand I shall write him an apology, or better still, make it in person."

His penitence was evidently not going to be content with half measures, and, considering that he had had so much the worst of the encounter, Ewen admired the spirit of it.

" I do not suppose that you can do either just yet," he

said. " Moreover, there's another difficulty. Where *is* Hector? "

" At his new property in Glenmoriston, I imagine."

" But he's not! The factor sent to me the day before yesterday to ask if I knew when he was coming, as he was aware that he designed to leave France some little while ago. He thought that Hector might have gone to Ardroy to visit us on his way further north, and Alison and I, indeed, half expected him. I did not know he had been here. What day did he leave? "

". Or, more correctly, what day did I drive him away," interposed Ian. " It was last Friday."

" Nearly a week ago! Then I fear some mishap has befallen him. Do you chance to know whether he meant to visit us at Ardroy, or was he going straight to Glenmoriston? "

Ian drew his brows together in an effort to recall some half forgotten words of that disastrous day. Suddenly the colour flooded over his face. " Ewen . . . I seem to remember something . . . I don't believe he was going directly either to you or up to Glenmoriston. He . . . yes, I am sure he said something about going to see Finlay MacPhair at Glenshian first."

An expression of anything but relief dawned on Ardroy's face. " What a crazy thing to do, alone! Glenshian and he last met at the sword's point, as I told you some weeks ago. I greatly fear some harm has come to him." He pushed back his chair and began to walk about. " Why, why was he so mad? "

Ian too got up, and with an increased pallor. " Ewen," he said, " if harm has come to Mr. Grant it is my fault. I . . ." he choked over it a trifle, " I had the meanness —there is no other word for it, I am afraid—to taunt him

with that accusation about the stolen letter which Glenshian made in front of me that day at Ardroy, a charge
which you told me was baseless . . . and which I nevertheless feigned that I believed. I fear that it is more than
possible that Captain Grant has gone to Glenshian to call
him to account for that slander."

His kinsman sat heavily down again. "Ian . . . what
possessed you?"

"I do not know," replied the young man, standing
very still. And then he added, but to himself, and with
his head a little turned aside. "Yes, I do know. . . ."

Ewen Cameron had excellent hearing, but the observa-
tion was plainly not meant for his ears, and he took no
notice of it. "Sit down again, at any rate, *'ille*," he said
gently. "Still and on, if you said that to Hector, I don't
wonder at anything which followed."

"No," said Ian as he subsided into his chair again,
"nor do I. At the time . . . well, all I need tell you is
that he struck me in the face for it." And, sincere as his
penitence appeared to be, he still could colour painfully at
the remembrance of that blow. "And I am afraid that
he may have gone to Invershian with the idea of doing the
same to Finlay MacPhair if he gets the chance. Ewen,
Ewen, if ill has come to him it is my doing . . . and
there's Jacqueline to think of!"

"No, 'tis not entirely your doing," replied Ewen con-
solingly. "Knowing Hector as I do, I strongly suspect that
he may have had it in his mind to pay a visit there in any
case. On my soul, there's something of the spider about
Fionnlagh Ruadh, for he has got me into his toils too!"

"You—good God, how?"

Ewen told him, thereby pretty well driving thoughts of
Hector and remorse out of his cousin's head for the time.

And when Alexander Stewart, returning, came up to his son's room he found Ian saying rather excitedly, " This convinces me that there was, as I have always thought, a great deal more than met the eye in that business of the steers found among yours."

" What's this? " asked Invernacree, as he shut the door behind him. " Ewen, my dear boy, I am very glad to see you, though I hear that you are in trouble of some kind. Someone else has been in the same condition," he added, laying his hand on his son's shoulder in a way which showed Ardroy that in their relations there was not now much amiss. " However, we'll not go into that. I thank God the consequences were not worse. What is your difficulty, Ewen? "

" This," said his nephew, the blue of his eyes seeming to deepen, as always when he was moved, " that Glenshian intends to cite me before the Sheriff Court at Inverness for stealing some seventy or eighty head of his best cattle —unless I pay him their full value before Michaelmas Day."

" Has Glenshian gone daft? " exclaimed Alexander Stewart. " *You*—steal his cattle! In any case you can easily disprove such a preposterous charge."

" No, not easily," replied Ewen grimly. " Glenshian has seen to that. Two of his beasts were found among mine last June."

Old Invernacree dropped into a chair and stared without words.

" The question is, how they got there," put in his son. " None of Ewen's people will admit to stealing them."

" Seventy or eighty head! " repeated the old laird, recovering speech. " And what, pray, are you supposed to have done with so large a number? "

"Hidden some, and sold the most."

"Glenshian must bring some evidence of the selling."

"I dare say he can contrive to do that. The buyers will prove to be MacPhairs—ignorant, of course, of where the beasts came from." Ewen gave a mirthless laugh. "His word is law round Invershian. But pay him what I never took I will not; though if he fulfils his threat and the case goes against me, I'm a ruined man. Do not imagine, however, Uncle Alexander"—Ardroy drew himself up to his great height—"that I will accept one Scots penny from you, for I will not. I only wished you to learn of the agreeable situation in which Glenshian has me. I do not know whether you can see a way out, for I cannot."

CHAPTER XVII

DELIVERANCE

Aug. 28th—29th.

Two evenings afterwards the worthy Mrs. MacGillonie, the wife of a tacksman on Lochiel's forfeited estate on Lochy side, was congratulating herself on having beneath her roof Cameron of Ardroy, the late Chief's cousin, and the latter's near kinsman, a Stewart of Invernacree, though not a little curious as to the errand which had brought them up this western side of the loch, less frequented by travellers, since there was no good road here, as upon the other. But she was not surprised that they had asked for shelter, seeing that it was growing dusk and was raining, and that the younger gentleman had his arm in a sling and got off his horse as if he were tired. She tried, without effect, to prise some information out of the gillie who had come with them, but found Angus MacMartin, for all his youth, as impenetrable as her own John could be when he wished.

Even had the good woman listened at the door, after removing the meal which she had brought up to the travellers, she would not have heard much to enlighten her. Ewen's chief preoccupation was now to induce his convalescent kinsman to convey himself quickly into the box bed in the wall which was to receive them both; moreover they had already thrashed out the two questions of the moment so thoroughly, both at Invernacree and during their two days' ride, that there was really no more to say.

Alexander Stewart had been unable to help his nephew except by upholding his already formed determination of defying Finlay MacPhair, and refusing to pay a penny of what practically amounted to blackmail. Fury shook the old Highlander at the thought of so impudent a claim; but its impudence did not preclude its being a very serious matter for Ewen. Both of them knew the ease with which Glenshian would be able to get his own dependants to come forward and swear what he wished. Invernacree's indignant sympathy over the wrong threatening Ewen had been the chief reason for his consenting to his son, with a half-healed wound, accompanying him back to Lochaber; for the fact of Ian's presence at the original " finding " of the steers might be of some value to Ardroy, though it was difficult to see exactly how. But Ian had another project in his own mind—to assist in the search for Hector Grant; and he had in consequence proved so obstinate when, nearing Loch Arkaig on the second afternoon, Ewen had tried to send him off to Ardroy with Angus—and Angus had shown such signs of rebellion at being required to desert his master—that Ewen had yielded, stipulating only that they should none of them go much further that evening, and in fact, claiming John MacGillonie's hospitality in less than an hour after that decision.

Ian was indeed by no means sorry to dismount at the tacksman's door under shadow of the green mountain wall; and, after the meal, inserting himself with no great reluctance into the box bed, was asleep in a few minutes. But Ewen remained a while at the window, with an un-uttered prayer in his heart that a vision which he saw painted upon the rainy mist outside might not come true, the vision of a man driven to sell the place dearest to him in the world, his home, through the deliberate and heartless fraud of an enemy.

He did not know how long he had lain asleep by his cousin's side when a persistent thudding sound penetrated his slumber. After a moment he realised that someone must be knocking on the farmhouse door, which was immediately below their window—and failing, it seemed, to attract anyone's attention. For a few seconds Ewen lay idly listening to the wayfarer's efforts; then, remembering the rain which was, or had been falling, he got out of bed, opened the window and looked out.

Down below he could make out in the grey light—for it was now after dawn—a man leaning against the door in an exhausted attitude, having momentarily ceased to beat upon it. But when the window above him opened he lifted his head.

"At last!" he said, in a hoarse and scarcely audible voice. "I can go no further . . . you must send . . . Cameron of Ardroy . . . at once! And for God's sake . . . open the door."

"I will come at once," responded Ewen. He got a light, hurriedly threw on a few clothes, said to Ian, who had awakened, "There's a man outside asking for me—it might be news of Hector; I'm going to let him in," and ran down the stairs.

None of the farmhouse people were stirring, so, rushlight in hand, Ardroy unbarred the door. The man outside all but fell against him. Ewen put an arm about him and led him to a settle; then, lighting a couple of rushlights on the table from his own, got a better view of the wet and exhausted stranger lying back there with closed eyes and blue lips.

"Send to Ewen Cameron of Ardroy," said the newcomer after a moment, and said it like a child repeating a lesson. "Ewen—Cameron—of—Ardroy."

"There's no need," observed Ewen, stooping over him. "By good fortune I am myself Cameron of Ardroy. What do you want with him?"

David Maitland opened his eyes. "Tell him . . . in a ruin on the loch there . . . I do not know how far . . . my fever's on me again . . ."

"Yes?" said Ewen, controlling his impatience. "Castle Shian, I expect. What of it?"

Maitland made a fresh effort. It was equally difficult to summon his words from a confused brain and to give them utterance through chattering teeth.

"There's a young man there . . . his name . . . Grant . . . chained to the wall . . . chained fast . . . two days . . . must get him away . . . I went there to . . . to . . ." He looked up rather wildly into the keen blue eyes. "But . . . that is . . . of no account . . . He said . . . Ardroy . . Cameron . . . set him free . . . I tried . . . too fast . . ." A violent shiver went over him and his own eyes closed once more.

Ewen turned his head and became aware of Ian standing behind him. "Why, 'tis Mr. Mait——" began the latter, but his cousin was already addressing him.

"Did you hear, Ian—Castle Shian, that's where Hector is . . . chained to the wall, by Heaven!—But first we must get this gentleman to bed; he's ill. I will carry him up to our room.—I think I can do it best alone, if you will hold the door open." . . .

He lifted Maitland from the settle like a baby, got him over his shoulder, and went slowly and steadily up the steep and narrow staircase with his burden. Ian followed.

" Castle Shian, you say, and chained to the wall! It's impossible!"

" We'll soon have him away," said Ardroy. " But first—see—we must get his messenger's clothes off; he is soaked to the skin. The bed is still warm, and he can have my nightshirt. The woman here must look after him until we return . . . unless you will, Ian? It would be better, you know."

But Ian, helping him to undress the practically unconscious Maitland, shook his head with decision. " I am coming with you. Do you think Castle Shian is guarded?"

" I don't know—useless to ask *him* now. I will raise some men though, as we go. . . . If Finlay MacPhair does not pay dearly for this!—Ah, here's Angus. Take your horse, Angus, go and rouse MacKail at the smithy up the loch, and tell him to get together the necessary tools for filing or undoing a chain. I will follow shortly.—What did you say, sir?"

The exhausted man in the bed had muttered something, but all that Ewen could catch was, " ocean " . . . " blood" and " hand."

" Fever," he commented, shaking his head as he turned away. And then, as the tacksman's wife appeared in the doorway, " Mrs. MacGillonie, pray do your best for this poor gentleman; he has rendered me a great service. Well, Ian, if you insist upon coming with me I suppose you must. Clothe yourself properly, at any rate." He himself threw on the rest of his attire, ran down the stairs, and could be heard calling for MacGillonie to help him saddle the horses.

Ian went again to the bed in the alcove. Yes, it was undoubtedly Olivia's Mr. Maitland: impossible to mistake that delicate, rather worn mask. He guessed him to be drowsy now, rather than unconscious. What could he have been doing here? Whatever it was, his presence had served Captain Grant well. Chained up in Castle Shian! Finlay MacPhair must really have gone mad!

He observed as much to Ewen as they rode fast along Loch Lochy side in the prevalent damp greyness. Ardroy said so little in reply that Ian hoped Finlay himself would not be encountered on the expedition, for, if he were, violence would probably take place despite all Ewen's vows. Two or three times Ardroy dismounted and went into a cottage, roused the man living there and gave him orders. Here, in Lochiel's country, Lochiel's cousin had no difficulty in getting any clansman to follow him. Last of all they turned up a little gully to a tiny forge, to find Angus and the smith waiting outside.

" Take him up on the crupper behind you," said Ewen to his attendant. " There are other men following us on foot, but we will not wait for them. They may not be needed; indeed, I hope not."

He was clearly alive to the disadvantages of an encounter with the MacPhairs, which would inevitably bring down upon both clans the hand of the English Government, firmly established in its military representatives on either side of them at Fort Augustus and Fort William. Otherwise, as Ian could see, he was spoiling for a fight.

"I must tell you, Ewen," he remarked suddenly, " that I have already met the gentleman who so nobly brought us this news. His name is Maitland, and he comes from Strathmory."

"You have met him already!" exclaimed his cousin,

8

turning in his saddle to look at him. "Why did you not say so earlier? Where, and when?"

"There was not time to tell you," said Ian, answering the first query and not the others, which he did not mean to do—at present. "And I cannot tell you aught about him, save that he is a Jacobite, was 'out' in the Forty-five, and is a friend of . . . Campbell of Cairns, whose coach, as you have heard, met with an accident near our house."

"I wonder what he was doing on Glenshian's territory at that time of night, and on foot," remarked Ardroy, but Ian could not tell him, and he himself was naturally more concerned with Hector's plight than with the man who had revealed it to them, so the subject was not pursued. Indeed the three horses and their four riders came, about half an hour later, in sight of their goal, and must exercise caution in case they were observed. A quarter of a mile or so from the ruined keep they pulled up, on Ewen's command, and dismounted. Angus, to his disgust, was left with the horses and instructed to detain the men, when they came up, unless they were summoned forward to the castle. Meanwhile Ardroy and Ian, and the indispensable blacksmith, would go forward very quietly, almost in the guise of scouts, for, though there was no evidence of such a thing, the tower might be guarded.

Slowly and quietly they approached the ancient fastness. In the east a faint red line hinted at sunrise. A number of hoodie crows flapped away from the broken battlements, and out of the very entrance, just before they reached it, scurried a rat carrying something white, possibly a bit of bread. But there was no sign of human presence, except what met their eyes when they got inside the ruin—Hector Grant, almost unrecognisable under his young beard, sitting amongst fallen stones and nettles, his back against the damp, bare wall and his head fallen forward upon his breast in sleep, the most forlorn figure imaginable. A rustling and squeaking, added to a sudden agitation of the jungle round him, hinted at the hasty departure of further animal life.

Under his breath Ewen swore a terrible oath. Next minute he was on one knee by the captive, who had not wakened, or at least had not moved. " Hector, Hector, we are here! you are saved! Hector, you are not injured, are you?"

And then Hector raised his head and looked at him vaguely. He had now completed a second night in this place, and was in considerably worse trim than when Maitland had come upon him several hours earlier. "You'll not be able to free me, Ewen," he said dis-spiritedly. " 'Tis only waste of time to try. Someone came and tried . . . the damned chains are too strong. But if you could only keep the rats away!"

Ewen put his arm round him. " A little patience, 'ille, and you'll be free. I have brought a smith with me. Come along, MacKail."

" A smith!" exclaimed Hector, a spark of animation coming into his dead voice. " Oh, Ewen!" For a moment his head went down on Ardroy's shoulder, and when he raised it he drew the back of his hand across his eyes.

Ewen got up and went to Ian, who had remained awkwardly and remorsefully in the entrance, thinking that Captain Grant might not like to feel that his late, if defeated, antagonist was viewing his present ignomi-nious situation. "Will you stand on guard here with this?"

asked Ardroy, producing and holding out a pistol. Seeing his cousin's look of surprise he added, " Have you forgotten that Lord Stowe procured me a ' protection,' and that I can carry arms again?   But do not use that if you can possibly avoid it.   Please God no MacPhair is stirring."

When he returned to the inner chamber the smith was kneeling in the nettles examining the chain. He looked up.

" If the gentleman will allow, Mac 'ic Ailein," he said respectfully, " it will be easier to get this chain apart where it will be going round the gentleman's body."

" The gentleman will allow anything," responded Hector with a laugh," especially as he has no desire to appear in public trailing a chain about with him. Set to work, blacksmith!   You might help me off with my coat, Ewen."

" How long will you take about it, think you, MacKail? " asked Ewen.

" I'm thinking it might be the matter of half an hour," replied the smith in an apologetic voice.

" Half an hour!   that's no time at all! " observed the captive.   " You'll get well stung by those nettles, I fear, honest man.—Oh, Ewen," he went on, taking to French, " I doubt if the angel who released St. Peter from his chain was half as welcome as you are!"

And in that tongue, which Ewen also spoke fluently, he gave his cousin a brief account of his adventures while the blacksmith's tools clinked and grated about him. Towards the end Ewen went again to the entrance, where Ian Stewart stood on guard, pistol in hand.   But all was quiet, save that a few blackheaded gulls were screaming noisily over the loch behind.

"All the better," commented Ardroy. "Unless Glenshian should come here in person, in which case we could have the smith chain him up here in Hector's place. By heaven, I wish he would!"

"Whom were you talking to out there? " asked Hector, looking up as Ardroy came back.

"To my cousin Ian."

"He's here with you—he has recovered, then?—For I suppose you know all about that affair?"

"He has almost entirely recovered, though it seems that he might have lost his arm over it."

"Lost his arm! " repeated Hector, looking rather shocked. "I am extremely sorry to hear that. Believe me or no, I tried to do him as little harm as I could."

"I am not blaming you at all," Ewen assured him. "And Ian—but I will leave him to speak for himself, later. Is that really giving, MacKail?"

For answer the chain slid like a heavy snake into the trampled weeds.

"*Ah, mon Dieu!* " exclaimed Hector, with a catch in his breath. He tried to get up, but was so stiff and cramped that Ewen had not only to assist, but partly to support him.

"Come, we'll get away as quickly as possible, and as quietly," he said, holding the captive up. "I have some of the clan a little way back, but you will understand, Hector, that though I would willingly throw Glenshian into the loch, I must for others' sake avoid a collision with his people, if possible." Hector nodded; not even vengeance attracted him at this moment.

At the entrance he came face to face with Ian Stewart. But Ian was holding Ardroy's pistol in his one available hand, and could not therefore extend that hand and take

Hector's in silence, as was his impulse, for by the time his cousin had relieved him of the weapon it looked for a moment as though the rescued captive was going to collapse entirely, and the opportunity was gone.

Holding him up between them, the two hurried him away towards the horses, unseen by any MacPhair. Yet neither then nor afterwards was Captain Grant heard to regret the ease and tameness of his eventual removal from Castle Shian and the revived methods of Red Finlay of the Battles.

But when the rescuers, riding slowly, and close on either hand to the rescued (lest, in spite of his disclaimers, he should slip off his horse) reached MacGillonie's farm, and Hector had been set down to a sound meal, his first for a week, Ewen turned his attention to the man to whose good offices the prisoner owed at least a speedier release than he might have had. It appeared that he was now asleep; but Mrs. MacGillonie reported that in a sensible interval the gentleman had told her that he had only a day or two left his bed after a week's illness, on hearing which Ewen became very uneasy, and formed a plan which he immediately communicated to Ian.

"I propose," he said, "that you and Hector ride on with Angus to Ardroy, while I remain here with Mr. Maitland—is not that his name? Mrs. MacGillonie, it is clear, has but the slightest knowledge of sick nursing. When you reach Ardroy you shall send hither that old chaise of mine, and I will bring Mr. Maitland back with me directly it is possible. He cannot be left here uncared for, perhaps to undergo another illness as the result of what he has done for Hector."

"No, indeed," agreed Hector between two mouthfuls.

" I'll never in this world be able to repay him for that. I cannot imagine what he was doing near that pestilential old ruin so late at night, but whatever it was I am thankful for it."

" Was he actually the only person who had come near you for two days? " asked Ardroy.

" Yes, except the gillie in the morning with food and water—and the rats." Hector gave a slight involuntary shudder. " The place has a name for being haunted, I was told."

" It is the most monstrous, the most intolerable behaviour that ever I heard of! " exclaimed Ewen anew, " and Glenshian shall be made to pay for it somehow! "

" I hope he will," agreed Hector. " I should prefer to make him pay in person, but I do not think, now, that such a course will be easy; he's too surrounded by gillies, to whom his word is law."

" Yes," said Ardroy with a gloomy intonation, " gillies who would swear, no doubt, to anything they were ordered to swear to." He looked across at Ian. " Fine talk on my part, is it not, to speak of making Glenshian pay for this outrage, when, before the year is out, it's likely he will have robbed me of every penny I possess, and more."

" *Au nom de Dieu*, how? " asked Hector with his mouth full.

" By proceeding against me at Inverness for stealing I know not how many head of his cattle. And since you too testify that his gillies———"

But Hector had reached across the table and gripped his brother-in-law's wrist in the clutch of extreme excitement. " Cattle! " he broke in, gulping a little.

" Cattle! That's the reason, then, I suppose . . . cunning devil! . . . But were there only *two* steers?"

" What do you mean—what do you know?" asked Ewen staring at him with some of the same excitement. Ian had jumped to his feet.

" I mean this," said Hector, very fast. " Two branded steers of Glenshian's were found in your herd some time ago, were they not?"

" Yes, yes. But how in heaven's name did you learn that?"

" By means of my Gaelic and the indiscretion of one Somerled MacPhair, who helped to put them there. Those steers, Ewen, were actually driven over to Ardroy two nights previously by Finlay's orders. Then that redheaded——"

" I was sure of it!" cried Ian exultantly in his turn. " I was sure there was something of the sort behind that affair! Ewen, you are saved! He cannot, he dare not proceed, now that we know this!"

The colour mounted into Ardroy's face. " I think I am, perhaps" he said, looking at the late captive in a rather dazed manner. " Tell me that again, Hector— tell me every syllable you overheard!"

CHAPTER XVIII

IAN DOES SOME HARD THINGS

§ 1

Aug. 29th—Sept. 1st.

THE greyness and the damp had lifted, even before the riders entered the gloom of the Dark Mile, and the length of Loch Arkaig, when they came to it, was sparkling in the sun and the breeze. At first the two young men said little to each other, though Hector spoke from time to time in a flippant and rather self-defensive manner about his experiences, much in the same spirit in which he had made Ewen's horse, which he was riding, caracole at starting, with the idea of showing that he was perfectly able to sit it, about which Ewen had expressed himself a little dubious. And indeed those same experiences had left their mark upon Hector, both in his pallor and in the loss of his customary military trimness, though he had somehow contrived to get hold of an indifferent razor from John MacGillonie.

Why, Ian Stewart wondered now, was it so difficult to make the apology for his own past conduct on which he had firmly resolved? Perhaps because it would have come more simply in that moment at Castle Shian, which for other reasons was impossible; perhaps on account of his ex-enemy's present attitude. Yet, though beginning was not easy, he was going to make that apology.

"You must guess, I think, Captain Grant," he said,

in the first convenient pause which ensued, " that I wish to say something to you. I desire to apologise without reserve for what I said that day on the hillside about your lost letter. I never believed it; I was crazy when I spoke."

" Oh, never trouble about that!" replied Hector easily. " I thought you were not yourself that day. . . . As I was saying just now, this man Somerled——"

He was off on his own experiences again, and Ian, who had found his words of regret hard to bring out, harder than he had anticipated, felt distinctly provoked. Surely an apology, made at considerable cost, merited a little more attention than this!

At the next opportunity he resumed doggedly: " I the more regretted what I said, when I heard that you had disappeared and were probably gone to Glenshian, for I feared that it was my repeating his slander which had sent you there to have it out with him."

" Then you were distressing yourself unnecessarily," Hector assured him, " for I should have gone there in any case. I had an old score to pay off. You are too punctilious. Moreover, we settled our difference by Loch Linnhe side—in a way rather unsatisfactory for you, I fear." He glanced at his companion's sling. " I, on my part, am exceedingly sorry to learn that your wound proved so much more serious than I intended—than I knew," he corrected himself.

Why, again, was it that Hector Grant always seemed to him to say the wrong thing? " You had, in short, intended to let me off more lightly?" enquired Ian with colour in his face and rather drily, and, before Hector could reply, added, " Yes, I had my lesson," and went on to talk of other subjects. By the time that their way

turned northward from the shore of Loch Arkaig and
began to mount, the two had subsided into comparative
silence. Yet Ian had meant to let his companion know
that it was anxiety on his behalf which had led him to
take this journey from Appin, in none too good trim himself; but he was not going to do that now. If Captain
Grant had shown the slightest curiosity as to why he
was here, his wound still imperfectly healed . . . but
no! One must, however, make allowances for the strain
of the last week in duresse.

Trying to do so, Ian's thoughts flew to Mr. Maitland,
and thence, naturally enough, to her whose image, for
all his efforts, was not long out of them. The bog-
myrtle still lay near his heart—brittle now and very
fragile. He supposed that the time would come when,
if he continued to carry it upon him, there would be
nothing left of it but small dry fragments. Better to
burn or bury it . . . on the day, perhaps, when he learnt
that she was married—if he ever came to hear of that
inevitable happening. And by this channel his thoughts
returned once more to Maitland. But it was absurd, he
told himself, to imagine that there could be any question
of *that*; Mr. Maitland was too old, and for all Ian knew
might be a married man, though somehow he did not
think he was.

Suddenly his heart beat faster. When Mr. Maitland
was brought to the House of Ardroy he would talk to
him, if he were well enough, about Olivia, but without
revealing his secret. On that he prayed that no obstacle
would occur to prevent that gentleman's speedy transfer-
ence to what Hector Grant, before setting off just now,
had not inaptly characterised as a hospital. And soon
afterwards they themselves arrived at that destination,

to the surprise and joy of Hector's sister, Alison Cameron, the satisfaction of Miss Margaret Cameron, who foresaw work for her skill in the general appearance of the one and the beslinged arm of the other, and the inconvenient curiosity of Donald and little Keith, as to how Cousin Ian's arm came to be in that sling at all.

§ 2

There followed two days of quiet—of quiet and of waiting for the arrival of the master of the house with the third invalid. Hector was a good deal taken up with his sister, and Miss Cameron decreed that Ian (whose long ride had not done his imperfectly-healed wound any good, if it had caused no actual harm) was not to exert himself. Indeed, now that the excitement of Hector's rescue was over Ian had no desire for further forays, and would sit for long periods by Loch na h-Iolaire with a book in his hand which he never read, thinking of his lost love. And also, with an increasing sense of dismay, of Jacqueline's lost lover . . . whom he had driven from her.

For though Hector Grant was perfectly friendly, and though he was here in the flesh within reach of speech, Ian was completely in the dark as to his present matrimonial intentions, which indeed Hector was hardly likely to confide to him again, even if they were unchanged. The position began increasingly to torment the young man; yet how could he, who had told Captain Grant to his face, and with a gross insult, that he should never marry his sister, how could he bring himself to say that he now only hoped that Captain Grant would do so?

And yet, unless Hector himself gave some sign, he would have to say that, for Jacqueline's sake.

So Ewen Cameron, coming, the third afternoon, upon his cousin by the loch, sitting propped up against a tree trunk with his eyes closed, stood looking at him rather ruthfully. Hector, whom he had already seen, appeared in his usual health and spirits, the latter heightened, if anything, by the rage which had been simmering in him since his release. But Ian looked so wan; he ought not to have been brought away from Invernacree . . . Ardroy came quietly nearer and Ian opened his eyes.

"You!" he said, looking up at Ewen in surprise. "When did you arrive? Have you brought Mr. Maitland with you?"

"Yes. I got here about half an hour ago. I am sorry if I woke you."

"You did not wake me. I heard a sound, but thought it was Donald. He was about here a little time ago."

"Was he? Ian, how goes that arm of yours?"

"Excellently, under Miss Cameron's care," answered his cousin. "And now I suppose she will have another patient to tend. How does that poor gentleman?"

"He was well enough to be brought here, and that is all one can say. Aunt Margaret now has him in her clutches. I don't think he was sorry to return to bed again, and, I flatter myself, to a more comfortable one than Mrs. MacGillonie's. I could not question him when I was with him there; I felt a delicacy about it, and moreover he was too ill. But he told me his name— which you had already done—and from some confused remarks which he let fall when feverish I could not avoid gathering that he had been an invited guest at Invershian, and had left hurriedly on account of some disagreement with that hound Finlay MacPhair. He seemed in considerable distress of mind to boot. You say you have met him before?"

"Yes," said Ian, arranging his sling with care. "I met him as I came back from Glasgow not long ago. He was then on his way into these parts."

"And he is, you told me, a Jacobite and a friend of Campbell of Cairns? That's an odd combination," observed Ardroy. "But I suppose it was Cairns himself who gave you that piece of information when he was at Invernacree?"

"No," admitted Ian rather unwillingly. "I did not know of this Mr. Maitland's existence then. It was Miss Campbell who told me . . . afterwards."

"The lady you pulled out of the coach," said Ewen, smiling. "I heard about that from Jacqueline the other day. And that feat, my dear Ian, might have proved the beginning of a very proper romance if the lady had not been of Clan Diarmaid. So it was she who told you this gentleman's history? . . . But what exactly do you mean by ' afterwards '? After you had met him? Where then *did* you meet him?"

There was no answer for a moment.

"Ewen," said the young man then, speaking with difficulty, "did my father say anything to you about . . . Miss Campbell?"

"Not a word. What should he tell me of her?" But Ian seemed unable to inform him. Ewen reached across and laid a hand on his wrist. "Good heavens, Ian . . . not that you *did* fall in love with her?"

But his cousin did not meet his gaze. He was look-ing across the loch. "That seems like Donald, climb-ing the *creag ruadh* yonder," he observed in a dulled voice. " I hope he will not slip." And then, as Ardroy did not even turn his head in the direction of his adventurous offspring, he met his eyes at last, and said, with a little gasp which he could not control, " Ewen, I wish I were dead! "

Ewen said nothing for a moment, but continued to look at him with those steady deepset eyes of his. After a silence he removed his hand. " I am glad you told me," he said gently. " Forgive me for my thoughtless words."

The breeze set the birch foliage over them swaying, and a cone fell with a thud from a neighbouring pine. " This arm of mine," went on Ian at last, without much coherence, " that is the reason . . . though Captain Grant does not even know of Miss Campbell's existence —from me at least. It was because I had said farewell to her for ever—that was up at Kilrain in Perthshire— and I was devilridden because my father had been so harsh. (But that matter's all put right now.) Yet, Ewen, I have perhaps wrecked Jacqueline's happiness too, for I have no notion now whether Captain Grant still intends to ask for her hand."

" Leave Hector to me," said Ewen with a consoling imperturbability. " I'll see to the matter; don't torment yourself over that. 'Tis only natural he should not speak to you of it. But, my poor Ian, I am more sorry for you than I can say. For, of course, there's nothing to be done."

" Nothing," said Ian, leaning his head back against the tree. He thought for a second of their conversation that June night at Invernacree. " Nothing. I recognized that at once. I did fight against it . . . My father has been kind . . . but I'll have to make my suit to Miss

Maclean in the end. . . . Sometimes I feel as if I were dead already, and that all this—even your beautiful loch —is an illusion. The last real water I saw was a burn in a wood at Kilrain."

His cousin did not try to offer him any consolation, for which Ian was grateful. What would be the use of being told, " You will forget her in time? " Either he should never do so, which was what he firmly believed, or he would hate to think that his memory of Olivia Campbell could ever be dimmed, were it by the passing of centuries.

" I think I see Hector coming to find me," said Ardroy, breaking the silence. " He is eager for a conference as to the next move against Glenshian. Shall we have it here and now?"

Ian nodded and got to his feet. Before Hector came up a mute hand clasp—no more—had passed between the cousins over the grave of Ian's stricken romance.

§ 3

But for twenty minutes or so after that the quiet shore of the little Loch of the Eagle rang with the expression of Captain Hector Grant's desire for vengeance, all the more fiery for having been kept some days in leash. And yet it was difficult to see how this desire was to find fulfilment, since Hector would not hear of any civil suit against Glenshian, his pride not enduring the prospect of having to stand up in court and admit that he, a Grant and a soldier, had been chained by the middle to a wall like a bear or a monkey. On the other hand, personal and individual vengeance, as he had just learnt to his cost, was too short in the arm to reach the well-guarded Chief, and a clan foray was impossible in these degenerate days. At last Ian, who was really more concerned with his cousin's case than with Hector's, suggested that the latter might perhaps find his best available satisfaction in checkmating Glenshian's monstrous design of ruining Ardroy—which must lie near the Chief's heart since he had taken so much trouble over the preliminaries. By what Hector had overheard, however, *he* now held the key to that position. And having learnt from his sister and Miss Cameron of the cloud of anxiety under which all at Ardroy had lately been living, Captain Grant agreed to this course, lukewarmly at first, abandoning with reluctance his taste for proceedings more violent and personal; then with a rush of something like remorse for not having sooner regarded the situation from Ewen's point of view.

"Indeed, my dear Ewen," he said, "I might have had the good feeling to think of this before, after your coming the way you did, almost single-handed——"

"Don't forget Ian," put in Ardroy.

"Faith, no, I'm not forgetting him.—We will do that, then, *Eoghain mhóir*, having such an excellent stick to threaten Mac 'ic Fhionnlaigh with. Yet, by the powers, I'm not going to leave him my horse and valise as a gift! You must demand those back, Ewen."

"I will," said Ardroy. Like Hector, he would much have preferred a more personal reckoning, but on the other hand he could scarcely yet fathom the depth of the relief which had come to him from the possession of that "stick" against Glenshian's machinations. Life had taken on a different complexion these last few days. "I will write a letter to Glenshian without delay, saying that I know he had those steers driven in among my cattle, and for what purpose; and that if he proceeds further against me not only shall I bring forward this damning fact, but Captain Grant will take action against him for assault and unlawful detention. That ought to give him his quietus—even though the part about Hector be only a threat. I will also demand the return of your horse and effects, Hector, by the hand of the gillie who takes the letter to Invershian."

They were all walking now in the direction of the house, but Ewen being intercepted, when they got round the loch, by one of his tenants who desired to speak to him, the two younger men found themselves alone together for the first time, as it happened, since they had ridden to Ardroy.

They went on in silence for a little while, Hector pulling a grass stalk thoughtfully between his teeth. At last he said, as if to himself, "Yes, I ought to have seen it in that light before. Poor Ewen, to think of that scoundrel having him on the rack all these weeks! Then you were here, Mr. Stewart, when the steers which he had sent on purpose were found—that almost incredible piece of villainy?"

Ian nodded. For the last minute or two his thoughts had left Finlay MacPhair and his victims to think of his own—Jacqueline. Ewen had indeed announced his intention of broaching that topic to Jacqueline's swain in order to save his cousin from drinking the worst of the draught which he saw ahead of him; but was *that* keeping his own promise to his little sister? The prospect was damnably unpleasant, but there was a strain in Ian Stewart which made him contemplate doing the thing for that very reason. He looked round; Ewen had gone off with the tacksman and they were unlikely to be interrupted.

"Captain Grant," he said, coming to a stop beneath a birch tree, "I have apologised to you for my . . . indefensible conduct, and you, I think, accepted the apology. But there's something else . . ." Here he stuck.

"Yes?" said Hector, throwing away the grass stalk.

"The . . . the original matter in question—I want to speak of that. My own extreme folly has made that difficult now."

"You refer to your sister," said Hector at once. "My suit to her offended you. I never thought that you in your heart believed the monstrous charge you made against me, and you have acknowledged that you did not. But you must pardon me for thinking that, if you had recourse to such a weapon in order to show your disapproval, you would dislike me as a brother-in-law very much indeed."

He had in truth put the case in a nutshell. Ian studied the heather at his feet. "I was crazy that day . . . And now, having paid pretty dearly for that madness, I have to ask you——" It was almost impossible to bring out the words.

"Whether I mean to pursue my suit," finished Hector quietly. There was no ungenerous exultation in his manner, but nothing, either, to blink the fact that it was this moment, and not that on Loch Linnhe shore, when he had run his traducer through the arm, which was repaying him for those wild words under the pine-clump. "But, Mr. Stewart, if I am to have your continued enmity on that score to reckon with——"

Ian's face was drained of colour. This was a strain

alike on pride and on bodily nerves. "If that were the case I should not have accompanied Ardroy from Appin with some hope of helping you out of Glenshian's clutches." It was not agreeable to plead this fact, especially as Captain Grant immediately responded, "You mean to say that you left home in that condition," he pointed to the sling, "on my account?"

"Only partly," muttered Ian. "Yet 'twas the least I could do, in the circumstances." Then he set his lips to the cup. "Mr. Grant, knowing now, as I did not earlier, my sister Jacqueline's sentiments, I can only hope that you—that you will fulfil the intention you announced of approaching my father on the matter."

The frustrated suitor was staring at him with such a curious expression that Ian felt a terrible sinking at the heart, and thought, "I have done it—I have ruined Jacqueline's life . . . unless she gets over her feeling for him!" and the blood beat so in his brain that he surreptitiously put out his only available hand towards the tree near him in order to steady himself. After a moment he saw, to his surprise, that Hector Grant was holding out one of his.

"Egad, I could not have done that!" he was saying frankly. "Mr. Stewart, I give you best! Let me also have the honour of telling you that I have not wavered an instant from my intention of asking for your sister in marriage."

Ian removed his left hand from the satin-smooth birch trunk upon which it rested, and it went into both of the late victor's.

CHAPTER XIX

§ 1

Sept. 2nd—5th.

NEXT morning Ewen stood by David Maitland's bedside and asked in his deep, gentle voice whether he was well enough to receive Captain Hector Grant, who owed so much to him, and desired to render thanks in person.

To Maitland, lying there clear at last of the circling mists of fever and weakness, his host appeared about eight feet high. A splendid fir-tree of a man—he remembered his carrying him up some stair or other; he remembered too, if dimly, his care of him in the succeeding two days. Now he had even more to thank Ewen Cameron for, and with a less clouded consciousness of it—his recent transportation hither, into the guardianship of this competent elderly lady. Camerons both, it was true; but he *had* done them a service . . .

"I shall be very pleased to see Captain Grant," he answered now; "but indeed I have no need of thanks." What would this handsome auburn-haired giant say if he were to add: "'Tis I who ought to thank Captain Grant, for I owe him, in a sense, my life?"

"Well, I'll not let him thank you overlong," said Ewen, smiling down upon him. Gratitude apart, he found this Mr. Maitland, with his refined and scholarly face, an attractive person even in illness, and the fact that he himself had nursed the poor gentleman for two days, without any adequate feminine aid, gave him a kind of proprietary feeling about the invalid.

At the door he turned, remembering something.

"By the way, sir, I am just on the point of sending a messenger to MacPhair of Glenshian demanding the immediate return of Captain Grant's horse and valise. Am I right in supposing that your effects also are at Invershian, because in that case I shall very willingly——"

He stopped, astonished at the hot colour which had flooded over the delicate, bloodless features on the pillow, at the look, as of extreme distaste, which contracted the mouth and brow.

"I . . . I thank you, Mr. Cameron. I prefer to hold no communication of any kind with Mr. MacPhair . . . I doubt not that later on——" He broke off, biting his lip.

"Certainly, we will leave the matter exactly as you please," said Ewen soothingly. "Communications with Glenshian are no pleasure to me either.—Yes, Hector, you can come in, but you are not to stay for more than ten minutes."

If the late captive was debarred by this fiat from spending long in the sickroom he made the best use of his time, and there was no doubt of the sincerity of his gratitude. Never, he declared, would he have suggested to Mr. Maitland such a journey, upon so wet a night, too, had he known that his benefactor was only recently risen from a sickbed. Maitland felt that this frank young man would probably have welcomed some corresponding frankness on his own part as to what he, fresh from that retreat, had been doing in that lonely spot in such weather and at so late an hour; but he naturally did not enlighten him, even though Mr. Grant showed, by what he said, that he supposed the invalid's previous illness to have taken place at Invershian, and though he gave him a summary of Finlay's behaviour to himself, without, however, acquainting his listener with the precise nature of the slander which he had gone to force Finlay to retract.

When he had left him David Maitland lay for a while in a kind of shuddering irritation. Why would everyone speak to him of Finlay MacPhair, that spider from whose web he had just broken free? He desired never to hear his name again. Glenshian might keep his horse and clothes for ever, for all he cared; he had sufficient money with him; he could buy or hire another horse and no doubt borrow a cloak. Yes, he had broken out of Finlay's web; that infamous schemer did not, probably, know where he was now, and he much preferred to feel that it was so. The air seemed easier to breathe.

For all that, Maitland was scolded when Miss Margaret Cameron came in, to find him flushed, and was told that he might have no more visitors till the morrow. And gradually the silence, the peace of the old house and his own weakness all worked to banish those repugnant memories; he ceased to see the sneer and the uncomfortable greenish-yellow eyes looking at him from the foot of the bed, and sank into a beneficent torpor and forgetfulness.

Next day his wardress pronounced herself more satisfied with him, and that no doubt was why, between sleeping and waking, he had a brief glimpse of a lady, still young, with an infant in her arms and a beautiful dark-haired child clinging to her skirts; and for one moment he was dreamily back in Italy years ago as a young man, look-

ing at an altarpiece in a little mountain church and wishing, for all his staunch Presbyterianism, that he could
take it home with him. Then he realised that this was no
Popish Madonna; it must be Ewen Cameron's wife with
her children. The little boy seemed much interested in
him, and his mother, smiling, had to whisper to him to
come away.

In the afternoon, feeling much more himself again,
he was lying listening to the childish tones and laughter
which floated in now and then with the sunlight through
the open window, when there came a discreet tap at the
door, a male voice asked permission to enter, and there
walked in, to Maitland's surprise, the young man whom
he had last consciously seen with Olivia Campbell upon
the hill road at Kilrain. He had his right arm in a sling.

"Mr. Stewart—Mr. Stewart of Invernacree, is it
not?" asked the invalid, slightly raising himself.

"The same, sir. I am glad to hear that you are so
much better. I have Miss Cameron's permission to pay
you a visit. I hope that I have yours also?"

"I am so completely in Miss Cameron's hands," replied Maitland, smiling, "that, even if I wished, I could
scarcely withhold it—not that I wish to. Sit down, pray,
Mr. Stewart. It is a surprise to see you here."

"I visit here occasionally, for Ardroy is my first
cousin," explained Ian, not enlarging upon the special
reasons for his presence this time. But Maitland, now
beginning to feel in a dim way that he had caught sight
of him that night at MacGillonie's house, asked whether
he had not played a part in the rescue of Captain Grant
from the ruined castle. Ian replied that he had, though
a very minor one; on which Maitland not unnaturally
said, " I suppose you took some injury to your arm in

that business? I did not know that there had been any affray over it."

" Nor was there," replied Ian, colouring. " I got this injury otherwise." He talked on indifferent topics for a while, and then asked whether Mr. Maitland had lately received any news of Miss Campbell. A few minutes sufficed to make it clear, even to the perceptions of an invalid, that Miss Campbell was the very subject about which he had come to converse. But this did not surprise David Maitland. Had not his " god-daughter " stayed a week under old Mr. Stewart's roof, and had not this young man been given the priceless privilege of rescuing her from a position of danger? If he had lost his heart it was not to be wondered at; what concerned Maitland was the state of Olivia's. What had the two, for instance, been saying to each other up the brae at Kilrain— why, in fact, had Ian Stewart been there at all? Olivia was kindhearted, but she did not suffer suitors over-gladly; yet Maitland knew from Mrs. MacUre that his present visitor had not only called at the cottage that morning and borne Olivia off for a walk, but had also had an interview with her alone the day before. So, lying there, he paid particular attention to Mr. Ian Stewart of Invernacree, and came to the conclusion that he liked what he saw of him, reserved young man as he seemed, but with a smile—probably rare—which quite transfigured his dark, intent face.

And when he had gone David Maitland lay thinking of Olivia, of Olivia whose home he had not visited (as she had pointed out at Kilrain) for more than two years —not since he had had blood upon his soul. But he still breathed the same air as she did. Should he not thank God for having held him back from the sin of suicide?

Dulled by illness, his own self-loathing had grown a little less sharp since that night; and he knew that Finlay MacPhair would never betray what he knew of him because it would go counter to that horrible and mercenary hope of his, which, for all that Maitland knew, he might still be cherishing in some modified form. This revived interest in Olivia's future stirred in his heart as the snowdrop's little green spear pushes through the frozen soil. If Olivia were really inclining to this young Stewart, and if he were worthy of her (or approximately so) then he might consider the means of aiding him. There was, it could not be denied, the gulf of clan and political hostility to be bridged, if possible. If only he knew what Olivia herself felt about the matter! Young Invernacree had not confided in him— why should he?—and had given him no inkling of the terms on which Miss Campbell and he had parted. He must learn more of him; in the days which must elapse before he could leave the house of Ardroy he might, per- haps, be able to penetrate his reserve. He wondered if Mr. Stewart's cousin, his host, knew anything of this attach- ment?

Maitland was vaguely thinking of Ewen Cameron, of this home of his, which seemed so pleasant, and the children—he supposed that they were his—whose prattle he had smiled over, when he heard Mr. Cameron's very voice, unmistakable in its tones, somewhere close below the open window. It sounded hurried.

"Ian, Ian, I want you! Where were you? Listen; the gillie I sent to Invershian with my letter has just returned empty-handed. It appears that MacPhair is away from home—or so he was told by those at the house. Consequently he had to leave my letter until such time

as Finlay should return, and to come back without
Hector's horse and effects."

The invalid heard his late visitor give an exclamation
of annoyance.

"And Hector must delay his visit to Glenmoriston no
longer," went on Ardroy. " He is much needed there.
I will lend him a horse."

" Do you think," asked Ian Stewart's voice, " that
Glenshian is really from home? "

" How can one say? Probably not . . . but he finds
it more convenient at this juncture to feign absence. . . .
Yet he is no coward, Finlay MacPhair, for all that he
betrayed Archie to his death."

Maitland, rigid, held his breath.

" But, Ewen," began Ian Stewart in lowered accents,
so much lowered that nothing of what he said was audible
in the room above save four words at the end. And they
were: " unknown man . . . information " and " Glenbuckie."

" Yes, I know that," responded Ardroy's deeper tones.
Evidently he had no idea how far they carried. " But
that man was Finlay's tool, probably his paid tool—I am
convinced of it. Sometimes I dream that I am meeting
him, and—" He checked himself. " But enough of that
subject. You must help me to persuade Hector to delay
no longer, but to set out at once for his inheritance. I had
rather, too, he were gone from these parts lest, after all,
he and Glenshian—" The two moved away out of
hearing.

Above, in Ardroy's best spare bed, David Maitland lay
like an effigy upon a tomb. Even here! . . . Yet, of
course, here—for in any Cameron house he might expect
to hear talk of Doctor Cameron's fate. . . . But not to

find it known that someone had sent intelligence from that obscure glen in Balquhidder. "*Finlay's tool. . . . his paid tool.*" "*Sometimes I dream that I am meeting him.*" Ewen Cameron had no need any longer to dream that. "O God!" said the betrayer, and threw his arm across his eyes.

§ 2

A couple of days later, in the early afternoon, Ian and Ardroy came slowly back from Loch na h-Iolaire with their fishing rods, and with five-year old Keith trotting between them, holding a hand of each, and making them laugh by his development of a theme of his own about caterpillars, in which creatures he was at this epoch deeply interested.

Hector, on the horse the loan of which had been more or less forced upon him, had been successfully persuaded to set off for Glenmoriston. Before he went he had sought out Ian, and had told him that he intended to present himself at Invernacree in about a couple of weeks' time to make a formal demand for the hand of his younger sister, and that he hoped he might rely upon Ian's support in the matter. Ian not only promised this, but offered on his own return to try to prepare the ground a little, on which the grateful suitor brought out a letter addressed to his lady-love. If Mr. Stewart would have the goodness to charge himself with that. . . .

"But I am not returning home for a while yet," Ian reminded the writer. "Perhaps you would rather find a speedier messenger?"

"I doubt if I could," Hector had replied. "And I

could not find one to whom I would sooner commit my correspondence."

"You honour me," replied Ian, not formally, to match the words, but giving his late foe that smile which was, as David Maitland had guessed, so telling if (or perhaps because) it was somewhat infrequent. And he took the letter. "None the less, if I have the chance, I will, if you permit it, send this on, for I am sure it is eagerly awaited." And as a matter of fact, he had found and seized such an opportunity soon after Hector's departure.

So he had fulfilled his promise to Jacqueline and laid at last the ghost of that unworthy impulse to deny her the happiness which he might not have himself. He hoped that she *would* be happy with Hector Grant; he had never thought to like him so well as he had the last few days. . . .

"Mr. Maitland is out of bed to-day, is he not?" he now asked suddenly. "—Very well, Keithie, if you think you can jump that little juniper you can but try!"

"Yes," answered Ardroy. "But, though I suppose he is better, he looks little better to me. He has at times so unhappy an air, as though he had somewhat on his mind. And from various things he let fall during those two days at MacGillonie's, I am sure he has, though I've no notion what it is."

"Something to do with his sudden departure from Invershian, perhaps," suggested Ian. "Although, to be sure, even before that he looked. . . ." He stopped reflectively.

"There is certainly something much amiss in that quarter," agreed Ewen. "And it was uncommonly odd of him to refuse the chance which I offered him the other day of recovering his horse from Glenshian. I told you, did I not, how the very idea seemed to horrify him? Yet I suppose—since he did not deny it—that his horse *is* at Invershian, and his clothes? He can hardly have travelled thither completely without effects. Was he mounted when you came upon him on your way back from Glasgow? "

" Yes, and had a valise on his saddle. The horse, of course, may have been hired."

Ewen shrugged his shoulders. " Well, 'tis no concern of ours, and I would not for worlds have Mr. Maitland think either that I am curious about his private affairs or that, owing him so much on Hector's account, I grudge him a nightshirt and razor, and the loan of a horse when the time comes. If he has quarrelled with Glenshian I but think the better of him for it.—Donald, haven't you yet learnt that it is useless to try and outrace Luath? "

For here his eldest son, who some while ago had vanished ahead, panted up breathless and crimson-cheeked in the wake of the great deerhound with his long easy motion.

" I wasn't racing him," he gasped, thrusting his hand into his parent's. " Father, do you know, there are soldiers coming up the avenue! "

Such potent memories of old perils hung round the phrase that Ardroy instinctively stopped, and even changed colour a little.

"—But I think one of them is Captain Paton, and I like him," finished Donald, regaining more breath. "There's a lady too riding with him. Perhaps the other soldier is an orderly, for he is riding some way behind."

" A lady? Mrs. Paton, perhaps.—The child gave me quite a fright," added Ewen under his breath to his cousin.

" You were not the only one alarmed," confessed

Ian. "Who is this Captain Paton approved of by Donald? "

" And by me also, for the matter of that. He is an old acquaintance of mine from '46—a very good fellow. Surely I have told you about him before now? He has been quartered at Fort William for some time, and occasionally rides over to pay us a visit; but he has never brought his wife with him before. She must have come to enquire after Alison—very civil of her."

By the time, however, that the little party got round the house to the porch only one scarlet-coated figure was to be seen there, just remounting with the reins of the other two horses over his arm. One of them bore a lady's saddle. Seeing Ardroy the soldier saluted.

" I was just about to take these 'orses round to the stable, sir, if convenient? "

" Do so by all means," said Ewen; and, aside to his cousin, " Did you ever expect to see me saluted by a *saighdear dearg?* As a matter of fact he *is* Paton's orderly. I expect we shall find Paton and his wife with Alison in the parlour. I should like to make you acquainted with him."

Outside the parlour door, when the two fishermen had got rid of the traces of their pursuit, they found Donald, a self-posted sentinel, important with information.

" It is Captain Paton, Father—I thought it was! But 'tis not Mrs. Paton with him—'tis a lady come from Fort William to ask news of the sick gentleman upstairs."

" News of Mr. Maitland," said Ewen, looking down at his heir. " Well, fortunately we can give the lady a tolerably good account. I wonder who she is—his wife, perhaps . . . What, are you not coming in after all, Ian? "

For his kinsman, a moment ago close upon his heels, was now several feet away, looking as if he had received a shock of some kind.

"I . . . yes . . . it would be strange if . . . no, it cannot be!" was his not very coherent reply. Then, making an effort to pull himself together, he said in a more rational tone, "Yes, I am coming in with you."

CHAPTER XX

IN A GREEN RIDING HABIT

Sept. 5th (continued).

IAN STEWART had thus had a moment's warning of whom—incredible though it seemed—he might find in Lady Ardroy's parlour. But the girl in the green riding costume who sat talking to her hostess in the large sunlit room, with the English officer standing beside her chair, had received no warning at all of who was to find her there. And, looking up as the door opened, she saw behind the master of the house a figure. . . . The colour rose in her face with the shock, rose and stayed there, burning. . . .

"Ewen," said his wife, "let me present you to Miss Campbell of Cairns, who has come over under Captain Paton's escort from Fort William to enquire for Mr. Maitland, an old family friend."

"Yes, I told Father outside that was what she had come for," observed Donald in a satisfied undertone.

Ewen bowed; Olivia curtseyed. Then it was Ian's turn. In a dream he heard some words or other of presentation; he fancied he heard Olivia saying that they had met already—at Invernacree. Her face swam before him under the little three-cornered riding hat which sat so deliciously upon her dark curls. The last time he had seen that face . . . unbelievable, impossible! . . . it had been very close to his, upon his breast. Still more incredible—he had kissed it. . . .

But now she did not meet his eyes—chance or design?

She had seated herself again, and was talking with animation to her host and hostess. On one side the long green habit lay in folds upon the floor, and Keithie, approaching, stationed himself upon it and looked at her gravely. Olivia put an arm round him as she talked, and he leant against her—a beautiful, dark-haired child such as one day, perhaps, she would have for her own . . . a child such as they two might have had. It hurt so bitterly that Ian could not bear the thought nor the picture which had suggested it, and he quietly removed himself so that he was more or less behind her, and could not see the little boy at all.

All these miles to visit Mr. Maitland! And supposing that he himself had been out, hours away on the hills, and had returned to find her come and gone? How much better! . . . No: a perfect sea of desolation engulfed him at the mere thought of such a disaster. Better this—though he could scarcely endure it—better at least to be able from where he stood to see the turn of her neck, the little tendril of hair by her ear. . . . Why had he not kissed that too when he had the chance?

Distinguishable words now broke through the sort of coma which enwrapped him. They were in Alison's voice.

"You would no doubt like to see Mr. Maitland himself for a few moments, Miss Campbell? I will go and ask my aunt about it, and prepare him for your visit.— You need not start back for a while yet, I am sure, Captain Paton."

"We must not delay too long, madam," said the soldier, as he went and opened the door for her. He had hardly shut it again before Ardroy was bending over the visitor.

" Miss Campbell, I want to ask Captain Paton's advice about a horse of mine. Will you forgive us if we leave you to be entertained by Mr. Stewart, since he already has the privilege of your acquaintance? Paton, you will not object, will you? I cannot make out what is wrong with the beast.—Come along with me, boys, to the stables."

He removed his younger son, who showed signs of reluctance, bodily from his station against Miss Campbell's chair; and in about thirty seconds Ian and Olivia were the only people left in the room.

Ian came forward then; he had to. Olivia also turned her head a little; and then they both said the same thing in voices of varying degrees of embarrassment:

" I had no notion I should find you here. . . ."

Despite the fact that of the two Miss Campbell was the more seriously handicapped by her memories, she was the first to recover from that embarrassment—or, at least, to affect recovery. She said, changing her position a little, and with some of her natural vivacity, " You have been told why I am here, Mr. Stewart, but I am still in the dark as to why you are! "

" Ardroy is my first cousin," said Ian briefly, as he had said to Mr. Maitland. But in Maitland's presence he had not felt so breathless.

" I did not know that! " remarked Olivia in a tone of surprise.

" But why are you in these parts at all?" asked the young man, words coming more easily now. " I thought you were returning home from Kilrain."

" It was my intention. But, before I left, there came a letter from my father enclosing one from my kinswoman Euphemia Campbell, who is married to an officer stationed at Fort William, proposing that I should visit them. My father wished me to go, so I went thither direct from Perthshire. And there, after a day or two, I heard that Mr. Maitland was lying ill at a farmhouse on Loch Lochy. My host was good enough to send a messenger to enquire, and the news was brought back that Mr. Maitland had been conveyed by Mr. Ewen Cameron of Ardroy to his own house. And while I was uneasy, wondering how he did, and how I should obtain further news of him, my kinswoman remembered her husband having mentioned to her that a brother officer, a Captain Paton, was a friend of Mr. Cameron's; and so this visit of mine has come about. But I did not guess. . . ."

The even fluency of her explanation of her presence failed suddenly, and she sat looking down at her hands in silence. Ian was silent too. The same memory was in the mind of each, the same place before their eyes, the same sound in their ears—the murmur of a tiny burn in a little oak wood. And it was plain what Olivia was thinking of, for a lovely colour began to rise once more and stain her cheek.

Suddenly she lifted her eyes. " You are an invalid too, I see, Mr. Stewart, for you carry your arm in a sling. I hope the injury is not serious? "

"I shall soon discard the scarf," said he, gazing at her.

" I am glad. . . It was good of Mr. Cameron to bring Mr. Maitland here. I wonder how he came on him."

" Mr. Maitland did a kinsman of his a service—Lady Ardroy's brother, to be exact. My cousin was only too glad to take charge of him."

" Has he been very ill—Mr. Maitland? "

Some perverse impulse tempted Ian to reply, " Not so

ill as I have," but he conquered it and contented himself with saying, "He was already better when he was brought here, and does well now; he has left his bed. But you will soon, doubtless, see his state for yourself."

Olivia was now looking across the room, out of the window. "This is fine country. I have enjoyed my ride. The sun shone all the way."

"Even in the Dark Mile?" asked Ian.

"The Dark Mile?" said she, struck by the name. "What is that?"

"Only a stretch of the road between Loch Lochy and Loch Arkaig which goes by that name—I do not know why, save that, what with trees and high crags, it is gloomy there."

"I think I remember the place," said Miss Campbell. She rose and went slowly to the window. Ian stayed where he was. Sitting in a chair in Alison Cameron's parlour, Olivia Campbell was a gentlewoman of birth and breeding come to pay a call; over there, standing by the open window, with the air of the hills blowing in upon her, she might resemble too much the Highland girl whom he had helped over the stepping-stones, and he might a second time . . . It was safer not to risk it. Yet he laid hold of the back of a heavy chair as a kind of anchor.

Then the door handle turned and Lady Ardroy came in, to find half the room between the two. But the danger was over, and Ian did not care at that moment what Alison thought of his manners. She went over to the guest.

"I see that you are looking at our prospect, Miss Campbell. It would be a great pleasure to Mr. Maitland to see you, and my aunt thinks it would do him good. Will you please to come with me? "

Olivia thanked her. Ian held the door open for the two of them, and Miss Campbell as she passed him, the folds of her habit on her arm, looked at him with a smile which he could not interpret. He stood there a moment like a dummy, still clasping the doorknob; then he shut the door rather hard. Next he found himself gazing at the chair where she had sat. He touched it; it was still warm, and, as no one could see him, he bent suddenly and kissed one of the arms.

After that he wandered about the room, thinking, Is she seeing him alone, and what is she saying to him? and trying to deduce, from Alison Cameron's continued absence, that she perhaps considered herself necessary as a duenna in the sick man's chamber. Then Ewen and Captain Paton came in again, and Ian made the better acquaintance of the English officer, who was after all a Lowland Scot. He and Ardroy seemed on very good terms, but Ian knew that this was less a testimony to the measure of peace and settlement which was gradually coming to the Highlands, than to their own earlier relations during the Forty-five.

And then both Lady Ardroy and Miss Cameron came in. So Olivia *had* been left alone with Mr. Maitland after all! Jealously the young man counted the minutes by the clock—eleven, twelve, thirteen. At the fourteenth the door opened and she entered. Nearly a quarter of an hour!

Refreshments were brought, and there was much talk of the part Mr. Maitland had played in Hector's affair, and of Ewen's gratitude on his behalf. Ian stood aside from it. Shortly afterwards, as he had foreseen, Captain Paton said they ought to be starting back, the horses were ordered round, and everybody gathered outside to see the riders off. It was Ewen who had the honour of mounting Miss Campbell, but Ian handed her her riding-switch, and for a moment his fingers touched hers.

"I hope your arm will soon be completely recovered, Mr. Stewart," she said kindly.

"I thank you, Miss Campbell," he replied with formality, and stood back at once, to circumvent an insensate desire which had rushed upon him to lay hold of her bridle and detain her.

Then she rode away down the avenue, his lost love, the scarlet-coated officer very attentive. Ardroy thrust his arm through Ian's as they returned to the house, but he said nothing; nor did Ian thank him for so considerately and swiftly removing Captain Paton and the children from the room. For one thing, he was by no means sure that he had reason to be grateful.

"So that is the young lady you rescued!" observed Alison. "She is so charming that I vow I forgot she was a Campbell!"

"And no kinswoman of Mr. Maitland's after all, as I hear," said Miss Cameron. "'Tis plain, therefore, that she came all this way in order to see you, her rescuer, Mr. Stewart."

"Since Miss Campbell had not the slightest notion that I was here, madam, that can hardly be," replied Ian as indifferently as he could.

"As if she would have avowed her knowledge of it!" scoffed Aunt Margaret. "'Tis pity, though, she had no chance of a word with you alone. Alison, you should have contrived it!"

"But——" began Alison——and was silenced by a look from her husband.

" Well, I expect to find the gentleman upstairs, who did see the bonny young lady alone, greatly set up thereby," announced Aunt Margaret, as she began to mount the stairs again, leaving the young man to whom that privilege had also been vouchsafed, by no means set up by it.

CHAPTER XXI

§ 1

Sept. 6th.

NOR, really, was it a condition of exhilaration in which Olivia's visit had left Mr. Maitland. Keen as his pleasure had been in seeing her again, much as he wanted, for her own sake, to discover her feelings about Ian Stewart, if she had but come two days earlier, before he had overheard that conversation beneath his window, he could have given her what she had always had from him—his whole attention. But almost every moment since that conversation had been for him a long and torturing warfare. There was a moral question to which he could find no certain answer. Was he bound to betray and incriminate himself in order to clear Finlay MacPhair from Ewen Cameron's accusation—Finlay who was only too anxious to claim the guilt of it, Finlay who had behaved so atrociously in that regard? Was *he* to tell Ewen Cameron whom he was harbouring, merely in order to lift the charge of final accomplishment of that bitterly regretted deed from the man who had " done the preliminary work " for it, and who would have given so much to have had Maitland's " luck "—the chance of sending that message about Glenbuckie? Must he do this?

9*

It was not fear for his own physical safety which held him back; Maitland was beyond caring for that now. It was the thought of the fearful shock which he should give to all in this house, where he had been made the centre of so much care and gratitude. His soul quailed at the idea, just because he liked them all so much, from his tall host down to his younger son, that little Keithie who had now been permitted to visit him in his room, and had there brought him an offering of a large moth and some exceedingly damp moss in a saucer.

He could face the prospect still less after Olivia's visit. She also would hear of the terrible revelation, through Ian Stewart if from no other source. It was too much to expect of him. In intention Finlay *was* guilty. He himself must get well and leave the neighbourhood as quickly as possible. The sooner therefore that he recovered the full use of his legs the better; and so next afternoon, half against Miss Cameron's wishes, he left his room and came downstairs.

In the big, pleasant parlour he found his hostess with her baby in her arms, the two boys playing in a corner, and Ardroy himself, who seemed just to have come in, for he had a fowling piece in his hand. Young Invernacree was not there. Warmly welcomed, the convalescent was conducted to the most comfortable chair near the hearth; there was question of lighting a fire for him; the children came running and little Keith showed a disposition to climb upon his knee.

And then all at once Maitland's eyes, straying up to the high mantel in front of him, beheld there, hanging under the antlers, a framed engraving which he might not have recognised but for the inscription. But that showed all too clear: "A True Effigies of Doctor Archibald Cameron, who lately suffered Death at Tyburn for High Treason."

It was like a blow on the head. The room whirled round him, yet still, by some awful magnetism, the picture held his gaze. He instinctively repulsed little Keith.

"I see that you are looking at the portrait of my unfortunate kinsman, Doctor Cameron," said Ardroy's voice through the mist. "I bought it last October in Edinburgh, although it little resembles him. But I had no other likeness."

Maitland wrenched his eyes away, murmuring some confused words of sympathy. The room had steadied itself, but his mouth was dry. Not that he feared discovery; for discovery—unless he betrayed himself—was practically impossible.

"He—Doctor Cameron—was a kinsman of yours?" he stammered out.

"He was my second cousin. But he was dearer to me than an elder brother would perhaps have been," answered Ardroy quietly, but with a note in his voice which made Maitland shiver. How could he ever tell him who was sitting there among them all?

It was too horrible. He wished with all his heart that he had remained in his room. He managed to answer the questions addressed to him by Miss Cameron, who fortunately came in at that moment, thereby creating a diversion; then, glancing at the window, he said, trying not to show the sense of suffocation which he felt:

"It seems a fine day; would it be possible for me to take a turn outside?"

"By all means," responded his host instantly. "I will come with you; you'll certainly need an arm. Donald, go and fetch Mr. Maitland a plaid or a cloak."

Maitland could not refuse that arm; indeed he was glad of support, for he found himself a good deal weaker than he had anticipated. Well, he had only to keep his head—and hope that there would be no more actual talk of Archibald Cameron.

But unfortunately Donald, who had come out with them, seemed inclined to pursue the subject, even if his father did not. For as they paced slowly to and fro in the sun in front of the old grey house, Maitland leaning slightly upon Ardroy's arm, the little boy on his other side remarked:

"Doctor Cameron came here once, Mr. Maitland, to cure Keithie when he was ill, and after that he was hidden in Angus's cottage up at Sloc nan Eun.—Oh, Father,"—he peered round the invalid,—"perhaps that is a secret, and I ought not to have told it?"

"It does not matter now, Donald," said his father, with so much sadness in his voice that Maitland was like to withdraw his arm. "Moreover, Mr. Maitland is one of us; he's a Jacobite too."

So Donald resumed: "And the redcoats took Father to Fort William because Doctor Cameron had been here, and he was there in prison a long time, and Uncle Hector too, and then they—"

"Never mind, Donald," interrupted Ardroy. "It will not interest Mr. Maitland to hear my adventures. And I think you had better run off now; you are fatiguing him, hanging on like that."

"Am I, sir?" asked Donald, looking up at the convalescent with his clear child's eyes. "I am so sorry." Maitland was not ready with an answer, but he held the boy's hand tighter, because in truth he did not wish to find himself alone with Ewen Cameron just then. But Ewen

himself said, a little peremptorily, " Off with you, now!"
and Donald, trained like most children in those days to
instant obedience, said cheerfully, " Yes, Father," and
ran back to the house.

" Nevertheless I am glad that my sons are able to remember Archibald Cameron," observed Ardroy after a
moment, " though they will never know the full extent of
the loss which they sustained when he laid down his life.
As a Jacobite, Mr. Maitland, you must recognise the great-
ness of the blow to the Cause, but, had you known Archibald Cameron personally, you would deplore much more
than that—the death of one of the best and noblest-
hearted men whom you could possibly have met.—But I
do not know why I am assuming that you were not
acquainted with him? You may have met him somewhere,
perhaps, during the Rising? "

Maitland had to pause to get his voice. Even then it
came with a gasp. " No . . . never."

Ewen looked at him in anxiety. " You are fatigued, sir
—this exertion is too much for you. Let me help you to
that bench yonder." His arm under the invalid's, he
guided him to it, and Maitland sank down, looking
ghastly enough to give colour to Ardroy's deduction.

He *was* near fainting, and yet he was not, for his senses
were not numbed; they felt sharper than usual and more
swift in operation. At the impact of that direct question
his first impulse had been an instantaneous, crazy desire
to say, " Yes, I knew him," and then to confess everything, whatever might be the consequences to himself.
But, almost as swiftly, came the knowledge that that
relief was impossible. As he had already felt, and felt
now ten times more acutely, to say, " It was I who
betrayed him," would be like driving a dirk into the breast

of the man beside him. It might be a sort of expiation for himself, but it could be nothing but a tragedy for Ewen Cameron. Even if he desired vengeance, as, being a High-lander, he probably did; even though he could now have it in full measure, Maitland knew in his soul that gratified revenge itself would be as nothing, weighed against the shock of the revelation. So there remained only one thing to do: to deny ever having met or seen Archibald Cameron.

"You should not have come out into the air," said Ewen solicitously, as he bent over him. "I'll go and fetch you a cordial, and then take you back to the house. Are you comfortable so? I will not be long."

He hurried off. The warm sun streamed down on to David Maitland, but he felt as cold as the dead. The heather-clad slopes in the distance smiled impassively; his presence was nothing to them. But the great deerhound lying, not far away, in front of the porch, watched him with vigilant, half-suspicious eyes. And the informer looked about him almost in desperation. He must get away at once from this happy household in which he felt like a poisonous snake, whose tongue might wound at any moment and shatter all its peace. But it was obvious that he could not get away yet; he was not strong enough in body for the attempt, and this semi-collapse of his would not make his kind and unsuspecting hosts any the more ready to let him go.

That of course was exactly the case, for in a moment Miss Cameron as well as Ardroy came hurrying out to him, and Maitland soon found himself banished anew to his own room, and scolded for having attempted a feat beyond his strength. Lying back in his chair there he wondered frantically how this was going to end. Once or twice his thoughts dwelt upon the loch which he knew lay behind the house. But, even if he succeeded in reaching it undetected, he could not drown himself in it, he saw now, without cruelly wounding several people—among others his poor wife, to whom he had written again since he came here, and Olivia Campbell—and without involving Ewen Cameron in who knew what unpleasantness, even suspicion. No, he could not take that way out. There *was* no way out.

Only yesterday Olivia had said half teasingly to him in this very room, " You find yourself, dear Godfather, as I did, in a perfect nest of Jacobites, but with more justification for your presence in it than I had at Invernacree." More justification! Great God, if she had only known!

He remembered now how he had caught at the name Invernacree and tried to get her to talk of the son of that house, now present in this. He had met with singularly little success; Olivia had slid away from the subject, but so naturally that he could not discover whether it was from real lack of interest in Ian Stewart—or from too much. Well, Heaven know that he, David Maitland, was hardly now in a position to lend a helping hand to such a match! Yet, partly because her happiness was always so much at his heart, partly in order to keep at bay for a little that hungry shadow at his back, he speculated on the problem, and for the first time it occurred to him to wonder in what light Ian Stewart regarded his, Maitland's, intimacy with Olivia. It was true that he might be putting upon it either of two constructions, each equally wide of the mark. Those at least he could correct if he had the chance.

Olivia, sitting there smiling in her green habit, Olivia,

come all this way to see him! And yet she would not
confide in him, not even a little. She had used to, sometimes. It almost seemed as if she had known what he was
now. Impossible! . . . And, if he could ever pray again,
that should be his prayer, that she might never know!

§ 2

At this stage of his reflections Maitland heard a curious
soft, undecided knock at the door, and a fumbling at the
handle, followed by the appearance of that engaging
little boy, Ardroy's younger son.

" I comed," he announced, running across the bedroom,
" to bring you something, Mr. Maittan'. It's in here."
He held forth a small wooden box.

" Another moth? " asked Maitland, and even out of his
despair could not keep a smile from his lips.

" Not a moth. A cattlepillar. You must keep it in
this box and not let it get out. But when it is a moth
you can let it fly about."

" I hope—I mean I expect—that I shall be gone before
it becomes a moth."

" Oh," said the donor, rather dashed. " I thought it
would like to be with the other moth. . . . Where is the
other moth? "

" I think your Aunt Margaret must have taken it
away."

" Naughty Aunt Margaret! " said the entomologist
severely; and then, placing the box on Maitland's knee,
removed the lid and with his small finger drew his
attention to its rearing occupant. Meanwhile someone
pushed open the door which he had left ajar.

" Keithie," said a man's voice, " who told you that you

might come in here? " It was Ian Stewart who stood in
the doorway. " I apologise for him, sir."

Keithie turned round with a commiserating air. " Poor
Mr. Maittan' had to go back to his room, and I knowed he
was all alone, so I brought him my *best* cattlepillar."

" That was very kind," said his cousin. " I am
sure Mr. Maitland is very much obliged to you. But
suppose you leave it with him now and go to Morag, for I
hear her calling for you."

Little Keith shut up the box and thrust it at Maitland,
about the middle of his waistcoat. " Good-night," he
said, and held up his flowerlike face, evidently expecting
a kiss.

If young Invernacree had not been there in the doorway, Maitland believed that he would have contrived to
get out of giving it. As it was he bent and kissed the child
of Archibald Cameron's race feeling as if he were indeed
the snake of his own tormented fancy. And he envied
the young man on the threshold, catching him up in his
arms and repeating the salute with unsullied lips.

" There, run along to Morag. I am sorry, sir," added
Ian as the little boy pattered away down the passage. " It
seems very hard to protect you from these children."

Anything to keep his own thoughts at bay a little. " Do
not go, pray, Mr. Stewart," said Maitland quickly, as the
young man was about to close the door. " Will you not
come in and sit down awhile? I am not really so relapsed
as might appear just now. 'Twas only the effect of the
fresh air, and the weakness of my legs. To-morrow I
shall do better, I hope; for indeed 'tis full time I returned
to my wife and family."

" Your wife! " exclaimed Ian in a tone of great
astonishment.

" Yes. Did you not know that I was married? Why, I have a son not so many years younger than you, I should suppose, Mr. Stewart; that is to say, he will soon be of age."

This unexpected news drew Ian within, shut the door behind him and placed him in a chair almost without his realising it. " I . . . I thought somehow that you were unmarried, sir," he said apologetically, " I do not know why."

" On the contrary, I am quite an old married man," replied David Maitland. He reached up as he sat, and, putting the little wooden box upon the mantelshelf, added, " Does that fact make any difference to you, Mr. Stewart? "

He heard the young man draw a sharp breath. " Any difference? What do you mean, sir? "

Maitland looked at him. " This, that being, I suppose, nearly twice your age, and married to boot, and an old family friend of . . . of a lady whom I think you admire, I wondered if I could prove of any service to you."

But young Invernacree did not meet his eyes. He was sitting near the door; Maitland near the window, but with his back to it. And almost instantly Ian Stewart left his chair and went and looked out of the window, saying nothing. His face was invisible. Maitland began to be a little sorry that he had obeyed the impulse to say what he had, though he had done it for Olivia's sake. If she . . . yet she had given him no clue.

" I am very much obliged to you, sir," came at last rather stiffly from the window. " But I fear you can do nothing. I . . . I a great deal more than admire Miss Campbell, but circumstances make it impossible for me to . . . in short, Miss Campbell is not for me."

" You mean by that, I suppose," said Maitland, screwing himself round in his chair to look at the speaker's back, " the general circumstances of your family's divergent politics, now and in the past?"

Ian turned from the window. " I mean a great deal more than that, sir. You are a Jacobite and were ' out,' I believe—as I was, though a mere lad then. You may remember therefore that Campbell of Cairns commanded the Campbell militia at Culloden, and where they were posted. My brother Alan, the heir, fell at Culloden. It is quite inconceivable that I should bring Miss Campbell home as a bride to the house which should have been his."

He was standing quite rigid, with his hands at his sides, staring straight out of the window again. The attitude, the hard, strained voice told David Maitland a good deal. He got up from his chair and came and laid a hand on the young man's shoulder from behind.

" Mr. Stewart—believe me, I have the right to ask, though I am neither her father nor, indeed, any relation— does Olivia love you?"

Ian stood unyielding under that hand. " No," he answered uncompromising, and went on almost immediately, " I believed so once. Perhaps for a moment she may have done so. I did think. . . . But now that I have seen her again I know otherwise. And it is much better so, sir—much better, since I could never marry her, with that between us."

The elder man sighed and removed the hand. " I hope you pardon my intrusion into your affairs, Mr. Stewart. 'Tis not mere curiosity, I assure you. What you have told me of the unfortunate barrier between you explains much. I think it partly explains why Miss Campbell would not speak of you when I saw her the other day—beyond expressing surprise at finding you here. But I think her silence meant also that you are wrong, and that she does care for you. I may, naturally, be mistaken. Yet I reflect that there have been times when she has not withheld her confidence from me—when it was of no importance."

Ian swung round. " Mr Maitland, don't torture me! Of what use to suggest such a thing! It can make no difference. I have done with her; it ended at Kilrain. She is a Campbell and the daughter of the man who has my brother's blood on his hands. God himself cannot wash that away from them." •

He spoke with anguish and passion in his voice, and he was pale. But David Maitland was paler still. He went back silently to his chair and put a hand over his eyes. Ian once more looked out of the window; then, roused by the silence, glanced round, saw his attitude, hesitated a moment and went over to him.

" Are you indisposed, sir? Shall I summon Miss Cameron?"

The convalescent dropped his hand. In the sudden grey pallor of his face his eyes had a strained, bright look. " No, no, I am quite well. I was only thinking how true, how terribly true your words were. Blood spilt can never be gathered up again—no, not by God Himself! All that one can hope for, Mr. Stewart, is that at the Last Day there may be some crumb of pardon for a man who never meant to spill it, but on whose hands, nevertheless . . ." He stopped abruptly. He was looking at his own. Ian thought his manner exceedingly strange, till he remembered that, as a Jacobite, he might have something of the same feeling about Campbell of Cairns, though he was his friend.

"I have my own opinion of the Campbells," said Ian slowly, "but I will admit that Campbell of Cairns did not direct his men particularly to kill my brother. Some might uphold that he was only doing what he conceived to be his duty."

David Maitland, looking at him with those bright, sunken eyes, and with the strangest expression in them, began to laugh. "His duty! That is the greatest snare of all, Mr. Stewart. When the ill angel who masquerades as the good suggests *that*—but I think I am talking nonsense. Forgive me—there's a breath of fever still in my veins. Suppose we turn to pleasanter subjects. You did not see what your little cousin gave me?" And he reached up an unsteady hand for Keithie's gift.

Ian thought the abrupt change of subject odder still, and almost wondered if Mr. Maitland's illness—his two successive illnesses—could have affected his mind. At the beginning of this conversation he had seemed so particularly well-balanced. He judged it time, at any rate, to leave him; perhaps to say a word about him to Miss Cameron.

"I thank you very much, sir, for your interest in my . . . in me," he said. "But that is all a closed book now; and I am afraid that I have tired you. I'll say good-night."

"Good-night," echoed Maitland after a pause. He looked at his visitor again with haunted eyes. "No book is ever closed . . . so long as we remain alive, Mr. Stewart. Remember that—to your profit!"

Ian shut the door gently behind him. He seemed to be back on the road to Kilrain, where he had first seen the cousin of that look.

And Maitland remained staring at the little wooden

box which he held, the sound of his own words in his ears. No, no book is ever closed till death turns the last page. And is it closed then? . . .

A little later there was another knock at the door, and in came Miss Margaret Cameron with a glass upon a tray.

" Now, pray, Mr. Maitland, do not rise! I have but come to see how you do and to bring you your draught; and also to suggest that after your fatigue of this afternoon you would do well to retire early to bed. I'll have your supper sent up here."

" I daresay, madam, that it would be well," acquiesced her patient. " But indeed you must not think anything of my having shown a slight weakness the first time I took the air."

Miss Cameron was turning down the bed. " 'Tis a pity you ventured into the air at all so soon. I had my doubts about the wisdom of it. And my niece tells me now that you had previously seemed distressed at the sight of the likeness—or rather of the unlikeness, for 'tis a mere libel on his features—of our unfortunate but heroic kinsman, Archibald Cameron. She told me how moved you appeared at it, sir, and it does you honour; but an invalid should not be called upon to endure sudden shocks."

" Shocks," repeated Maitland rather faintly. " Shocks . . . why—yes, yes, it was unexpected, I'll admit. Though of course," he went on, trying to work off his agitation unperceived through speech, " such a portrait may very naturally be found in a Cameron household."

" Aye," said Miss Margaret, busying herself now with a water jug, " and may well be found, above all, in this

one. Do you know, Mr. Maitland, that my nephew
Ardroy, who was devoted heart and soul to Archie
Cameron, and nearly got himself killed in the effort to
save him from capture in Glenbuckie, was actually on
the scaffold with him, wearing the dress of the minister
who should have attended him thither, and that 'twas he
who received the Doctor's last words, and heard him with
his own ears pardon his murderers . . . Bless us, what's
wrong with you?"

She set down the ewer with a thud, and hurried across
the room. David Maitland had fainted.

CHAPTER XXII

§ 1

Sept. 8th.

" Not the smallest article has been performed of what was expected and at first promised," declared Finlay MacPhair with emphasis, " not the smallest article! Not only is the five hundred pounds per annum boggled at— though God knows 'tis a small enough sum to ask, considering my position and influence—but the very journeys I took for the late Mr. Pelham are still unpaid. And as for the intelligence which I sent three years ago concerning the coming of Doctor Cameron and my cousin Lochdornie to the Highlands, I might as well have kept it to myself. On my soul, 'tis the most infernal treatment!"

Thus declaiming, the misused Chief tramped up and down the stone floor of his dining-room in deep indignation. The day was drawing to its close; supper was finished, but the recipient of this plaint still sat at the table finishing his wine, a neat, middle-aged gentleman in a particularly close grey wig, a sober blue coat and snuff-coloured breeches. Mr. Bruce looked something between a merchant and an attorney, and had small appearance of being what he really was, a " court trusty," a secret agent deputed by the English Government to keep an occasional eye upon another secret agent. What was

270

odder still, the latter, who had just so passionately bewailed his treatment by that Government, was perfectly aware of the fact, and Mr. Bruce knew that he was aware of it. The position was thus robbed of much of its awkwardness.

The guest emptied his glass and wiped his lips carefully with his napkin. "My dear sir," he observed in a pleasant voice, "you know that I desire to serve you in any reasonable manner. It is undeniable that you suffered a great loss in the death of your patron, the minister, last spring, particularly in no longer having him to urge your merits upon the Government. I am but a poor substitute for the brother of my Lord Newcastle."

"Yes," said Glenshian moodily, "the cursed erysipelas which carried off Mr. Pelham has much to answer for, in putting a Highland gentleman to shifts for money, when money is actually owing to him!"

Mr. Bruce raised his eyebrows. "Shifts? You are in difficulties again?"

"I am never in aught else," growled his host, "since the fines on my estate are not remitted—and that's a scandal almost as bad as the other! You may remember that about this time last year, when I succeeded to it, you obliged me with a small loan?"

"Aye, that I remember very well," assented Mr. Bruce with a little smile. "Very well, indeed. 'Twas in Edinburgh, about mid-October, the very day that you told me you had a scheme on foot. . . ."

"It came to naught," said Glenshian with a hasty scowl. "It came to naught because in the end I had to do with a fool . . . I had spent money on the business too."

"I am sorry to hear it," said his companion, still

equably, " and I regret, too, that my own circumstances do not permit me to tear up your note of hand."

" I should not wish you to do so," responded the Chief haughtily. " I prefer to honour my obligations. And I hope soon to do so, for I have another scheme which, if it succeeds, should bring me in a comfortable sum and very likely rid this neighbourhood of a most pestilential enemy of mine, or at the least cripple him . . and disgrace him into the bargain."

The " court trusty " shook his head. " Are you already at quarrelling with your neighbours, Glenshian, and you not yet settled here a twelvemonth?"

" This ' neighbour ' has been in my path these two years, before ever I came up here," answered Finlay with his lip curled back, kicking as he spoke at a stool "—he and his kinsman by marriage. But I have him at my mercy now. By Michaelmas Day the laird of Ardroy will not be holding his head so high, I fancy. That's one of the matters which took me to Inverness, so that I had not the pleasure of being here to welcome you upon your arrival." Warmed, apparently, by the thought of his transactions in Inverness, from which he had only returned a couple of hours ago, to find Mr. Bruce already arrived to see him, Glenshian sat down once more at the table and refilled his visitor's glass and his own. " Come, pledge me, good ' Twenty-one,' as you pledged me last year when you assisted me with the rent-roll after the old man's death."

The court trusty complied with much amiability. " To the success of your undertakings, Mr. ' Pickle '! And, speaking of rents, how do they come in now?"

But at the question Glenshian scowled anew. " Very ill. Since the troubles, many persons have come on to my land and taken possession of what farms they please; and it is the devil's own work either to uproot them or to get them to pay. I have an unopened letter about one such encroachment in my pocket now."

"But," said Bruce with the flicker of a sidelong glance, "you have come to a very advantageous arrangement with some of your wadsetters, have you not?"

Finlay put down his wine glass. "What do you know about that, pray?" he asked suspiciously. "Whom have you been talking to?"

"Nobody in particular," replied Mr. Bruce mildly and mendaciously. "You forget that the doings of a powerful chief like yourself are public property in the neighbourhood. I understand that you succeeded in persuading some of your wadsetters further west to give up their mortgages and pay rent, did you not?"

"Aye," said the young Chief; and he added with a contemptuous smile, "the fools! To be frank, however," he went on, "I failed with my wadsetters in Glenshian itself. I shall be even with them some day yet for that. . . . Now, look you, Bruce, to come back to this five hundred pounds per annum which, as I was saying, I must absolutely receive from the Government before I undertake to do anything—five hundred pounds paid twice a year without fail. But you can tell my Lord Newcastle that for that sum there is nothing honourable he can think of, but I am able to perform. For instance, I would be willing . . . But come, we'll discuss that by the fire, unless you will drink some more claret? No? Find yourself a seat, then, while I take a glance at the letter I spoke of, for it came in my absence."

Thus invited, Mr. Bruce got up and went towards the hearth, followed by his host, who had brought out the letter from his pocket, torn it carelessly open, and was beginning to read it as he advanced. But all at once he ceased advancing. . . .

At the string of curses in Gaelic and English which some high, unfamiliar voice was pouring out behind him, Bruce whipped round to see Glenshian, with a distorted, livid face, holding a paper in his hand as one might hold a wriggling serpent.

" Good God, what's amiss? " he asked in alarm.

" Amiss—amiss! " Looking round blindly as though to find some object on which to vent his wrath, the young man caught hold of the end of the linen table-cloth hanging in a long point over the edge of the supper-table, tugged at it and then flung it violently back, sending plates, wine and glasses into a confused, clattering heap in the middle. " *Amiss!* Everything has gone agley . . . ruined . . . all my careful plans! May the devil cut the ears off Hector Grant and the tongue out of Seumas's mouth! . . . But the latter I'll do myself! " He strode furiously to the bell which stood on the far end of the table and began to ring it like a tocsin.

In the middle of the clangour appeared old Roderick, out of breath.

" Roderick, you old fool, how long ago did this letter come for me? "

The ancient considered. " I am thinking it would be about two days after you went away."

" Did you know that it came from the laird of Ardroy? "

" Yes, Mac 'ic Fhionnlaigh. That is to say——"

" Then why the devil did you not say so when you gave it to me? I thought it was only about that Cullachy affair. . . . And why in the fiend's name did you ever admit that damned spying Captain Grant to this house? You're at the bottom of the business after all, you doited old carline!" And he actually shook his aged retainer till Roderick's few remaining teeth clacked together. "'Tis Hector Grant who has wrecked . . . no matter what . . . and I cannot settle with him! But I'll settle with Seumas that he'll not go chattering again in a hurry! Send him to me in my own room!"

"What has Seumas been doing?" enquired Bruce, as after a horrified glance at the supper-table, the old man shuffled out again.

"Talking!" replied Finlay fiercely, "— a thing it will be long before he does again!" And without apology he went striding out, pausing only to snatch down a heavy riding whip from the wall.

The guest thus deserted stood a moment rubbing his chin, more than a little uneasy at this tornado of rage and its possible consequences. Yet if the Chief of Glenshian chose to flog one of his gillies for misdemeanour he could hardly interfere. So he finally sat down by the inviting peat fire; yet, looking again over his shoulder at the havoc on the supper-table, observed half aloud, "I wonder if by chance our "Pickle" is a trifle unsettled in his wits?"

And, not having been idle in the neighbourhood before Glenshian's return, he thought of the stories which Colonel Trapaud of Fort Augustus had related to him over a bowl of punch—stories of the Chief's haughty and overbearing behaviour alike to the English garrison there and to his own tenantry.

"He has refused my officers the right to shoot over his land because, not having taken the oath to the Government, he may not have a fowling-piece himself—as if that were *my* doing!" said the Governor indignantly. "And he has forbidden his tenants to sell us any peat, which does more harm to those poor devils, whose only chance it is of earning a small pittance, than it does to us, since we are to be supplied with coal next year. I have pointed that out to them and drawn the moral—not in Glenshian's favour, as you may imagine. And then that sharp practice with his small wadsetters, about which I have told you—that has not made him popular; when he tried the same game nearer home they refused stoutly to give up their rights. Yes, he is alienating all but the most devoted, so that I have hopes his own arrogance will be his undoing."

The secret agent had listened to the soldier, nodded thoughtfully and said little. He was pleased; and he was not pleased. For if Glenshian's undoubtedly great local influence diminished, so would his potential usefulness to the English Government. This dilemma engaged his reflections now, by Glenshian's fire. Fionnlagh Ruadh's overwhelming sense of his own importance— though he *was* important—joined to the crazily violent temper of which he had just given a specimen, made him a difficult instrument to handle. And yet . . . he had his points. A confessed and trusted Jacobite—and in English pay since 1750—it needed craft, a cool head, and a certain amount of personal courage to combine those positions for five years without arousing the suspicions of a single soul.

Mr. Bruce picked up a peat with the tongs, lit his long pipe, stretched out his legs to the blaze, and wondered idly where the flogging or other chastisement was taking place. Perhaps Glenshian's personal retainers liked that sort of thing; perhaps the adage should run, " A woman, a gillie, and a walnut-tree . . ." All the same, *he* would not care to lay a horsewhip about the shoulders of some of the natives here. But then he was not MacPhair of Glenshian. . . . Five hundred pounds per annum! He wouldn't get it!

Nor, if he really were a trifle unbalanced in his mind, would he be worth it. Mr. Bruce slowly brought out a little pocketbook and made in it a short and cryptic memorandum.

§ 2

" Beat me—kill me if you must," said Seumas, unresisting in his master's grip, " but as God sees me, I have never breathed a word of that journey to a living man. Then how much less before your enemy?"

Finlay loosed him almost with reluctance. He had not yet used the whip on him. For, after all, Seumas, abuse him as he might, was of an almost abject fidelity, proved, now, by some years of ill-paid service in France and England.

" Would you swear that on the iron?"

" Aye, and pray to God to send me to a dishonoured grave in a far land if I spoke not the truth!"

" Then who *has* talked? The laird of Ardroy has written me a letter in which he says that Captain Grant—maledictions on him for forcing himself in here and obliging me to keep him prisoner!—overheard the story of the driving of the branded steers, and so, if I proceed with my intention of summoning Ardroy himself before the Sheriff Court——" Glenshian did not finish, but ground his teeth. " Someone must have talked before Captain Grant—and he having the Gaelic all the while! Who was it?"

Seumas offered no suggestion.

"Who went with you that night?"

"My half-brother Somerled."

Finlay gave a sort of snarl of comprehending rage. "And it was Somerled whom I put in charge of Hector Grant. The dirty traitor! Fetch him here!"

"Mac 'ic Fhionnlaigh . . ."

"Fetch him here!"

Seumas went; and in a little returned with that stalwart gillie whose face at one time was only too familiar to Captain Grant. That officer would, however, have been gratified to observe the apprehension upon it now.

Evidently his half-brother had already acquainted him with the reason of his summons, for before Glenshian had time to get out his furious question—if indeed he even meant to ask one at all—the culprit had confessed.

"Aye, I spoke of it, Mac 'ic Fhionnlaigh—I spoke of it one day to Roderick . . . because it was so clever a trick to have played upon the Cameron——"

"You spoke of it to Roderick! When—where?"

"It was one day when he came for wine," faltered Somerled.

"For wine—in the very next cellar to Mr. Grant! You fool, you fool, did you not know of that grating!"

"I knew of it. But Roderick was sure that the gentleman had not the Gaelic."

Glenshian consigned Roderick to a much deeper place than a wine-cellar. "How dare he make such a statement! But you——" he had Somerled by the throat now —"do you know what you have done? Ruined all my schemes, lost me hundreds of pounds, and my revenge on Cameron of Ardroy—my just and well-planned revenge!" He threw the big gillie from him and snatched up the whip.

Somerled made no resistance; he only tried to keep his arms across his face to shield it from the rain of blows. He uttered no plea for mercy nor even a cry of pain; the only sounds were Finlay's own hard breathing and the whistle and thud of the lash. But at the end Somerled was crouching, not much more than semi-conscious, in a corner; and it was at this stage that Seumas, who had stood and gravely watched the execution of justice, ventured to come behind his irate Chief and catch his arm. Finlay turned like a madman and struck him on the mouth. But he had been checked for a second, and in that second the wretched Somerled slid completely to the floor and lay there on his face.

"Mac 'ic Fhionnlaigh, is it not enough?" pleaded Seumas, the blood running down his own chin. "Of a truth he has deserved it all, and more—but if you kill him, they will perhaps hear of it at Fort Augustus . . ."

"Take him away, then!" said his master, out of breath. He flung the whip on the floor. "Throw him outside somewhere—then come back to me."

Seumas, tugging at his dazed kinsman, got him somehow to his feet and helped him from the room. Finlay, as though he had not been within measurable distance of murder, was already absorbed in the re-reading of Ardroy's letter. Then he put it back in his pocket, and stood biting his nails in an even blacker and deeper absorption, and suffering the pangs of an emotion which very seldom troubled him—regret. He was bitterly sorry that he had ever kept Hector Grant a prisoner and so given him an opportunity of overhearing what he had. The mortification of learning, nearly a fortnight ago, that the captive had been rescued with such ease from Castle Shian had been bad enough, yet there had been a certain element of compensation in that cup. The forcible removal of Captain Grant had in fact ended a situation which was becoming awkward for its originator, faced on the one hand with his prisoner's absolute refusal to submit to his terms, and on the other with the impossibility of keeping him indefinitely a captive. Wounding to his pride as was the episode of the rescue, it was not nearly so galling as to be called to book by Governor Trapaud of Fort Augustus and reported to the English Government for his high-handed conduct—a consequence which was well within the bounds of possibility. But now he had not only been deprived of his prisoner but, with that prisoner, of the secret which formed the corner-stone of his nefarious plot against Cameron of Ardroy.

It was only too true; he was checkmated. He dared not move further in the matter. He would have to send to Inverness to stop the pending proceedings. All the time that he had recently been there this accursed letter, lying at Invershian, had been making a fool of him. Once more he took it out and read its short, uncompromising phrases. No, he would get no damages out of Ewen Cameron now, no sweet revenge for that glove flung into the gutter in Edinburgh last autumn, nor for the accusation Ewen had launched at him in June . . . in fact, unless he were careful, Ewen Cameron might get damages out of him. "Assault and unlawful detention;" yes, since the English, damn them, had taken away the old jurisdiction of the chiefs, a jury was very unlikely to pass over his chaining up of a gentleman in a ruined castle on the plea that that gentleman had obtained admission to his house and uttered threats against him. . . .

Moreover the immediate return of Captain Grant's horse and valise was demanded, and he would have to comply—damn Ardroy and all his kin! Finlay tore the letter to pieces, threw the pieces on the floor and ground them with his foot.

Glancing up he saw that Seumas had returned, and was standing looking at him with a gloomy interest.

"For God's sake wipe that blood from off your mouth!" said his master irritably. "Listen! That horse of Captain Grant's—I suppose it is still here—must go back to him at Ardroy without delay. Do you hear?"

"Yes, I hear," answered Seumas, who was well inured to this manner of address. "It shall go. And is the other gentleman's horse to go at the same time?"

"What other gentleman? Do you mean Mr. Maitland? But, you fool, he is not at Ardroy—Heaven knows where he is."

"He *is* at Ardroy, Mac 'ic Fhionnlaigh—that is to say, he was there when the laird's letter was brought."

"Nonsense!" said Glenshian sharply. "That's the last place in the world he would have gone to."

"Nevertheless," persisted Seumas, "he is there, ill . . . unless the gillie lied."

His master's face suddenly lit up. *Could* it be true—Maitland fallen into Ewen Cameron's hands? "My God!" he said under his breath, "what a jest that would be! How did you come upon this tale, Seumas?"

"I learnt it from the gillie of Ardroy's who brought the letter," responded Seumas promptly. "While you were away I had already heard a rumour that the gentleman whom you had fetched here in a chaise was lying ill at some farm on Loch Lochy, where it was said that Ardroy himself was nursing him. I asked the Cameron if this were true, and he answered that not only was it true, but that the laird was just after bringing this Mr. Maitland to his house as a guest, and that he was in the best bedchamber and was having every care."

" The best bedchamber . . . every care . . . *Maitland!*" The young Chief went off into a wild burst of laughter. But he stopped laughing as abruptly as he had begun, his yellow-green eyes dilated and, as if wishing to hide, even from this *âme damnée* of his, some idea too visible on his face, he swung on his heel and went from him towards the empty hearth.

" Yes," he said after an instant, in a slow tone of enjoyment, " in that case, Seumas, I shall certainly send Mr. Maitland's horse to Ardroy. (I wonder whether he will ever ride away on it.)" Then he turned and faced the gillie. " See to it that a trustworthy man sets off with both beasts to-morrow morning, and that he takes the valises of Captain Grant and Mr. Maitland as well.— I'll have no one accusing me of larceny," he added to himself. " There will also be a letter for Mr. Cameron of Ardroy . . . yes, there will undoubtedly be a letter." He smiled, stood a moment in contemplation of some vision of his own, and then roused himself. " You can go now, Seumas. But be careful that someone goes with the horses who can keep his mouth shut better than that cursed half-brother of yours."

Seumas, instead of taking his dismissal, came nearer, his thin, swarthy face transformed with eagerness. " Grant me a favour, Mac 'ic Fhionnlaigh! Let *me* take the horses and your letter!"

" As you please," answered Finlay carelessly. He had already gone to an escritoire and was unlocking it. " No, you cannot go; I may be needing you to-morrow."

"Ah, Mac 'ic Fhionnlaigh, I beseech you to let me go!"

"In the devil's name why, man?"

"Because it might be," responded Seumas with a dark, inward look, "that I could wipe out the disgrace which Somerled has put upon us . . . and show you that one of my father's sons knows how to be faithful to his Chief, and to his Chief's inmost wish." The last words were so low as almost to be inaudible.

"I don't doubt that *you* are faithful," said Finlay carelessly. "Yes, you shall go then, for you have perhaps the wit to bring me back certain intelligence from Ardroy: how for instance—— But I will give you instructions in the morning, and the letter whch you must convey, and give into the hands of the laird of Ardroy himself. Come to me betimes to-morrow."

Seumas was murmuring thanks. He picked up the horsewhip and laid it on a table. "You were right to use this, Glenshian. And when I return you shall use it on *me* if I have not pleased you."

But the Highlander's protestations appeared to make little impression on his master; he had already sat down to the escritoire with a pen in his hand. For some seconds after Seumas had gone he sat there nibbling the end with a malicious gleam in his eyes. It was in this very room that that fool of a Maitland had refused to comply with his suggestion. And now, through some chain of events not yet clear, Maitland was an honoured guest at Ardroy, of all places in the world! Ewen Cameron had brought to his own house—had, if report were true, himself tended in sickness—the very man who. . . . And Ewen had accused *him* of being the cause of his precious kinsman's execution!

Finlay burst, for the second time, into a loud laugh; began to write slowly and carefully; paused, surveyed what he had written, then dashed off a few more words at the end, signed the letter with a flourish, folded it, and sealed it with care and a sort of relishing slowness.

When he went back to the other room Mr. Bruce was comfortably smoking by the fire.

"You have been the deuce of a time away," he observed, but with perfect placidity.

"I ask your pardon for it. I had some business to transact which involved . . . the writing of a letter." He showed the sealed, addressed letter in his hand.

"More business relating to your . . . financial schemes?" hazarded Bruce.

"No," answered his host, looking down at the letter. "I doubt there's money in this, for I am making restitution."

"Paying back, in short?" observed Mr. Bruce, knocking out his pipe.

"Aye, paying back, as you say—and with interest . . . paying two men at the same time!"

"Egad, I'm sure that's very laudable," replied the "court trusty," beginning to refill his pipe. But halfway through he stopped, and fell to studying his companion with some intentness. The young Chief, half sitting on the arm of his chair, was staring down into the peats on the hearth with a secret little smile which even to the rather phlegmatic Bruce—who was, however, no fool—contained something sinister and cruel.

And indeed the red heart of the fire seemed to the gazer to hold a possibility even more seductive than he had foreseen when he penned his letter. David Maitland was but a poor scrupulous creature, and, despite the fact that he had crossed him, he did not really care very greatly what happened to him . . . though something would undoubtedly happen when this letter reached its destination. But, when one remembered what Doctor Cameron's memory appeared to mean to Ewen Cameron, was it too much to hope that he might, in a moment of ungoverned fury, wring Maitland's neck? And then— could the dreamer himself plan a more satisfying revenge than that which the law would take upon his enemy, without his having to lift a finger? He saw in the fire the man who had lectured and insulted *him*, a common criminal flying from the neighbourhood to which he could never dare return—there was no amnesty for murder; he saw him leading a hunted life of shifts and disguises, and then he saw the inevitable end—quite soon, it might be—on the gibbet erected for a crime less easily exonerated by the world than Jacobitism. The Grassmarket at Edinburgh . . . a shifting, vociferating crowd, awaiting the hangman and the tall, pinioned murderer . . . the seed of that possible consummation slept in the letter which he held, with its big, blood-red seal. The sending of it to-morrow was only the putting of a match to a train already laid by circumstances, it was true; yet, in the knowledge that his hand would apply that match, Finlay MacPhair had an almost delirious sensation of power, as of some Olympian chess player bending over two pawns, one of which, at his bidding, should sweep the other from the board, and then be swept itself . . .

He got up, slipped the letter almost caressingly into his pocket, and stretched himself like a large cat. " Let us go to bed, Bruce. I must be up betimes to see that some orders are duly carried out."

The court trusty rose. "You have recovered, I perceive, from your recent disappointment?"

"Entirely," replied his host. "Matters are turning out more favourably than I anticipated . . . Money is all very well, but there is one thing that is dearer . . . to a Highlander."

"And that is?"

Finlay slapped him affably on the shoulder. "You have lived too long in England, Bruce, to appreciate what it is. Come to bed!"

CHAPTER XXIII

THE STREAM IN SPATE

§ 1

Sept. 9th.

A LITTLE of the nip of September was in the air, though the sun's heat almost kept it under. The Allt Buidhe at Ardroy, coming down from the mountains, had more than a hint of recent rainfall in the pale amber waters whence it took its name; and indeed it had been raining fairly persistently for two days. But the afternoon was bright, if with a windy and an ephemeral beauty, and the young man slowly crossing the footbridge over the racing stream stopped to look at the view.

In old days the footbridge had been unguarded, but Ewen Cameron, after his firstborn, a couple of years ago, had fallen into the burn and nearly been carried away, had caused it to be railed for the better safety of his children; and on one of these rough wooden rails Ian Stewart leant for so long that it was plain he was no longer admiring the scenery but thinking. And his expression would have shown that his thoughts were not merry ones.

At duty's call he had said farewell to Olivia Campbell for ever—so he had believed at the time. He had kissed his love and departed; he had found a token from her in his hand and had ridden away. He had been incredibly strong-minded at very great and searching cost. And yet, ever since Olivia's most unexpected visit here five days ago, he had been at intervals a prey to a strange

10*

and inexcusable mood of indignation, much as after his
height of renunciation at Kilrain he had come home and
picked a quarrel with Hector Grant. He was increasingly hurt, resentful and bewildered because Olivia had
seemed changed to him—so light and cold and civil, so
concerned about Mr. Maitland (though on that score he
might certainly now feel easier, since the good gentleman
had turned out to be already married) and on such good
terms with that redcoat escort of hers. Days had passed,
but he could rehearse every word she had said to him—and
all those she might have said; every look of hers—for
others. She had never loved him. The scene in the
oakwood had been merely a surprise to her; it meant
nothing. And that she had not spoken of him to that
father confessor of hers, as the latter had avowed, meant
clearly that she had nothing to confess. Had he not
been right after all in his first impression of her at
Invernacree—that she was a finished coquette? And on
the little bridge, as if wind and stream had brought them,
there came back to him the words of the old spaewife,
years ago, who had told him that he would love a woman
who was other than she seemed.

Why, since he had most definitely refused to think
of marrying her, Ian should consider that Olivia was
nevertheless bound to a barren constancy, the jealous and
illogical heart of a lover alone could tell.

He was leaving Ardroy for home to-morrow, and had
come out here—it was about half a mile from the house
—to try to settle the thorny question of his behaviour
when he reached Fort William and Maryburgh on his
way thither. The best course would be to ride straight
through, though in the natural order of events he would
have stopped at Maryburgh for an hour or two. But he

dreaded the neighbourhood while Olivia was in it; he wished there were some other way of getting down to Appin. Yet he did not know which seemed to him the more unbearable prospect, that of chancing upon her as he passed or of not doing so.

Ian propped his chin on his fists. No, he must have the strength of mind to ride straight through without drawing rein. It was the only safe course. All was over; how often had he not declared it—to her, to his father, to Ewen, to Mr. Maitland! Why, then, did he so foolishly preserve those bits of bog-myrtle which she had probably never laid after all in his sleeping hand, or, if she had, only as a jest to fool him with? It was odd— when she had been here the other day he had completely forgotten his possession of them. But now he pulled out the stolen letter of hers in which they were folded, slid them out into his palm, and looked menacingly from them to the hurrying burn below his feet.

It was easy, almost too easy. One jerk of the hand, and the brittle fragments had vanished in the racing yellow swirl of the Allt Buidhe. The letter too— Grizel's property though it was—he ought to burn it; but this grave would serve as well as a fiery one. With hands that shook a little he tore across and across Olivia's announcement of her coming visit to Kilrain, and went on tearing until a drift of snowflakes fluttered in the breeze, and then sailed like shaken petals down the stream. Gone—the last trace of her. . . . Ian bowed his head upon his folded arms on the rail. He had no sling now to hinder such a posture.

And thus, a while later, he was found by Donald, as he came running lightly along the path to the burn.

"Oh, Cousin Ian, what are you doing? Are you looking for trout? Angus says there are none in the Allt Buidhe; and I've never seen one there. Besides, the burn is running very fast this morning."

Ian had promptly raised his head. "Very fast," he agreed.

Donald picked up a stick and threw it in. "Look where that has gone to already! Throw in another, Cousin Ian, and we will have a race."

Ian roused himself. "I have already thrown in my offering, Donald, and it is gone."

The boy looked at him, a little puzzled at his tone. "You speak as if you were sorry, cousin."

"Perhaps I am," said the young man. "Perhaps I am not. . . . Well, *laochain*, where are you off to?"

"I was walking with Mr. Maitland," answered the boy. "But he does not go very fast, and he was only in the garden. So he told me to leave him, and I did. Then I came this way, and saw you on the bridge. If you are walking anywhere may I come with you, as you are going away to-morrow?"

"Certainly," said Ian, laying his hand on Donald's shoulder. He was a charming and promising boy, this young cousin of his. "Where would you like to go?"

"Let us start by the *bealach* and go down to the place where you can see Loch Arkaig below."

So they set off, Donald chattering as they went.

"Mr. Maitland is much better, isn't he? He says he will be able to start home in a couple of days now. I think he wants to go very much."

"Well, naturally," said his cousin. "He wishes to get back to his family."

"Keithie is being a nuisance to him, I expect," resumed Donald with brotherly frankness, "for he means to give him his very largest caterpillar to take home with him, the shaggy one. The caterpillar he gave him the other day—the day when Mr. Maitland was taken worse —was not truly his best one, though he said it was."

"Keithie doesn't give me any caterpillars to take home with me," observed Ian. "But, on the whole, I am not sorry."

Donald's next remark was on a different topic entirely. "Cousin Ian, did you ever have to hide in a barn, among the hay—after the battle of Culloden, I mean?"

"No, Donald, I did not have to hide anywhere. But your father did."

"I know," said the boy. "But he was very badly hurt, and he could not enjoy it. And he never hid in a loft or a barn—I asked him. It must be so delightful to sleep the whole night all among hay, with nobody knowing that you are there."

"I suppose it might," said his cousin rather absently, without noticing that Donald's youthful countenance was that of one cherishing a bright dream not impossible of realisation.

The two crossed the burn and walked on the track which wound through the heather. In ten minutes or so they began to approach the cleft in the hills sometimes locally called a pass, though it could hardly claim that dignity. But it had at least the distinction of being the highest point of the rough road coming up from Loch Arkaig, and also the property of acting as a sounding-board, for before Ian and Donald had turned the corner into it they heard the beat of hoofs, and knew that there were riders there. A moment later, when they came into the little damp, rocky defile, they saw them, advancing at an easy trot. And they were a lady in a green habit, with a soldier following behind.

" Oh, Cousin Ian, there's Miss Campbell!" exclaimed Donald, very needlessly indeed.

Ian stopped; his heart also, it seemed to him. He looked at his companion, and made up his mind instantly what to do—if Miss Campbell pulled up, as she probably would.

Olivia perceived him, and the trot dropped to a walk. Ian uncovered and went forward, and they met. She pulled up.

" Good morning, Miss Campbell," said the young man, and before Olivia had time to do more than echo the same greeting he went on: " Will you allow me to send the orderly on ahead, and Donald with him, and permit me to walk with you the rest of the way? I have something I wish to ask you."

He did not know it, but his abrupt if humbly phrased request was uttered much more like a command. Olivia looked a little surprised, hesitated for a second, and then said, " Certainly, if you wish it, Mr. Stewart."

Without further words Ian beckoned to the soldier, who had discreetly halted at a distance. " Orderly," he said, as the man came up, " you will go on ahead to the house, and I will escort Miss Campbell thither. Take this young gentleman with you. Up you get, Donald! Will you have him in front of you or behind?"

" In front, if you please, sir," replied the redcoat, stooping from the saddle.

Mercifully Donald was aglow with pleasure at this prospect. Had he objected he would have found himself astride the orderly's horse all the same. Ian waved them forward.

"You are in a very autocratic mood this afternoon, Mr. Stewart," observed Olivia laughing, but not quite easily.

"You pardon me, I hope?" asked the autocrat, his hand on her bridle.

"There seems very little choice," responded she. And as her horse moved forward again, with Ian at its head, she asked, "How does Mr. Maitland to-day? I could not be easy without news of him once more."

"Then you will be relieved to hear that he is much better; indeed he is at this moment walking in the garden."

"Oh, I am glad to hear that!" exclaimed Olivia. "He must in truth be stronger.—And you, Mr. Stewart—I am rejoiced to see that you are able to abandon your sling. But to find you still here is a surprise. I thought you gone to Appin by now."

"I go to-morrow."

A little silence ensued, during which they came out of the fern-clad walls of the defile into the wider stretch of moor and mountainside. Away amongst its trees sparkled Loch na h-Iolaire, and Olivia's eyes were on it. How he would have loved to show it to her—but he never would. . . .

"Had I known that you were leaving to-morrow," she observed suddenly, "you might have brought me news of Mr. Maitland, since you must pass Fort William."

"But you are such a notable horsewoman, Miss Campbell, that it would not have been necessary."

Olivia looked down at the top of his head. He sounded cross; was it possible that he was jealous of her coming all this way a second time to see Mr. Maitland? Everything was possible with a man, but how extraordinarily foolish,

especially when he himself would have none of her.—
Foolish and dear!

"How far are we from the house now?" she asked.

"About three quarters of a mile."

It occurred to Olivia that if she dismounted it would
take longer to cover that distance than at her horse's walk.
"I feel a trifle stiff, so I think I will get out of the saddle
and walk a little," she announced. "And since you have
deprived me of my escort, Mr. Stewart, I fear you'll have
to lead my horse yourself."

Ian had not foreseen her dismounting, and that he
would consequently have her in his arms for a brief
moment. He could, however, pretend to himself that it
was Jacqueline whom he was helping off her horse.
Fortified by this remarkable and not very successful piece
of dissimulation he received her as she sprang from the
saddle—a light enough burden—and they set out side by
side, the wind bringing to them in little warm puffs the
scent of the heather.

Without saying much they came to the bridge, and to
an unexpected difficulty, for Miss Campbell's horse
showed an invincible objection to crossing it. Ian tugged
and urged him, but he would not set a hoof upon it.

"Surely," said Olivia, "he cannot imagine that it is
too narrow for him! The horse I was riding the other day
did not think twice about going over it."

"Perhaps he will consent to go through the burn, even
though it is somewhat in spate," suggested Ian. "'Tis
not very deep here, and the bottom is good." He
scrambled into the saddle and succeeded in getting the
animal through without much trouble. Olivia, on the
bridge, stood and watched the performance.

"A thousand thanks, Mr. Stewart," she said, as he

gained the bank. "But what a foolish beast—though this is, indeed, a beautiful burn to go through." She lingered a moment on the bridge, gazing down at the joyous little tide of the Allt Buidhe, while Ian, swinging off her horse, and thinking how much he should dislike a side-saddle, stood on the further bank waiting for her.

"It looks," said Olivia suddenly and rather mischievously, leaning on the rail, "it looks as though someone had been tearing up a letter here." And she pointed down stream to where three or four small fragments of paper, carried by the wind, showed white among the stems of a water weed.

Behind her horse Ian coloured suddenly. The next moment he had knotted the reins to the end of the rail and had stepped on to the bridge himself. "You are quite right. Someone has been tearing up a letter here. It was I; and the letter was yours. And that brings me to what I want to ask you, Miss Campbell."

She turned a startled face on him. "A letter of mine! I have never written you a letter, Mr. Stewart!"

"I know that. The letter was to my sister Grizel. But I . . . I had it in my possession . . . till this afternoon. It was foolish of me. Just before you came I tore it up and threw it into the burn, and with it something else from your hand, I believe, which I had kept till then. Of that—and it is what I desired to ask you— you have, perhaps, some knowledge?"

Her cheek answered that question. It was crimson. She said, "Oh, Mr. Stewart!" in a small voice, and clapped her hands over her face like any schoolgirl.

"You did put the sprig of gall in my hands, then," he asked rather harshly. "Why?"

Olivia did not answer, and he could not see her face.

But a movement passed across her shoulders, and Ian concluded that she was laughing.

"It was, I admit, an amusing prank," he continued. "It must be gratifying, too, to learn that I kept your posy so long. But, you see, I have thrown it away at last —of my own free will!" he concluded defiantly.

A very low voice murmured something which sounded like—but surely could not be—"I think that you have thrown me away also!" There was a catch of tears, or laughter, in that voice.

Ian dared not come nearer; he was already not far off, since the bridge was very small. Olivia removed one of the hands from her face and began to run it agitatedly along the rail; and Ian saw upon the cheek thus revealed something bright . . . She had not been laughing; it was . . . the other thing!

At that glittering drop he remained staring incredulously, while the bridge for a second or two might have been a boat upon an unquiet sea. Below his feet the Allt Buidhe sped on, with here and there a leap of foam; the tethered horse champed his bridle impatiently. Very slowly Ian approached, and then abruptly caught the little hand which strayed along the wood, bent his head, and put his lips upon it passionately. Pinned to the rail, it contracted and moved beneath the imprisoning kiss.

"What is the use of that?" asked Olivia's voice above him, with a note in it he had never heard, like a child half angry, half sorrowful. "I cannot be your wife, so why . . ." The hand escaped.

Ian lifted his head and looked full at her. The grey eyes and the dark blue met; and the two upon the bridge were plunged into a stream infinitely stronger and swifter than the Allt Buidhe. All consideration of where he

was went from Ian, all his costly scruples and his difficult loyalty.   He caught both her hands.

"You do love me, you do love me, Olivia?   Heart of
my heart, little white love, let me hear you say it . . .
this once!"

§2

"But you must know it," said Olivia softly, a moment
or two later.   "You must know that if it were not so I
should never have permitted you to . . . to kiss me;
. . . And I should not have made you the gift which
you have just thrown away."

Ian's arms tightened round her.   He was holding more
than her hand now, and the little three-cornered riding-
hat rested against his shoulder.   He would have liked
to take it off, if she would have permitted it, but did not
wish to spare a hand for the purpose.

"You did make that gift then!"   How brightly the
sun shone!   "By what magic did you come there when I
was asleep?"

She glanced up at him.   "Is it chivalrous to demand
that of such a poor, foolish, besotted girl?" she demanded
reproachfully.

"Yet how could you know——"

"I did not know!   I thought that, having given
Elspeth the slip, I should be alone there.   You can hardly
guess my feelings when I saw that I was not alone!   I
really fancied that I was bewitched.   And then I so
feared that you would wake, and learn my foolishness."

"*I* could hardly have reproached you with that, *mo
chridhe!*   And yet I must avow that it was mere chance

—at least, I believed it mere chance—which led me to the wood. But when I recognised where I was, and remembered "—Ian drew a long breath—" then I stayed."

" And fell asleep! Was that remembering?"

" But I dreamt of you, beautiful spirit of the place!" said he eagerly. " I dreamt that you were standing there —and that could not have been wholly a dream. I even tried to speak to you!"

" Indeed you did not . . . or at least, you had no success. You were as sound asleep, sir, as——"

" As Endymion?" suggested Ian.

" You flatter me," said Olivia, sparkling.

" And myself too, perhaps. But the bog-myrtle? Why did you——"

" Oh, Diana knows, perhaps," said she, half laughing. Then her look grew dreamy. " I saw a patch growing not far away, and since it is the badge of our clan . . . and you lay sleeping under an oak, your own emblem . . . I believe I thought it might prove . . . a kind of charm."

" A charm . . . to make me stay longer at Kilrain?"

" That," said Olivia, laughing outright, " is a question which the panel does not feel bound to answer. Moreover, who knows what a charm may not accomplish in some other, unintended way. At least I thought 'twould puzzle you! Yet I think it must have worked upon me instead." She looked at him, quite serious, the smile gone, but with a light in the depths of her eyes, clear as sea-water, but not of its colour—grey like the dawn. " Do you know why I fell in love with you . . . Ian?"

He caught his breath at the sound of his name in that

voice. It came winging to him like a word from Paradise.

"I could not guess. . . . Who could divine any possible reason for a thing so wonderful . . . so unlikely?"

Olivia held him by the lapels of his coat. There was mischief as well as tenderness in her gaze. "It was because I could not make you do as I desired!"

But at that avowal, which should have lifted him to the supreme pinnacle of pride, Ian awoke and perceived whither the two of them were fast being swept—towards a shore they could never reach. And the bright world turned dun and cold . . . For a moment speech was not possible; but he was able to slacken his hold of her, before he said sadly:

"It is not my will that stands out against you, Olivia. It is Fate."

Her hands dropped instantly from his coat; he saw the colour leave her lips, her eyes change. "I thought we had done with Fate! If not, why are we——"

"Because we are bewitched," broke in Ian desperately. "Because you are so beautiful and I love you so . . . and am so despicably weak."

Olivia Campbell, very pale, had retreated the little space to the rail of the bridge. "And so——" she began, with a flash in her eyes.

"And so little a man of honour—say it if you must, for it is true!" he cried, retreating himself. "Oh, I should have let you ride on . . . I should never have spoken to you again! There's nothing left me now, not even your good regard . . . I wish the sword which went into my arm a while ago had gone through my heart instead!"

He said it as if he meant it, and he did mean it. A

sword thrust in that region would have spared him this moment.

Olivia suddenly twisted her hands together. " Oh, my grief!" she said brokenly; " Was I harsh? . . . 'Twas because I was bewildered. Ian, Ian, how can you say such a thing! " And she, who rarely wept, broke into weeping. " Ian, I cannot let you go, I cannot!" Then she stretched out a pitying hand. " Was it a sword, then, that wounded you? There's a sword in my heart too. Can't you pull it out? . . . You could, you could, but you are so thrawn . . . and I love you for it, yet I . . ." She became inaudible, partly from tears, partly because she had turned away and buried her face in her hands.

Ian stood with his arms at his sides. His resolution was nearly worn down; he dare not touch her again. Yet he could not, could not leave her sobbing like that! The moment he was a trifle nearer—no distances were other than trifles on that narrow bridge—Olivia, still sobbing, turned and clung to him; and he tried to comfort her, not knowing what words he used, save that they were vain.

So employed, it was no wonder that he was unaware of the slow advent of a man along the path to the bridge. Moreover, the bulk of Olivia's horse, which had moved across the end, somewhat blocked the view, even had he been looking that way; and the beast partly hid the couple on the bridge from the newcomer too. But as the horse moved aside at his approach the latter stepped on to the planks, saw them and stopped dead.

The footsteps on the sounding wood did reach Ian's senses. With Olivia still in his arms he turned his head, and saw David Maitland.

" Olivia," he whispered, " Olivia, there is someone here—Mr. Maitland."

Even that name did not rouse her as he thought it would; she went on sobbing quietly. After a long moment Maitland came further on to the bridge.

"Mr. Stewart, I do not wish to intrude, but perhaps I can be of some service to you. I know now . . . . what I wanted to know."

Then Olivia did lift her head, putting her handkerchief to her eyes, and trying to restrain her sobs.

"I did not mean you to . . . see me like this, God-father . . . I came hither to enquire for you . . . and I was . . . tired with my ride . . . I thought I was . . . going to be h-happy . . . and I find I am not. You cannot move a Stewart, I find; his clan is more to him than——"

"For God's sake do not talk like that!" cried Ian, at the end of his endurance, and careless that Maitland heard him. "You know that I am yours to the last drop of my blood; but I cannot marry you. I would give the rest of my life," he added illogically, "if only I could!"

Maitland came quite close and said in a low voice, "Will you leave Miss Campbell to me for a few minutes? You will not, I think, regret it."

At any rate, thought Ian desperately, he could not make the case any worse. It was out of the question for the elder man really to help him, but the scene must be ended somehow; he at least could not bear much more. He answered rather abruptly: "Yes, I will take Miss Campbell's horse on to the house, and you can follow with her at your leisure." And seeing that Olivia was now looking at him out of tear-drenched eyes, he explained gently, "I am going to leave Mr. Maitland to bring you to the house," and taking her hand, kissed it almost without emotion.

But as he unfastened her horse's reins he took a last glance at her. She was looking neither at him nor at Maitland; she had moved to the other side of the bridge as if to let the wind which blew downstream play on her tearstained face. Her back was towards her old friend, who was standing gazing at her very gravely. Then Ian, bridle in hand, turned away from the place where he had learnt beyond doubt that Olivia Campbell loved him, and where he had come through the worst moments of the tormented journey begun in the field of daisies on Eilean Soa, which must stretch away in front of him for the rest of life.

§ 3

"Olivia," said Maitland at last, gently. "Olivia, my dear . . ."

"Yes, Godfather?"

He came to the rail beside her. "My dear child, I wish with all my heart that I could help you! You do truly love that young man?"

"I do truly love that young man," she repeated, as if it were a confession of faith. Her eyes were fixed upon a distant mountain peak. Then, with an effort at once heroic and pathetic, she added, "'Tis unfortunate, is it not, since he refuses to marry me. That is to put it bluntly indeed, yet not too bluntly. He says that there is too much to keep us apart."

"Yes, I know what it is. He told me."

"You have talked to him about it?"

"Once. I wished to sound his feelings for you. They

are sincere; I have no doubt of that. And now I know yours, Olivia."

"You could hardly mistake them, coming upon me thus," avowed Olivia, trying to smile. "But what is the good of learning all this, dear Godfather; though I know it is your affection for me which makes you desire to go into the matter."

"No," answered Maitland, looking at her narrowly, "it does indeed seem of little use. That barrier . . ."

"It is terrible to be so helpless, to have happiness—for I know I should be happy with him, and he, I think, with me—to have happiness put almost into one's hand and then snatched away."

"Perhaps," said Maitland slowly, "happiness, like most things that we desire, has to be paid for."

"Ah me!" said Olivia sighing, "as if I would not be willing to pay for it!"

"Would you? How much, I wonder?"

"I'd pay—Godfather, why do you look like that? You are not a warlock, are you? How could there be a bargain, with a price? But if there were, I'd pay it, gladly!" The tears came back for a moment into her eyes. "But there is nothing that I can do. I cannot bring Alan Stewart to life again."

Maitland sighed. "No, my dear, you cannot.—Well, let us be going to the house, if you are sufficiently recovered to face the kind people there."

Olivia turned and put her hand into his arm. "And tell me how far *you* are recovered. What a thoughtless creature I am, keeping you standing thus while I discourse of my own woes!"

CHAPTER XXIV

" ASK MR. MAITLAND . . ."

§ 1

Sept. 9th (continued).

ONCE before, doubting his own resolution, had Ian conveyed himself bodily from the neighbourhood of Olivia Campbell until such time as he could ride away from it altogether; now he did much the same until she should ride away from his. And so, while Olivia was resting, and being entertained by Alison Cameron and chattered to by the little boys, he, her lover, was lying on his face under the pines at the farther end of Loch na h-Iolaire.

He lay there so long, so motionless, so much like a man slain, that the wild things of the wood began to disregard his presence, and from a bracken frond above his head a spider swung down an experimental gossamer and tethered it to his coat collar.

After a long time he stirred and got to his feet, frightening a young hind which had come down to the loch for a drink. Dazzled by the sunlight, he shaded his eyes a moment, then looked at his watch. Olivia must surely have started back by now. Slowly he went along the smiling loch side, and more slowly still turned off towards the house. If she were not yet gone, but upon the point of departure, he risked meeting her if he went in by the front of the house, so he bent his steps towards the stable-yard, thinking that he could there discover whether the horses from Fort William were gone.

They were gone; he had successfully carried out his unheroic plan. But in the yard, in charge of an unknown gillie, were, oddly enough, two other strange horses, one of them a grey which nevertheless seemed somehow familiar. So did the other, when he looked at it again. The swart-faced gillie, too, Ian fancied that he had seen before; but *he* came out of a different department of memory. His own mind, however, was so numbed by that hour of seeming death under the pines that he had not much interest in recapturing a more exact recollection. The only feeling of which he was really conscious was the beginning of a bitter ache which throbbed already like a bruised nerve—an ache of reproach for not having said farewell . . . It was too late now.

In the hall he met Ewen.

"Miss Campbell has gone, I think?" he observed listlessly.

Ewen gave him a look. "About a quarter of an hour ago." And in a lower tone he added, "You had the courage to remain away from the house, of design?"

"Or the cowardice," answered his cousin. He went towards the stairs, but Ardroy stopped him.

"I wish you would come into my room for a few minutes, Ian. I have just had a letter about which I should like to consult you."

His tone was peculiar, and looking at him again Ian saw that something was wrong. He wrenched his own mind from following Olivia.

"I will come with pleasure. What is it?"

Ewen waited until he had shut the door of his little sanctum behind him.

"The first point is that Glenshian has suddenly sent back Hector's horse and effects."

"Ah," said his cousin, "I thought I had seen that horse out there before. (I came in by the stable yard.) And the grey, too—why, is not that——"

"Yes, it is Mr. Maitland's," replied Ardroy rather drily. "From the same quarter."

"But you knew that he had been at Invershian. And the horse has been sent back very conveniently, for Maitland proposes to leave the day after to-morrow, does he not? What is there amiss in that? The surrender of both horses shows, on the contrary, a desire on the part of Glenshian to mend his ways."

Ewen had sat down at the writing table and was drumming upon it with the fingers of one hand in a manner unlike him. The other, as Ian now saw, was clenched over something. "Yes, if he had only sent the horses and baggage. But he has written me a letter also."

"About those damned cattle of his? But he *dare* not now——"

"There's not a word in it about cattle. I think he has abandoned the idea of citing me for theft, though he characteristically does not say so. And, as I do not put the least faith in anything which comes from him, I do not believe what he has written here, this . . . this horrible allegation. It's a lie—it must be! But all the same I wish to God he had not made it."

"Do you think, my dear Ewen," asked his cousin, "that Glenshian is likely to write you a letter of compliment? But what new charge is he bringing against you now?"

"There's no charge against me," said Ardroy. "I almost wish there were, for I could better deal with it.

But look at this!" And out of his clenched hand came a missive which he smoothed, and threw across the table very much, had Ian but known it, as he had thrown into the gutter another object which Finlay MacPhair had touched.

Ian read:

Mr. MacPhair of Glenshian presents his com-plements to Mr. Cameron of Ardroy and is att pains to send him herewith, in adition to Mr. Grant's horse and valise, which he has not the liest desire to retain, those belongeing to one Mr. David Maitland who left his house in haste about fowerteen days since, and hath not returned nor writt to claim them, for the which he doutlesse had his own good resons. But Glenshian has no fancy for being putt to the expence of keping Mr. Maitland's beast longer, and deputes the charge of it to Mr. Cameron, with whom he under-stands Mr. Maitland has obtained shelter.

Here the lofty and impersonal style of the letter suffered a sudden declension, for underneath was written in what seemed to be the same hand, though the slope of the letters was different:

I vow it neer makes me die with laughing when I reflect on whom you are so carefully tending, as I hear. Ask Mr. David Maitland what he was about in Glenbuckie (the word was heavily underlined) *in the March of '53, or rather, what he did immediately after. You'll find the truth a matter of great surprise to you, as it was to poor A—— C——.*

At this epistle Ian sat staring, and could feel himself turning pale.

"My God!" he said after a moment. "He means—no, he can't mean!—that it was David Maitland who sent that information about Doctor Cameron!"

"Don't say that you believe it!" cried Ardroy sharply.

"Of course I do not—any more than you do. The idea is preposterous. Maitland, *Maitland* Glenshian's tool, whom he is now betraying? No!"

"But what," asked Ewen uneasily, "has Glenshian to gain by writing such a monstrous thing to me?"

"He has two aims, I think. First, he wishes to perturb you, in which he has succeeded; secondly, to produce some kind of unpleasantness between you and your guest, with whom he has obviously had some violent disagreement. In both he has been actuated by nothing more than sheer malice. You have checkmated him over the cattle; he is bound to have another blow at you."

"Yes, I suppose that must be it," acquiesced Ewen slowly. "It cannot be anything else—dirty traitor that he is, seeking to fix his own guilt upon an innocent man—a man of Maitland's type, too! He might have selected someone more probable."

"Why not burn the letter and think no more about it?" suggested his cousin.

"No, I cannot do that. I cannot allow Maitland to go in ignorance of what an enemy is saying of him."

"No, I suppose not," agreed Ian rather dubiously. "And yet that is playing into Glenshian's hands. He is no doubt hoping to create animosity between you."

"But why should there be animosity? I can make it quite clear to Maitland that I do not believe a word of what Glenshian hints at, especially since I know how deeply Finlay himself was concerned in that betrayal."

"Where is Mr. Maitland now?" asked Ian.

" He has gone on a horse of mine to set Miss Campbell a little on her way. I shall not say anything about this letter until there is a chance of discussing it with him undisturbed—not, I think, until after supper to-night."

Ian strayed over to the window. How far had Olivia ridden by now; and what had Maitland said to her by the bridge which *he* " would not regret?" Regret . . regret . . . how could there be anything but regret? He was sorry that Maitland, who had shown him unexpected sympathy, should have this evening to go through a distasteful scene. Life indeed was clouded just now . . .

When he turned again Ewen was still sitting at the table frowning, with his chin propped on his fists. " I wish nevertheless that I knew what it was which took Maitland to Invershian at all, and what drove him so abruptly away," he said. " I'd liefer think there was no connection between a man to whom I have taken a liking and one whom I despise and detest."

" Well, you'll no doubt get the matter cleared up to your satisfaction this evening," returned his kinsman.

§ 2

Ian happened to be sitting with a book in the window of the living-room at Ardroy when, about half-an-hour before supper, the other guest came riding slowly back to the house. Maitland's head was dropped upon his breast, and he appeared buried in thought. In other circumstances Ian would have gone out to meet him, but now he felt a certain constraint, due to his recent conversation with Ewen. Besides, the poor gentleman looked tired. So he let him be.

Had he known, it was of him that Maitland was thinking as he returned, of him and Olivia, and so deeply that his own never-failing source of torment, all the sharper since Miss Cameron's revelation of Ardroy's actual presence at Tyburn with his cousin, had for the time ceased to gnaw at him. He went upstairs to his room and, never noticing the presence of his recovered valise in a corner, threw himself on the bed, for the ride had fatigued him, and lay staring at the ceiling. What was the right thing to do? Olivia had said that she would pay any price. Would she pay *that*—willingly?

Downstairs Ian continued to read his book, or tried to do so. He had not seen Ewen since their interview, for Ardroy had subsequently gone out. As the clock neared the hour the family began to assemble for supper, first Miss Cameron, then Ewen, then Maitland himself. The latter came over towards Ian and the window, which was still open. It occurred to the young man, on the approach of the convalescent, to shut it, and he was just on the point of doing so when a small figure made its appearance outside, and Donald, seizing his opportunity, thrust in his head.

"Mr. Maitland," he exclaimed, "do you know that your horse has come back from Invershian as well as Uncle Hector's? I have been talking to the gillie out there, and——"

"Why are you not in bed?" interrupted his father, coming to the window. "Do you know what time it is? Be off, you young rascal!"

Donald disappeared with celerity. But the pebble of information which he had flung in, though it was not news to Ian or Ardroy, seemed to have struck David Maitland as though it were a real missile. Ian, who was nearest, observed him draw his breath sharply and put his hand over his mouth with the instinctive gesture of one who desires to suppress an exclamation. And Ian knew that Ardroy's eyes also were fixed on the elder man, and that he had seen his discomposure.

"Mr. Maitland's horse sent back?" commented Aunt Margaret. "I think Master Finlay might have been a thought more prompt about it, with Hector already gone off on that beast of yours, Ewen! Did he not send any letter—any excuse about Hector's?"

"Yes, he sent a letter," answered Ewen briefly, in a tone which plainly implied that he did not wish to pursue the subject. "Ah, here's Alison. Alison, my dear, do you know that Donald is still running loose outbye?"

"Morag has just captured him," answered his wife smiling, and they all took their places at the table, where, after he had fulfilled his duties as master of the house, Ardroy began to talk firmly about a scheme which he had in view of planting that recently introduced tree, the larch. Ian, and Alison too, obediently followed his lead, but Miss Margaret Cameron, always independent, clearly preferred to continue investigating the matter of the returned horses, which, she averred, was of far more general interest to the present company than non-existent trees.

"I feel a certain concern in that redheaded young gentleman since my encounter with him in this room in June. You are sure 'tis horses he has sent this time, Ewen, not steers?"

"I have not seen them, Aunt Margaret, but I imagine that they know the difference in the stables.—Ian, why has Uncle Alexander never taken to the larch?"

"My father's old-fashioned, as you know," answered Ian, and pursued the larch a while longer. Maitland took little part in the discussion, and did not appear to be eating much . . . but that might be ascribed to recent illness. Ian wished that he could avoid observing him, but, sitting almost opposite, he could not.

"Perhaps, Ewen," suggested Miss Cameron, with mischief in her eye, "you would do well to ask Glenshian his opinion of larch-planting. Being young, and new to his estate, and knowing nothing about the subject, he'll be sure to have one."

But here Lady Ardroy turned Miss Cameron's flank by asking Mr. Maitland how he found himself after his ride, a topic which immediately diverted Aunt Margaret's attention, though, leading as it did to questions about Miss Campbell, and at what point her escort had parted from her, it was not altogether the subject which Ian would have chosen.

By now the daylight had somewhat waned, and Angus MacMartin, who was serving, lighted the candles.

"The gillie from Invershian is having some supper, I hope?" asked Ewen in an undertone, and Angus replied that he was. Ian, who guessed rather than heard the question, contrived to keep his eyes from seeking Maitland's face across the table . . . though surely it was rather absurd to be so scrupulous. And yet . . .

Ordinarily, since there was no drawing-room at Ardroy, the ladies did not retire farther than to another part of the large parlour. To-night, however, the Fates appeared to have decided to clear the board at once for Ewen's explanation with his guest, for Alison, when she rose, announced her intention and Aunt Margaret's of spending the evening in the latter's bedroom over some unspecified task which male eyes were apparently not to rest upon.

"Very good," said her husband; and when, after holding the door open for the two of them, he came back to his place at the head of the table, he dismissed Angus in a manner which told that astute and devoted young man that he was not to enter the room again unless he were summoned. So Ian knew that his kinsman was going to bring forward the matter of Glenshian's letter here, and in front of him. He rather wondered that Ewen had not invited Maitland to his own room, where they could be more certain of privacy, but came to the conclusion that he wished to make the business as informal as possible, lest it might look as if he were bringing an accusation against his guest.

So the three of them sat at the long table finishing their claret. Ian, instinctively desiring to postpone the unpleasant moment which was coming, engaged Maitland, with fair success, in small talk. But, the instant it died down, Ardroy, who had taken no part in it, began with his customary directness:

"Mr. Maitland, I have this afternoon received a letter from MacPhair of Glenshian, sent with the horses of whose return you have heard. I think you ought to see it, for in it he makes an allegation against you so monstrous that, were I not convinced of its falsity, I should hesitate to acquaint you with it."

Maitland leant suddenly back in his chair. By this movement of his the hand which had been on the table near his glass disappeared below it. He sat quite still for a second or two.

"Glenshian and I have quarrelled," he said at last, in

a voice so unlike his usual one that Ian had to look twice to be sure that it was he who spoke.

"I guessed that," said Ewen gravely. "And I assure you, sir, from my experience of Glenshian, that I do not believe a word he says upon any subject. But it would not be just to you to keep this charge of his from your ears."

"May I . . . know what it is?" asked Maitland, in that voice which gave an impression of creaking as it came forth.

Ewen instantly extracted the crumpled letter from his pocket-book and passed it to him.

Whatever devilry on Glenshian's part Maitland expected after this warning—and he hardly knew what he did expect—it was not that which now stared him in the face. For he did not immediately read the whole letter; the underlined word *Glenbuckie* at the end caught his eye at once, and he knew that he was lost. The one thing which he had thought Finlay MacPhair would never do he had done—for the sake of revenge!

Yet, as a man might clutch at a mere tuft of grass before sliding down a precipice, he gained a moment's respite by slowly reading the letter through. Then he looked up . . . and did not need to feign consternation.

"I do not understand . . . What is this that Mr. MacPhair is hinting at? 'Glenbuckie'? That means——"

"It means," said Ewen with visible reluctance, "that he is accusing you of acting as his tool in the betrayal to the English Government of my cousin Archibald Cameron. I know that Glenshian had a tool—the man who actually sent the letter which brought my kinsman to the scaffold. He is charging you with being that man."

There was still, perhaps, foothold as well as hand-hold. "I am no tool of Glenshian's," replied David Maitland with emphasis.

"I never believed it for a moment," said Ardroy with an air of relief, and Ian too was conscious of the lifting of a heavy weight. "Why, as you told me the other day, you never even knew Doctor Cameron."

Maitland shook his head, since there appeared to be a tacit question in the remark. Speech seemed to have withered on his lips. He brought up one of the hands which had been clutching the other under the table, and, trying to keep it steady, drank off a gulp of wine. He did not know that on the back of that hand, so deeply imprinted as to be visible by candlelight, were the nail-marks of the other, and that they lasted while he drank, and a little after.

But Ian, across the table, saw the marks, and they affected him very unpleasantly. His sensation of relief deserted him again. Either there *was* something in this charge of Glenshian's, or Maitland, since hearing of the letter, had been anticipating some other accusation. For one thing he had not expressed what one might have looked for, an indignant, a horrified surprise at the charge; moreover he was obviously in a state of extreme tension.

Ardroy seemed to be sharing his cousin's renewed uneasiness. He reached forward and possessed himself once more of the creased paper.

"Mr. Maitland, what is behind this letter?" he demanded rather sternly. "I can see that you know. And, as Archibald Cameron's kinsman, I have a right to know too. You can speak freely before Mr. Stewart."

Maitland pushed back his chair and looked over his

shoulder at the uncurtained windows behind him,
through which all he could see now was a dark mass
of mountain slope topped by a lighter mass of sky. The
view did not help him. He turned back to the table
again. What should he say, what should he say?

"I begin to believe," said Ardroy, fixing on him that
very blue, steady and now somewhat imperious gaze,
"that you know who the informer was!"

Maitland was silent, half mesmerised by those eyes.
They might be merciless eyes too. An immense fatigue
had invaded his brain.

"Answer me, please," commanded Ardroy. "Be
easy, I'm making no shadow of accusation against *you*.
But you know who he was . . . and Glenshian knows
that you know it!"

He must say something! Truth came easiest. "I
know at least why the . . . the informer did it."

Ewen jerked forward, his hands gripping the edges
of the table. "*Why!*" he exclaimed fiercely. "Good
God, as if there could be any reason but one!"

"It was not the reason that you think," said Maitland
almost inaudibly.

"Whatever it was, since you know it, I demand to hear
it! I demand it, Mr. Maitland!"

Maitland made a struggle, but his heart was not in
it. "You will not believe it, so what use to tell you,
Mr. Cameron?"

"I dare be sworn I shall not," answered Ewen scornfully. "Nevertheless you will tell me, if you please!"

"Not here," retorted Maitland, and he gave the frac-
tion of a glance across at Ian. Olivia's lover was the
last person he desired to be present at . . . whatever
might be about to happen.

Ewen got instantly to his feet. Heavens, how tall he was, and how the candlelight below him threw up the strong lines of his mouth and chin!

"Come to my own room, then, sir, since you are so particular to shield Glenshian's tool."

Maitland rose. "I have said already that the man was no tool of Glenshian's," he answered in a low voice.

Ian perceived the slip. *That* was not what he had said! His blood checked and ran for an instant very chill. Oh no, no, it could not be! . . . He was reading a wrong implication into the difference between the two phrases Mr. Maitland had used. For Ewen, already on the way to the door, had not so interpreted the last. It was true, perhaps, that he had not heard it . . .

Nor did Maitland seem to be aware of what he had said. His face, as he passed out of Ian's line of vision, had almost the appearance of a sleepwalker's, and like a sleepwalker he went out of the door which Ewen held open for him.

CHAPTER XXV

" *HE FORGAVE . . .* "

Sept. 9th (continued).

" WELL, Mr. Maitland?"

Ardroy had turned the key in the lock and stood in the middle of the room. By the hearth, with his hand on the back of an armchair, David Maitland faced him; he had refused a seat. For a second or two he could almost see himself standing there, as one sees an actor on the stage, interested, perhaps moved by the situation, expectant of the words he is about to speak, but aware that the whole business is at bottom nothing but a play.

" The man who did this thing," he began slowly but quite steadily, his eyes fixed on a little frizzle of horse-hair escaping from the worn top of the chair, " this man was once a convinced Jacobite like yourself, and had given proofs of his conviction. But during those sad years after the failure of the Rising he had come, much against his will, to see how utterly vain were the hopes upon which it had been based, and what a disaster to Scotland, to all whom he loved, would be a repetition of——"

The Highlander with an impatient movement cut him short. " Suppose that after all we leave that part to the end, and that, since you know so much of the traitor's mind, you tell me first how he had the chance of doing what he did—and who he was!"

Maitland dropped his hand from the chair back. " That last I cannot tell you, Mr. Cameron."

" You mean that you will not?"

" Do you wish me to act the traitor too?"

" He was surely not a friend of yours!" exclaimed Ewen in a tone of repugnance.

" I knew him well . . . once," answered Maitland very slowly.

" Is he still alive?"

Maitland nodded.

" And in enjoyment of a pension from the English Government, no doubt," commented Ewen in a tone of great bitterness. " Unless Glenshian, the arch-traitor, contrived to keep all the money for himself."

A fleeting vision of Glenshian's face the other night, lusting after that visionary blood-money, came and went, and with it the unnatural feeling of being exterior to all this departed also. " The man I speak of did not betray for money, Mr. Cameron. He would sooner have shot himself. Yet he has been paid—my God, he has been paid!" Maitland's voice began to shake a little. " Two years of the most bitter, the most unceasing remorse, when, if he could only have given his own life instead of the life he so mistakenly sacrificed (thinking merely to deprive a conspirator of the chance of doing further harm) he would have asked no greater boon of Heaven!"

He ceased, staring straight in front of him, and the room was filled with an aching silence. But Ewen, very white, had recoiled a little until he was brought up by the table behind him. No one could easily believe that those heartwrung accents came from the lips of a man who was merely pleading for another, even for a friend whom he had known well . . . once. The ghastly suspicion provoked by Glenshian's letter, which Ewen had flung aside, now hissed deafeningly in his ear.

"It is not possible that, after all . . . it's not possible!" he whispered, out of lips as dry as Maitland's
own.

And then Maitland saw, too late, what he had done.
The passion and sincerity of his own remorse had betrayed him. Nor could he fight any longer for foothold;
he was worn down by the unceasing torment within, by
the pressure of this place with its talk and its memories
of the man whom he had sacrificed. It was the end;
he only longed to make it complete.

There was a pistol lying on the mantelshelf; he had
seen it as he came in. He went and took it by the barrel
and held it out. "I do not know if this is loaded. If
it is, use it on me, and I will thank you with my last
breath."

But Ardroy made no motion either to take or to
repulse the weapon; he only stood looking at the man
who offered it.

"There must be a mistake. You don't mean what
you are saying. It was not *you!*". A lock of tawny hair
had fallen disordered over his forehead, and emphasized
his paleness and the ice-blue of his eyes, full of the pro-
foundest horror.

"I do mean it," answered Maitland. "I am the most
unhappy man on earth. You would be doing me a kindness." He continued to hold out the pistol.

And now Ardroy, his eyes still fixed upon him, took
it. Away at Invershian Finlay MacPhair must surely
have held his breath.

"I will come with you wherever you wish," added
Maitland unemotionally. "For you were better not do
it in here, where the sound of a shot—"

Ewen Cameron gave the strangest laugh. "Why

should I play executioner? And the thing's not loaded. And I swore at Archie's burying that I would not . . . Nevertheless, to make sure—" The heavy pistol went crashing through the window out into the darkness beyond.

"Now sit down," said its sender, his voice pulsing with a fury and an agony not less terrible for being held in leash, "sit down where the man you betrayed once sat, and tell me—" he drew a long choking breath, "tell me, not about these noble motives of yours, but how you compassed it!"

Maitland sat down where he was bidden. He was not conscious of fear, only of regret for the pain that he was inflicting. He had told himself so many times recently, when confession had tempted him, that it would be stabbing Ewen Cameron to confess. Now he was doing it. He wondered if Ewen would hear him out; he had never seen a man so pale. The pistol was gone, but the Highlander, he knew, could easily kill him with his bare hands. That did not greatly matter; but he hoped he might be able first to finish all he wanted to say. . . .

Outside the night pressed against the window, and found an entry too, through the shattered pane. Every now and again the twin candle flames on the table bent and wavered, wavered and straightened themselves again.

"I must tell you," began Maitland, with his eyes upon those flames, "that my wife, who is partly Highland, had a little property on Loch Voil which she had for some time wished to dispose of. Early in 1753 Mr. Ferguson, a neighbouring laird, made an offer for it, and we decided to sell it. That was what took me to the Braes of Balquhidder in the March of that year. And I must also tell you, Mr. Cameron, for it has much bearing upon my . . . upon the step I took . . . how painful an impression I received from the still partly demolished condition of Balquhidder itself, which, as you perhaps know, had suffered a partial burning at the hands of the Government troops after the Forty-five, and in which there were still many poor houses in ruins."

He paused a moment. Ardroy's gaze, sombre, freezingly hostile, and full of pain, was fixed upon him, but nothing came from his lips. Maitland went on in the same level tones:

"The sale of the property being almost a foregone conclusion, I had brought with me the necessary documents, drawn up by a lawyer. All that Mr. Ferguson and I needed, in the little inn at Balquhidder to which we had adjourned after visiting the property, was a couple of witnesses. We were just about to summon the landlord when two persons passed the window—there was some kind of a local cattle fair going forward—and Mr. Ferguson said, 'There is Duncan Stewart of Glenbuckie; I will ask him and the gentleman that's with him to serve as witnesses for us.' In a moment he came back with the two of them, and on his explaining what he wanted Mr. Stewart said that he would willingly append his signature to the deed, but that he feared his friend would be unable to do so, having, he said, hurt his hand. This he said somewhat meaningly, I thought, and the gentleman with him, whose right hand appeared quite uninjured, gave a little smile as though he were amused. Mr. Ferguson laughed and said, 'You mean, Glenbuckie—we're all friends here—that his name would not have a very good appearance upon any legal document just now.' And at that I looked again at Mr. Stewart's companion, and recognised him for Doctor Archibald

Cameron, whom I had seen more than once during the Rising, though I had never spoken to him."

A pause. Ewen's lips moved. " Poor Archie! "

" Doctor Cameron said that he would find a substitute, and going out he returned with a farmer of the neighbourhood, and so the deed was signed. Mr. Stewart and the Doctor left almost immediately, but from something which was said in talk it was clear that Doctor Cameron was staying with Mr. Stewart at his house. I knew already that he was pretty generally supposed to be in the Highlands working for the Cause, but also that his whereabouts had naturally been kept very secret.

" All the way back to Perth I was turning the situation over and over in my mind, with the ruins of those poor cottages at Balquhidder still before my eyes. Here was a man whom I admired and respected doing his utmost to rekindle the fires which should burn the rest of them. For I was as sure as of anything under heaven that an attempt which had failed when it had had the Prince in person to lead it could never succeed now, wanting him. And what of the waste of lives—of the lives of young men above all? I fear I thought first of my own son, scarce of age, whom there would be no restraining . . . but not of him only. . . . I wished with all my soul that I had tried an appeal to Doctor Cameron. But I knew that it would have been in vain. There was no means of stopping him so long as he was in Scotland and at liberty.

" And as I went, picturing another and a more hopeless civil war sweeping once more over the fair countryside . . . more blood, more fire, more ruin, and all to no purpose . . . I prayed that Archibald Cameron, brave and single-hearted as I knew him to be, might somehow be checked in what he was doing."

" If you had known," broke in Ewen, shading his eyes suddenly with his hand, " how little, God help him, he *was* doing . . ."

" And from that," went on Maitland after a slight pause, " it was not a very far cry to speculating on the means which might put a stop to his activities. He might, for instance, be recalled—or he might be captured."

Ewen went abruptly to the dark, broken window. But the speaker continued steadily.

" He naturally ran the risk of capture and of imprisonment every hour that he was in Scotland. Yes, Ardroy—" Maitland got to his feet—"I swear solemnly by the God above us, the God in Whom I firmly believe, from Whom I hope—even I—for pardon, I swear that no vision of anything worse crossed my thoughts! "

But all that Ewen said, and without turning round, was, " Go on! "

Standing now, Maitland went on. His voice had dropped.

" You can guess the next step. . . . It was at Perth that it came to me that I had myself the power to stop him. . . . All night long I lay awake wrestling with the thought, and whether I were wrestling with angel or devil I could not tell. The idea of giving up a fellow-Jacobite to a captivity which might last for years was so shudderingly repugnant that at first I could not face it. Yet, on the other hand, there was the heavy thought of all the consequences which I have rehearsed to you—"

This time Ewen swung round from his station. " Captivity! " he said in a hard voice. " You knew, you must have known, that Archibald Cameron was attainted in '46, that he had a death sentence hanging over him . . . and you talk of ' captivity'!"

"I knew that he had been attainted after the Rising. But how many ever dreamt that that seven-year-old sentence would be put into force? Did you, Mr. Cameron?"

"The Government might not have been able to enforce it had they brought him to trial. And brought to trial he would have been, as I believe, but for Finlay MacPhair."

Maitland looked bewildered. "Ardroy, I am telling you the truth as at God's judgment bar! Finlay Mac-Phair, whom I have no cause to love, is for nothing in what I did. I had not then made his acquaintance."

"That was not what I meant," said Ewen. "But you have made it now; you have been with him, you have quarrelled with him, you are—In God's name, David Maitland, what *are* you to Finlay MacPhair?"

"A bitter disappointment, I am glad to think." Life and animosity sprang into the dead voice. "You wish to know why I was recently at his house? It was because, having somehow ferreted out my identity as the sender of that letter to the Lord Justice-Clerk, Glenshian caused me to go there so that he could discover whether I had been paid by the Government for the act, and if not, whether I could be induced to abandon the credit of it to him, so that he himself could claim the reward. He wished to recompense himself for the services he had already done the Government, for which, so he said, he had not been adequately paid. That, though you may not credit it, is what Finlay MacPhair wanted with me at Invershian, and why I walked that night straight out of his house."

Ewen had come back to his former place, his face alight with the fierce eagerness of a hunter who sights a long pursued quarry.

" He acknowledged to you that he had worked for the Government in this matter—he acknowledged it?—Pshaw, Mr. Maitland, you need not hesitate to give evidence against the dirtiest scoundrel who walks this earth, when you could do it against a man like Archibald Cameron! "

Maitland put his hand for a moment over his eyes. " You hit very hard, Mr. Cameron! " He removed it and added, somewhat oddly, " I think I had rather you did . . . Yes, Glenshian acknowledged it. Yet, at the same time, as you see, it was not he who actually informed. I do not say he does not wish it were. But the belief which I overheard you discussing with Mr. Stewart below my window is not justified. Glenshian neither actually betrayed Doctor Cameron nor did any tool of his betray him. . . . And now, since you know the truth about me, you know it about him also."

" I have to believe that hound cleared of the ultimate charge, and you—*you*—guilty! "

" Yes," answered Maitland, but with difficulty. " Yes. I am guilty, and he is innocent. No doubt I should have—"

Ewen made a gesture dismissing Glenshian for the moment. " Go on, if you please, with what you were saying. You were doubtless about to tell me that by morning, that time in Perth, you saw yourself as the saviour of Scotland! I hope the mood lasted. Perhaps not until the seventh of June and Tyburn . . . Saints in Heaven, to think that scaffold, which I trod with him, was raised by *you!* "

" 'Twas partly for your own sake that I did not want you to know it," murmured Maitland. The words would hardly come out now; he put a hand to his throat. " I

hoped that I could get away from here without your
learning it. . . . One day more . . . and I should have
succeeded. When I came on Captain Grant that night I
was about to drown myself . . . I was filling my pockets
with stones to that end. If you could have used that pistol
just now . . . only God knows I would not make you a
murderer also. But since expiation is denied me I know
that I am—" He staggered suddenly.

"Sit down," said Ewen, catching him by the arms. He
put him back in the chair. "I will fetch you some water."

Maitland clutched at him. "No, no! I need none
. . . There's but one thing . . . if you could tell me
that you believe me when I say that I only foresaw imprisonment for him. . . . I suppose I cannot hope for
that . . . I can hope for . . . nothing now."

He lay back and closed his eyes. Ewen gazed at what
this last hour had made of the sensitive and beautifully
chiselled face. Weakness there was perhaps, but not a hint
of baseness. And yet—he had betrayed a comrade.

Nevertheless, a man with that face might have been
so moved by the prospect of calamity falling upon his
country as to contemplate such a step and remain the while
blind to the doom hanging over his victim . . . Ewen
tried to think what Archie himself would do were he
now in his place—but he knew. He knew it as if his slain
kinsman were in this room, where not three years ago he
had sat in the very chair now occupied by his slayer . . .
he knew it penetratingly.

He took a step towards Maitland as though to lay a
hand upon his shoulder and then drew back. No, he
could not touch him in that spirit. But he said, standing
upright, and looking a little as if he himself were facing
a firing party:

"Mr. Maitland, I cannot say that I entirely believe you. But I think I am near believing you; and after a while, perhaps. . . ."

Maitland opened his eyes. "And, when you do . . . will you forgive?"

But Ewen turned away without answering.

"*He* forgave," said the broken voice. "And you heard him."

CHAPTER XXVI

A LIFE FOR A LIFE

§ 1

Sept. 9th (continued).

A SOUND like splintering glass, which he had heard in the living-room, where he still remained, had made Ian very uneasy, and he came out into the hall to listen. But he heard nothing more, and going back he waited, it seemed to him, for an interminable time. At last he thought that he heard someone go upstairs; and about three minutes later he himself went to the door of his cousin's room. There was no sound of voices within; he tapped, there was no answer, so he entered.

The candlelight glinted on Ewen's auburn hair as he sat in one of the chairs by the hearth, with his head bowed between his hands. Maitland was not there. Ian came to a standstill.

"Ewen, it's surely not that—that Glenshian was right!"

The head made a movement of assent.

Somehow the length of the interview seemed to have told Ian that already. And then there was Maitland's own slip. Yet all he said, after one sick moment, was, "Where is he?" But he did not mean Glenshian.

"Gone to his bedchamber, I believe," answered Ewen almost indifferently.

"Not gone altogether?"

"No. He wished to leave to-night, but I would not have it. Nothing—not even *that*—can alter the fact that I brought him here as my guest. . . and am indebted to him."

He rose, very haggard. "I am going out. I cannot stay under the same roof with him . . . though he swears he only took the step he did to prevent a renewal of bloodshed, thinking it would merely mean imprisonment for Archie! My God, that a man could be so deluded. It is enough to send one crazy!"

Ian looked at him dizzily. Maitland—Olivia's Mr. Maitland—really had done this terrible thing, from whatever motive. He was but dimly conscious of following his cousin from the room, yet a few minutes later he was walking with him in the half-darkness along the path towards the loch behind the house, having indeed some ado to keep up with him, for Ewen walked as though he were driven by the furies. At the margin of Loch na h-Iolaire he stopped, and there, whilst the scarcely seen water lapped at the shadowy reeds, he told Ian the story.

"Just a chance meeting," he ended, "a chance meeting—no more—of a few minutes with a man who, if he is to be believed, wished Archie no harm—was moved, one might even say, by high principles and regard for others—and there's Archie, Archie . . ." He obviously could not finish.

"And Glenshian?"

Ewen recovered himself. "Glenshian had no hand in it. A better man than he played the villain's part."

"Are you . . . what are you going to do?"

"Nothing. What can I do? I cannot bring Archie back. Moreover there's my oath."

Ian looked away to the mountains looming vaguely

across the loch. He still only half realised the truth. Ardroy now began to walk on again, beside the loch this time, and they had tramped in complete silence nearly to the end of it, when he suddenly gave a harsh laugh, " So 'twas not Finlay MacPhair after all who twisted that rope. I have been misjudging him, Heaven help me, though one would have sworn that was impossible! Had I not better apologise? "

His tone was so bitter that Ian glanced at him apprehensively. Deep down beneath Ardroy's calm and self-control there coursed, as his kinsman knew, passions stronger than most men's. " I would leave Finlay alone were I you."

" Particularly as his regret is that he cannot claim the guilt," retorted Ewen. " Pah!—let us not talk of him! I will tell you what I mean another time. My head is so hot that I can scarce think or speak. I shall stay here awhile." Kneeling down he dipped his face into the water, then, going back a little distance, sat down against a pine bole.

Ian threw himself on the ground at a yard or two's distance; he too found thought difficult. The man so speculated upon these two years, the execrated unknown informer was . . . the gentle, attractive David Maitland —Olivia's "godfather "! He had confessed; so one *had* to believe it.

Ardroy was silent for so long, his arms folded, his head sunk upon his breast, that at last Ian began to think that he had fallen asleep. It must, surely, be very late; he pulled out his watch but was unable to distinguish the figures. The slight movement roused his cousin, who was evidently not asleep after all, for he raised his head at once.

" You are still there, Ian? "

" Yes. Do you mean to return—" The end of the sentence was broken into by a shrill noise, an unmistakable whinny, followed almost instantly by a sound as though some large and probably frightened animal were plunging through the undergrowth at no great distance.

" Why, that's a horse! " exclaimed Ewen, jumping up. " How came it out of the stable—there are none loose! "

He looked suddenly in the direction of the house, now nearly a mile away, to which their backs had all this time been turned as they sat. It was still invisible by reason of the intervening trees, but in the sky above was written an awful answer to his question.

" O God! " he said under his breath, and started without another word to run wildly in that direction, and Ian with him.

§ 2

After Maitland had gone up to his room he sat for an uncounted space of time on the edge of his bed, so battered by the seas of emotion which had broken over him that he had now been swept into some deep impassive place where they surged harmlessly above his head, a drowned man . . . or one lost for ever in that Dark Mile which had bulked so largely in his feverish journey of a while ago, although he had never reached the actual place.

. . . Or had he come through it, since there was now neither hope nor fear left for him? No, nor even ex- piation, for Ewen Cameron had forsworn revenge; he had told him so.

Without moving from the bed he looked out at the

night. Not very dark. Ardroy had said that he would not have him leave as he had left Invershian, for he had eaten his salt. That rendered even an enemy sacred. And indeed, unless he wished to burden Ewen Cameron with the responsibility for his death (having laid far too much upon him already) he could not safely set off at night in this unknown and mountainous country. Nevertheless all his impulses were towards doing so. How could he face Olivia's lover to-morrow?

Moving like an automaton, he got up at last from his bed, left the room and went along the passage to the window there, from which he could see the irregular square of detached buildings behind the house—stables, granary and the like. In one of those was his recovered horse. Probably the door was not locked. And he continued to stare out, already seeing himself in the saddle, miles away. . . .

Suddenly he came to life, gave an exclamation, and flinging open the window leaned out. Was that *smoke* eddying and curling from the bottom of one of those buildings, that on the left nearest to the house? Maitland leant out further to make sure, for the light was very deceptive. Yes, it was undoubtedly smoke. As he came to that conclusion he saw, though indistinctly, a human form standing below apparently observing the same phenomenon. Fortunately, then, there was someone astir. He shouted down, " You there, do you know that that place is on fire?"

And at that the half-seen man turned and bounded out of sight into the darkness. Gone to summon help, no doubt. But it was for him, Maitland, to make known without delay to someone in the house what he had seen. He went back to his room, seized a candle and set out.

But he could find neither Ardroy nor his cousin anywhere. Then, since the gentlemen of the house had vanished and he was not acquainted with the servant's quarters, he must rouse the ladies. It was quite possible after all that Ardroy was in his wife's room.

He was not, however, for Lady Ardroy, coming after a moment to the door with a shawl about her, said that she did not know where her husband was. She took the news of the outbreak without undue alarm, and on hearing exactly where it was—in the stables—said that it would not be necessary to rouse the children at all and run the risk of frightening them. The great thing would be to get the horses out at once; no doubt by now helpers had been summoned and were doing this, but in case they had not, if Mr. Maitland would go and rouse Angus MacMartin—she indicated his quarters—he and the stable lad could set to work.

But it was Maitland himself and a half-naked Angus who some three minutes later were hastily unbarring the door of the burning building. Not only was there no sign yet of other helpers, but even the stable lad was nowhere to be seen, and there was no time to be wasted in shouting for anyone. Kicking and plunging, the four terrified horses were somehow got out, a difficult and dangerous business too, as was proved at the end when the last animal, which had been particularly unmanageable, reared, lashed out violently and sent Angus to earth with a broken arm. Then it galloped out of the policies after the rest, which there had been no time to tie up.

By now Lady Ardroy and Miss Cameron were out in the yard, and both hurried to poor Angus. Maitland helped him up, half fainting and repeating wildly, "What can be keeping the men?"

"And where in the name of the Good Being is the laird himself?" exclaimed Miss Cameron.

Alas, Maitland, if he did not know the answer to that question, could well guess what had driven him away. He began to shout his name and Ian Stewart's, for already, from lack of helpers and of water it was too late to save the stables; and other buildings, even the house itself, might be endangered.

All at once Alison Cameron gave a scream so terrible that it cut through his own voice like a knife.

"In the loft there . . . look . . . *O God, it's Donald!* "

She ran forward. High up in the stable, in the end facing the house, was an aperture which at first sight Maitland took to be a window. And his blood seemed turned to ice in his heated body, for at it, half veiled in smoke, had appeared the head and shoulders of a little boy.

"Good God, how did he get there?" he exclaimed, loosing hold of Angus and running too. Alison was crying distractedly up to the child, "Donald, Donald, jump down to us, darling! We will catch you!"

"But we must have a sheet or a blanket," interposed Maitland hastily. "Otherwise—"

But Donald's childish tones came down to them sharpened by terror, "I . . . I can't. 'Tis too far . . . And I can't climb over this. . . ."

And then Maitland saw that the supposed window was really of the nature of an open doorway for the reception of hay or corn into the loft, blocked at present, however, across its lower half, by a deep boarding.

"I'll come up to you, Donald!" he shouted. "Stay there—keep your head out in the fresh air.—A ladder, quickly!"

The chief danger to the child was, he believed, suffocation from the smoke, for there was as yet no light behind him to suggest the presence of flames. From somewhere Miss Cameron and the crippled Angus were bringing a small ladder. " But, God be merciful to us, it will be much too short!" cried the distracted young Highlander.

This was obvious. " Is it the only one you can find. Then we must try raising it upon something—that mounting-block yonder."

It took the four of them to shift the block, for it was the solid trunk of a tree. Even as they got it into place Alison gave another cry: " He's gone—he's disappeared! " and looking up Maitland saw that it was only too true. Overcome, no doubt, by the smoke, Donald had slipped down out of sight behind the planking.

The ladder was reared up on the block and steadied, and Maitland ran up. It was of no more use than if it had rested on the ground, for he just failed to reach the sill of the doorway with his fingers. And since the boy was no longer visible, and made no reply when he shouted, he could not encourage him to try to climb over the obstacle and let himself down into his arms on the ladder.

" God in Heaven," he thought as he slid rather than climbed down the ladder again, " there's nothing for it but to attempt it from the inside.—Is there not a trap-door up to the loft from the stables?" he asked. " I though I saw one."

" Aye," said Angus, " and a ladder up to it, fixed to the wall in-bye."

They ran to the door of the burning building. A volley of thick, suffocating smoke came out at them, as if in wrath at their temerity.

"Get me a rope, if you can!" commanded Maitland. "I may have to lower him." He tore off his cravat, steeped it in a butt of water standing there, and tied it over his mouth and nose. Angus came running with a short piece of rope and several yards of cord. As the rope was plainly inadequate, and Donald could not weigh much, Maitland took the cord and wound it round him, Angus, nearly out of his mind, imploring him the while to let him go up in his place.

"No use, with one arm," answered the elder man. "This business needs two. But you can come in with me and show me the ladder—I am not sure of the exact spot. And then go back to the ladies . . . *Now!*"

They plunged in. Partly owing, perhaps, to the direction of the wind, the actual fire was still confined to the further corner, where it had originated. But the mere smoke was more thick and deadly than Maitland could have believed possible. Yet somehow he was clambering up the wooden ladder clamped to the wall, and was fumbling to push open the trap-door above his head. "I have it—I can do it!" he shouted down through his mufflings, and in spite of them paid with a fit of coughing for having attempted speech. Then, exerting all his lately depleted strength, he pulled himself up and through, and found himself on the floor of the loft.

Up here the heat seemed greater. There was not much of the hay which a romantically-minded little boy was like to lose his life for having slept in; it was mostly piled in one corner, and, miraculously enough, had not yet caught fire. Donald himself, a pathetic little figure, lay face downwards by the boarded aperture. A few strides and the rescuer had him in his arms, was raising him up to the fresh air and tying the cord round his body.

It was safer than throwing him down to two women and a one-armed man below, and there was not time to wait for the sheet or blanket which, so far as he knew, had not been brought.

Just as he lifted the inanimate child over the planks two men burst into the yard. Yes, there at last, thank God, was Ewen Cameron, breathless and shouting. In a moment he had thrown aside the useless ladder; and it was into his arms that Maitland lowered Donald through the smoke. The cord was not quite long enough; he had to let him drop the last few feet.

Ewen gave the boy one passionate kiss and passed him immediately to his mother. " Quick, Maitland! " he shouted up. " No time to lose—the roof's catching, I think. I'll throw the rope up again—no, this cord would never bear you. . . . Drop, then—drop!"

But, as Donald had flinched from jumping, so did Maitland from clambering over the planks and dropping. It was too great a distance. Not a young man, and newly convalescent, he was now completely exhausted, shaking from head to foot and almost asphyxiated with the smoke. He could not make a success of the attempt; he knew that. Tearing away the cravat from his mouth he shouted down, " No . . . by the way I came . . . trap-door!" and ran back across the floor.

Thick eddies of smoke were now curling up through the open trap-door, and, just before he got to it, a pile of hay heaped against the nearest wall suddenly flared up and fell forward like a fiery cataract. Maitland jumped back just in time, but, though he was not actually touched, the mere heat singed the clothes on his body from neck to ankle, as well as the unprotected hands which he instinctively put up to shield his face and eyes. . . .

Before he even knew it he was back at the aperture, the only possible way of escape now, and was starting to climb over the boarding to let himself drop. . . .

Ardroy and Ian, who, on hearing what he had shouted to them, had run round to the stable door in order to drag him out when he appeared down the ladder, had seen, directly they got there, that no human being could come alive by that route, for through the mouth of the trap-door was hanging a mass of blazing hay. They ran back again, and were just in time to hear a cry, and to see Maitland fall sideways from the aperture, betrayed by the un-expected slipping forward of the boards which blocked its lower half.

He came down right across the mounting-block which had been placed underneath for his attempt to reach Donald by the ladder.

CHAPTER XXVII

LIGHT IN THE DARK MILE

§ 1

It was the second day after the fire, and the wind was flinging the rain against the window of Ewen's room with such force that the panes were little but a blur of sliding water. Through one, indeed, over which a sheet of paper had been roughly pasted, it was finding a slow entrance drop by drop, brimming over the window-sill to form a tiny pool on the floor. Ian Stewart, standing in front of the window with his hands behind him, watched the process with half-seeing eyes.

Water enough now, and to spare! If only this drenching rain had come thirty-six hours earlier, could it have arrested the tragedy? Or if Donald had never been inspired with that fatal desire of spending a night in the loft —or had been seen as he slipped from the house to carry it out: or if Alison Cameron had not decided (as Ian now knew that she had) against having the children roused when Maitland had given the alarm, since otherwise the boy's absence would have been discovered, and in time, perhaps, to rescue him at less cost. Or if Ewen and he had not left the house that evening under the stress of emotion and taken themselves out of earshot. Or, supposing a sharper watch had been kept on that gillie of Glenshian's who had spent the first part of the night here, and had then so mysteriously vanished, could the catastrophe have been prevented altogether?

A drop trembled on the edge of the sill, detached itself, and went to the floor. Of what use were a hundred surmises, when upstairs a man's life was trickling away like this rain-water which spilled itself with such silent persistence? And two nights ago this quiet room had echoed to the clash of agony and passion; yet nothing of all that remained, save the witness of the broken window, and a fleck or two of blackened paper on the hearth, where Ewen, early next morning, had burnt Glenshian's letter to ashes. Even Alison must never know what it had contained.

Impelled by a sudden draught, several drops now hurried themselves off the window-sill at once. The door had opened; Ian turned and saw Ardroy shutting it behind him. His face was greyed with vigil and strain.

"How is he?"

Ewen looked at first as if he had not heard the question. Then he answered slowly, "Awake, and asking for you."

"For me!" exclaimed Ian. The information seemed to set flowing some spring of hope in him, and he said impetuously, "Ewen, do you not think that, after all, there is some chance for him? There must be, there must be!"

Ardroy's tired face turned a shade greyer. "There is not the smallest hope; the surgeon said so. You know that his back is broken, besides the internal injuries. Morrison said that the end would be quite peaceful; that he would suffer less and less. Indeed he is in no pain at all now. We have to face it . . . though I don't know how to do it."

Ian turned away. "Does he know?"

"Perfectly well. When I said just now . . . he had asked me point-blank whether I had told you of . . . of his action in regard to Archie . . . when I said in reply that it should always remain a secret between you and me, and that if ever he came here again he would be received as what he was, the man to whom I owe my son's life—God knows why one makes these pretences of a future for the dying, but one does—he answered that I must know well he could never come to this house again, because he should never leave it." Ewen's voice cracked a little. "Yes, he knows."

Ian was quite silent. A gust tore at the window and passed on.

"And now," went on Ardroy, looking down at the hearth, "he would like, it seems, to see Miss Campbell, if it be possible. I am therefore going to ride over to Fort William at once, and, if she desires it, bring her back with me."

The colour mounted to his cousin's face. "Bring her back? I . . . I had best be gone before she comes, then."

"That's as you wish, of course," answered Ewen, still staring downwards. "But go in and see him soon. I think he must have something of importance to say to you."

§ 2

Upstairs it was just as quiet, save for the rain lashing in the same way against the window. And David Maitland's sense of hearing not being in the least dulled, the sound of that assault was very present to him, as he lay there with his eyes closed. It did not distress him; he almost welcomed it, for he knew that he would never be out in conflicting elements again—in any sense. He had forced the surgeon to tell him the truth, though, since he had no feeling below the waist, it had been easy to guess it, directly he had recovered consciousness. The Dark Mile was over for him, and he had come out, against all hope, into a place where there was a glimmer of sky overhead, even, at moments, sunshine. Never, in that wild rush through the smoke, not even in the moment when he saw that he was trapped, had the shadow of an idea of expiation visited him—he had thought solely of the child's danger. But now, lying here waiting for the end, it was impossible not to know, and with a measureless content, that he had been allowed to make reparation after all. If he had murdered Archibald Cameron he had not only saved Ewen Cameron's heir, he had probably saved Ewen Cameron himself also. Ewen had said that, and much more. . . .

And here was young Stewart. He must rally all his forces for what he had to do.

" Do you remember a conversation we had in this room, Mr. Stewart. . . . not very long ago? "

Maitland's voice, slow, even, and apparently produced without effort, was a surprise to Ian. But the face on the pillow, when one looked at that . . . He averted his eyes from it, and found them fixed on one of the injured man's scorched hands, swathed in bandages, which was lying outside the bedclothes.

" Yes, I remember very well," he answered with some difficulty.

" You cannot doubt, after what happened at the bridge that afternoon . . . how long ago is that?"

"It was but the day before yesterday," replied the young man, hardly believing it himself.

"Is that all? . . . As I say, you cannot doubt, after that, that Miss Campbell returns your sentiments . . . Are you still of the same mind that you were then? You said, if I remember rightly, that you would give the rest of your life to be able to marry her."

"Mr. Maitland——"

The bandaged hand half raised itself. "Believe me, I am not torturing you for pleasure, Mr. Stewart."

"Then . . . yes, I mean that—as much as ever I did, God help me. But I . . . I have turned my face from it," said Ian unsteadily. "And it does torture me to speak of it." Then he was ashamed for having spoken of any pain of his own.

The sunken eyes studied him in silence; and when Maitland spoke again it was very slowly.

"Mr. Stewart, I have it in my power to put into your hand a key . . . which would unlock the barrier between you and Miss Campbell."

Forgetting that he was at the bedside of a badly injured man, Ian abruptly pushed back his chair, and sprang up. "Sir . . . I don't understand . . . how can you——" Further words failed him.

"Had I not been dying I should not contemplate doing it—yet," said Maitland, his brows a little drawn together. "For it means that I must betray a trust. I dare say," he went on, with a smile about his bloodless lips which was only just not sardonic, "that you think that must be a small consideration to me, who have betrayed a man . . . but it is not so."

Ian made some inarticulate sound. He could not believe that he was hearing aright. Or was Maitland feverish?

"And I hesitate again very much to put this key in your hands," went on the quiet voice—no trace of fever there—"because the price of using it is heavy."

"As if I would not pay any price!" burst out the young man, the sweat beginning to bead on his forehead. "Sir, sir, if you have any pity . . . ."

"I have," answered Maitland very gravely, "and that is why I hesitate. For it's not you who will pay that price, Mr. Stewart."

"You mean that she—that Miss Campbell will?"

And on the pillow David Maitland moved his head a little in assent.

"Then do not—" began Ian, but could not bring out the words. They were too hard to say. He sat down again and hid his face in his hands.

There was a silence; then a long sigh from the bed. The young man looked up. "Can I do anything for you, sir?"

"Nothing, thank you. Nothing but swear your most inviolable oath that if I give you the means of marrying Olivia she shall never repent it."

"But," said Ian with a beating heart, "if she has to pay so heavily, how can I tell whether she would not repent it?"

"That is the risk," said Maitland, half to himself. "But she said, like you, that she would pay any price . . . any price . . . It is treachery to Cairns. Yet if you love one another. . . ."

"At least, sir," besought Ian in an agony, "at least give me this key, this secret. I need not use it, but give it to me!"

"You think you would not use it?" The smile came

again, faint and not untender. "You are young, and in love."

Nevertheless, fixing his eyes on the end of the bed, David Maitland began in a voice which, though firm, sounded as if it came from a great distance. "Listen then, and may God forgive me if I do wrong. . . . Olivia is not Campbell's daughter at all, nor his wife's— nay, nor mine neither, don't go thinking that! She has not a drop of the blood of Diarmaid in her veins; but she is involved in no dishonour—she is not illegitimate. She is the daughter," his voice changed slightly, "of a very beautiful and gracious lady, own sister to Mrs. Campbell, who was a Lindsay, and of Robert Urquhart of Drumgarve, the husband who deserted her and was killed in a duel in France the year afterwards."

"But why then, . . ." stammered Ian, his tongue hardly able to articulate.

"Because Mrs. Campbell's own daughter died in infancy, and her grief was so great that her husband almost feared for her reason, so that when, soon afterwards, her sister Mrs. Urquhart died, leaving a girl of six months old, already fatherless, they adopted the little Olivia. The boys already born to the Campbells were too young to realise that she was not their own sister, and a few years sufficed to make it all but forgotten among acquaintances and servants, particularly as there was a strong resemblance between Olivia and her supposed mother—not unnatural, with so close a tie of blood. Mrs. Campbell died when Olivia was five. I believe that Cairns meant to tell Olivia the truth when she came of age, but he could not face it—she was too dear to him. I doubt if he will ever tell her now, of his own free will. That is why I am breaking the silence of more than twenty years . . . for the sake of Olivia's happiness."

His voice, which had weakened, died down altogether, and there was absolute silence, for even the rain had stopped.

A long time afterwards, so it seemed to him, Ian had sufficiently recovered to ask in awed accents, " But you, sir, how do you know this secret? "

Maitland was looking at the foot of the bed as though he saw someone standing there. He said, " She was more beautiful even than Olivia is. I had known her well; but I never saw her again after her marriage. I helped Cairns over the business of the adoption, and we have been friends ever since. And now I am betraying him . . . for Olivia's sake."

Ian ran his hands through his hair. " He . . . he may deny it. What proof is there? "

" Proof enough—locked away in my desk at Strathmory. The key is yonder."

But Olivia's lover stood up trembling. It was like a cup of water held, just out of reach, before the eyes of one dying of thirst. " O, Mr. Maitland, how can I tell her the truth . . . how can I cause her such a shock, such grief—even though it sets me free to marry her? If she loves Mr. Campbell as a daughter she may hate me for it! And once done it cannot be undone."

" Like most things," came faintly from the bed. " Well then, Mr. Stewart, if she arrives in time, I will tell her myself. And if she loves you as I think she does, she will not reck so much after all of the cost. She will come through the dark to you . . . only a mile or so of darkness . . . I am tired; I think I will sleep now."

§ 3

Down again to Ewen's room and the pool of rain-drops. Ian hardly knew how he got there. He harboured no thought now of leaving before Olivia's arrival; he was staring at the clock. Hours before she could be here. And what if she never came, if she could not face see-ing her " dear Mr. Maitland " *in extremis?* But she was brave; she would come . . . to find her old friend dying and to learn that she was not what all her life she had supposed herself to be—a Campbell and her father's daughter.

What then if he spared her that disclosure—what if he asked the dying man not to tell her about her parentage, and kept his own lips sealed; never, as he had said, used the key? . . . But Ian was not so deluded as to imagine that he would ever be able to do that indefinitely.

How quiet it was . . . and, after all, the sun was coming out! Upstairs David Maitland, the informer, who had sent a hero to death, was himself dying the death of a hero. But he, Ian Stewart, in this over-shadowed house, could think consecutively of one thing only—life with Olivia. He hated himself for doing it, but he could not tame his thoughts. Nevertheless there still ran between himself and her a chill enough stream, for all that a bridge had miraculously been thrown across it. Would she set foot upon that bridge—come . . . what was it Maitland had said . . . come through a mile of darkness to him? (Odd; could he have been referring to the *Mile dorcha*, and if so, how had he ever heard of it, though it was true that he must have driven through it when Ewen brought him here? Olivia too—but he remembered then that it was he himself who had told her of the place.)

"My aunt is not at all easy about Mr. Maitland's condition," said Alison to Ian at the midday meal, where they were alone. "I hope Ewen will soon be back." Her eyes filled with tears. "All on Donald's account . . . I can't bear to think of it!"

Ian asked where Donald was, and was told that it was thought wiser to keep him in bed until to-morrow, not because he had suffered any physical hurt, but because, though he seemed quite free from reminiscent fears by day, his sleep was haunted by such alarming dreams. For that reason, and also because the pursuit of his fancy had not contravened any actual command, the boy had not been punished—save that from his point of view confinement to bed was in itself a punishment.

The afternoon was endless—sunny and endless. Towards the close of it Alison took him to the sick-room for a moment or two, and Ian saw indeed a great though indefinable alteration. Maitland seemed to have gone much further away since the morning. He was very drowsy. Yet, as Ian stood looking at him, he opened his eyes, recognised him, and said, "Has she come yet? . . . No matter . . . do not be afraid!" And then, with a change of tone, "Where is the little boy with the caterpillars?"

"Do you wish to see him?" asked Alison, hesitating a trifle. He signified by the least movement of the head that he did, and a few moments later Ian heard through the half-open door Keithie's little pipe commenting on the situation: "Poor Mr. Maittan's ill again!" and he was brought in. He was too small to realise the impending presence of death, and was no more frightened or abashed than a bird hopping about on a tree in yesterday's battlefield, but he was sympathetic. " Poor Mr. Maittan'!" he said, as Alison lifted him up. " I will truly give you my best cattlepillar when you go away. . . . Are you going away soon?"

"Yes . . . very soon," said Maitland faintly, smiling up at him. " Will you kiss me, little Keith?"

Keith bent forward at once from his mother's arms, and David Maitland received that fresh and dewy salute with a look so full of content that Ian turned away with a constriction in his throat.

Outside the door Alison rather anxiously asked him if he thought that the dying man would ask to see Donald also, because she had not prepared the child for any such summons, and ought now to relieve Aunt Margaret in the sick room. So Ian offered to go up to his small cousin and stay with him awhile, and, if he were sent for, to explain to the best of his ability what it meant. " Though I doubt," he added, looking at the closed door, " whether Mr. Maitland will ask for anyone further now."

Not even for Olivia, he thought, as he went up to Donald, to find the late adventurer tossing restlessly in a jumble of bedclothes which almost engulfed the book he had been reading. When, he asked eagerly, could he get up; when could he come down and thank kind Mr. Maitland for saving him from the fire? Later on, perhaps, Ian told him; adding that Mr. Maitland might possibly send for him, in which case he must not make a noise in the room, for he was very ill. Deciding not to add anything further until it was necessary, he then offered to read to the boy, and was willingly handed *Robinson Crusoe*.

Page after page of the immortal castaway's doings did

he read aloud without taking in more than a few words here and there. But no summons came, and though he tried to listen, while he read, for any sound of arrival outside the house, he heard none.

It was not until Donald had at last fallen asleep that there was a familiar step in the passage. Ian jumped up. The door opened and Ewen beckoned him forth.

"You must come quickly," he said. "There is only just time—he is going fast."

"Miss Campbell——"

"She is there, with Alison. I did not think it would be so soon. Yet perhaps——"

There was no "perhaps." They had to stoop to see if he were still breathing. But years and sorrow had so rolled away from the face on which the two who knew his own bitter secret looked down that it was not possible to feel regret. And after a moment Maitland's eyes opened; they first sought out Olivia, and then looked from her to Ian, and he murmured almost inaudibly, "There is . . . no time now . . . for me . . . but . . . tell her . . ."

They were the last words he spoke; yet his last look was for Ewen, kneeling at the bedside; and the last faint movement he essayed was that of his bandaged left hand towards him. Ewen put both of his over it. The smile which came then stayed long afterwards.

CHAPTER XXVIII

THE KING OF LOCHLANN'S DAUGHTER

§ 1

Sept. 12th.

COUCHED in the warm heather about half a mile off, Ian Stewart stared at the old grey house which confronted with close-curtained windows the almost incredible brilliance of the September day. It held death—its silence, its blind air of withdrawal, were tributes to the august visitant; and no more than any of its grown inmates was Ian likely to forget that guest. Yet for him it held love too, a love which might soon be flown unless he put out his hand and caught it. But what if, in the capture, he crushed its wings past reparation?

In the night it had seemed to him that he could never bring himself to tell Olivia the secret of her parentage. But because this was a new day, and one drenched in that unearthly beauty of which September holds the secret, so still that the fall of a leaf was an event, and even the murmur of the distant Allt Buidhe faintly audible— because of all this, and because he was young and desperately in love, Ian lay there and pulled at the heather-stems, and knew that he could not let Olivia go away unenlightened. The life which pulsed so strongly in his veins this morning—only in her could it find its full satisfaction; and with Olivia, as he knew, it was the same. Now at last the barrier was gone, and those two streams could mingle . . . And yet he could not but dread the moment of disclosure.

Before he came out here, half an hour ago, Ian had talked with Ardroy in the little room where yesterday the rain had found its slow entrance, and where to-day the drawn curtains made a curious twilight which the radiance without nevertheless found means to penetrate. Ewen was certain now that the fire had been the work of the gillie from Invershian, and when his cousin had objected that, if the MacPhair's aim had really been to burn Ardroy's property, either by his master's direct orders or on his own initiative, he would scarcely have chosen the stables instead of the house, Ewen had replied very grimly that he had *not* chosen the stables, which was why one knew that the fire had not been caused by accident.

"If you go round to the policies and look carefully," he explained, "you will find clear proof that he did try to fire the house itself—from the outside. I only discovered it this morning. But there was nothing sufficiently inflammable; and he either could not get inside or was afraid to risk the attempt. So in the end he took the easier course, and set fire to the stables, hoping perhaps that the flames would spread to the house, though he must have known that the wind was in the other direction. I suppose he thought that the horses would at least be burnt, poor beasts, including those he had brought back—perhaps unwillingly."

"Or," had said Ian hesitatingly, "since there was . . . Donald up there asleep in the loft . . . do you think he can possibly have known of his presence? Surely not—it is too horrible a thought!"

In the darkened room the two Highlanders looked at each other almost furtively. Both knew that the annals of their native land had in the past been stained by crimes just as horrible. Then Ewen went and twitched the window curtain over a chink of sunlight. " I like so little to investigate that possibility," he said in a low voice, " that I vow I am glad I have not the means to do it. Donald himself, though he does not seem to know the exact time at which he started to carry out his fatal escapade, is sure that he did not see the strange gillie when he went into the stables and climbed up through the trap-door. Whether the gillie saw him is another matter, and one which we shall never know. I could never bring the crime home to Glenshian, because he could always disclaim responsibility for the gillie's action. And even if he is responsible, he has failed. What has been brought about was probably no part of his intention."

He was silent a moment, while into Ian's mind there shot the memory of a fierce June sunset, gleaming windows, and a small boy crying out: " Our house is on fire!"

Ewen lifted his head. " Have you seen *him* this morning?"

" No," said his cousin.

They went up together, and in the stillest room of all that still house Ardroy removed the cloth from the quiet face.

" I am glad that Archie forgave him, as he did, without even knowing who he was," he said. " I wonder if they have met by now?"

Ewen had a downright belief in the next world and a rather disconcerting habit of speaking of his dead friends—and since the Rising he had lost two by violent deaths—as if they were in an adjoining room. For Ian the dwelling-place of the departed was more remote. He looked down at David Maitland and wondered . . .

"God rest him!" said Ewen gently, and replaced the covering.

§ 2

Ian roused himself at last from his communion with the heather, got to his feet, and then stood still. The great vista of mountain and moorland before and around him, always fine, was this morning of an unspeakably intensified beauty, serene yet searching, so that between the silver stems of two birch trees, early yellowing, the deep hyacinth blue of a distant peak smote the senses with a stab like pain. What had death to do with a day of such profound loveliness . . . And what had human passions? . . . Or was it, on the other hand, the trembling nearness of the fulfilment of his heart's desire which gave the day its transcendental quality? Everything that the young man looked at, even his own hand in the sunlight, seemed of a new and troubling significance, as if he and all that his eyes rested upon this morning existed in some other world.

Wondering a little if he were going fey, he set off towards the house, to see for himself that ugly thing of which Ewen had told him. In the golden radiance the wreckage looked more than ever hideous, even though the rest of the outbuildings had escaped, and the heavy rain had soon put a stop to the sullen after-smouldering of the fire. Round the gutted stables the ground was strewn with charred debris and half-burnt beams; but it was not to look again at those that Ian had come here, and after a little search he found, in a dark angle of the exterior of the old house itself, the proof of what Ewen had told him. And it was a sight more repellent somehow than the wider ruin behind it, though there was so little of it—just a few half-burnt bits of wood piled up in a corner, with a slightly-blackened wall above them. By the extent of the discolouration, more fuel must have been used than appeared now; finding his attempt fruitless, the gillie had perhaps removed the bulk of it to escape detection. But enough remained . . .

Ian stood gazing at this testimony to a malice truly devilish with such revolted attention that he did not hear a door open near him. But, something cold and wet being thrust without warning into his hand, he discovered it to be Luath's nose. And the deerhound was not unaccompanied; a little way off a lady and a small boy were standing looking at the blackened skeleton of the stables—Olivia and Donald.

Ian was aware of a great commotion in his breast. Mechanically he caressed Luath's head, and the great dog responded by rearing himself up and putting his paws on young Invernacree's shoulders—always an embarrassing mark of regard. Its recipient heard Donald's fresh voice, untouched by any emotion other than a somewhat awed excitement.

" That was the stable, Miss Campbell—doesn't it look strange? I will show you where I was—up there; you can still see . . Oh, there's Cousin Ian!"

Ian threw off Luath and came forward to salute her who was not, and never had been " Miss Campbell," ashamed all at once that he was aware of so momentous a circumstance while she was still ignorant. That blue cloak with the swansdown cast about her—surely it was the same which she had been wearing when he had lifted her out of the coach and had helped to carry her along Loch Linnhe? Ah, he had thought her lovely then . . . and ever since; but now that face was more than lovely to him.

Olivia responded very quietly but composedly to his greeting. He saw that she was paler than usual, and had wept; yet it seemed to him that a night of grief had but endowed her with a diviner beauty.

" This is painful for you," he said in a low voice. " I hope you did not allow Donald to——"

" No," said Olivia quickly, " I was already on my way. I wanted to see the place where——"

" I went up to the loft," broke in Donald eagerly, " by the ladder against the wall in the stables; but you see, Miss Campbell, that's all gone now—no, here's a piece——"

But at this point his revelations were cut short by the advent of Morag, his young Highland nurse, who apologetically requested permission to withdraw him, Lady Ardroy having sent her to find him. That the summons was instantly if unwillingly obeyed was no doubt due to the presence of " Cousin Ian."

Olivia looked relieved as the boy disappeared into the house. " I thought that perhaps he ought not to come. But he does not know yet, I think, what his going up that ladder cost . . . Will you explain to me just what Mr. Maitland did, Mr. Stewart?"

That " Mr. Stewart " hurt like a knife; but how else, after the parting on the bridge, could he expect her to address him? And in sight of the smoke-blackened remains Ian went through the story of the rescue. He did not say anything about the origin of the fire, and happily

Olivia appeared to have no suspicion of incendiarism, nor to have observed what it was that he had been looking at a few moments previously. It was, however, a little difficult to account satisfactorily for his and Ardroy's absence from the house that evening; he could only say that, having something of importance to discuss, and the night being fine, they had walked up to Loch na h-Iolaire for the purpose.

Olivia heard it all without flinching. " Yes, I see . . . I understand. He first tried to reach Donald from outside, then he went up where the ladder used to be, in there. Then in trying to let himself down from the loft. . . ." She stood awhile in silence, her face working slightly, but she did not break down. And at last she said, " Just the death I should always have expected my dear Godfather to die, giving his life for another's. . . . And now there is but one thing more to ask you— what was it that he said you were to tell me? "

It had come, the longed-for, dreaded moment.

" Let us go from here first," said Ian, paling. " It is too difficult and too strange to tell you here . . . and needs too much courage."

" Courage? " echoed Olivia. " But surely there was no lack of courage here? "

" God knows there was not," assented he. " But this needs a different kind."

" In me? "

Ian bowed his head. " Yes. And in me too. Courage to hurt you—perhaps terribly."

" I do not feel as if you could hurt me any more," said Olivia.

And those words, uttered with an exquisite but unreproachful sadness, ended Ian's attempt at disclosure ere it was begun. The smoke-blackened spot where they stood seemed for a second to be shot with myriad points of light, and then grew blacker than before. He took time to breathe and then said quite quietly:

"I will not tell you then. There is . . . no need." (*No need!* cried his cheated hope to him—*no need!*) "And in that case I——" He broke off. Was this, out of so many leave-takings, to be the last, the true farewell?

"But I think there *is* need," said Olivia, looking at him very gravely. "I should not have said that about your hurting me; for it has not been your fault. . . . And you must surely do what Mr. Maitland desired you to do. 'Tell her!' they were the last words he uttered. I must know what he meant; if it needs courage, I must find it."

Ian was staring at a half-consumed beam upon the ground. "It is I who have not the courage," he said, with something like a groan.

"Is it so terrible? Shall I be so unhappy? My dear Godfather would never have wished you to tell me if that were so."

"No, that is true," replied the young man more calmly. He raised his head and looked at her again. "I will tell you, then, as he urged me to do. If he had had the strength he would have told you himself. Only I must implore you to come elsewhere. We are not even very private here.—You have a cloak, I see?"

"I will come wherever you wish," said Olivia, gathering it about her.

§ 3

It was natural, being already behind the house, to go towards the loch, even without any fixed intention of reaching it. But five or six minutes walking in silence through the still, sunflecked wood, and they were there.

Loch na h-Iolaire this morning was no loch, but a mirror. Not only were all the tawny heights on the further side built downwards in its depths, in a similitude no less bright in colour, and in detail no whit less perfect than the originals, but in that crystalline cup there even moved the little waterfall which tumbled down the lowest slope of Meall Achadh—a tiny white snake alive amid the unstirred heather and motionless birch trees of that reflected world. The feeling of being in some other plane of existence again grew strong upon Ian Stewart; the magic of this golden day was so profound that, even at such a moment of crisis, it could penetrate and bewilder senses like his, deeply troubled with the warfare of the mind—with pain and regret and apprehension and faint hope. Yet . . . was hope so faint?

Olivia turned at last from gazing. She was waiting, though she said no word. But now he knew how to begin.

" If you will allow me," he said, standing at a little distance, " I will go back to the dream I had of you in the oak wood at Kilrain, because it was—that is, it might be—a kind of presage . . . You know the legend of the children of the King of Lochlann or Norway, how they were changed by sorcery into seals? "

" Yes," said the Highland Olivia, " I know the legend."

" When you had been a little time at Invernacree,"

continued Ian, "I thought of you as one of those, because, from the first, I was a man bewitched. And you
know, perhaps, that, as the tale goes, a seal-woman wedded
to a mortal man can always go back to her native element
so long as she retains the skin which covered her as a
seal; and that therefore the only way in which a man
can be sure of retaining this enchanted bride is to possess
himself of the skin. In my dream, where you were the
King of Lochlann's daughter of my fancy as well as
. . . Olivia Campbell, I thought that you came and laid
the magic covering beside me, as if you were renouncing
your privilege for me. And when I woke, I found in
my hand, not indeed the skin of the seal, but . . . a
sprig of bog-myrtle." His heart was beating hard, but
he managed to keep his voice steady.

"How long ago that seems now!" said Olivia almost
to herself, looking again at the imaged water. For a
moment she said no more; then, her eyes still on those
deep-plunged mountain-sides, she answered the thought
behind the allegory of his dream. "But what the gall
stands for I have no power to renounce. How, if I
wished, could I make myself of other blood than I am?"

He came a step or two nearer. "No, no one can do
that . . . And yet, a spaewife told me years ago that I
should love a woman who was not what she seemed."

Now she was startled; she looked straight at him with
that beautiful fearless gaze of hers. "Not what she
seemed! Ian, what are you trying to tell me?"

The young man clenched his hands till the nails ran
in. "Something that, though it will make you sad, could
make us happy—make us, if you have the courage and
the will . . . happy together."

"*Together!* You mean . . .?" The colour rose in

Olivia's face like dawn over snow; one of her hands too shut itself quickly. "You mean that . . . somehow . . . there *is* a way out for us—a way over the river you spoke of that day at Kilrain? Was that what my dear Godfather meant when he said, the last time I was here, that happiness must be paid for?"

"Yes, that is what I mean—what he too meant, no doubt. There is a way; but it is a dark and difficult way for *you* . . . Only, if you would take it for my sake, my very unworthy sake, when I have told you . . . Olivia, will you—will you?"

One starving look at her, standing there in the windless glory, and Ian dropped to a knee and pressed the hem of that blue cloak of hers to his lips. In his heart was a silent prayer for pardon that he should ask her to suffer on his account, and the intuitive feeling also that he must give her time. . . . She was a woman, and would show some reluctance, were it only to repay him a little of the humiliation of his own persistent refusal. But when, getting to his feet again, he saw the look which she was bending upon him, he could have cried out in mingled exultation and self-abasement.

For as this day was not as other days, so was his love not as other women. She had a soul as nobly clear as the water by which she stood, and gallant as any paladin's. She did not even wait to learn the price required of her.

"I think I would come across yonder loch to you— and that with no bridge at all! Only tell me the way quickly . . . I will be as brave as I can."

And with a gesture at once simple and royal Olivia Urquhart gave him her hand.

THE END